Contents

they serve in his office building is anything to write home about, but it's decent enough to drink and strong enough to tide him over till the evening. Which is way more than he can say about the coffee served on the rest of the Coast. Why is it such an ordeal to find a café that makes consistently good coffee? How hard can it be? The coffee machine does all the work anyway.

God, he misses Sydney. Misses being able to walk into any café, even in the middle of nowhere, and get a spectacular cup of coffee. But beggars can't be choosers.

Fifteen minutes later, after grabbing a lightning quick shower and brushing his teeth, he's already in the car, checking for road work updates. The highways here are such a mess, it's something new each day. Case in point; Gold Coast Highway lights up with red and orange, as does Sunshine Boulevard. Of-fucking-course this has to happen when he's (almost) late for work.

He updates the GPS to lead him via alternative routes around the beaches and starts the car. *ETA 32 minutes.* Well, it will be cutting it close, but he should be fine. At least he has no appointments until ten. Oh yeah, that's right—another appointment where he'll have to tell the person he's letting them go. Why did Amanda think it was a good idea to schedule the meeting for the morning? On the other hand, maybe it's better to get it over with and focus on other things.

Taking a left turn onto Seagull Avenue, he passes by yet another café. He's seen several on his way, paying them no mind, but something about this one makes him slow down and take a closer look. Why? He hasn't a clue. The place looks like nothing special from the outside, and the few tables and chairs lined out front have seen better days. The name alone almost makes him bail. Who the heck names a business *Lost and Ground*? A serial killer, perhaps.

He pushes onto the gas pedal, passing the café, but only getting as far as the end of the block before a strange feeling in his gut compels him to stop. He's set on ignoring it—there's no reason to lose more time stopping for coffee when he has a perfectly adequate café at work. Still, he finds himself glancing into the rearview mirror.

Frustrated, he turns the car around. He pulls up to the curb in front of the café, disregarding the 'no standing' sign. He doesn't have time to look for a parking space. It won't kill anybody if he stays for a couple of minutes.

Out of curiosity, he googles the place before deciding to go in. The sheer number of high ratings stuns him. Over 500 with an average of 4.9. Yeah, right. He'll eat his watch if at least half of these haven't been paid for.

Either way, he's already here. Might as well go in.

The second he steps inside and spots the queue, he knows he made a mistake. Jesus. Where have all these people come from? This isn't even the main road.

Just as he's about to turn around and leave, the divine smell of coffee, sugar, and spices fills his nose, making his mouth water. He blames it on them when his legs carry him further inside, joining the line of people waiting to be served. He tries not to check the time whenever the line moves inch by slow, miserable inch. Why the fuck is it taking so long?

Once he gets a proper look, he can see why. There's only one person behind the till and one behind the coffee machine. No wonder the line is moving excruciatingly slow, especially since most people seem to be ordering fancy, diabetes-inducing, basic-bitch drinks that can barely be considered coffee. Who the heck puts whipped cream on a latte?

As the line moves by a couple of feet—fucking finally—Ellis gets a view of the person taking orders. He expects to see some wide-eyed, disheveled kid on the verge of a mental breakdown, but he couldn't be more wrong.

While the guy behind the counter looks rather young, he's decidedly not a kid, though he might still get asked for his ID. His hands are flying over the till with surprising speed, incongruous with the time Ellis has spent waiting for his turn. Not only does the guy look perfectly composed; to Ellis' irritation, he even indulges the customers in some corny small talk. He seems to be *enjoying* the pointless chitchat, Jesus Christ. What a weirdo.

Fucking great. Just tell each other your whole life stories, why don't you?

Ellis grinds his teeth, trying to recall all the stupid meditation techniques he's succumbed to in his attempts to manage anxiety and stress. It might finally come in handy now and prevent him from flipping his shit in a public place swarming with people.

You can always leave, you know?

Yeah, he knows. So why doesn't he? Whenever he thinks of turning around and marching out, the strange feeling in his gut from before makes a comeback, rooting him to the spot. He must be coming down with something.

It's fine. He'll get his coffee and fuck off, making sure to avoid the place in future. Should be easy enough, because there can't be anywhere else with such a ridiculous name.

He takes a deep breath when it's almost his turn, the woman who ordered a simple, medium cap tapping her card to the terminal. He watches as the barista steps away from the till and grabs a new takeaway cup and a pen to write—

The fuck?

Ellis fucking bristles. He assumed the barista would write the type of the coffee on the cup, but he's sure that the short order the woman placed shouldn't take up the whole circumference of the cup. Did he just write his number on there?

"Are you kidding me?" Ellis hears himself speak. Both the woman and the barista snap their heads up to look at him with identical shocked expressions.

"Sorry?" the barista says.

From up-close, he looks even younger; all smooth skin and a mop of unruly, shaggy blond hair. He's tall though, almost as tall as Ellis, give or take an inch or so. For some reason, that little observation annoys him. A pair of wide, amber eyes fix on him, swimming with confusion.

"There's a line of people waiting to order, and yet you seem to find the time to flirt with a customer and write your number on the cup.

Good to know that you have your priorities straight. I'm sure your boss would love to hear it."

He doesn't feel any better once the words are out, his anger spiking when a voice inside his head that sounds exactly like his dad speaks. *Resorting to making threats over stupid coffee? How pathetic are you?*

He doesn't realize he'd closed his eyes until someone clears their throat and he's prompted to open them. The woman from before has moved on, and now it's just him and the guy behind the till.

The barista doesn't look like someone who was just reprimanded, rather harshly, by some dickhead in an Armani suit. There's a softness in his gaze as he rakes it over Ellis' face, a softness that has no place here after what Ellis just said. It's making him uncomfortable, at a loss for how to react. His throat feels dry and uncooperative, and he has to resist a sudden urge to turn around and hide in his car. His brain really must be playing tricks on him, because he swears that there's a golden glow to the guy's eyes that wasn't there a few seconds ago.

Thankfully, the guy blinks, breaking the weird not-quite spell that had Ellis in a chokehold for a moment. His eyes are a perfectly normal color—of course they are—and Ellis can breathe again.

"I'm sorry to have made you wait. What would you like?" the barista asks, not a trace of resentment or sarcasm in his voice.

Ellis exhales in a whoosh, pulling himself back together with the hope that he'll leave this strange place within the next few minutes.

"A long black, the largest size you have. Two extra shots," he parrots his usual order and watches as the barista reaches for a large cup. Halfway through Ellis' order, he stops, eyebrows raised.

"You want...five shots?"

"Can you count?"

The guy hesitates. "Our large has three shots."

"So you *can* count. Good on you," Ellis snarks, too aggravated and out of sorts to feel guilty. The guy is probably seconds away from losing his shit.

"Sugar or milk?" he asks in that same, gentle voice.

"No, I take mine black." Just like his heart.

The barista nods, typing the order in the till. "Anything else to go with it?"

Having foregone breakfast, Ellis has been eyeing the pastry display. The cinnamon rolls in particular look sinful, and he hasn't indulged in so many carbs in a long time. But the last two minutes have effectively killed his appetite.

"No."

"Can I have your name?"

"You can just call out the order, no?" How many people can possibly have the same order as him?

The guy's eyes flick to Ellis again, a slight tilt to his head, like he's studying a fascinating creature.

Probably never seen a dickbag like you.

The barista licks his lips, causing an unfamiliar, stabbing sensation in Ellis' chest. "That will be $6.50." He lets Ellis pay, then calls out, "Hey, Zeke? Could we swap for a bit?"

The other guy—Zeke—pokes his head out from behind the coffee machine. One of his eyebrows slowly arches up and his eyes jump between Ellis and the barista.

"Sure thing. Let me just pour this one."

"Thanks." The barista looks at Ellis, giving him a small, startlingly caring smile. "It won't be long." With that, he takes Ellis' cup and goes over to the coffee machine.

Ellis sighs. What are the chances he won't end up with spit in his coffee? It's a testament to how desperate for caffeine he is that the thought doesn't bother him as much as it should.

He heads to the other end of the counter to wait for his order. He slumps slightly against the edge, exhausted now that the anger and frustration have bubbled over and left him burned out. And he still has a whole day of paperwork and meetings ahead of him. Fuck.

Before he can sink into the endless chasm of misery–aka thinking about all the things he has to do–a steaming cup appears in front of him.

"A long black, two extra shots," the barista says pointedly, nudging the cup towards Ellis.

That was super quick. Given how many people were there before him, Ellis expected to be waiting for quite some time before his coffee was ready. It seems that his rampage chastised the barista enough to prompt him to work faster and, apparently, jump the queue and make his drink first.

Except, when he looks up and their eyes meet, the guy is not looking chastised. His gaze is curious, and there's a barely-there curve to his lips that makes Ellis want to step back and lean closer at the same time. What the hell is going on with him today?

"Apologies for taking so long. I hope we didn't make you late for work," the barista says, expression open and earnest, and totally fucking with Ellis' head.

He reaches for the cup, holding it in front of him like a shield. "It's fine," he grunts, because what else is he supposed to say to that? He's not going to start oversharing by explaining he's the great CEO now, and thus doesn't have a boss, but still has to stick to his schedule because he has responsibilities towards the company and—

The barista pushes a small paper box towards him.

"I didn't order this," Ellis says with a frown.

"It's on the house."

"I'm not a charity case. I can pay if I want something," he argues, even as his mouth waters at the scent of sugar and cinnamon.

The barista's minuscule smile grows into a full-blown grin. He gives Ellis a quick once-over, causing a rush of heat to sweep through him. "I'm aware. It's just something to make your day a little better."

Ellis blinks, so out of sorts it's not even funny. "How's food going to make my day better?"

"It's scientifically proven that sugar stimulates the release of endorphins and dopamine," the barista says, clearly having an answer for everything. "Non-scientifically, I believe everyone could use a little sweetness in their life."

Ellis really wants to retort, but the guy's open, earnest face forbids him to open his mouth. Plus, he can feel his stomach growling, his appetite renewed with vigor now that he has smelled something good. Swallowing his pride, he reaches for the box, ignoring the clenching sensation in his stomach at the guy's beaming smile.

"Thanks."

"You're most welcome," the barista says. "By the way, I don't write my number on the cups. Just so you know." He steps away from the counter, slowly disappearing behind the coffee machine. "See you around."

Ellis doesn't bother correcting him on that one—there will be no seeing him again. What a weird guy. Again, not surprising. Gold Coast is full of weirdos.

He leaves the café in a rush, letting out a huge breath when he's back in the security of his car, no strange, confusing baristas around. Setting the box on the passenger seat, he raises the cup to take a sip. The coffee better be worth the toll this visit has taken on his mental health.

The coffee never makes it to his mouth.

He brings the cup to eye-level, reading the words he wrongly assumed indicated his coffee order.

They do not.

You deserve good things.

He stares at the words in a stupor, a kind of numbness spreading through his limbs before it transforms into a raging turmoil of emotions.

He grips the cup tightly, just short of crushing it, but realizing last minute that it's full of scalding liquid. He closes his eyes, focusing on his breathing to quell the surge of anger that's climbing its way to the surface.

Who the fuck does the guy think he is? What makes him think he can act like a shrink to complete strangers?

Ellis is _this_ close to marching back into the café and having words with the obnoxious barista, but gets himself together quickly. He's already running late, and who knows what would happen if he went back in there. The guy probably writes random shit on the cups anyway, thinking it's cute or something. That at least explains what he wrote on the woman's cup before Ellis lost his cool.

Satisfied with his reasoning, Ellis finally brings the cup to his lips to take a much-needed sip of the nectar of the gods. The moment it touches his tongue, an involuntary moan rumbles out of him. He tenses, embarrassed, even though there's no one around to witness his reaction.

He stares at the cup in bewilderment. How on earth is it so good? It must be that he's so tired and desperate that even an average coffee would taste like heaven.

He takes another sip, half-expecting it was a one-off and it won't taste as good the second time. It wasn't a one-off. In fact, it tastes better with each sip, and as he slowly works his way through the whole cup, he swears he can feel the coffee traveling through his bloodstream, waking him up and chasing away all the tension that's been piling in his body like poison.

By the time he's halfway through the cup, he doesn't even care he's going to be late for work. He sighs, sinking into the seat and letting the warm feeling sweep through him. He better enjoy it while it lasts. Letting his head roll to the side, he zeroes in on the paper box. His stomach gives a loud rumble of agreement.

He reaches for the box and flips open the lid, not surprised but still elated when it reveals the cinnamon roll he was eyeing earlier. Fuck it, he can go off the rails once in a while. He'll even survive the stomachache the dairy will likely end up giving him.

He digs into the roll, tearing off a piece of warm, fluffy dough. Once he pops it in his mouth, fireworks go off on his tongue. He soaks up the taste, tearing off another piece and licking his sticky fingers.

Yeah, work can wait.

Chapter 2

Blue. That's his new favorite color. Not just any blue, though. The sea after the storm when the first rays of sun are starting to peek through the gray sky. That kind of blue.

An hour ago, Gabe had no idea that eye color existed. Now it's all he can think about as he absently polishes glasses, still hot from the dishwasher.

Zeke marches up to him, giving him a judgmental look. "Either you're having a stroke, or that dumb expression has something to do with Mr. Tall, Dark, and Asshole from before."

Gabe scowls, just barely restraining himself from defending the nameless stranger. "Now that you mention it, I do feel kind of dizzy. And I can't feel half of my face."

Zeke snorts, slapping a hand on the counter. "Spill."

Groaning, Gabe puts down the latte glass he's been polishing for several minutes. It's probably shiny enough by now. "There's nothing to spill. He needed a pick-me-up. I tried to give it to him."

That's putting it mildly. It's been a long time since Gabe has felt so much pain and loneliness in anyone. But this man with soul-deep sadness in his eyes, and walls around his heart taller than Everest...

Damn, Gabe nearly threw himself across the counter and gave him a much-needed hug. Since he had a feeling it wouldn't have been taken well, he went with the next best thing: a cinnamon roll.

"Are you talking about the freebie—which you will pay for, by the

Gabe clutches his proverbial pearls. "I would never." He totally would. Hell, he totally has. Cal's donut obsession is too damn endearing to not indulge it.

"I'll have the Cherry Ripe, please," Cal says, so freaking polite all the time. He's eyeing the donut like it's manna from heaven.

See? How is Gabe supposed to stay unaffected? But Dawson is watching him like a hawk, so no sneaking more donuts today.

Tongs in one hand and a paper bag in the other, he fetches a donut from the display and hands it to Cal, who's likely seconds away from having drool drip out of his mouth.

They all look at Donut when he lets out an impatient whine and walks around in a circle.

"I'll take him outside," Cal volunteers with a smile that's just this side of tight.

Gabe suppresses a snort. From what he's heard, Donut constantly has a bone to pick with Cal.

"Okay. I'll be right out." Dawson hands him the leash, pressing his lips together when Cal takes it from him like he's being handed a weapon.

"You look good. I take it things are going well?" Gabe asks when Cal's out of earshot. He takes the cups over to the coffee machine, and Dawson follows.

"Yeah. Really well," he says, a shy smile playing on his lips. He ducks his chin and rubs the back of his neck. "I think we've had our second first date."

"Yeah? What did you do?" Gabe asks, wanting to soak up the happiness radiating off Dawson. It's so rare that he gets to recharge from someone else and not the opposite.

"Cal was intrigued by that Paint 'n Sip place around the corner, so I made a booking for us."

"Oh yeah, I've been to that one. It was fun! Did you like it?"

Dawson hesitates on that one. "Eventually. It was...unnerving. Holding the brush after so long, you know?" Almost five years, if Gabe remembers correctly. "But then I kinda sank into it and—" He waves his hand vaguely through the air, chuckling a little. "Honestly, the best part about the whole thing was Cal's painting."

"He's that good?" Gabe asks with surprise. He doesn't know Cal all that well, but he doesn't seem like the artistic type.

"He's that *bad*," Dawson corrects, his shoulders shaking with suppressed laughter. "So I tried to pick something easy peasy, right? Basic shapes, not much detail..." He trails off and pulls out his phone, giving the screen a few swipes until he finds what he's looking for. "This—" He turns the phone so Gabe can see. "Was supposed to be a cactus."

"Oh my god." Gabe slaps a hand over his mouth. "Is that a dick?"

"It's a cactus dick," Dawson manages between giggles.

Gabe loses it then, a laugh bursting out of him. "That's priceless. God, I love that so much. You took it home, right?"

"Took it home?" Dawson gives him an incredulous look as he pockets his phone. "I made sure it's hanging on the wall."

"You didn't."

"I did."

Their laughter grows in volume, a few dine-in customers turning to see what the commotion is about. Gabe shoots them an apologetic smile, trying to tone it down.

"I don't think Cal's happy," he points out. Cal is glaring at them from outside, his lips pursed in an unhappy pout. He clearly knows what they're talking about—Dawson must have teased him about the painting a lot. It just sends Gabe into another fit.

Dawson throws a glance over his shoulder, waving at Cal. It just makes Cal glare harder. "Guess I better make it up to him," Dawson says with a shrug.

"Another donut?" Gabe offers.

Dawson rolls his eyes. "Sure."

"It's good to see you happy," Gabe tells him a couple minutes later when he's handing Dawson the drinks and paper bags with the donuts.

"Thanks. I am," Dawson admits, sounding almost shy. "It's all so weird, still."

"I bet." Who wouldn't find it weird if their asshole husband got into an accident, only to wake up with complete memory loss and a personality that's 180 from who he used to be? "But weird doesn't mean bad."

"No, I know." Dawson looks at Cal who's picking up Donut's poop with a less than ecstatic expression. "Doesn't make it any less scary."

"The best things in life usually are."

"Thanks, Yoda."

"Be nice to your barista," Gabe warns. "Or you might end up with something extra in your drink."

Dawson's eyes narrow. "You wouldn't."

"Try me."

"You know what? I think I'll leave a scathing review on Google."

"Go ahead. It will get lost among the hundreds of raving ones."

"We'll see."

By the time Dawson and Cal leave, Gabe is back to his high spirits, even though his mind occasionally wanders to the sad stranger from this morning. He'll likely never see him again, so he can only hope the man will get all the good things he deserves.

Chapter 3

"How do you like your new job?" Ellis asks, propping his phone against a pile of files so he doesn't have to hold it. He's not normally one to make personal calls at work, but Jordan is technically his employee, so it counts as work-related, right?

"It's alright. Not really different from what I did before." Jordan smirks at him from the other side of the screen. "Just proves that I did everything for you when you were still here."

"Fuck you," Ellis says, fighting a smile.

Damn, he misses his best friend, with all his misplaced remarks and twisted sense of humor. Jordan's had his back for the past seven years, always ready to step in when needed. He didn't even hesitate when Ellis asked him to take over for him in Sydney.

"What about you?" Jordan inquires. "You look like shit."

What a shocker. "I feel like shit. I *am* shit."

"Ellis," Jordan says disapprovingly. He's been subjected to Ellis' pity-parties way too often, even more so in the past month. "Come on, man."

"Don't *come on* me. You know how many people I had to fire in the last eight years?"

"Well..."

"Two," Ellis cuts in. "You know how many I have to fire now?"

Jordan lets out a sympathetic sigh. "Ellis."

"Six, Jordan. *Six*. And not because they showed up to work high as a kite or because they were harassing a secretary. No, it's because my fucking brother fucked up and now everyone else is taking the fall." There he goes, getting himself all riled up again.

Jordan barely blinks at the outburst. "It happens more often than you think."

"Not here," Ellis grits out. "Not on my watch."

"It wasn't on your watch," Jordan reminds him.

"No. I'm just the one who has to deal with the aftermath."

He could really use a drink these days, but ever since he found out about Cal's addiction, he's been careful not to fall down the same rabbit hole.

"It sucks, Ellis. It does. But there's nothing else you can do."

"That's not quite true." The more Ellis thinks about it, the more he's warming up to the idea.

Jordan's eyes narrow in suspicion. "What do you mean?"

"I could cut people's hours."

"And by hours, you mean their pay," Jordan points out. "They'll end up leaving anyway."

Ellis purses his lips, drumming his fingers on the desktop. "Maybe I wouldn't have to cut their pay."

Jordan's features fill with confusion, which is quickly replaced by dismay. "Ellis William Reeves, you are not paying them out of your own pocket. Are you nuts?!"

Ellis shrugs uncomfortably. "I wouldn't be paying all of them."

Jordan has to visibly take a second to compose himself. He takes a deep breath before speaking again, sounding much calmer now. "What about Cal, huh? You gonna cut his pay too? Maybe *he* should be paying these people. It was his fault, after all."

"He doesn't remember that."

"Doesn't change anything. You've always had to clean up after him. And now he decides he doesn't want to come back? The least he could do is take some responsibility."

He's not wrong, but the mere idea of doing so makes Ellis cringe. He can't simply walk up to his clueless brother and dump all this stuff on him. Cal has his own shit to deal with. Plus, if Ellis started whining, it would put more stress on Dawson too.

"Yeah, well, this isn't exactly a run of the mill situation."

"Same difference."

"I'm not cutting Cal's pay," Ellis says with finality.

"Cool. You're not cutting yours either," Jordan informs him, not even giving him a chance to protest. "Ellis, for the love of god, grow some balls and deal with this like an adult. It sucks ass, but it is what it is. Deal with it and move on. Okay?"

"Fine," Ellis grunts, surrendering but not happy about it.

"Good. Work aside, how're things?" Jordan switches the subject. "Made any friends yet?"

"Ha ha, very funny," Ellis says with an eyeroll. He's not exactly notorious for making friends easily. Hell, the only reason he became friends with Jordan is because he was bullied into it. Jordan is one persistent fucker.

"Met a girl?"

"Oh, yeah. Amanda," he jokes.

"Cal's PA?"

"My PA."

"Ah." Jordan's lips curl in a knowing smile. "Is it true what they say about her?"

"It's not untrue." He leaves it at that.

Jordan whistles. "Nice. You need someone to keep you on your toes since I can't."

"I don't know. You seem to be doing just fine long-distance."

Jordan laughs, his head thrown back. This banter is what Ellis misses the most, though he never thought he'd say that.

"Speaking of, how about I fly up once the dust has settled?" Jordan offers.

Ellis perks up at the suggestion, but quickly dismisses it. "You really don't have to baby me." They'll both have their hands full in the foreseeable future, and Jordan knows that. He just offered because he thinks Ellis will work himself into an early grave if he doesn't keep an

Gabriel flashes him a smile. "Won't be long."

"Wait," Ellis says before Gabriel takes off to make the drink. He fishes out his actual wallet, glad that he always carries a bit of cash on him just in case. He pulls out a tenner, holding it out to Gabriel. "That's for the cinnamon roll. The other day," he explains when Gabriel just stares at it uncomprehendingly.

"That's not necessary. It was on the house."

Ellis clenches his jaw. "I don't like taking free stuff."

He feels like a bug under the microscope with the way Gabriel's eyes study him so intently. Then those same eyes soften, and he doesn't feel like a bug anymore. He feels...*somehow.*

"Not everything has to be hard-earned, you know?" Gabriel says, his voice matching his gaze, making that squirmy sensation from before return with a vengeance.

"Yeah, it does," Ellis disagrees. "What's the point if it just falls in your lap?"

"Maybe you just deserve good things," Gabriel says in a half-whisper. But the words ring loud and uncomfortable in Ellis' head, making him want to run, to hide. Most of all, they make him want to scream at Gabriel that he couldn't be more wrong.

He swallows it all down, one-handedly folding the note and putting it in the tip jar instead.

If Gabriel looked bummed before, now he looks completely dejected. It stings in a way it has no business to. They're strangers. Gabriel was kind to him when he had no reason to, but that's all.

Gabriel mumbles an obligatory 'Thanks', before moving towards the coffee machine.

With a sigh and a bitter taste on his tongue, Ellis goes to wait at the end of the counter. He can see Gabriel working from the side, but instead of watching, he angles his body away and pulls out his phone. There's an unread text that he didn't notice while he was paying. Suppressing a groan—could work wait until he is actually at work?—he unlocks the screen.

Some of his agitation bleeds away when it turns out it's just his brother-in-law. And the text is actually a picture. Dawson has been sending him a lot of those, especially since he and Cal got a dog. This one is no exception.

Donut the dog. It's a stupid name, but it kind of goes with Donut's silly face, now staring at Ellis upside down from the screen, his tongue lolled out to the side, legs in the air. His paws are wet and covered in sand because duh, they're on the beach. Or they were when Dawson took the picture.

An involuntary smile grows on Ellis' lips even as something else, something sharp and nasty twists in his gut. He ignores it, crumpling it into a ball and shoving it somewhere deep inside him where all unwanted things end up.

Another text comes through, another picture. It's of Cal, still on the beach, seemingly mid-nap. His eyes are closed, his mouth slightly open, and Donut is lying next to him, his butt practically pressed against Cal's left cheek.

The picture comes with a caption. *You can just feel the love LMAO*

Ellis almost smiles again. Cal had called him when they took Donut home from the shelter, going on and on about how happy he was that Dawson finally got a dog, but afraid Donut would kill him in his sleep because he hates Cal's guts. Ellis advised him to take the spare bedroom and to never step between a man and his dog. He doesn't think Cal listened.

Swallowing down the lingering bitter taste, he locks the screen and shoves the phone into the pocket of his slacks. God, what kind of asshole isn't happy for his own brother? Or his brother-in-law who he knows has been through absolute hell and deserves to be happy? Fuck, what's happened to him? Ellis has always been a grumpy ass, but he's never been that much of an ass. Maybe he can blame it on the heat. And sand. Fucking Queensland, seriously. This place is terrible for his mental health.

A movement from the corner of his eye gets his attention. He turns towards it just in time to see Gabriel securing a lid on a cup full of rusty-brown liquid. What did Ellis order again?

"Okay, here you go." Gabriel slides the cup towards him. "A medium—"

"Ellis," Ellis blurts out. "My name is Ellis," he clarifies, so as to not look like a complete moron shouting out random names.

There really should be a law about the way you can look at a stranger, because the way Gabriel is looking at him right now? Yeah, that should be illegal. No one should be allowed to smile like the fucking sun at the guy who's been nothing but a rude dickhead.

"Hi, Ellis," Gabriel says, and yeah, another thing. No one is allowed to make Ellis' name sound like *that*. "I'm Gabe." Before Ellis can tell him that he already knows, someone clears their throat. Turns out that Zeke's been watching them through the kitchen pass. Gabriel hooks a thumb over his shoulder to point at him. "That's...no one important."

"Hey!" Zeke shouts in indignation, then salutes Ellis. "Name's Zeke. The one who actually owns this place."

"Co-owns," Gabriel corrects.

"That's what I said."

"You—" Taking what looks like a calming breath, Gabriel turns back to Ellis. "Sorry. Don't let our bickering keep you."

"It's fine." Ellis checks his watch. "I still have time."

"You work nearby?"

Before Ellis can reply, his phone chimes with a text. He's almost relieved to find it's not Dawson, but Amanda.

Did he just wish his work was calling him instead of his, well, family? Jesus, he really is fucked up.

"I spoke too soon." He waves the phone at Gabriel. "Have to go."

"Of course," Gabriel says and...does he sound disappointed? Can't be. Ellis must be imagining shit. "Take care, Ellis. It was nice seeing you again." Could he at least say it a little less earnestly?

Ellis gives him a curt nod. "Bye."

It's not until he's at work and pulling up into his usual parking spot, his drink untouched in the cup holder, that he realizes he never actually apologized. Great. That means he'll eventually have to go back, right? And why is it that the thought doesn't bother him all that much?

Not wanting to dissect it, he reaches for his fancy mystery drink, taking a cautious sip. A firework of flavors bursts on his tongue, making him take another sip before he even swallows the first one. God, how has he lived his life without knowing this thing existed? He could've been drinking this the whole time. It's like Christmas in a cup. Not that he celebrates Christmas, but you know...

His tense muscles gradually relax, and he can feel his nervous system calm down. And isn't caffeine supposed to have the opposite effect? Strangely enough, he doesn't feel sleepy. He doesn't feel particularly energized either. He just feels...pretty okay. Hell, he doesn't remember the last time he felt *really* okay.

A curious part of him brings the cup to eye-level, a little wary of what he might find. Except there's nothing on there, no mysterious message. Ellis has to push down an unexpected surge of disappointment.

"You're fucking ridiculous, Ellis." He lets out a derisive laugh and brings the cup to his lips.

This. This could be his good thing.

Chapter 4

EVER SINCE A CERTAIN someone had wandered into his café two weeks ago, Gabe has been a disaster, his mind all over the place. Zeke hasn't been helping either, taking the piss any chance he gets, hoping to wind him up. And wound up, Gabe is. Not even the new *Guardians of the Galaxy* is enough to distract him from the thoughts of stormy blue eyes and a whiskey-smooth voice he could listen to for hours.

"I'm gonna go out on a limb and say it's not the movie that has you so jittery," Ash comments smugly after they've entered the cinema lobby, making their way to the counter.

Gabe should've seen it coming. His cousin never leaves the therapist behind after he clocks out. Not that the job is to blame. Ash has always loved to pry, sticking his nose—and other body parts—in other people's businesses. It made sense he would go ahead and get paid for it.

Gabe decides to play dumb for the sole purpose of stalling. "Why not? You know I love the *GOTG* franchise. And this one is supposed to be epic. I mean, it's Rocket's story." The trailer was heart-wrenching. He just hopes no one will die, he's too emotionally strung out right now to handle that.

Ash gives him a flat look. "Nice try. What's up?"

"You still like to sit all the way in the back?" Gabe asks when it's almost their turn.

"Seeing as I'm still far-sighted, yeah."

Gabe gives him an unimpressed side-eye and turns toward the girl behind the till with a smile, ordering their tickets.

"Put that back." Ash grabs Gabe's wrist when he attempts to pay.

"But I asked you to the movies."

"And here I am." Ash grins, retrieving his wallet.

Gabe scowls. He only has two rules when it comes to paying. You either pay for what you ordered and the other person does the same, or the person who invited the other pays for both.

Ash, of course, doesn't give a crap about the rules. Gabe knows that in Ash's eyes, he's still the lanky kid five years younger than him looking for his place in the world. It's annoying. But also kinda sweet. Well, as sweet as Ash can get.

Gabe puts his phone away with a sigh. "Okay. I'm buying popcorn."

"Sounds good to me."

"It's so cute that you're arguing about who's going to pay," the girl behind the till says dreamily. She nods towards Ash and gives Gabe a wink. "He's a keeper."

"Aww, he knows," Ash says, voice a few pitches higher than normal. He slings an arm around Gabe's shoulders, pulling him into his side. "Isn't that right, pumpkin?" He lets his arm drop only to slap Gabe's ass, pulling a horrified yelp out of him.

The girl giggles.

"I hate you," Gabe hisses while Ash pays. "If you swat my ass again, you're gonna lose that hand."

"So violent." Ash clicks his tongue in disapproval, pocketing their tickets.

Throwing a glance over his shoulder to make absolutely sure Ash's hand isn't in the vicinity of his ass, Gabe heads towards the snacks section. He gets a large popcorn and a soda for each.

"So, are you going to tell me what's up, or do I have to drag it out of you?" Ash asks innocently.

Gabe whips around to glare at him. "You can't just do that whenever you feel like it." He braces himself just in case Ash does try to sneak around in his mind. Gabe has practiced blocking him out long enough that it's not really a big deal if the fucker tries something, but it's still annoying.

Ash grins. "Pretty sure I can."

Gabe thrusts the snacks at him. "I can't believe you're a licensed professional."

Ash hums, taking a sip of his soda. "Are you done stalling?"

Gabe gives a resigned sigh. "I met someone." That's overstating it, really.

Ash perks up like a dog with a bone. Then his eyes narrow. "Wait, you're talking about a person, right? Or have you found another stray cat—"

"He's a person," Gabe grunts. So he has a weakness for furry faces. Who doesn't? Animals are far less complicated than people, and that's saying something considering Gabe can read anyone like a book with an extra-large font.

"And he's a *he*. Nice," Ash says approvingly. His gay ass always gets more excited at the prospect of a penis. Which means Gabe is not getting out of this conversation unscathed. A note for the future self: next time, get obsessed with a female customer.

"Don't start," Gabe begs, knowing it's futile.

"I'd ask how you met, but considering you live at the café—"

"I don't live at the cafe."

"He's a customer, I assume."

"...Yes."

"Hmm." Ash smirks. "Hot?"

Gabe opens his mouth, closes it and lets out another, wistful sigh. "Beautiful." So beautiful he could cry. People like Ellis shouldn't technically exist. Surely, there must be a law for how beautiful a human being can be.

"That's what I said." Ash rolls his eyes. "Show me."

"What? No!" Gabe takes a step back, reinforcing the barrier in his mind.

"Come on."

"I don't want you to objectify him."

Ash grins slyly. "I already am."

Gabe makes a face. No, he doesn't want Ash to objectify Ellis, but that's not the main reason he doesn't want to let him poke around in his noggin.

Aside from practically growing up together, Ash has dug around inside his mind often enough that there is virtually nothing he doesn't know about Gabe. Most people would find that scary, but he finds it quite relieving. There's something freeing about having someone who knows him to his core and loves him anyway. Naturally, it helps that Ash has mojo of his own, having inherited that particular trait from his dad. Which means Gabe can be open with him about his own powers.

But Ellis? Despite their short acquaintance, Gabe feels extremely protective of him. Having to listen to Zeke bitch about Ellis based on how he behaved the first time they met makes him grit his teeth. And Ash, being a therapist, loves dissecting people. Gabe isn't comfortable with letting him do that to Ellis.

Unfortunately, since he knows Ash as well as Ash knows him, he also knows his cousin won't leave him alone until Gabe breaks.

"Fine," he relents grumpily, holding up a finger before Ash can start. "Just a peek. Then you fuck off."

Ash arranges his fingers into the Star Trek greeting. "Scouts honor."

With an involuntary huff of laughter, Gabe brings the barrier down a smidge, letting the thought of Ellis rise to the surface. Given how much time he spends thinking about the man, it hardly takes any effort.

He can feel the exact second Ash's consciousness nudges his, then the exact moment he encounters Ellis. His teeth flash in a shark-like smile that makes Gabe want to take a long, hot shower asap.

"Well, hello," Ash drawls. Gabe can feel him poking around. "Such a preppy fellow. Damn, red would look good on him."

"Okay, that's it. Get out." His protective instincts kicking in, Gabe gives him a mental shove.

Ash physically stumbles back a step, a wince passing over his face "Ow." He massages his temples. "Chill, Gabby. I won't touch your boy."

"He's not my—" Ash's skeptical expression forbids him to finish that sentence. He looks away, hoping to hide the color that has risen to his cheeks at hearing Ellis be referred to as his boy. "I don't even know him."

"You said, I quote, that you *'met someone'*."

"Yeah." Gabe checks his phone. The movie has officially started, but there's no need to rush since the first fifteen minutes are always just commercials. "What cinema are we in?"

Not fooled by the change of topic, Ash checks their tickets, and continues interrogating him on their way to the movie.

"When?"

"Hm?"

"When did you meet him?"

"About two weeks ago?" Gabe feigns uncertainty, knowing full well which day and time it was that Ellis first showed up, all grumpy and sad and beautiful. "He's only come to the café twice."

"It's not like you to get hung up on someone like that."

As if Gabe doesn't know. He might struggle with a savior complex, but he doesn't normally get invested. Not anymore. He likes to think of himself as more of a...guide. Nudging others in the right direction and vanishing when they don't need him anymore. Well, it's more like the people leave when they don't need *him* anymore, but that's fine. He's fine with creating a positive impact on someone's life and then staying behind. It's enough. It is.

"I'm not hung up. I just..."

"Can't stop thinking about him?" Ash supplies unhelpfully. Something in Gabe's expression must give him away because Ash's eyebrows lift up in realization. "Ah. I got it."

Gabe's instantly suspicious. And wary. "You don't get it."

There's no one checking tickets, so they just continue straight to their cinema.

"He's one of them, isn't he? A lost soul?" Ash makes a *tsk tsk* sound when Gabe remains stubbornly silent. "Gabby…"

"I know," he says miserably, pushing open the door to Cinema 6. By the sound of it, some car insurance commercial is playing on the screen.

"You can't save them all."

"I *know*. Okay? I know." He slurps at his soda, his heart getting heavy at the vivid memory of how it felt being near Ellis that first time. Not that Ellis was particularly happy the second time they met, but it wasn't as…intense. Hell, he even chatted with Gabe. And laughed a little! It was such a beautiful sound. "It's just… God, Ash, he's so…sad. So fucking sad." He looks at Ash. "How do you do it?"

"Do what?"

"Your job. How do you talk to people who are in so much pain every day without completely losing it?"

Ash used to be his role model, the reason Gabe went to study Psychology. While learning about the human psyche in a more clinical manner was interesting, it had soon become clear to him that this wasn't a career path he wanted to pursue. No way would he be able to sit through patient after patient and not meddle. That's not to say Ash is the epitome of professionalism. His methods are questionable at best. But he gets the job done, and he's just fine. Sure, a little messed up in the head, but what therapist isn't a little coocoo?

Ash seems to mull it over, as though he himself doesn't know how he does what he does. Gabe can relate. Not many people know about his powers, but those who do always ask how he handles it. Most of the time, he has no idea how to explain.

They find their row before Ash comes up with an answer. Gabe uses the torch on his phone to find their seats, shuffling carefully down the aisle.

"16, 17…oh, sorry guys." He always feels bad when he has to ask people to move so he can get to his seat. "We just need to get—Oh. Hey!" His vision having adjusted to the lack of light, he recognizes Dawson and Kieran.

The initial confusion clears from their features, and they smile at him. "Hey, Gabe!" Dawson whisper-shouts over the commercial, blinking in surprise when he notices Ash. "Hey, Ash! Small world, huh."

Ash smiles back. "It is." His gaze shifts to Kieran, curious. As far as Gabe is aware, the two of them haven't met.

"Are you sitting next to us?" Kieran asks, he and Dawson standing up to make room.

"A little further down, actually, but..." Gabe shrugs, figuring they might as well take the seats here since the row is empty otherwise. They can always move if someone comes who has the tickets for the seats. "We can park here."

"Great!"

Gabe sits next to Dawson, with Ash on his left and Kieran on Dawson's right. He taps Ash's arm, nodding at Kieran. "This is Kieran, by the way. Kieran, that's Ash."

Kieran's friendly smile freezes. "Ash..." He turns to Dawson. "Your shrink?"

"My therapist, yes," Dawson corrects, his tone suggesting that his going to therapy is something he has discussed with Kieran before and did not enjoy.

Kieran huffs. "Yeah, whatever."

Okay. That's interesting. Plenty of people are judgmental about therapy, but Gabe had no idea Kieran is one of them. He's so chill most of the time.

Ash leans forward, angling his body so he can see Kieran. "And you're Dawson's best friend."

"Yup." Kieran pops the *p*, then does a double take. "Wait, you guys talk about me?" He glares at Ash accusingly, then Dawson, then Ash.

Gabe clutches the popcorn to his chest and slides down the seat, trying to blend into the fabric.

"I can't discuss my patients," Ash says haughtily, making Gabe groan. Why is it that Ash enjoys conflict so much?

"Dude, you recognized my name. Obviously, you talk about me."

"Guess you answered your own question, then." Ash shrugs, the picture of indifference.

Gabe elbows him, but only gets his arm.

Kieran's nostrils flare. "You—"

"Kieran..." Dawson says pleadingly. Miraculously, it works. Kieran settles—somewhat—though the energy in the air is enough to choke Gabe.

He coughs to disperse it. It doesn't do much. "O-kay. Awkward."

When the commercials end and trailers start, the air has cleared up a little, allowing Gabe to relax. It doesn't last long.

"How are you, Dawson?" Ash asks.

"Good. I have a good story for you when I see you next."

"Oh yeah?"

"Yup. It involves painting and cacti."

"Sounds like an intriguing combination."

"Dude, seriously?" Kieran snaps, glaring daggers at Ash. "He's your patient. Are you even allowed to talk to him outside of work?"

"We're just chatting, Kieran," Dawson says irritably.

"You usually pay him for chatting. Pretty sure there are some rules about this."

"Would you rather I talk to you?" Ash suggests, an infuriating smirk blooming on his lips. "Maybe you should swap seats with Gabe here, so we can get to know each other."

Oh, for Christ's sake. Lesson learned: no going in public with his stupid cousin ever again.

"No, thanks." Kieran sniffs. "I don't have three hundred on me to pay you for a *chat*."

Ash hums, and that's...not good. "Shame. You sound like you could use my services."

Yup, there it is.

Kieran takes a breath so sharp it can be heard over the speakers, already halfway out of his seat, white hot rage flashing in his eyes. "The fuck did you just—"

"Kieran!" Dawson snaps at the same time that Gabe hisses, "Ash!"

Ash continues to smile while Kieran glares. Gabe starts crying on the inside, and almost on the outside.

Eventually, everyone is saved by the opening *Marvel* credits appearing on the screen.

"Oh, hey, the movie is starting!" Gabe announces with fake enthusiasm, but the relief is real. Once everyone has marginally calmed down, Gabe leans into Ash's space and growls, "You always have to stir shit up, don't you?"

Ash doesn't even take his eyes off the screen. "Only when the situation invites me."

"Yeah, right." Gabe scoffs, trying to focus on the beginning of the movie. It lasts all of twenty seconds before a wave of something hot and tacky rushes over him. He frowns when he feels a tingle in his belly, his skin suddenly hot despite the aircon. He looks around, trying to find out who it's coming from because it sure as hell isn't from him. It dawns on him when he feels Ash shift in his seat, crossing his legs, and another wave slams into him.

He gags, slapping Ash's chest. "Oh my god. Gross! Stop it now!"

It's bad enough when it happens with random people, but feeling his own cousin's arousal? That's just yuck!

"I'm not doing anything," Ash lies.

So not only does Ash love conflict. It clearly gets him off.

Gabe could've lived his whole life without that particular knowledge.

He leans closer so he doesn't have to whisper. "Kieran is straight and clearly biased against therapists. And he's a friend. Don't you try anything."

Ash chuckles darkly. It sounds dirty. It feels dirty.

Gabe is so putting bleach in his bath today.

"They're all straight until I get my dick in them."

Gabe manages not to hurl into the popcorn, but it's a close call. He shoves the box at Ash. "I lost my appetite."

Ash happily takes it from him. "More for me."

Gabe suffers through the movie, unable to focus on what's

happening on the screen because he's too busy blocking out Ash's horniness.

The awkwardness from before grows tenfold when the movie ends, and the four of them make their way out of the theater.

Once outside, Gabe lets the horny-cousin-repelling-shield down, taking in a relieved breath. Summoning a smile, he turns to Dawson and Kieran. Kieran still has daggers in his eyes.

"Well, it was nice bumping into you, guys. See you tomorrow?" Kieran pops into the café here and there, but Dawson shows up more often than not.

"Probably not," Dawson says regretfully. "I have to be at the shelter earlier than usual. But Tuesday, maybe."

"Alrighty. Say hi to Cal for me."

"Will do." He looks at Ash. "I'll see you Friday."

Ash smirks. "Looking forward to our *chat*." Then the fucker winks, his smirk growing when he gets a reaction out of Kieran, who looks like he's about to lose his shit. Dawson better be ready to pay bail.

Before Ash can do any more damage, Gabe gathers his frustration into a small ball of energy and flings it at him.

Ash jerks like getting electrocuted, a noise of surprise escaping him. His attention snaps to Gabe, and he glares.

"You okay there, Ash?" Dawson asks with concern.

"I'm fine. Just a cramp," Ash says without taking his eyes off Gabe, who juts his chin out defiantly.

"Okay, well...we better go," Dawson says with a nervous laugh. He frowns at his phone. "I just noticed I have, like, twenty missed calls from my obsessive sister. I should call her back before she sends out the cavalry."

"Of course," Ash says easily, smiling again. "From what I've heard of her, she actually might."

Dawson's eyes grow a little wide. "She totally might. Anyways, see you!"

"Have a good night," Ash says, then looks at Kieran with an

unreadable expression. "You too, Kieran."

Kieran's eyes narrow. "Kiss my ass."

"Kieran!" Dawson chastises, horrified.

Ash grins predatorily. "Only if you ask nicely."

Kieran pales, then turns crimson, sputtering something that was probably meant to be an insult but comes out a jumbled mess.

"I'm so sorry. We're leaving. Kieran!" Dawson barks, grabbing his best friend by the collar and dragging him away.

Gabe stands rooted to the spot, fighting the urge to cry. Is it possible to die of sexual frustration that's not even your own?

"Damn, I'd love to spank that attitude out of him," Ash groans and, to Gabe's absolute horror, reaches down to adjust his dick through his pants.

Gabe turns on his heel, striding away to grab his scooter. "I'm going home."

"Ah-ah-ah, not so fast." Ash blocks his way. "We haven't finished our chat."

Now he wants to talk about Ellis? Hell no. It would make everything feel tainted.

Gabe opens his arms. "There's nothing to say. I fucked up. I've met the guy twice and now I'm attached."

Ash rolls his eyes. He's always told Gabe he tends to get dramatic. "Does he have a name?"

"Ellis," Gabe tells him reluctantly. He points a threatening finger. "Don't you dare go digging around in my head."

Ash scoffs. "I don't have to. It's written all over your face."

"What is?"

"That it's too late for you to back out. Trying to cut yourself off never works, it just leaves you miserable," Ash says solemnly. Ugh, how did the tables turn so quickly?

"So you're saying I should run with it?" Gabe asks with disbelief. He thought Ash would be the first in line to discourage him from it.

"Always the better option than running *away* from it."

Gabe folds his arms on his chest. "Am I talking to my cousin or a therapist?"

"They're the same person."

Gabe's not sure how to feel about that.

"I don't even know if he likes guys." There have been...tells, but nothing solid to go off of.

"He doesn't have to like guys. He just has to like you," Ash says it like he's explaining something obvious to a total dumbass. "And let's face it, it's more important to you to save his soul or whatever than it is to pursue a relationship with him."

Gabe scowls. Damn Ash for knowing him so well. "I hate it when you're right." The chances are that once he manages to bring a little more light to Ellis' life, he'll stop being so hung up on him. After all, the most important thing is that Ellis is happy. With or without Gabe in his life.

"Sure you do. Come on, I'll drive you home."

Not really wanting to be in closed-in quarters with Ash and his dick, but knowing how persistent Ash can be, Gabe collects his scooter and follows him to the car. For the ride home, he makes sure to put up the barrier again. Just in case.

Chapter 5

ELLIS PINCHES THE BRIDGE of his nose, trying to fight off the headache he feels building. His vision has started to blur from the incessant staring into the computer. He should probably give in and get a pair of glasses like his doctor is telling him to, but he simply doesn't look good with them on. Contacts aren't an option, since he'd rather die than let anything touch his eyeball. The eye exams are bad enough.

Normally, he tries to avoid having to take work home with him, but it's been happening a lot this past week. He's been getting distracted at work, and there's no point pretending he doesn't know the reason. No matter what he does; his mind keeps wandering to deep, amber eyes and wide, heartful smiles. To kind words Ellis has no right to but craves deeply.

In short, Gabriel is fucking with his head, and his work. That just won't do. No matter how good the coffee is, or how settled it makes him feel, Ellis can't go back. It's not conducive to his productivity. Or sanity, for that matter.

The ringing of his phone gives him a reason to take a much-needed break, though he really shouldn't take any if he wants to get this done tonight.

Cal's name flashing on the screen makes him sigh. What does he need this time? Cooking advice? Complaining about being bullied by his dog?

He accepts the call. "Cal, hey."

"Can I talk to you for a minute?" Cal blurts out instead of a greeting, sounding frantic. Oh dear. Did he turn all the laundry pink again? Last time he did, he called Ellis in a complete panic, afraid of what Dawson would say when he came home.

"Is it urgent? I'm quite busy."

"Did you know Dawson wanted to apply for a divorce?"

Ellis freezes, the headache and work instantly forgotten. He pushes his chair back and stands up. "He told you."

It doesn't make sense. Dawson has been fighting him—fighting everyone as far as Ellis knows—tooth and nail to ensure Cal wouldn't find out about their past. Ellis let a comment or two slip about Cal's drinking, but that was that. It's been almost two months since the accident and Dawson seemed so happy with the direction things have been going. Why would he tell Cal now?

"You did know," Cal says, voice tight with betrayal.

"I found out by accident," Ellis says defensively. It's not fair to put blame on him. For him, this was a lose-lose scenario from the start. His options were to tell Cal the truth and risk ruining everything, for all of them, or not tell him and risk losing Cal over a lie. Like he is right now.

"So did I," Cal says, resolving Ellis' confusion. Does that mean Dawson *hadn't* told him?

"How?"

"I found the divorce papers in his nightstand. I wasn't going through his stuff," Cal adds in a rush, as though he's worried Ellis would judge him. He's the last person who can judge anyone. "I don't understand, Ellis," Cal admits quietly, voice as small and broken as Ellis has ever heard it. "I thought... He seems happy with me. And just now, he..." There's a pause, an intake of breath so big Ellis can hear it through the phone. "He asked me to hold him. He was in pain and needed sleep, and he asked me to hold him."

"Cal." Ellis feels his eyes well up. And isn't that a first? He's not a crier. Neither is Cal. Their whole family line might as well be carved from stone. "I don't know what to tell you. I'm sorry."

"You knew," Cal reminds him, sounding angry again. Okay, angry is good. Ellis can work with angry. He knows how to handle angry. "So you must know the reason."

"I do," he confirms. "But it's not mine to tell. You need to talk to Dawson." There's no way he's making things any worse than they are. And yeah, maybe it's selfish and cowardly to dump all of this on Dawson, but it doesn't mean he's wrong. Even if Ellis didn't know the truth, it would still be up to Dawson to tell it.

"Thanks," Cal grits out, clearly not sharing Ellis' views. Ellis calls out to him before he can hang up, earning an irritated, "What?"

"Just... Whatever he tells you, keep an open mind. You're a different person than you were before, but Dawson remembers both of you. It might be hard for you, but it's harder for him."

Ellis can't even imagine what a mindfuck this must have been for Dawson. Ellis and Cal had barely tolerated each other before the accident, reserving their interactions to business talk and biting each other's heads off. But getting used to this new Cal has still been an adjustment.

Cal doesn't say anything, the line going quiet for a long moment before the call disconnects.

That went well.

Giving his desk a glance, Ellis shuts his laptop and puts all the papers back in their folders. Someone up there clearly doesn't want him to get any work done. Why else would he be plagued with thoughts of Gabriel—a guy he barely knows—and then have his brother drop a bomb?

He grabs himself a can of gin and tonic from a 12-pack and settles on the sofa, his phone laid next to him in case Cal calls again. In the meantime, he might as well watch something. At least he'll make use of that *Netflix* subscription he rarely uses.

His two most-watched shows come up when he opens the app. Deciding between *Gilmore Girls* and *Lucifer,* he settles on *Gilmore Girls.* He likes how it allows him to turn off his brain for a bit.

It doesn't last. His phone rings not long after. Pressing pause on the TV, he picks up. "Cal?"

"How could you not tell me?" Cal hisses, sounding on the verge of tears.

"I didn't know until recently," Ellis starts to explain. "He told me the night of your accident—"

"Two months?! You've known for two months, and you let him stay with me?!"

"Hey!" Ellis snaps, standing up fast and accidently dropping the remote on the floor. "I told him not to do it. I told him I'd take care of it. Of you. But he was adamant."

"So you just backed off?"

And Ellis bristles. He's so fucking tired of being held responsible for other people's messes. "I'm not his mother to order him around. He had enough of that from you."

Once the words are out, silence hangs heavy between them. Guilt slams into him like a freight train, but he doesn't take the words back. They might be insensitive, especially given Cal's current predicament, but that doesn't make them untrue.

"You should've fought him on this," Cal persists, but he doesn't sound angry anymore. Just resigned. Guilty.

Ellis swallows, dropping back down on the sofa. "You didn't remember, Cal."

"I could've still hurt him."

"Have you?"

"Of course not!"

"Then let it go," Ellis says gently. He's hardly someone to go to for advice, but even he knows that nothing will come out of trying to change the past. "Go talk to him. Ask him what he wants. For once, let him decide for himself."

Once again, Cal hangs up without a goodbye. Ellis can only hope he won't do anything stupid. He makes a mental note to reach out to Dawson tomorrow if he doesn't hear from Cal.

Well, this whole mess has one silver lining. He finally managed to stop thinking about Gabriel.

He picks up the remote from the floor and presses *play*.

Ellis should be listening to the presentation. He really should. Instead, he checks his phone for the third time in ten minutes. Still not a word from either Cal or Dawson.

"Ellis?"

He looks up at the sound of his name. He's not sure who said it, but everyone's attention is aimed at him.

"Yes?"

"Are you alright? Should we take a break?" That's Steve, the head of finances, whose presentation Ellis has been ignoring.

"Yeah, sorry. You can—" His phone goes off, startling him. Relief and trepidation play table tennis in his stomach when he glimpses Cal's name. He stands up abruptly. "Actually, I need to step out for a minute. Excuse me." He disappears into the hallway, picking up as the door shuts behind him. "Cal?"

"Hey. I'm downstairs. Are you free?"

"Downstairs? As in here? In the building?"

"Yes."

"Jesus," he breathes, running a hand over his face. "Can you call next time?"

"I'm calling now."

"That's not—" He cuts himself off, groaning. Seriously, how is this his brother? "I'm at a meeting. Come on up. Amanda will let you into my office." Technically, Cal's office. "Can you wait half an hour?"

"I can wait."

"Good. Do you have your card?"

"I do. Which floor is it?"

"27th. I'll let Amanda know you're coming," Ellis promises. He hangs up, shaking his head. Seriously. How is this his life?

He smooths down his suit before stepping back into the conference room, sparing another apology. If he was distracted before, there's no way anything from the presentation is going to register now. He'll just have to get Steve to send him the slides so he can go over it again.

The next thirty minutes drag like an old lady with a hip replacement, followed by a series of questions and a long-ass discussion Ellis has no chance of following. He gets a few weird looks as he basically runs out of the meeting, rushing to his office. Amanda gives him a curious look as he breezes past her desk but, bless her, she doesn't say anything.

He swipes his card to open his office, spotting Cal sitting at his desk, immersed in his phone.

"Sorry for being late. The meeting went a bit—" The sound coming from the phone makes him stop in his tracks. Surely, that can't be...

Oh, but it is. And it's *loud.*

Ellis slams the door shut. "Are you watching porn?!"

Cal pauses the video, putting the phone down, his face the picture of nonchalance. "It's for research."

"Research," Ellis echoes dryly.

Cal nods. "Yes.

"Can't you do 'research' at home?" Ellis grunts, counting down from 100, so he doesn't strangle his brother.

"I was bored."

"Bored."

Cal cocks his head. "Why are you repeating everything I say?"

Ellis throws his hands up, his voice a pitch higher. "I don't know! Maybe because you show up unannounced—"

"I called you when I was downstairs.

"—and watch porn in my office, where anyone can hear you! I don't want to be explaining this!" He only recently started to settle in here. People are not used to him as they were to Cal.

"Did you hear anything from the outside?" Cal asks, giving Ellis a pause.

"That's beside the point!"

Cal sighs, ducking his head as though he finally understands Ellis' frustration. "Sorry."

Ellis runs a hand over his face—he's been doing that a lot recently—and spreads his arms. "Well, I'm here." He runs his gaze over Cal, trying to gauge how yesterday went based on what he looks like. *He's watching porn, so it probably went fine.* "Is everything okay? How did it go with Dawson yesterday?"

His brain supplies a handful of possible scenarios that might've taken place, but Cal totally blows him away when he says, "We had sex."

Well, that explains it. "Uh...okay. I was kinda hoping you'd talk it out first." He doesn't bother reminding Cal of TMI. The concept is probably lost on the guy, anyway.

"We did," Cal says. "Twice, actually. This morning too."

"And? All good?"

Cal contemplates it for a second. "All good."

"I'm happy to hear that." His lips pull into a small smile, but it leaves quickly. "What do you need from me? Came to rip me a new one?"

Cal shakes his head. "I need to talk to someone who knew me before. To...understand why I did what I did. What kind of person I was."

Ellis really, really doesn't like that idea. But the way Cal is looking at him is trusting. Hopeful. He can't really blow him off now, he owes him that much.

"My lunch break isn't long enough for that but...sure. I can do that." He gives Cal a stern look. "If you promise me not to beat yourself up about what you learn."

Cal's features twist into something pained. He must have already guessed that whatever Ellis is about to tell him won't be pleasant. "I'll do my best. I promised Dawson."

"Good." Heat crawling up his neck, Ellis nods towards Cal's

phone. "I'll probably regret asking this, but what's with the porn?"

Cal heaves a sigh. "Yesterday was amazing. I'm just not sure I did it right."

Ellis holds back a snort. "It's pretty easy to tell if you did it right or not."

Cal's lips purse in thought. He blinks up at Ellis, his expression lighting up with hope. "Could you teach me?"

Ellis frowns. "Teach you what?"

"How to have sex."

Ellis staggers back. Surely, he must have misheard. He takes in Cal's earnest expression, the absolute cluelessness of it. He closes his eyes, pulling a deep breath in. "There's so much wrong with that sentence, especially when spoken to your brother."

"But—"

"Let me make it clear that we each play for a different team," he cuts in. "I sleep with women." Something inside him reacts to that claim, like a nudge in his mind, trying to alert him to something. He brushes it off, too busy to investigate every single weird feeling that rises inside him. "Dawson very much isn't a woman."

Unfortunately, Cal keeps talking. "But the principle is the same. You still need to—"

"No. *Hell* no!" Ellis steps back until he's pressed against the door. "I'm not talking to you about gay sex." No hate, he just doesn't want to think of sex and his brother at the same time.

"But—"

Out of desperation, Ellis covers his ears, screaming. "Lalala, I can't hear you!" God, he hopes no one is currently in the hallway to hear this shit. He'd never live it down. He'd have to resign.

Cal isn't impressed. He looks at Ellis in disappointment, honest to god pouting.

Slowly, Ellis drops his hands to his sides, ready to clamp them over his ears again if Cal so much as hints at anything remotely sexual.

He clears his throat. "Okay, here's what we'll do. We'll take my car and go get lunch, and I'll tell you what you want to know. About you and our family," he adds, in case Cal gets any stupid ideas. "And we never, ever talk about what just happened here. Understood?"

Cal has the audacity to roll his eyes, as if Ellis is being unreasonable. "Fine. Where are we going?"

Ellis regards him suspiciously, then says, "I'm craving Indian. You okay with that?"

Cal shrugs. "Sure."

The ride to the restaurant is tense and awkward, and it continues even when they sit at a table and order their food. Figuring it's better to get it over with, Ellis bites. "Okay. What do you want to know?"

Cal's face darkens, his fingers curling into his palms. "Did I... Was I always like that?"

Ellis doesn't need him to clarify. *Was I always an abusive drunk?*

"I don't know how to answer that, Cal," he says apologetically. "I had no idea about the drinking or about...Dawson. Not until I came here and he told me." He drums his fingers on the table, wondering what to say. "I can't tell you when it all started because I wasn't there. You and I, we aren't close."

Cal's expression turns into something resembling regret. "Because of me?"

Ellis sighs. "Because of everything. You. Me. Dad. Because of our fucked up lives."

"What do you mean?"

"How much do you know? Did Dawson tell you about our family?"

Cal takes a minute to reply. "He said our dad died of a heart attack years before we got married. That's when I took over the company." Distaste flashes across his face. "He said that you and I don't see each other much. Or didn't used to because you moved to Sydney to run the office there." He shrugs. "That's it."

Their food arrives then, and Ellis is grateful for the short time it earns him to stall. There's a rock in his stomach, his appetite gone, but he forces himself to eat.

"Did he tell you about Mum?"

"He said she wasn't in the picture, but he didn't know much. Apparently I never talked about her."

No, of course he didn't. "Yeah, that tracks," Ellis bites out, shoveling food into his mouth.

"How do you mean?"

"I wouldn't be keen on talking about the woman who walked out—well, more like ran out on us when we were kids either." And really, it shouldn't hurt like this after all this time. He's not a kid anymore.

Cal's eyes grow wide. "She walked out on us?"

"Yup. Packed her shit and left before I was old enough to remember her." He tries to sound unaffected, but his voice cracks towards the end.

"Oh." Cal pushes his food around, a furrow between his brows. "Why?"

Ellis gives a bitter laugh. "Who the fuck knows. Probably grew tired of taking care of us."

"What makes you think that?"

"It's what Dad said." Among other things.

"That's it?"

"What other reason is there? She left. Period. The end. Whatever her reasoning was, it doesn't change the fact that she abandoned us." He hates how hard his voice shakes even after three decades.

Cal isn't satisfied with the explanation. "What about me? I was older than you. Did I not remember her?"

He did. Too much, too often. He never failed to rub it in Ellis' face, even going so far as to blame him for Mum leaving— *'Everything was okay until you came along.'*

Ellis didn't want to believe it. Contributed the vile words to Cal's own pain looking for an outlet. But that all changed when Dad admitted Ellis wasn't planned, that they never meant to have a second child. He never said Mum leaving was Ellis' fault, but how could it not be? It all makes sense. He was never wanted. No wonder Cal hated him.

Ellis reaches for his water, throat dry like a gravel road. "You remembered a little, but you were still really young," he lies. It's for the best. Ellis would give anything to rid himself of his childhood memories. Cal doesn't know how lucky he is.

"But—"

"Look, this isn't why you came to me today," Ellis cuts him short. He can feel himself starting to slip into the past. "You wanted to know about yourself. Well, here it is. Dad was always strict, especially with you, but at least you had Mum. Then Mum left, and you were stuck with me and a tainted memory of her. You were the older brother, so of course Dad would be tough on you, preparing you to take over and shit. He never cut you any slack."

Cal mulls it over, then asks, "And you? How was he with you?"

"I didn't matter, Cal. You were the golden child. You had his eyes on you all the time."

Ellis used to be so damn envious of Cal, of the attention he got from their dad. Sometimes he still is, because even negative attention is still attention. But a part of him is relieved he never had to experience the stress Cal must have lived through. The stress of always needing to be perfect, never making a mistake. The spitting image of their dad.

"I'm not a shrink," Ellis says. "And I have no intention of defending you. No way. But honestly, looking back at the way we were raised? It's not quite surprising you turned out to be...you know."

"You turned out fine," Cal shoots back.

Ellis laughs, but there's no humor in it. "You have no idea how fucked up I am, Cal."

Cal eyes him critically. "Are you an alcoholic?"

Ellis lifts a shoulder. "I enjoy a drink or two."

"But it's not an addiction."

"No." Though he can see how easy it would be to go down that road.

"Have you been in a relationship?"

"Not a serious one."

"Have you hurt any of your partners?"

The no is on the tip of his tongue, but he makes himself ponder it. "There have been times I was a jerk."

"But have you hurt them? Intentionally. Repeatedly."

He sighs. He gets Cal's point. "No."

"Then you're not nearly as messed up as you think you are."

"I have my issues." It's not fair to compare who is the more fucked up one. Ellis might not go around drinking his ass off and beating his partners, but he knows that wherever he goes, he leaves something bad behind.

"Doesn't everyone?" Cal challenges. "You might not be perfect, but you're a good person. You were there for Dawson and you didn't even know him that well. You took care of my screw-ups, dealt with the police and the company, and never asked for anything."

"You're family," Ellis says, fidgeting uncomfortably. He's no hero, or whatever Cal sees in him. Ironing out other people's messes is the one thing he's good at, especially since he's unable to sort out his own shit.

Cal, the bastard, doesn't wanna back down. "Based on what we just spent nearly an hour talking about, it's clear that blood doesn't mean much. I was terrible to you our whole life, our mum walked out on us, and our dad was a controlling asshole." He pauses. "You might be right, someone was bound to turn out like him. I'm just glad it wasn't both of us."

Ellis' chest constricts, making it hard to pull in a proper breath. He looks at Cal, really looks at him, shocked by the wave of affection that comes at him out of nowhere. The man in front of him might not be the brother he knows, but it's a brother he always wished for. Minus the sex talk.

"There's no one at this table who's like him," he says, making sure his voice brooks no argument.

Cal must get it because he smiles, holding Ellis' gaze. "I hope so."

Something passes between them; kinship Ellis has never felt with his brother before. He hopes it's not the last time he feels it.

He returns the smile. "Okay, the moment is over." Cal laughs at that. "Tell me something good. Read any interesting books lately?"

"I started reading *Me before you,* but couldn't finish it after Dawson told me it doesn't have a happy ending."

Even though he's known about Cal's sudden affinity for romantic fiction for a while, it still feels very weird to hear him talk about it. Just how hard of a hit did Cal's brain take in that crash?

"I thought you're only into fantasy."

"Mainly, not only."

"Next time you'll tell me you're reading *Fifty Shades.*"

Cal's expression turns curious. "I don't know that one. Is it good?"

Ah, Jesus. Then again, Ellis walked right into that one. "On second thought, if you're going to dive into that particular rabbit hole, you might as well look into gay romance. Maybe you'll learn a thing or two."

"Any recommendations?"

Ellis chokes on air. He was just teasing, but of course Cal would take him seriously. "Uh, no? Ask your husband. You're on the same team."

"Team?"

Ellis has to close his eyes and pull in a steadying breath. "Gay, Cal. You're both gay."

"Oh. There are teams for that?"

Ellis screams internally. What the hell is his life?

Chapter 6

"WOULD YOU STOP?"

Gabe unwillingly tears his gaze away from the entrance to glare at Zeke. "What?"

"You're like a puppy waiting for his human to come home."

Gabe sputters, a rush of heat flowing to his face. "What's that supposed to mean?"

"Oh, nothing. Just that you've had your eyes glued to the door waiting for Mr. Asshole to come through for the past week."

"I have not—"

"And I'm pretty sure that spot you've been cleaning for fifteen minutes is as shiny as it gets."

Gabe drops the cleaning cloth he's been running over the whole counter, not just one spot, thank you very much. "Fuck you, Zeke."

"Aww, I'm flattered, but we both know I'm not the one you want. Although I'm a much better catch."

Gabe is saved from being charged for very voluntary manslaughter by a customer coming in. He plasters on a smile which widens when he sees Cal.

"Look who the cat dragged in." He glances behind Cal, puzzled not to see anyone with him. He and Dawson are attached at the hip these days. "Where's your better half?"

"Working."

Cal's face takes on that ridiculously smitten expression all lovebirds tend to get when someone mentions their SO. His energy becomes so sweet Gabe feels the urge to cough. And that's saying something, considering he lives for sugar!

"Ah, I see." He waggles his brows. "Thought you'd sneak out and get a dose when he's not keeping a tight leash on you, huh?" Cal's donut obsession is honestly adorable. A little worrying, sure. But adorable. Also, very flattering to Gabe, who actually bakes all the stuff in the café.

Cal smiles sheepishly. "Yeah, but I didn't come straight here. I was with my brother. Ellis is now running the company, so I don't have to." His smile vanishes then, expression falling. Gabe is about to ask what's up when something else registers in his under-caffeinated brain.

"Ellis," he repeats slowly, licking his lips. "Tall, dark, and broody?"

Cal chuckles at the description. "Um, yes? That would be my brother."

What are the odds? Then again, he shouldn't be so surprised. How had he not seen it before? He's sure Dawson mentioned his brother-in-law at some point when Cal had his accident and Ellis had to fly up here; possibly another time after that. Has Ellis' name ever dropped? He can't remember.

"I should've known. You're practically twins." That's stretching it a little, but similarities are undeniably there, just not very obvious unless you're looking.

"Not really..." Cal says dubiously, making Gabe laugh.

Sure, Cal's features might be different under the scruff, but their hair and eyes are the same—though in Gabe's very unbiased opinion, Ellis' eyes are prettier. Deeper. They're almost the same height, and if Cal hits the gym a little more after he's healed, his frame will fill out to match Ellis'.

"You've met him?"

Not wanting to give away how bummed he is that Ellis has only visited a couple of times, Gabe puts on a mask of indifference. "He's popped in for a coffee a time or two. Anyway, what are you after? Wait. One hot chocky and one donut?" he asks before his resolve crumbles and he starts interrogating Cal for information.

Cal ducks his chin, like he's embarrassed for being so predictable. "Yes, please."

"To have here?"

Cal looks around, scrunching his nose when he spots the few occupied tables. "I'll take it away."

Gabe chuckles. He likes his introverted customers, they're so funny. "Sure thing." He grabs the donut first, then scribbles Cal's order on the cup, pausing when a familiar, tingly sensation sweeps through him, turning into a ringing in his ears that lasts no longer than a few seconds. Once it stops, words flash in front of him in a golden swirl, burning bright before they start to fade.

If you don't like your story, rewrite it.

He quickly writes the words on the cup before he forgets them and passes it on to Zeke while Cal pays.

Well, that was a first. Cal's never got a message from him before. Or more accurately, there has never been a message to pass on to him. Does it mean something is happening with Cal? Maybe Dawson too? The message was kind of ominous, to be frank.

Once Cal's collected his order and bid them both goodbye, Zeke walks over, leaning against the counter as he watches Cal leave. "Huh. Who would've guessed?"

"That he and Ellis are related?" Gabe guesses. He's under no impression that Zeke won't eavesdrop if given a chance.

"That you've met your future brother-in-law and didn't even know it."

Gabe lets out a groan. "Seriously. Will you stop?"

Zeke has the nerve to look offended. "Moi? What did I do?"

"Oh, please. You've been giving me shit for weeks."

"But I do it with love."

"Well, stop."

Zeke sighs, feigning disappointment. "You won't let me have any fun." He huffs, turning around, then back to look at Gabe. "You know, I can predict the future. Want me to tell you what's coming for you and your loverrr?"

"You can't predict shit."

"Sure can!"

"You can draw and read—very inaccurately, may I say—a pile of tarot cards. That doesn't mean you can see the future."

Zeke crosses his arms. "I also read tea leaves."

"Again, inaccurately."

"Not true!"

"When we met, you told me I'd be dating a guy named Tyler in three months."

Zeke makes a face. "I was close enough."

"I met *Taylor* in six. And she was a girl."

Zeke throws up his hands. "Tyler, Taylor, it's the same! And since when do you care about gender, huh?"

Gabe shakes his head, holding his hands up in surrender. "I give up."

"You're ungrateful, you know that? I offered to give you a glimpse into the future."

"I'm happy with my present."

"Fine. How about your present self goes and makes some more cookies? The freezer is running low."

"Gladly," Gabe retorts, making a beeline for the kitchen. He undoes his waist apron, exchanging it for a full-length one as he turns the oven on and starts lining up the ingredients for the cookies. Finally, some much needed reprieve.

Adding ingredients to the mixing bowl, Gabe tries to focus on the feeling of the dough forming under his hands instead of daydreaming about impossible scenarios in the future.

Fucking Zeke. This is all his fault.

Chapter 7

THE LUNCH WITH CAL, despite the topic of conversation, had put Ellis in a strangely good mood. Well, an *okay* mood. Turns out there might be something about opening yourself up to another person. Not that Ellis is planning on repeating the experience anytime soon. He's not equipped to withstand such an emotional rollercoaster. Once in 34 years is enough.

So yeah, he'd felt a little lighter, at least until he got back to work and received an updated report from the finance department. That effectively returned his mood to its default gloomy state.

The sun has already started to set by the time Ellis' stomach growls, signaling how long it's been since lunch. When he ignores it in favor of opening another document, the universe sends him a further reminder in the shape of his relentless assistant.

"What are you still doing here? You're not sleeping here again, are you?" Hands propped on her hips, Amanda arches a perfectly shaped eyebrow.

"Please, come in," Ellis says drily. After weeks of being barged in on, jumping out of his skin every time, and giving Amanda a scolding which yielded absolutely no results, he's given up. The mini heart attacks aside, it's not too bad having a PA who could run the company if Ellis ever drove himself into a ditch from sleep deprivation.

Amanda's other eyebrow joins the party, indicating she's waiting for a response.

"I'm not sleeping here. I never slept here."

"You slept here twice last week."

"I didn't sleep here. I napped."

"It's only a nap if it's during the day."

"Well, I woke up and went home."

She rolls her eyes, tucking a blonde lock behind her ear. "Didn't you just buy an apartment? Is there something wrong with it or what?"

"I did and it's fine." For four walls and a roof. It's still better than Cal's pretentious, sterile apartment.

Folding her arms on her chest, Amanda gives him a scrutinizing look, wrapping it up with an ominous, "Hmm."

"What?" Ellis looks down at himself, checking if there's something wrong with his suit.

"You need to get laid," Amanda says, as if talking about the weather.

Ellis gives her a flat look. "Are you offering?" he taunts. He's not going to give her the satisfaction of showing how uncomfortable he is. Amanda takes too much pleasure in making people—and especially Ellis—squirm.

Seriously, if she wasn't so brilliant at her job...

Amanda shrugs, popping the top button of her shirt open. "Since you asked so nicely."

Ellis falls back into his chair, gripping the edge of the desk before he can topple backwards. "Amanda!"

Her evil laugh booms through his office. "Gosh, you're so easy to wind up." She stalks towards him, her heels clapping against the linoleum floor. She leans over the desk, giving Ellis a flash of her cleavage that's most decidedly intentional. "Chill, will you? But really, if letting off some steam will make you less insufferable, I volunteer."

"Charming," he says with a glare.

"I'm just trying to be practical. It would make both our lives easier."

"You're making this offer truly irresistible."

"I try. I'm a very good PA, after all." She winks.

"Is that why Cal kept you around?" Ellis retorts, regretting the words right away. His brother might be a brand-new person after the memory loss, but that doesn't mean Ellis is comfortable with the idea of Cal being a cheater on top of being a jerk. Ellis wouldn't be able to ever look Dawson in the eye again, knowing something he doesn't.

"Unfortunately, both me and your brother love dick. Alas, I had to make do with alternative solutions."

Ellis lets out an inaudible sigh. Thank god. Yes, sure, Cal being gay should've told him something, but one can never be too sure, especially given his drinking problem. People do stupid shit when they're drunk—like driving and ending up in a nearly fatal car crash.

"Alternative solutions?" he asks against his better judgment.

"You know...coffee. Massages. The occasional spanking."

"Amanda..."

"Figuratively speaking, of course."

"Of course." He rubs his temples. "Go home, Amanda. There's no point in both of us being here."

At first, Amanda doesn't move, and when she does, it's to lean further over the desk and reach for Ellis' face. He freezes in surprise, hoping he's hiding his spooked expression well when her manicured fingers trail across his cheek.

She smacks her lips, making a disappointed sound. "Damn, I could slap those cheeks."

Ellis swallows. "No, thank you."

"Such a waste." She hums and pulls away. "Don't stay too long. See you tomorrow."

"See you," he replies to her retreating form, fighting a sudden urge to take a very hot shower. He knows Amanda was just jerking him around—okay, maybe that's not the best choice of words. But the interaction has left him feeling kind of...filthy. Not that he's a prude. At least, he doesn't think so, and Amanda, despite being almost a decade older, is a ridiculously attractive woman. Just a tad intense.

Who is he kidding? She's *way* too intense and Ellis is...mellow. And he likes mellow. Some of his ex-girlfriends have called him boring, but what's so wrong about wanting things to be easy and uncomplicated?

He checks the time, deciding to give it until seven before going home.

He almost makes it. It's only 7:34 when he gets into his car, the thought of his fluffy mattress and hot shower extracting tension from his body.

The shrill sound of his phone ringing pulls him out of his reverie. It's unlikely the call is work-related, which leaves Dawson or Cal. Hopefully, it's nothing serious. Cal said everything was okay.

Ellis huffs when the name that flashes across the screen doesn't belong to his brother or brother-in-law. Taking a calming breath, he picks up.

"Erika?"

"Hey, Ellis," she says in a sweet voice, as if she didn't scream her lungs out at Ellis the last time they spoke. As if *he* was the one who got caught blowing a guy from the customer service department in the bathroom during the last company event. "It's been a while, huh?"

"It has."

"How are you?"

"Fine. Why are you calling, Erika?" He's so not in the mood for this.

"Um...well. Okay," she lowers her voice, pretending to be bashful. "There's no easy way to say this. My pill must've failed because I...I'm pregnant."

Ellis wasn't in love with her or anything, but they *had* dated for almost half a year. And while seeing his girlfriend with another guy's dick down her throat is irrefutable proof that she cheated on him, the reminder still stings.

"Congratulations." What else is she expecting him to say?

Erika giggles, like the situation is funny. He supposes it's a good thing she's not freaking out about being a future mum. "Likewise. You're the baby daddy, dummy."

Right. He should've seen that coming. "Am I, now?"

"Yes, of course!" She laughs. "Who else would it be?"

"You tell me." He's under no illusions that the guy at the function was a one-off.

"Jesus, are you still upset about Brian? It was just a blowjob, come on. I never slept with him."

Ellis isn't going to dive into a long-winded, pointless discussion about what officially counts as sleeping with somebody.

"If not with him, then with someone else. Because it's not mine."

"Of course it is! I'm twelve weeks along."

And the event was ten weeks ago, just a couple of weeks before the whole thing with Cal and the company went down. Which only reinforces his belief that Erika *was* cheating on him all along. In retrospect, Ellis should be glad that they broke it off right before he had to move to the Gold Coast.

"Then you might want to hit up the guy you fucked twelve weeks ago."

He hears a sharp intake of breath before all hell breaks loose. "Fuck you, Ellis! Just because you're afraid of commitment and admitting that—"

"I'm sterile."

Whatever she was about to say never makes it out. "W-what?"

"I can't have kids. I underwent a vasectomy years ago." One of the first things he did after graduating.

"You..." she seethes. "How did I not know about this?! I was in a relationship with you for months! I deserved to know if the guy I was dating couldn't have kids!"

"Erika, let's stop the bullshit." He's tired and so fed up with being taken for an idiot. "Neither of us was pretending that this was something it wasn't. Neither of us was planning a white-picket-fence future with the other."

"That's completely beside the point!"

"Let's talk about something else, then," he says, keeping his voice empty of emotion. "Like the fact that you were going behind my back. Or that when I caught you, you tried to make it my fault because, let me paraphrase, 'I didn't pay you enough attention'. Or that you're trying to manipulate me into raising someone else's baby. Either way, it doesn't concern me."

She's quiet at first, breathing harshly, loud enough to hear through the phone. "You're such an asshole, Ellis! Fuck you and your guilt-tripping. If you weren't such a boring, workaholic fuck, I wouldn't have to go and seek comfort elsewhere!"

And there it is again.

"You definitely didn't mind the perks that came with me being a workaholic. I don't remember you complaining about me working so much when it got you nice jewelry or dinner at a fancy restaurant.

She sputters indignantly. "I was trying to be an independent woman and give you space!"

"Thanks for your consideration. Now that there are almost a thousand kilometers between us, feel free to forget about me."

"I won't listen to this," she grits out. Ellis can hear her pacing. "How about you sort out your daddy issues before spewing judgment all around you? Just go and live your boring, dull life with your piece-of-shit company while you can, because no one will ever stand to be around you. You're going to die alone, Ellis. And you'll deserve it."

The call disconnects.

Erika didn't say anything he hadn't heard before. Yes, he's boring. Yes, he's a workaholic who doesn't even like his job. Yes, he judges people because people are stupid. He knows all that.

So why does it hurt?

He's not without fault. He was well aware what kind of person Erika was, be it her affinity for pretty, expensive things or the need to be the center of attention. Ellis could give her the former. He's not good at the latter. So none of this is a surprise, is it?

He might complain about people using him for the money all the time, but what has he ever done to change it? Throwing money at people is easier than connecting with them. It's his fault his relationships are so superficial.

He throws his head back against the headrest, hating himself a little more when he dials Erika's number. She lets it ring five times, likely trying to prove a point, but eventually picks up.

"What do you want?" she snaps.

"Are you going to keep it?"

"How dare you— Of course I'm keeping my baby!"

Fine, then. "The father, will he help you raise it?"

She hesitates. "What is it to you?"

"I want to know if he's competent to be a parent."

"More than you would be, that's for sure," she says with derision, as if she hadn't tried to rope him into parenthood just now.

"When it's born...if something happens and you struggle raising it...I can help. Not raise it but...I can send you money. If you can't afford a babysitter, or daycare, or...I don't know. Something. I can help."

Working in marketing pays well, but no one can predict what might happen down the road. Erika might struggle when she's on maternity leave, or some other issue will pop up. She's beautiful and will have no problem finding a guy, but that doesn't mean the person would be willing to take care of someone else's kid.

It might not be Ellis' baby, but just by knowing about it he feels kind of responsible. If he can do something to ensure it has a good life, materialistically at least, he will do it. No kid should grow up with only one parent, but if they have to, they should be taken care of.

"I don't need your money or your help," she bites out after a long moment of silence. "I don't need anything from you. Don't call me again." She hangs up.

Well, then. That's one more thing sorted.

Waking up the following morning, Ellis feels more miserable than usual, and that's saying something. Yesterday's events, starting with the bizarre lunch with Cal, to getting an earful from Erika, have opened a can of worms he'd hoped to keep shut forever.

His life in Sydney never felt particularly fulfilling, but it was *his*. Even though he couldn't run away from his past in a spiritual sense, the physical distance sure helped. Now he doesn't even have that. Coming back to the Coast has awakened feelings he's spent years and years building walls around. He can feel it; this void spreading through him like cancer. He has no doubt it will completely consume him one day, probably sooner rather than later.

It's not like he never tried to fill the void. It's just that everything he's ever tried only made him feel emptier, pushed him further from what he wanted. Not that he knows what that is. There might have been a time when he did, when he was looking for...something. Whatever it was, it's long forgotten. Most days, he doesn't even know who he is, who he *truly* is under the suit and glamor. For all he knows, there's no one else and *this* is who he is.

Erika was right about him. He's a miserable dick with a mountain's worth of daddy and mummy issues, and he'll always be alone, just as he deserves. It's for the best. Why should he barge into someone else's life and ruin it, like he always does?

Exercise. That's what he needs to clear his head.

He brushes his teeth and throws on a baggy t-shirt and his favorite track pants. As displeased as he was to leave his apartment in Sydney, he has to give this much to his new one: the building has a fantastic gym. It's not just treadmills and rowing machines, but a variety of free weights, and even bars and plates. He saves so much time when he doesn't have to travel to a public gym, not to mention he hates working out with so many people around.

He heads to the kitchen to refill his water bottle, making a mental note to keep an eye on his fluid intake. They're coming into the summer now, and he almost forgot how hot Queensland gets during that time. At least he lives in the Southeast and not somewhere up North, like Townsville. His soul would probably evaporate in the heat.

Running the tap, his eyes steer involuntarily to the empty coffee cup with the *Lost and Ground* logo in the corner. His cheeks burn even though there's no one around. He still doesn't know what compelled him to bring the cup home with him, he just remembers how everything inside him rebelled when he went to throw it away. It reminded him of the time his dad made him get rid of his favorite toy—a dinosaur plushie—when he turned ten, because he was *'too old for toys'*. Sneaking an empty, dirty paper cup into his apartment definitely made him feel like a child. How embarrassing.

It's just that whenever he reads the message Gabriel put on the cup, the storm constantly raging inside him just...settles. Not for long, not completely, but enough that he can breathe without feeling like there's a hand around his windpipe that just keeps squeezing.

He has no illusions about being special, Gabriel likely writes random messages for people all the time. But when reading the four words, no matter how incorrect they are, he can't help but feel like Gabriel meant them specifically for him.

You deserve good things.

He really doesn't. And if Gabriel knew him, he'd agree. Still, the possibility that Gabriel, despite their brief interaction, might actually believe Ellis is worth more than chewing gum stuck to someone's shoe makes him want to be that person. Someone who truly deserves good things.

It's not going to happen. But a guy can dream.

Worthy or not, Ellis ends up at *Lost and Ground* again. He tried to stay away, he really did, but to no avail. He's like a freaking kid who knows he's not supposed to touch a hot stove but is unable to help himself. There's something about the place that keeps drawing him in, making him believe that the potential burn might be worth it.

Are you sure you're still talking about the café?

He shakes his head to dismiss the inconvenient thought and gets out of his car. This time, he doesn't park in front of the café but at a parking lot down the street. For some inexplicable reason, he doesn't feel good about ignoring the 'no standing' sign. He never cared before, so what the hell?

He takes a moment to check his reflection in the side-view mirror. His morning has been rushed because he managed to lose track of time while at the gym, getting too much into his head. He'd only had time to take a quick shower and had to forgo breakfast. He's even forgotten his tie, but thankfully keeps a bunch of spare clothes at work for emergencies.

His hair, on the other hand, is a proper mess. He hasn't gone a day without pomade since his hair had started doing that weird curly thing in his early twenties. It's a necessity, one of those things he'd take with him on a deserted island. His hair has a mind of its own, sticking in all directions and curling slightly whenever there's a hint of humidity in the air. Just another reason why he hates this place. He uselessly runs a hand through the unsalvageable mop, before making a beeline for the café.

Similarly to his first visit, the place is buzzing with people. The queue isn't as long as before, but it still makes him look at his watch to make sure he has enough time. He makes a mental note to start coming here a little earlier.

Already planning on becoming a regular, huh?

Gritting his teeth at the annoying voice in his head, he shuffles forward when the line moves, giving him a better view of the counter and the person behind it. A feeling of déjà-vu washes over him.

Gabriel, in his usual fashion, is smiling broadly at the woman he's serving. She must've said something funny because Gabriel laughs, his head thrown back. Good mood is oozing off him, so potent the air in the café is practically saturated with it.

Ellis finds himself staring stupidly at Gabriel, like he couldn't look away if he tried. He's met a few people who could quite literally light up the room, where you could feel the entire atmosphere change the second they walked in.

But Gabriel...he's like the freaking sun, the warmth radiating from him drawing everyone in. To Ellis' chagrin, he's no exception; wanting to get closer though he knows he shouldn't. He's the exact opposite, carrying certain darkness with him wherever he goes. Maybe that's why he feels so drawn to the café. It's as though the darkness starts to dissipate when he's here, like it can't withstand being close to Gabriel's light.

He wonders if Gabriel has mind-reading skills, if he can hear Ellis' thoughts, because he suddenly stills, a pen in one hand and a cup in the other. He lifts his head, a frown furrowing the space between his brows, and his gaze zeros directly in on Ellis.

Ellis' breath catches, no air flowing into his lungs as he waits to see Gabriel's reaction. His heart leaps into his throat when Gabriel's frown vanishes and his lips pull into the broadest smile Ellis has seen on him so far.

He's probably thinking very highly of himself, but Ellis could swear Gabriel rushes through the three customers before him, sparing only a few words to each before writing down their order and moving onto the next person.

Before Ellis knows it, it's his turn.

Only, he forgot what he wanted to say. He stands there like an idiot with his mouth half-open but no sound coming out.

Gabriel saves him, his already huge smile broadening the slightest bit. "You're back."

Ellis, with his above average IQ, manages to squeeze out, "Yes."

Head tilting to the side in a bird-like manner (which is not cute, by the way), Gabriel's eyes travel around Ellis' face, studying him. His lips twitch. "Rough night?"

Heat crawling up his neck, Ellis lets out an embarrassed chuckle. "I look that bad, huh?"

"Nah." Gabriel winks. "A little disheveled, but you're still gorgeous."

Ellis freezes, his eyes probably popping halfway out of their sockets. "What?"

Gabriel mirrors his expression. "What?"

"You said—"

"I didn't say anything." Gabriel quickly drops his gaze to the iPad and clears his throat. "Now, where were we? Right." He clasps his hands together. " A large long black, two extra shots?"

His mind stuck on the word 'gorgeous', it takes Ellis a few long seconds to process the question. "Actually...I think I'll have the other drink. You know, the one you made for me last time?"

Gabriel looks at him in surprise. "You liked it?"

"Yeah. It was different. I liked the spices."

"Cool." Gabriel grins. "So, one dirty chai on oat?" He hovers his hand over the selection of cup sizes. "Medium?"

"I'll have a large today."

"Great." Gabriel scribbles on the cup and puts the order through the iPad. "Anything else?"

A 'no' on the tip of his tongue, Ellis hesitates. He still hasn't eaten breakfast, and the spicy-sweet scent floating from the pastry cabinet gives his stomach all sorts of ideas. "I'll have a cinnamon roll too. Which I'll pay for," he adds with a pointed look.

Gabriel, the minx, rolls his eyes. "Yeah, yeah." He grabs the tongs and a small paper box. "Should've known you'd have a sweet tooth. Runs in the family, huh?"

Ellis goes to say that no, it actually doesn't, before Gabriel's words register. "What do you mean?"

"Your brother and his donut addiction?"

"You know Cal?" Ellis asks like a moron.

"He's a regular. He and Dawson. And the doggo."

"Huh." Makes sense. The café is kinda conveniently stuck between Ellis and Cal's apartments, though it's definitely closer to Cal's. "How did you know we're related?"

"I just found out yesterday. Cal popped in solo this time to stock up on some donuts while his hubby wasn't around. He mentioned having lunch with his brother, and your name came up."

"Oh."

Ellis can't keep the surprise from his face. Cal talks about him? It takes incredible effort not to interrogate Gabriel about what exactly Cal said.

"It explains why we only met recently," Gabriel carries on. "You're new to the area, right? Sydney, was it?"

"Yeah," he confirms. "I'm still...adjusting."

Gabriel is about to say something else when an irritated voice from behind Ellis quips, "'Scuse me? If you're done chit-chatting, I'd like to order my coffee."

Ellis is torn between telling the lady to mind her business, and apologizing for clearly having become one of those people who share their fucking life stories with strangers. Oh, how low he has fallen.

"Sorry! I'll be right with you," Gabriel apologizes, sounding genuinely remorseful. It reminds Ellis of the first time he was here.

He still hasn't apologized for that.

"Sorry for holding you up too," Gabriel says to him.

"It's fine," Ellis reassures him. "I have no meetings this morning."

"Cool." He smiles, tapping on the iPad. "That'll be $12.50."

Ellis pays silently, but continues standing there even after the payment has gone through. He wants to say something. Feels like he *should* say something. And for whatever reason, he doesn't want to move away just yet.

The way Gabriel's looking at him suggests he might feel the same.

"The pick up station is over there," the lady from before speaks, pointing to the far end of the counter.

"Right. Sorry," Ellis says without looking at her. He exchanges a strange, tense smile with Gabriel and goes to wait for his order, spotting Zeke behind the coffee machine. He's a little bummed Gabriel won't make his drink.

"Howdy?" Zeke grins at him over the top.

"Hey. Zeke, right?"

"You got it, sugar." Zeke winks, calling out the drinks he's just made and moving onto the next order. "What do we have here?" he says to himself, studying a docket. "Hmm. I see you like my milk."

"Pardon?" He's not sure he heard right.

Zeke laughs. "I make the powder for chai latte. It's a very special recipe. Has a secret ingredient."

Not wanting to be rude for once, Ellis plays along. "What secret ingredient?"

Zeke leans forward, beckoning Ellis to do the same with a curl of his finger. Ellis does, albeit reluctantly.

"Magic," Zeke says ominously.

"Magic," Ellis repeats flatly. "Right." God, he really wishes Gabriel was making his drink.

Something must show on his face because Zeke grins knowingly. "I see how it is," he says. "Stay right where you are." He saunters over to Gabriel, grabbing him by the hips and whispering something into his ear.

Something ugly spreads through Ellis' stomach, an acidic taste coating the back of his tongue.

Stupid heartburn. He really should look into an alkaline diet.

Hands still on Gabriel's hips, Zeke manhandles him—there's no other word for it—all the way to where Ellis is standing.

"There you go! Can't have you looking like a kicked puppy, can we?" He gives Ellis a wink.

"What?"

"Gabe here will make your drink. I know he's your favorite." He winks again. Ellis is starting to think it might be a neurological issue. "You're his too, by the way." With that, Zeke skips over to the till, taking over Gabriel's spot.

"Well," Gabriel breaks the awkward moment and laughs. "I guess I have a date with the cold room after I've made your drink."

It takes Ellis a second to understand the reference, and blood rushes to his face when he gets it.

"Uh..."

"I'm so sorry about him," Gabriel carries on, now sounding a little frantic. It...should not make Ellis feel all fluttery. "He's chaos incarnate, I swear. You have no idea how many times I've thought of slipping a tranquilizer into his coffee."

An unexpected laugh burst out of Ellis. "Perks of the job."

"Huh?"

"If someone pisses you off, you can take it out on their drinks," he explains, remembering how he was convinced Gabriel would spit in his coffee after the shit he'd pulled the first time around.

Gabriel chuckles, looking a little taken aback, like he hadn't expected for Ellis to have the ability to make jokes.

"Believe it or not, I've never felt like doing that. Most of our customers are pretty lovely, and those who aren't usually don't come back anyway."

"I did. I came back," Ellis says, feeling uncertain all of a sudden. Gabriel has been perfectly polite—friendly, even—but that doesn't mean he actually wanted Ellis to come back. He's probably just too nice to say it.

But what about all those times he's smiled at Ellis? Is it just an act?

Suddenly, Ellis feels like throwing up.

"You did," Gabriel says simply, but it doesn't feel simple at all. There's tenderness in his tone, and his expression, and he's looking at Ellis like he knows what he's thinking. He's been doing that a lot, actually.

"I was a dick the first time I came here," Ellis says.

Gabriel gives him a smile that's infinitely patient. "You were obviously stressed out of your mind. We all have off days, I'd never hold that against you."

Ellis swallows thickly, his heart starting to pound. "Most of my days are off days."

Gabriel frowns. "Well, your brother doesn't remember who you are, and, from what I hear, you're the big boss now? That's a shitload of stress and responsibility. Trust me, you're doing just fine."

When Ellis only stares at him, Gabriel deflates, remorse filling his features. "I'm sorry. I shouldn't have said that. It's none of my business—"

"No," Ellis stops him. "No, you're... Please, don't apologize." He runs a hand over his face in frustration. How did they end up with Gabriel apologizing to him? That's not what he wanted.

He can't believe how well Gabriel can read him. Talking to him makes Ellis feel exposed, stripped bare with all his dark secrets out there in the open.

What he doesn't understand is why it's not as scary as it should be.

It's kind of...nice. That there's someone who can see through the layers of bullshit into his very soul and not judge him for it. Dangerous, but nice all the same.

Someone clears their throat. Loudly.

"Shit," Gabriel utters, frantically perusing the amount of dockets that have accumulated while they were having a heart-to-heart. "I'm sorry. Orders have piled up like roaches."

"No, I'm sorry. I didn't mean to distract you."

"It'd be hard not to. You're a very distracting man." Gabriel makes a desperate sound, somewhere between a groan and a sob. "God. I totally have a date with the cold room after this."

Ellis laughs, really laughs, tears springing to his eyes while his heart slams against his ribs like he's had ten espressos in a row.

Gabriel stares at him in stunned silence, his mouth slightly agape and eyes half-lidded. Then he licks his lips, Ellis' gaze instantly drawn to them. His hammering heart comes to a sudden halt before starting to beat even faster.

Gabriel's eyes slide shut for a moment. When they open, they have that golden glow Ellis was sure he imagined the first time around. To be fair, he's not sure he's not imagining it again. He's been experiencing a lot of weird phenomena lately.

Reaching for a sharpie, Gabriel scribbles something on Ellis' cup. Excitement flutters in Ellis' stomach. Gabriel has already written down the order, so that means this must be one of his messages, right?

When he's done, Gabriel pushes the cup and the paper box with the cinnamon roll towards Ellis, his eyes wide and hopeful.

Ellis reaches for the items, a jolt of electricity zapping through him when their fingers brush.

He swallows, whispering for some reason, "Thank you, Gabriel."

"You're welcome," Gabriel whispers as well, as though he too can feel the fragile spell hanging around them, reluctant to break it. "See you around?"

Without hesitation, Ellis replies, "Yes."

It takes all his strength to turn around and walk out. He manages in the end, forbidding himself to look back. It's fine, he'll be back tomorrow. He can last that long, for fuck's sake.

When he's in the security of his car, suddenly feeling ten degrees colder, he finally gets a look at the cup. He doesn't breathe as he starts reading, and by the time he's finished, his vision is blurry.

Whatever you're looking for is looking for you too

His eyes burn, but he doesn't cry. Instead, he laughs. It makes him sound like a lunatic, but he laughs.

Because for some inexplicable reason, it feels like he's already found it.

Chapter 8

"THAT WAS FUN!" ZEKE exclaims when the morning rush finally dies down. He's always enjoyed working under pressure, gets a kick out of it or something, but Gabe suspects his good mood has more to do with how Zeke humiliated him.

"Where do you think you're going?" Zeke demands when Gabe strides past him in his hurry to get to the cold room.

He whirls around, pointing a threatening finger. "I'll deal with you later." And he will. Once he clears his throat chakra.

He runs to the cold room, sliding the door shut behind him. "FUUUUUUUCK!" Damn, that felt good.

He thunks his head against one of the shelves in tandem with his chanting. "Fuck fuck fuckity fucking fuck."

He's going to kill Zeke. Hell, he'll look up fucking voodoo and turn Zeke's miniature into a pincushion. He'll make him suffer.

Not that Gabe needs help when it comes to embarrassing himself. He can do that brilliantly on his own. His filter is malfunctioning on a good day, but with Ellis it's pretty much non-existent. Ellis is still his customer, a relatively new one at that, and Gabe called him gorgeous. And distracting! To his face! Talk about cringe.

Not as cringe as the ass comment, though.

Oh god. Did that really happen? Yup, it did. Forget about calling a guy you barely know gorgeous. Nothing tops admitting to said guy that you like to eat ass.

"At least I didn't tell him I'd like to eat *his* ass."

Great. Now he's thinking of Ellis' ass. More specifically, he's thinking of—

Nope. Not going there. It's only morning and he has to get through his shift in one piece.

Shouting another half-hearted 'fuck' for good measure, he pats his overheated cheeks, straightens his apron and slides the door open.

Zeke is standing in the middle of the kitchen, one of his brows arched and a self-satisfied smirk on his stupid mouth. "Feel better?"

"You..." Gabe growls.

"Yes?"

Gabe throws himself towards the baking station and makes a grab for the wooden spoon. He holds it out like a sword, giving Zeke a seething look.

Zeke's smirk drops. "You wouldn't."

"Wouldn't I?"

Eyes darting around, Zeke snatches the thing closest to him which turns out to be a whisk. "Ha!" he shouts victoriously, taking a defensive stand. "What's your problem, anyway."

"My pro—" Gabe chokes out, shaking the spoon threateningly. "How could you do that to me?!"

"Christ's sake, it's like having a child," Zeke says with an eyeroll. "Seriously, with all your mojo and shit, how can you be so dumb? He likes you!"

Gabe melts a little. He didn't want to get his hopes up. When he likes someone, it's tricky to differentiate between which feelings belong to whom. He thought he felt something from Ellis this morning—a kind of curiosity and intrigue, and, possibly, a tiny bit of attraction. But he instantly disregarded it as projecting his own feelings onto Ellis. It's not unusual. With his gift, there's quite a large margin for error. Sometimes his emotions just bounce off the other person and he gets confused.

He can't afford to go out on a limb. Especially when that limb is Zeke's!

"If he does, that's not a green light for you to scare him away! He's...reserved!"

Zeke scoffs. "Reserved, my ass. He was a dick the first time you met and now he doesn't know how to act. I was helping out!"

"You were doing the opposite!"

"He looked pretty damn happy to me when I dragged you over."

That gives Gabe a pause. "He did?"

"Yes!"

"Oh." He hates the spark of hope lighting up in his chest. Dangerous territory. Abort! "It doesn't matter. You humiliated me! Intentionally made both of us uncomfortable!"

A corner of Zeke's mouth curls upwards. Oh, how Gabe would love to feel it against his fist. "Yeah, that was fun."

Gabe is saved from committing a first-degree murder by someone calling out, "Hello? Anybody here?"

Dammit. There's no way he can go out and serve customers. Zeke must come to the same conclusion because he puts the whisk down, giving Gabe a supercilious smile.

"How about you go cool down while I serve?"

"I hate you," Gabe grumbles as he slaps the spoon on the counter and stalks back into the cold room. He has a feeling he'll be spending a lot of time there in the near future.

The following morning, Gabe almost drops a tray with freshly baked cinnamon rolls when he exits the kitchen to find Ellis standing in the middle of the café. He looks as gorgeous as usual—no surprise there—but there's something different about him. He seems...softer, for the lack of a better word, and Gabe instinctively picks up on the nervous energy emanating from him. Or maybe it's Gabe who's nervous? Ugh, why is it so hard to tell?

Nervous or not, Gabe can't help the huge smile that always seems to appear whenever Ellis is around. "Hey! You're early!" He only flipped the sign to *open* ten minutes ago.

"Hi," Ellis says, looking unsure as he sweeps his gaze around the café. "You're open, right?"

"We are. That's not what I meant," Gabe says with a small chuckle, setting the tray down. The cinnamon rolls can wait.

"Oh." Ellis shuffles his feet. "Yeah, I figured I might as well pop in before the crazy rush starts."

"Good thinking. Give it twenty minutes and we'll be slammed." Weekdays are all the same. People start pouring in at 8:30 on their way to work, then again at noon when they're on their lunch break. Mondays seem to be the worst.

Ellis is being smart, getting up earlier to avoid the mayhem, but Gabe feels bad for him. As much as he loves coffee, he's not sure he'd be willing to wake up earlier just to avoid waiting in line.

"Nice apron," Ellis says, voice strange. And is he blushing?

Gabe's gaze drops to his own chest. He has a whole bunch of funny and cute aprons and never remembers which one he threw on in the morning. Today, he apparently went with the one saying *I like big buns and I cannot lie*. Ah, Jesus.

"Oh yeah, thanks." He laughs nervously. "I bake everything we sell, so... *Buns*. You know? Like food. The bigger the better. Not like...um..." *Oh. Dear. God.*

Ellis looks like he's contemplating if he should leave or call Gabe an ambulance.

He does neither, but seems to be holding back from laughing his ass off. "Yeah, I...figured that's what it means."

"Right. Of course."

"So, you like your job?"

Gabe releases a breath. Finally, something he can talk about. "I do. I mean, it has its ups and downs like anything, but it combines a lot of stuff I enjoy."

Ellis raises an eyebrow. "Like buns?"

Gabe turns beet red, and chuckles. "Baking in general, but yes. Also, coffee. Drinking or making it. Customer service comes naturally to me too."

Ellis makes a face. "I don't know how you do it."

"What?"

"Deal with...people." He says 'people' in a way someone might say 'excrements'.

Gabe laughs. He has to laugh, overtaken by a wave of affection. God, this man is precious. And so contradictory. But mainly precious.

"Don't you do the same thing? Being a CEO and whatnot."

"In a way, but it's different. I deal with numbers. Proposals. Contracts."

"Sounds sexy," Gabe says, then groans. Here he goes again. "I'm sorry. I tend to put my foot in my mouth if I haven't had my coffee yet."

Ellis must be getting used to Gabe's antics because instead of shocked silence, there's only a short pause, and then he laughs. "Only when you haven't had your coffee?"

Relief loosening his shoulders, Gabe decides to go with the flow. Ellis already knows what a disaster Gabe is. He might as well be himself.

"It's rude to call someone out like that, you know?"

Ellis' reaction isn't what he hoped for. There's a hint of a smile, but his mood shifts, something that feels like guilt tainting the air around him.

"I'm a rude person, so..."

Oh.

Gabriel Emmett Cleaver, do not throw yourself at a likely straight man, just to give him a hug.

Repeating the mantra like a prayer, Gabe says softly, "I don't think you are. I think you're just..."

"What?"

Hurt. Sad.

Lonely.

"Tired," Gabe says. It's safe, and it's true. "Having your usual?" he asks to fill the silence when Ellis doesn't say anything. Gabe can feel his discomfort, and kicks himself for being the cause.

Ellis nods. "Please." He sneaks a peek at the abandoned cinnamon rolls. Gabe notices only because he can't seem to be able to take his eyes off Ellis for even a single second.

Smiling encouragingly, he nods towards the tray, lifting an eyebrow in question.

Ellis bites his bottom lip, two spots of color appearing on his cheeks. He gives a small nod, looking embarrassed, as though it's unmanly or something to have a weakness for pastry.

The irony isn't lost on Gabe. He'd bet his favorite pair of socks that Ellis is secretly a cinnamon roll himself.

He wouldn't mind getting a bite.

The mood is a little awkward but not unpleasant while Gabe works. He puts a cinnamon roll in a box and draws a smiley face and a little heart on the lid. Ellis follows him to the coffee machine, watching silently while Gabe steams the milk. There are so many emotions Gabe has to keep in check in front of Ellis, and he takes the opportunity to pour them into making the drink.

"I do deal with people sometimes," Ellis says suddenly as Gabe transfers the milk into the cup. "It's...unpleasant."

The fact that Ellis went back to that particular topic gives Gabe the impression something has been bugging him.

"Something happen?" he asks, hoping he sounds laid back and not like he's dying for Ellis to share the smallest tidbits of information about his life. Which he isn't. Not even a little. Nope.

Ellis answers with a derisive laugh. "Where do I start?"

"I assume it has to do with what happened before Cal's accident?" Gabe says, and instantly wants to smack himself.

Ellis' intense gaze fixes on him for a few seconds, but thankfully Gabe doesn't feel annoyance or anger coming from him, just...surprise.

"How much do you know?"

Gabe shrugs. "The condensed version. Something went down at work, Cal took it hard." He hesitates. "Self-medicated. Cue car crash. Then you showed up to pick up the pieces."

Ellis licks his lips. "That...pretty much sums it up." He seems almost relieved he doesn't have to give Gabe a rundown on the whole thing.

"I'm sorry," Gabe says. "I can't imagine the stress you must be under."

Ellis stares at him as if Gabe said something groundbreaking, then averts his gaze, aiming it somewhere in the general direction of his shoes.

Jesus, is this the first time someone actually acknowledged his struggle? Surely not. When Cal was talking about his brother, he mentioned all the things Ellis was doing for him and for Dawson. Said how grateful he is. So why does Ellis seem so out of sorts now?

"It was the stupidest thing," Ellis starts. "We had a project lined up, but it fell through because Cal never signed off on it."

Gabe's eyebrows shoot up. He did not expect something so...anticlimactic. On the other hand, that would explain why Cal took it so hard. "Well, fuck. How did he miss it?"

"My guess would be his 'self-medicating' had something to do with it," Ellis says tersely. "It was literally there on his desk. So fucking stupid."

"Wasn't there someone to, like, remind him of the deadline?"

"The project manager. He was in charge, so technically it was his fault."

Gabe cocks his head. "You don't think it was?"

"He had stuff going on at the time—his wife was about to give birth..." He waves a hand. "It was a whole thing. Didn't mean much when I had to fire him." He gives Gabe a pinched smile. "See why I don't like dealing with people?"

Oh.

So it's not just the stress.

No hugging straight guys, he repeats again when he feels his resolve inching dangerously close to a breaking point.

Ellis, on the other hand, seems dangerously close to bolting, as if talking about what bothers him is socially unacceptable.

"You know, if you wanna change jobs there might be a position open here," Gabe jokes, though he wouldn't be opposed to having access to Ellis on the regular.

Ellis takes the bait, tipping his head back and giving a throaty laugh that does terrible things to Gabe's heart and...other body parts.

"I honestly don't know which is worse."

Gabe feigns offense. "Wow. Fuck you too." He doesn't have time to worry if he went a bit far because Ellis laughs again.

"Speaking of, why don't you hire someone? Is it you and Zeke all day, every day?"

"Zeke is..." Gabe searches for the word. "Territorial. And I can't blame him. We put a lot into the café and, let's face it, it's hard to find someone who would love it as much as we do." He pats the countertop gently. "It's our baby."

Their baby, and second home. As much as he wants to kill Zeke half the time, Gabe's always reluctant to go home after a shift, sometimes even staying behind to read a book on one of the sofas instead of his bed. He might've spent a night here once or twice too. Or ten times. The café has everything he needs after all: a kitchen, coffee... Okay, so maybe there's no shower but there's a whole ocean just a street over. Sometimes he wonders why he bothers paying rent on his apartment. He could easily live here.

Ellis slides his hands into the pockets of his suit pants, growing a little tense. "So...are you two..."

"What?"

Ellis clears his throat. "Like, a couple?"

A beat passes, then another. Gabe staggers back a step. "Oh my god. Eww. Eww! No way! God." A shiver wrecks his body, and not a good kind. The yucky kind.

"Okay," Ellis says with a nervous chuckle. "That answers it." His shoulders relax, as though the answer pleases him.

"Why would you say that? Now I'll have to bleach my brain."

Ellis chuckles, giving the back of his neck a rub. "Sorry. You just...you seem really close."

Do they? Yeah, probably. Zeke is like an older brother to him. Or another irritating cousin.

"He bullied me into befriending him. I had no choice."

"Right. Because you're such an unfriendly person otherwise."

Gabe narrows his eyes at him. It earns him another laugh. Goddammit, it's such a beautiful sound. If only he could bottle it up.

"Anyway, the hours aren't too bad," Gabe returns to the original topic before he can say something inappropriate again. Like how he's going to think of Ellis' voice and his laugh when he's in his bed and—

Focus, Gabe.

"We close at three on weekdays and at two on Saturday. And we always have Sunday off," he rambles.

Ellis purses his lips in thought. It wouldn't take much for Gabe to lean over the counter and—

Seriously? Get a grip, you pervert.

"I guess you win," Ellis says at last. "Your job is less miserable than mine. And you get all the coffee you want."

"Don't you have something at the office?" Gabe asks, praying his face isn't too flushed.

"You get all the *good* coffee you want."

"Ah. Gotcha." Mournfully, he looks at the drink and the cinnamon roll sitting on the counter between them, all ready for Ellis to take and enjoy. Not wanting Ellis to go just yet, he scrambles for something to talk about. "Do you miss Sydney? You look like you miss it. Did you even have time to adjust? It was all quite abrupt, wasn't it?"

If Ellis is surprised by the sudden switch, he doesn't show it. "Sydney was...simpler." He hesitates before continuing. "Me and the Gold Coast, we have a history. But...I guess it brought me and my brother closer. And my brother-in-law, so..." He shrugs. "Silver linings."

"It brought you to my café, too," Gabe says. He never thought he'd be grateful for someone getting into a car accident, and while it makes him a horrible, horrible person, he can't deny it's true. *Thanks, Cal, for taking one for the team.*

Ellis' expression goes from perplexed to incredibly soft, his eyes full of the same vulnerability Gabe saw before. It lasts a beautiful few seconds before it shuts down.

"Yeah. The only decent café in a ten-mile radius."

Gabe huffs. "I know I should take the compliment, but god, you're dramatic."

Ellis smirks. "It's been said."

The conversation comes to a lull again, and Gabe rushes to remedy that. "So...you don't miss Sydney too much? No one got left behind?"

He cringes. *Smooth, Gabe. Smooth.*

Something dark passes across Ellis' face. "I was happy to leave behind my cheating girlfriend, if that's what you mean."

"Oh, shit. I'm sorry." Great. He did it again. Foot meet mouth.

"It's fine," Ellis says, in the way that someone who's decidedly not fine would. "The timing was kind of perfect, actually. Though she did think she could rope me into coming back when she tried to make me her baby daddy."

Gabe's jaw drops a little. "Wow. That's...intense." He taps his fingers on the counter. "I feel like a right prick to ask this, but..."

"I'm sure. It's not mine," Ellis assures him. He doesn't look upset about Gabe's nosiness, thank god. "I'm shooting blanks. It was a choice, so you don't have to feel sorry for me."

It takes Gabe a few long seconds to process everything he just learned. Most of all, he's surprised how much Ellis has shared with him. It's clearly something he's been bottling up and hasn't had a chance to talk about. As sad as the revelation is, it makes Gabe feel kind of special. He's used to people sharing—sometimes over-sharing—things with him. He knows the effect he has on others; his warm, welcoming energy and friendly personality give the impression he's a great confidante. Which he is, by the way.

So, yeah...he's used to people confiding in him. But it's another thing entirely to have a person you're crushing on confide in you.

"Your ex is an idiot for cheating on you," he says at last. It's not lip service—he means it. If Ellis was *his*...

"Guess I had it coming," Ellis says. "I'm not exactly the most attentive boyfriend."

"There are better ways to ask for attention. Doesn't mean she had to go and fall on another guy's dick."

Ellis' eyes widen, his mouth falling open.

Gabe lets out a groan. "And I'll stop talking now."

"Please don't," Ellis says so quickly Gabe doesn't even have time to panic. "I...like talking to you." He mostly whispers the last part, but Gabe's spent so much time with his eyes glued to Ellis' lips he could probably read the words anyway.

Gabe's stupid face splits into an even stupider grin, his heart thundering. "I like talking to you too."

For a moment, time stands still, something important stretching between them. It feels like they've crossed a line, leaving the employee/customer territory and moving into an uncharted one. One that Gabe would like very, very much to explore.

The sound of someone speaking makes them both flinch. Gabe searches for the source, seeing five people walking into the café at once, followed by Zeke who is, as per usual, late for his shift. When he spots Ellis, he grins like the dick he is and waves.

Ellis looks like he's coming out of a trance, but manages to wave back.

"Didn't you say twenty minutes?" he says to Gabe.

Gabe heaves a sigh. "I was wrong."

Ellis huffs. "I take it back. Your job sucks."

It would be so easy to end the whole interaction on a humorous note, to keep the banter going.

Gabe finds he doesn't have the strength to do it. He looks at Ellis and he just...*wants*.

"Well, seeing you makes it better, so...you know..." He pushes the cup and the box towards Ellis. "You could keep coming here. Make my job a little less sucky."

Ellis seems to have stopped breathing as he stares at Gabe, reaching for his items. "I'd think the opposite is true." And fuck, he sounds so resigned, like he actually believes it.

"You'd be wrong," Gabe says firmly. Unable to help himself, he brushes his fingers against Ellis', who shivers at the contact. "I'll see you tomorrow?"

"See you tomorrow."

Chapter 9

ZEKE IS ANNOYING ON a good day, but when Gabe offers to do the opening shift on a permanent basis instead of alternating how they normally do, he becomes positively insufferable.

"That have anything to do with Mr. Grumpy popping in first thing in the morning?" Zeke asks with a smirk.

Gabe doesn't dignify it with an answer. Zeke should be grateful, given how much he hates mornings.

Seeing Ellis bright and early the next morning makes suffering through Zeke's constant bullying totally worth it. Gabe's high spirits last for hours, until Zeke manages to burn their last batch of red velvet cookies because he got sucked down the rabbit hole of funny cat compilation videos.

Insert a dramatic sigh.

Gabe has a moment of panic (aka being a complete and utter moping mess) when Ellis doesn't show up on Friday. Maybe Gabe said something weird yesterday that freaked him out? Wouldn't be the first time his big mouth scared someone off.

But then Ellis turns up amidst the morning rush, way later than he ever has and looking a little disheveled, like he worked late and slept for shit. And fuck, Gabe wants to feel sorry for him, but the whole messy appearance is doing *things* to him. He starts to wonder if this is what Ellis looks like first thing in the morning, all soft and warm with sleep, and probably grumpy as hell without a drop of caffeine in his system.

Fuck, why is that so cute?

It's not lost on Gabe that Ellis found the time to come here despite being in a hurry. His heart leaps to his throat when Ellis' eyes find his over the queue, tired and underlined with dark shadows, but brightening when they see Gabe.

Gabe grins like a lovestruck idiot, but it's worth seeing Ellis's reaction, his cheeks changing color and lips curling into a heart-stopping smile.

But the smile won't last if Ellis ends up being late for work because he had to wait ages for his coffee.

It's a testament to how corrupt Gabe's work ethic has become whenever this man is involved when he barely hesitates putting the pile of orders on hold and starting on Ellis' coffee right away. He's done it before, but that was a different situation. He has no excuse this time.

He beckons Ellis over when he's done with his coffee and drawing a heart on the cup. No messages today either.

Ellis frowns slightly at the two people in front of him and carefully extracts himself from the queue, heading towards Gabe. He blinks when he sees the cup and a boxed up cinnamon roll that Gabe took the liberty adding to the order.

"Is that mine?"

"I figured you're in a bit of a hurry."

Ellis runs a hand through his hair self-consciously. "I must be more of a mess than I thought."

Don't say he's gorgeous. "You're fine." There. That sounds normal. "But you've never come here so late."

"Long night," Ellis confirms Gabe's theory, shooting him another of those thought-annihilating smiles. "Thank you. And sorry that I can't stay and chat."

"That's fine. I've probably talked your ear off by now anyway."

Ellis chuckles, the sound low and dark, and compromising Gabe's already poor self-control. "Don't underestimate how much I can handle."

Gabe raises an eyebrow. "Is that a challenge?"

Ellis shakes his head almost fondly and reaches for his items, stopping at the last second. "Ah. I haven't paid yet."

"Leave it. You can do it on Monday," Gabe says, blushing a little at his blatant admission that he expects Ellis to be back.

Ellis doesn't seem to notice, simply saying, "On Monday, then."

Ellis shows up on Saturday, a laptop tucked under his arm and, for the first time, not wearing a suit. How can dark jeans and a simple gray tee look so good on someone? Holy hell, Gabe can see the outline of his nipples!

Lord have mercy on my poor, depraved soul.

"Are you listening?" Zeke huffs impatiently, probably having asked a question which never made it to Gabe's deteriorating brain.

"Nope," he says without taking his eyes off Ellis for a second.

Zeke's eyes follow in the same direction, and he huffs again. "You're so whipped, Gabe."

"Uh-huh." What's the point in denying it?

Ellis smiles when he sees Gabe, just a quirk of lips that has Gabe's stomach doing some elite-level gymnastics, and approaches the counter.

"Hi."

"Hola," Zeke greets, smirking.

Gabe discreetly steps on his foot, earning himself a jab between the ribs.

"Hi!" he squeaks. "You know it's Saturday, right?" he teases, as if he's not cheering on the inside.

Ellis rolls his eyes. "I do. Not that it matters. In my line of work, days kinda blend together."

"Please tell me you're not going to the office today."

"I'm not." He holds up the laptop. "I brought work with me."

As happy as Gabe is to not have to wait until Monday to see Ellis' lovely face, he hates how much the man works. "Yeah, you can't do that. It's one of the conditions of entry that you can't bring work with you."

"Is it?" Ellis quirks an eyebrow and makes a show of looking around. "Where can I read these conditions?"

"It's on the front door. In very, very small print."

"I see." He presses his lips together. "What am I allowed to do then?"

Gabe shrugs. "Sip coffee. Chill."

"And Netflix," Zeke blurts out.

Ellis blinks at him confusedly. "What?"

"Hm? Oh sorry, sometimes I talk to myself." He waves a hand and laughs. "Let me give you some privacy." Which apparently means stepping towards the coffee machine four feet away and pretending to polish it.

"I will kill you," Gabe mouths at him, then plasters on a smile as he turns back to Ellis. "Seriously, Ellis, you'll work yourself into an early grave. And if you die here, you'll turn into a ghost and haunt the place. We'd lose all our customers."

"People pay good money to visit haunted places. I'm sure you could turn it around."

"He's not wrong," Zeke says, dropping the act of minding his own business. "Hey, that's actually a great idea! Maybe we could—"

"We're not turning the café into a haunted house." He's so done with Zeke's occult ideas. His offer to brew a love potion and sneak it into Ellis' drink was the worst of all. Morally speaking. Practically, it would probably only end up giving Ellis a case of diarrhea.

"You won't let me have any fun!" Zeke cries.

"You and I have very different definitions of fun," Gabe grumbles, turning his attention back to Ellis, who's watching him with intrigue. "What?"

"Nothing. Just...you're so young. Sometimes I forget you own the place."

"Co-own," Zeke quips.

"And how old do you think I am?" Gabe inquires.

Ellis cocks his head, eyes raking all over Gabe's face and causing a warm, tingling sensation in his belly. "Twenty-three? Twenty-four?"

Gabe laughs. No one ever guesses right. "In your defense, I do get asked for my ID a lot. But I'm 29."

Ellis stares. "No, you're not."

Gabe chuckles. "I'll take it as a compliment."

Ellis looks perplexed by the revelation. What does Gabe's age matter, anyway? "You have some good genes. Honestly, I'd never have guessed."

"No one would. What about you? You can't be older than 35."

"34. Though, I suppose my job has added some wrinkles."

Gabe doesn't like the insecurity in his voice. "Well, if it has, they look good on you."

"Thanks," Ellis mumbles, sounding embarrassed. God, this man is so freaking precious. He looks around a little helplessly.

"Gosh, I'm sorry." Gabe wants to face-palm. "I'm taking up your time when you need to work."

"I don't mind," Ellis says quickly.

"Okay. Cool." Gabe tries not to grin like a total loon. "Having your usual?"

"I'll skip the cinnamon roll today, I've already had breakfast."

"Hmm. I guess a man can't live on cinnamon rolls alone."

"Unfortunately. I'm still surprised they don't give me a stomachache." He elaborates when Gabe gives him an inquiring look. "Dairy tends to mess up my digestion."

"Oh, there's no dairy. We use soy milk, and oil instead of butter. Can't really taste the difference."

"Yeah, I couldn't tell," Ellis agrees, sounding impressed.

"I mean, it doesn't make it much healthier."

Ellis smiles. "No, I know." He brings up his phone. "Don't forget to include my order from yesterday."

"Yeah, yeah," Gabe retorts. He totally forgot.

"How about you take a seat? I'll bring it to you," he suggests once Ellis has paid. Gabe would love to hold him hostage and talk to him until his brain liquifies, but a couple more people have come in, waiting their turn.

"Okay. Thank you. I'll be sitting somewhere…" He waves in the general direction of the tables.

Gabe sends him a wink. "I'll find you, don't worry." He may or may not watch Ellis' retreating, uh, backbody. Sue him, he's only human. Mostly. Probably.

"Swap?" Zeke asks with a knowing smirk.

"Bite me," Gabe replies and lets Zeke take over the till, starting on Ellis' order.

He wills his hands to remain steady as he carries the coffee to Ellis' table, cursing himself for filling the cup to the brim. Ellis watches him approach with a soft expression that has Gabe almost spilling the coffee. Placing the cup on the table, he pauses when he takes note of Ellis' strange expression.

"Something wrong?"

"Nothing." It's definitely something. "You always draw hearts on the cup. Should've known you'd find a way to put one in a drink-in order." He nods at the heart sprinkled on top of the coffee with cinnamon powder.

Gabe knew those stencils would come in handy even outside of Valentine's Day. Hopefully he didn't go too far.

"What can I say; I wear my heart on my sleeve. And coffee, as you can see." Despite the joking tone, Ellis' expression looks more serious than amused.

"Yeah, I can tell." He licks his lips. "You should be careful with it. Someone could take advantage."

Gabe melts a little at the concern, but a part of him wonders if Ellis is speaking from personal experience. The way his energy just dimmed a notch suggests so, and it takes major effort not to pry.

"I'm not worried. I'm very good at reading people," he says to put

Ellis' mind at ease.

Ellis' gaze flicks up before he quickly averts it. "So, what's with the messages? Do you, like, google motivational quotes and put them on the cups?"

Gabe takes the change of topic in stride. "I used to do that a lot when we first opened. I'd have a list of quotes, and every morning I'd write them on at least three sleeves of cups." A feeling of nostalgia expands in his chest at the memory. Setting up his business was so exciting and terrifying. "They were a bit repetitive, but the customers loved them. But within a few months we started getting busier and there was no time. So now I only write something when I feel...compelled to do so."

Naturally, Ellis isn't satisfied with a half-baked explanation. "Compelled?"

"It's...hard to explain." *Yeah, very helpful.*

"That's okay," Ellis says easily. "I probably wouldn't get it anyway, considering I have the emotional range of a rock."

Gabe frowns, his protective instincts unraveling. "That's not true."

"Huh?"

"That's so not true. You're a very emotional person." One of the most emotional people Gabe's ever met. "Just because you don't always show it doesn't mean you don't feel profoundly."

His little outburst is followed by a long stretch of silence and Ellis' stunned expression. While he wouldn't take the words back—someone needs to tell Ellis his perception of himself is completely askew—he wishes he'd picked better timing. And maybe hadn't reacted so fervently. It looks a little sus.

"I'm sorry. I keep sticking my beak where it doesn't belong. I'll let you work, Zeke is about to kill me if I don't help." He points to the counter where Zeke is glaring daggers at him as he hurries to serve a long line of people that has accumulated while Gabe was being a Chatty Cathy. He spins around, striding away and pretending he didn't hear the soft-spoken, "Gabriel".

"Everything okay?" Zeke asks with a frown.

"Yup," Gabe lies, and plasters on a smile as he takes Zeke's place behind the till.

He keeps sneaking glances at Ellis here and there, damn near swooning as he watches him do, well, pretty much anything; frowning at something he reads, wiggling his fingers before he types, licking his lips after taking a sip of coffee... Everything he does is so hypnotic. And cute. And sexy. And cute.

So. Fucking. Unfair.

And it gets worse when Gabe catches him looking back. When it happens, they both quickly look away like a couple of eighth-graders. How lame.

Ellis packs his stuff up a couple hours later, taking the empty cup to the counter.

"You didn't have to," Gabe says, though the thoughtfulness makes him a little giddy.

"No? Oh, okay, let me take it back," Ellis says, pretending to take it away.

"No!" Gabe yelps, laughing, making a grab for the cup and accidentally getting Ellis' hand.

Oh, this is bad. His skin is smooth and warm, and Gabe is overtaken by a strong urge to slide their palms together and intertwine their fingers.

"God, you're such a smartass sometimes," he says affectionately and slowly removes his hand, pretending he can't see Ellis' stricken look.

"Guilty as charged," Ellis says. "I changed my mind. I'll have a cinnamon roll. To go."

"What happened to cutting down?"

"Sometimes you have to live dangerously."

Gabe snorts. "I agree." He puts a cinnamon roll in a takeaway box while Ellis pays and draws a little heart on the top.

"You don't bother me," Ellis suddenly blurts out, his expression pinched. "You never bother me. And I'm sorry if I made you feel like you do. It's just...you can be a bit intimidating."

"Me?" Gabe touches a finger to his chest. He's been called a lot of things, but intimidating isn't one of them.

Ellis avoids looking at him as he speaks. "I don't know how to act around you. I've never met anyone like you."

That, Gabe can believe. "I'm sorry that I make you uncomfortable."

"It's okay," Ellis says, finally letting their eyes meet. "It's not *bad* uncomfortable, if that makes sense."

"It does," Gabe says, thinking what to say next when Ellis suddenly laughs. "What's so funny?"

"This isn't my usual route." He gestures outside at the street. "The first time I came here, it was because I was trying to avoid congestion. I saw this place and it just...drew me in." He gives another soft laugh. "I almost changed my mind when I saw the queue."

"I'm glad you didn't." He doesn't believe in coincidences and has no doubt that Ellis finding his way here was always meant to happen. He keeps that belief to himself.

Ellis' smile turns shy. "Yeah, me too. I'm glad I found you." His eyes widen. "The café, I mean. Obviously."

"Obviously." Gabe wills his thundering heart to calm the fuck down before it bursts out of his chest like it does in cartoons. "Hey, I know it's hard to break a habit, but you never have to act around me. I like the person you are."

Ellis' reaction isn't what he'd hoped for. The air around him becomes heavier, like a shadow has been cast over him. "How do you know what kind of person I am?"

"I told you."

"Right. You can read people." Skepticism is heavy in his tone.

"I can," Gabe says firmly. He grabs a sharpie, his hands shaking when he thinks about what he's going to do.

He flips open the box with the cinnamon roll and scribbles down his number alongside a short note and his initials. It comes out crooked but hopefully legible.

"Contrary to what you might believe, I'm not the only one who wears his heart on his sleeve." He closes the lid and pushes the box towards Ellis, who takes it with a confused frown. "I'll see you Monday?"

"Yeah," Ellis promises.

Gabe can only hope. There's a good chance he just flushed everything down the toilet.

Guess I'll find out soon enough.

Chapter 10

MONDAY MORNING HAS ELLIS standing in the shower for a good twenty minutes, staring unseeingly at the charcoal gray tiles while hot water runs in rivulets down his body. He can feel himself turning into a cooked lobster but can't get himself to move. Because once he's stepped out, he just needs to put his clothes on and he'll be on his way to get coffee.

And he'll see Gabriel.

At the thought of warm, kind eyes and a cloud-breaking smile, his insides do something strange, a tingling sensation spreading through his abdomen and tinkering off into a low thrum under his skin.

He shivers, leaning forward to rest his forehead on the tiles. Good grief. He's too old to have a sexual identity crisis. Definitely too old for Gabriel—who might be, as it turns out, pushing 30, but his bright, curious personality makes him too innocent. Way too innocent for the likes of Ellis, who only knows ruthlessness and manipulation.

Didn't sound so innocent when he was dishing out all the sexual innuendos.

Great. Now he's thinking of Gabriel and sex. That's the last thing he needs.

His dick must be of a different opinion because it twitches, a rush of blood heading in the same direction as more thoughts of Gabriel take over his mind. Goddammit!

With a grunt of annoyance, Ellis switches the water off and steps out, drying himself with harsh strokes as if that could help him get rid of unwanted thoughts. He has more pressing matters to think about. Like the message Gabriel left him on Saturday, and what answer Ellis is going to give him.

Yeah, go ahead and pretend there's anything to think about.

There's plenty to think about. So many things to consider. Just because Ellis might feel...a certain way doesn't imply he should go for it. Innocent or not, Gabriel is too good for him. Just remembering their first meeting has Ellis wanting to slam his head against a brick wall. Gabriel might have forgiven him, might even sympathize with him, but he doesn't deserve a grumpy ass like Ellis, that's for sure.

But then he thinks back on the moment he was sitting in his car on Saturday, the box with a cinnamon roll in his lap, waiting to be devoured. He can still feel the violent jolt of his heart as he flipped the box open, as he skimmed his gaze over what he'd assumed was another mysterious message. Instead, he found ten digits followed by four words that opened a door to what he'd promised himself he would never touch.

Have dinner with me? G.

His pulse spikes even now, just thinking of it all: the anxiety, the confusion, the fear. And the flicker of hope that set off a fire in his heart.

"Fuck it," he growls, making quick work of taming his hair and throwing on his clothes, sans the tie. He doesn't have the patience to faff with it right now.

He checks the time, cursing when he sees how long he's been stalling. But if he hurries, he'll get to the café nice and early, before anyone else comes in. It will be just him and Gabriel, and Ellis will have the chance to tell him...to tell him...

His phone goes off just as he grabs his car keys, and he frowns at seeing Dawson's name. It's not like him to call so early, unless...

With an ugly, foreboding feeling settling in his gut, he accepts the call. "Dawson? Is everything—"

"Cal's at the hospital." Dawson's voice breaks on the last word.

"What? What happened?"

"I don't—He just collapsed. Couldn't breathe. I called an ambulance, but they wouldn't let me ride with him."

Hearing Dawson's growing panic ironically quells Ellis' own. Having something or someone else to focus on always helps him to keep his mind straight and to do what he does best—fix things.

"Where are you?" he asks calmly as he leaves the apartment.

"Home. I'm just headed to the garage—"

"No," Ellis cuts him off. "You're in no state to get behind the wheel. Wait for me, I'll be there in five." At least he'd had the foresight to get an apartment so close to Cal and Dawson's.

"But—"

"Dawson. Breathe," he orders gently when he senses Dawson is on the verge of hyperventilating. "It will be okay. I'm on my way."

"...Okay."

Seven minutes later, Ellis pulls up in front of Dawson's apartment building. He grabs his phone to give Dawson a call when the passenger door opens, startling the living hell out of him.

Dawson slides into the seat, looking exactly as Ellis pictured he would based on how he sounded on the phone. His eyes are wide and red-rimmed, and he looks like he's about to hurl.

"Thanks for picking me up," he says mechanically.

"Don't mention it," Ellis says, putting the car in motion. "Uni Hospital?"

"Yeah."

Thanks to morning traffic, it takes them over half an hour to get to the hospital. Ellis' stomach twists into knots as they enter the emergency room, the whole situation too similar to the last time.

Last time, Cal pulled through two invasive surgeries. He'll be fine, Ellis reasons.

Seeing as Dawson is still visibly shaken, Ellis instructs him to take a seat and approaches the lady at the reception. She's nice, and Ellis tries his hardest not to snap at her when she tells him they need to wait for a doctor. Instead, he grits out a begrudging 'Thanks' and goes back to

Dawson.

"We need to wait, don't we?" Dawson asks with resignation when he sees Ellis' sour face.

"Yeah." He collapses into the chair next to him, feeling the beginning of a pounding headache creep in. God, he needs coffee.

Fuck. Coffee.

His chest constricts, his fingers twitching with the urge to pick up the phone and text Gabriel to let him know why he's not coming this morning. He nearly laughs when he remembers how hastily he saved Gabriel's number after the initial shock had worn off. And yet, it took him a good 36 hours to pull his head out of his ass and put a name to his feelings.

"We need to stop meeting like this," Dawson says suddenly, letting out a small, humorless chuckle.

Ellis allows himself a small smile. "We really do." The stark contrast between their interaction two months ago and now almost makes him laugh for real. It's kind of insane how quickly he's come to care for Dawson in such a short time, after all but ignoring his existence for the past six years.

The contrast between Dawson then and now is even more startling. Two months ago, right in this waiting room, Dawson was kind of a mess. But he wasn't a shivering, shaky mess sick with worry. Two months ago, Dawson wasn't crazy in love with his husband.

So much has changed for Ellis too. Two months ago, he'd never even dream of having a civilized conversation with his brother, let alone sitting down for lunch with him. Laughing with him.

Two months ago, he didn't know about baristas with soulful eyes and inappropriate jokes who could light up the whole room with one smile.

Two months ago, his heart wasn't on the line.

"Ellis?" Dawson says in a small voice, his eyes quickly welling up. "What if..."

Ellis swallows. "He'll be fine. He's tougher than you think."

"He's already beat the odds twice. But doing it a third time...no one is that lucky."

Ignoring the voice in his head that's been whispering the same thing, Ellis says resolutely, "He'll be fine." Acting on instinct, he slowly slides an arm around Dawson's shoulders and pulls him to his side for a loose hug, feeling awkward as he does so.

Dawson has no such qualms, leaning into him and resting his head on Ellis' shoulder. Albeit reluctantly, Ellis has to admit the human contact feels... Well, it doesn't feel *terrible*.

Thankfully, a doctor approaches them within a few minutes, hope blooming in Ellis' chest when he sees the man's pleased expression. The hope transforms into relief when the doctor promises Cal will be just fine, explaining Cal suffered a mild heart attack which luckily didn't require surgery, just administration of some clot-dissolving drugs.

"You'll be able to see him shortly," the doctor assures them before excusing himself.

"Fucking genetics," Ellis grumbles when they're alone.

"From your dad?" Dawson guesses, already familiar with their family's medical history.

Ellis grunts, tasting bitterness on his tongue. "He can find a way to mess with our lives even when he's not here."

Dawson's fingers curl gently around his arm. "To be fair, Cal has been eating a lot of donuts," he says with mirth.

Ellis huffs. "I've heard." He feels a pang in his chest when he remembers where—*whom* he heard it from.

"Thank you for being here," Dawson says, looking up at him with big, soft eyes. "You're always here."

He shrugs uncomfortably. "Family is family."

"You were there for me when I needed you too," Dawson reminds him.

Ellis fixes him with a firm look. "You *are* family, Dawson." He hates how vulnerable Dawson looks, hates himself for being one of the reasons for it. "I'm sorry we spent so many years being strangers."

"Me too," Dawson says wistfully. A sheepish smile curls his lips. "I feel like the moment warrants a hug."

Ellis feels his own lips twitch, and he quickly covers it up by rolling his eyes. "Sure." The hug is awkward and unfamiliar, different from the one he gave Dawson to comfort him. This time, it's for his own benefit too, and he's not sure what to do with that.

Not long after, the doctor comes back to let them know Cal is stable enough to have visitors, but isn't awake yet.

"I'll never get used to this," Ellis says as he takes in Cal's unconscious body. At least this time there are no bruises on his face, and he's not hooked up to twenty different machines.

"Me neither," Dawson agrees, taking a seat next to the bed. He carefully takes Cal's hand that has an IV inserted into it, cradling it gently between his palms.

As Ellis watches them, a peculiar feeling grows in his chest, a sort of hollowness that feels like a long-forgotten memory.

His phone vibrates, and he looks away from the scene in front of him, almost grateful for the distraction. He curses when Amanda's name flashes on the screen. He lets it go to voicemail, and curses again when a dozen unread messages glare at him. Between his erratic thoughts involving Cal or Gabriel, he completely forgot about work. Unbelievable.

He turns to Dawson. "I'll be right back. Just need to step out for a bit to cancel the rest of my schedule."

Dawson blinks up at him disorientedly. "You don't have to do that. Look at him." He nods at Cal. "He's not waking up any time soon."

Ellis hesitates. As much as he'd like to keep an eye on Cal, he'd rather not wait around for him to wake up. There'd be no point anyway, and he'd just end up being an anxious mess. On the other hand, he doesn't want to leave Dawson alone.

"What about you?"

"I'll need to go home too, for Donut. But I'll be back later. I'll let you know if anything changes."

That makes Ellis feel a little better.

"How will you get home?"

"Uber. Or I can call Kieran." He gives Ellis a small smile. "Don't worry about me."

Yeah, no such luck.

"Call me if you need me," Ellis says after giving it a thorough thought. Here goes hoping that work will help him focus on something else.

Once in the car, he gives Amanda a call to explain the situation, leaving it in her scarily capable hands to reorganize his schedule.

Amanda is waiting for him when the lift opens on his floor, holding a large cup of what he assumes is coffee in one hand and an iPad in the other.

"Figured you'd need this," she says, her features softened in sympathy. "You okay?"

"Swell," he deadpans, taking the coffee with reluctance. The logo tells him it came from the small café on the ground level, and he suppresses a sigh. Gabriel has totally spoiled him. "Thanks for this."

"Anytime, sugar," she says, grinning when he glares at her. She turns the iPad towards him. "Your 10:30 will be here shortly."

His head spins at the tightly packed colorful blocks filling the screen. He grunts noncommittally, knowing Amanda never takes his shitty attitude personally, and heads to his office.

Regarding the cup in his hand judgingly, he takes a small, cautious sip and instantly gags. The fact that the coffee didn't come from *Lost and Ground* aside, his tastebuds must have reprogrammed because black coffee just tastes vile now, like bog water. He dumps the whole thing in the trash. He'll just have to go through the day uncaffeinated and miserable. It's fine. The day was off to a shit start anyway.

Once at home, Ellis collapses onto the sofa, suit and all. He'd planned on going back to the hospital after work, hoping Cal would be up by then, but no such luck. Dawson instructed him to get some sleep instead, promising he'd call once there was any news. Ellis has no doubt Dawson himself will be staying the night at the hospital, but he didn't call him out on it. Dawson probably wouldn't be able to sleep anyway.

Ellis doesn't think he will either. Not yet, at least. His body is exhausted, but his brain won't settle, constantly sending mini doses of adrenaline through his veins. He fiddles with his phone, so, so tempted to dial Gabriel's number. To hear his voice. He knows Gabriel would listen, would know what to say to make Ellis feel better.

Just because he'd listen to your whining doesn't mean he should.

He dials Jordan's number. The call connects on the second ring.

"As I live and breathe," Jordan teases right off the bat.

Glad that he decided against a videocall, Ellis allows himself to grin. "Go fuck yourself."

"I was about to, but then you called."

Ellis' face contorts into a grimace. "I hate you."

He can hear the smirk in Jordan's voice. "You started it."

"Yeah, yeah. Instant regret."

"You're so delicate. Something on your mind?"

Right. It's not like Ellis to call for the sake of calling. While he knows that Jordan doesn't mind being his unpaid shrink, it doesn't make him feel any less of a dick. If only expressing his emotions didn't take such monumental effort. It would be much easier if someone could just read his mind.

Golden-brown eyes flash in his mind, his heart giving a particularly powerful thud.

"You could say that. It...has been a day." He gives Jordan a quick rundown on the situation.

"Fucking hell," Jordan says after a few seconds of heavy silence. "As if getting in a car crash and getting your memory wiped wasn't enough."

"According to the doctors, the two are likely connected. I don't mean the accident, but the surgery," Ellis adds. "But I guess our great genetics don't help either."

Jordan hums thoughtfully. "And stress. Can't be easy to try to fit into your old life while remembering nothing. At least Cal doesn't have to worry about work now. The same can't be said for you."

"I'm fine," Ellis says, not wanting the conversation to steer towards him.

"Right. That's why you're calling me."

"I thought you'd like to be updated on all the drama."

"That too. I hate that I can't be there for you. I hate that you're so far away."

The emotion in Jordan's voice gets Ellis a little choked up, like there's something he wants to say but when he tries to put it into words, they just lodge in his throat. He misses his best friend too, though he hasn't had much opportunity to dwell on the feeling with everything that's been going on since he moved here.

"It's one hour on the plane. It's not too bad," he reasons. Not that he'd have time to fly down to Sydney anyway.

"It's different. I was used to seeing you at work all the time."

"Which I assume was the highlight of your day," he mocks.

"It was," Jordan says without hesitation. "I miss you. We should call more often."

Ellis sighs, loving the idea, but knowing he'll never stick to it. "We should."

Jordan's voice is lighter when he speaks next. "I'd suggest calling after work, but I'd hate to impose on your *Gilmore Girls* time."

Ellis groans, cursing his drunken ass for spilling that particular fact. "Sod off."

"So sensitive."

They don't talk for long, Ellis' eyes drifting shut intermittently. His responses must be slow because Jordan huffs, ordering Ellis to *'take his workaholic ass to bed and get proper sleep'*.

Ellis grumbles something, getting a grumble in response, and hangs up. After a quick shower, he falls face first into bed, but manages to shoot off a text to Dawson, wanting to check on him. He has no illusions that Dawson might have gone home to rest, the little hypocrite.

Ellis: How are you doing?

Dawson: Been better.

Dawson: Been worse too.

Ellis: Fair. Seriously, Dawson. Anything you need, just ask.

Dawson: Thank you. Same to you.

He puts the phone on the nightstand and switches off the light. He's asleep in seconds.

There's way too much light in his room when he wakes up. A quick glance at the dark phone screen makes it clear he forgot to plug it in last night. Again. Seriously, he's been such a scatterbrain these past few weeks. He should probably go get himself checked. This isn't normal.

He should still make it to work on time if he hurries. Except...that means he won't be able to stop at *Lost and Ground*. But maybe if he—

No. Even if he could make it, he'd have to rush. Just barge in, grab his coffee and go straight to work. There's no way he's going to show up and leave in five minutes flat when he needs to talk to Gabriel. When Gabriel is expecting an answer. And there's no way Ellis will be short with him. There's also no way he'll talk to Gabriel about...*that* with other customers around. He'll have to stop by early, so it's just the two of them.

Tomorrow. He'll go tomorrow.

Dawson calls when Ellis is already at work to tell him Cal's up and kicking. He all but forbids Ellis to come running like a worried parent, and convinces him to stop by after work. Apparently, Cal won't be released until noon tomorrow.

He makes Amanda shuffle his schedule around so he can leave early, not wanting to risk Cal being asleep by the time he gets there. He texts Dawson once he parks at the hospital, unsurprised that Dawson is still there. Dawson graciously agrees to step outside to give Ellis and Cal some privacy. Hopefully he'll survive five minutes without being glued to his husband's side.

"How are you feeling?" Ellis asks as he drops ungracefully into the chair at his bedside. It's just as uncomfortable as it looks.

Cal sets aside the e-reader in his hands. He's probably reading another vampire novel. "Good, all things considered." He fidgets, his eyes meeting Ellis' with some difficulty. "You didn't have to come. They're releasing me tomorrow."

Ellis scoffs, even though Cal has a point. "Happy to see me, are you?"

"I *am* happy to see you," Cal says with such honesty it takes Ellis aback. "But I know you're busy."

Yeah, but when is he not? "I can make time for my brother." The last thing he wants is to turn into their dad.

Cal winces and drops his gaze to his lap, a muscle in his cheek jumping.

Ellis tenses, looking around for the call button in case Cal is having another episode. The machines keeping tabs on his blood pressure and heart rate don't register anything strange, but maybe there's some delay. What does he know? He's not a doctor.

"Are you okay?"

Cal nods stiffly. "Yeah." He licks his lips and looks up. "Thank you."

"For?"

"Everything. All you've done for me and Dawson."

It's Ellis' turn to avert his eyes. He shrugs. "You'd do the same for me." He's not quite sure that's true. At least not when it came to the old Cal, before he lost his memories and turned into this...clueless, earnest guy stupidly in love with his husband and eager to nurture their brotherly bond. Ellis is still getting used to this new Cal, to having a brother who doesn't despise him and blames him for everything that's gone wrong in his life.

Sometimes, he misses the old Cal, as fucked up as it sounds. He *knew* the old Cal, knew where either of them stood and what they were to each other. Sometimes he just misses the familiarity. He doesn't know how to act around this new Cal, doesn't know the rules. And he sure as hell doesn't know how to act when Cal is being all nice and sweet, something Ellis would never have associated with his brother before. But...he likes him. A lot. More than anything, he likes the idea of having a real relationship with him, of having family. One that doesn't think of him as a mistake, a failure.

"So." He clears his throat, his voice thick with emotion. "I know the doctors said the heart attack was due to your surgery, but you should definitely watch your diet. You need to keep your cholesterol low."

Cal frowns, pursing his lips. "Dawson cooks for me."

Ellis rolls his eyes. "Don't blame this on your husband. Maybe cut down on the donuts too."

"Dawson said the donuts aren't to blame," Cal says like a petulant child. Seriously, who is this guy?

"They probably don't help either. Seriously, Cal." He fixes him with a stern look. "You don't want to kick the bucket at fifty-eight like our old man."

Cal cocks his head. "What old man?"

Ellis takes a very slow, very deep breath. "Our dad, Cal."

"Oh." Cal's brows furrow contemplatively. "I don't think fifty-eight is old."

"For fuck's sake..." Ellis has no choice. He's either going to hug Cal, or strangle him. He goes with the former, mindful not to hurt him. "You're fucking ridiculous sometimes." At least like this Cal can't see the smile that's threatening to take over Ellis' face.

"Sorry?" Cal croaks, hugging him back awkwardly.

Ellis tightens his arms around him for a second and lets go. "I'm glad you're okay," he mumbles, covering it up with a cough. "I'll head out. Pretty sure Dawson is pacing the hallway waiting for me to get out."

"That's not true. Dawson likes you," Cal tells him. So. Damn. Earnest.

"That's not what—" He huffs, shaking his head. "Anyway. I should go."

Cal nods, looking a little bummed. "Thank you. For coming."

Standing up, Ellis gives his shoulder a very manly pat. "Stay away from the hospital."

"I'll try my best."

Ellis means to go see Gabriel the next morning. He really does. Sets up his alarm to wake him up early and all.

He never makes it to the café, staying in bed for half an hour, doubt and fear creeping in like a thief.

Gabriel is...not unlike Cal, Ellis realizes. Both of them are open and honest, innocent but also kind of insane, and see the bright side to everything.

And Ellis is...the exact opposite. Which is probably why he feels such an intense pull towards Gabriel, who's the light to his darkness. He's open where Ellis is reserved, warm where Ellis is cold.

Maybe opposites do attract, but that doesn't mean they should exist side by side. And just because Gabriel might see something good in him doesn't mean he should deal with the bad.

Ellis' life is too much of a mess. *He* is too much of a mess, and while he suspects Gabriel would confidently take on any baggage Ellis might drag in with him, he shouldn't have to. Ellis doesn't want him to. As much as a part of him is dying to have someone like Gabriel in his life, bringing some color to his gray existence, it wouldn't be fair. Sooner or later, Gabriel would be miserable, and he'd come to resent Ellis.

Everyone does, eventually.

He sighs. Time to find a new decent café.

By the time Friday rolls around, Ellis is ready to resign. Change his name. Flee the country. Anything. He just needs a goddamn break. And sleep. So much sleep. And food.

His stomach is growling so loud he swears it echoes through the lobby as he heads towards his office. Thank fuck it's lunchtime.

"Someone is waiting for you in your office," Amanda announces by-the-way when he passes her desk.

He whirls around. "You let them in?"

"Relax," she says like he's the one being unreasonable. "Go on. I guarantee you won't mind."

Fat fucking chance. "Who is it?"

Infuriatingly, she just smiles and coaxes him to go on.

Ellis stomps to his office and throws the door open, a biting remark on the tip of his tongue.

"Jordan?" His mouth might be hanging open a little.

Jordan swivels in Ellis' chair, grinning wildly. "About time. I was getting bored."

Ellis stares at him as it slowly sinks in that his best friend left on a working day to come and see him. That being said, he'd have appreciated a warning. He's too old for surprises—his heart may not be able to take it.

"At least you weren't watching porn."

Jordan blinks at him. "What?"

"Nothing." Shutting the door, Ellis approaches him. "What are you doing here?"

Jordan shrugs. "The weather in Sydney's shit. I needed some vitamin D."

Yeah, right. Ellis might have believed it if Jordan wasn't pasty white and would turn lobster-red after two minutes in the sun.

Jordan stands up, spreading his arms wide. "You gonna hug me or what?"

Lips twitching, Ellis steps forward and lets himself be pulled into an embrace. What's with all the hugs lately? It must be the Gold Coast. It turns people mushy or something.

"Are you okay? You seem...off," Ellis asks when they've pulled apart, noticing something strange in Jordan's gaze, like his mind is somewhere else.

"Shouldn't I be asking you that?"

"I'm okay. Cal's okay. Everything's back to normal." Which is good. Normal is good.

"I didn't think that word was in your vocabulary," Jordan teases.

Ellis punches his shoulder. "You really didn't have to come all the way here just to make sure I don't have a meltdown."

"Maybe I just missed you," Jordan says, smiling because the fucker knows how uncomfortable this kind of talk makes him.

"How long can you stay?" Ellis asks instead.

"Flying back on Sunday afternoon." That's only two days. Ellis tries not to let his disappointment show. "By the way, I need your keys.

You don't mind me crashing at your place, do you?"

Ellis levels him with a flat look, grumpily handing over the keys. "How nice of you to check in with me first."

"If you don't want visitors, why did you get a two-bedroom apartment? Not that it matters. I would've just slept in the bed with you."

"The fuck you would."

Jordan gives him a sly grin. He always loved winding Ellis up. "It's your lunch break, right? Let's go grab something. And then we can grab drinks after you've finished."

"Sounds like a plan. What are you gonna do in the meantime?" Even if he wraps up work early, Jordan will have to entertain himself for at least five hours.

"Wander around. Explore." There's a glint in his eyes that Ellis knows too well.

"Have you been on *Grindr* again?" The business trip to Melbourne from three years ago is still fresh in Ellis' mind. He's never sharing a hotel room with him again.

"Maybe I have, maybe I haven't."

He's sure Jordan's just messing with him. Like, 98% sure.

"No fucking in my apartment."

Jordan's face falls. "Not even the sofa?"

"No!"

"You're no fun."

"And you have too much fun." The tension that's been building up throughout the week drains a little as they settle into the familiar banter. "I missed you too," Ellis admits in a quiet voice.

Jordan eyes him intently and throws an arm over Ellis' shoulders. "Of course you did." He grins. "So, lunch?"

"Lunch."

Chapter 11

"Gabe," Zeke sighs out his name, probably fed up with Gabe's moping and endless staring at the door.

Gabe can't blame him; he's been useless the whole week, getting orders wrong and moving at a sloth's pace. Even his customers have noticed and been trying to cheer him up. It made him feel all kinds of guilty because that's *his* job. That's why he ditched his psychology degree and opened a café, to actually get close to people and make their lives a little better.

He can't afford to be a heartbroken mess. One of the downsides to his gift is that no matter how he feels, his emotions roll off him in intense waves, influencing other people. Normally that's not a problem, since he's the type of person to see the glass half-full, but when he gets like this... Maybe he should go home. Except he can't leave Zeke here alone. Not that he's much help, but still.

"I'm fine," he says, hoping that if he repeats it enough times, it will be true. "I knew there were only two ways this could go. This is one of them."

Zeke scowls. "He's a dick."

"He's not a dick just because he's not interested," Gabe says tersely, feeling a strong compulsion to defend Ellis. Zeke is biased, so of course he'd bitch about Ellis to make Gabe feel better, but that's the last thing he wants. He *gets* it, gets why Ellis never showed up.

It's his own fault for acting so recklessly and ambushing Ellis like that. The poor guy gets skittish at the faintest display of emotion, and Gabe went and all but professed his undying love. Okay, so he just asked Ellis on a date, but he can imagine how freaked out Ellis must have been. Not to mention that Gabe is quite positive he's never dated a man. What did he expect, really?

"Not because of that," Zeke disagrees. "But there aren't only two ways for this to go. He could've always let you down politely and kept coming here anyway."

"Yeah, because that wouldn't be uncomfortable for him at all," Gabe grumbles, though he wishes for the same thing.

Despite all Zeke's teasing, Gabe is not in love with Ellis or anything. A simple 'no thanks' from Ellis would've put him in line and made him cut down on all the flirting. He has some dignity, after all. In time, he could've started seeing Ellis as a mere customer and settled for making his day better with good coffee and some friendly chat. It's a shame he's never going to have the chance because his eagerness scared Ellis off.

Zeke slips a tea towel from his shoulder and slaps it on the counter, his face stormy. "Fuck that. Your feelings are more important than his comfort."

Gabe huffs. "They really aren't. You're just biased." Something tells him Ellis doesn't get to bask in any type of comfort in general.

Zeke opens his mouth, but Gabe is saved from a rant by a customer walking in. Zeke narrows his eyes and ominously promises, "Later."

Summoning some semblance of a smile, Gabe turns to the customer. The man stops in the middle of the café, gaze sweeping over the interior with curiosity.

Gabe feels a pang in his chest as he takes in the man's appearance. He's not wearing a full suit, but the whole attire reminds Gabe of Ellis—down to the expensive-looking slacks, shiny shoes, and a pristine white shirt (Ellis alternates between white and blue). No tie, though.

Smile firmly in place, Gabe calls, "Hey there! How are ya?"

Slowly, the man's gaze reaches him. "Hey. I'm good." The gaze turns appreciative when he runs it over Gabe from head to, well, his waist, which is where the counter cuts off. "Very good," he reiterates, voice significantly lower.

Gabe tries not to groan. Normally, he's happy to indulge in some harmless flirting, but today is so not the day. Technically, any day since he'd met Ellis has not been the day.

"What can I get you?" he asks, ignoring the obvious interest in the man's eyes. Hopefully, he doesn't sound annoyed. His shitty mood is not the guy's fault.

Stepping forward, the man places his both palms on the counter, adopting a relaxed, suggestive pose.

Gabe prays hard that the man is not going to say something cheesy like '*Your number*', or worse. He's not sure he'd be able to keep a straight face.

"A medium flat white. One and a half pumps of hazelnut syrup."

Well, that's a relief, even if he always finds those particular orders amusing. At least the guy didn't ask for a decaf half-strength abracadabra what-the-fuck-ever. Not that Gabe would judge him for it.

Okay, he totally would.

"Sure thing." He grabs a medium sized cup and writes the order down. "Anything else?"

"That's it," the man says simply, though he hasn't taken his eyes off Gabe.

"Great. That will be $6.30." He puts the order through, pointedly keeping his eyes on the iPad.

"This is a cute little place," the man comments after he's paid.

Gabe suppresses a sigh, both at his own attitude and the man's attempt at small talk.

"Thanks."

"Been here long?"

"About five years."

The man hums. "Interesting name, by the way."

That makes Gabe groan and look up, the man's eyes sparkling with mirth. "Not my idea." He *might* sound a little defensive.

"It was mine!" Zeke announces with pride. "Hi, I'm Zeke."

The man slowly looks at him, as if surprised to see another person there. Giving him an acknowledging nod, he turns back to Gabe. "And you are?"

"Gabe."

"Jordan." He offers his hand for a shake, a small smirk curling a corner of his lips. Under other circumstances, Gabe might have found that smirk attractive. "Nice to meet you."

"Likewise." He slides his hand into Jordan's, mindful to not send anything through the connection. It's hard enough to keep his emotions in check as it is, but pushing them back when it comes to physical contact is ten times harder.

Some of them—probably disinterest and mild frustration—must seep through regardless, because the smirk disappears from Jordan's face, his intense energy growing muter as if someone turned down the light in the living room. He quickly schools his expression and lets go of Gabe's hand.

"Are you new to the area?" Gabe asks, feeling a little bad for the guy now.

Jordan's aura instantly brightens, and so do his features. "Visiting a friend, actually. Only here for two days before I'm going back to Sydney."

Gabe nods, smiling, this time genuinely. He loves listening to people talk about their passions and their loved ones. Their energy always turns into something warm and beautiful.

"Shame that you can only stay two days. Do you get to see each other often?"

"We're in the same business and used to work together. In Sydney. But he went through some hard-core family drama and had to relocate here." He sighs. "I do miss the fucker."

Gabe tenses up. That...sounds awfully familiar. It *could* be a coincidence, except it checks out all too well. Family drama? Sydney? Relocating to the GC? Yeah, no. Also, coincidences *never* happen to him. Ever.

"You should bring him along. We're open on Saturdays too," he suggests innocently.

Jordan laughs. "Yeah, I might, though I'm pretty sure he's been here before. I found some cups with your logo in his kitchen. No idea why he kept used cups, but I figured; Ellis is a huge coffee snob, so your coffee must be good."

Shit. He was right. Jordan *is* talking about Ellis and—

Wait a second.

"He keeps the cups?" he asks, voice a little squeaky.

"Weird, I know." Jordan laughs again.

"Did you ask him about it?"

Why would Ellis—*Oh.* Gabe's written a couple of messages for him, hasn't he? And Ellis kept them? God, that's just so adorable and kinda yucky and sad and adorable.

Pull yourself together, for crying out loud.

If Jordan's noticed Gabe's obvious fishing, he doesn't show it. "Haven't had the chance. He's at work, but he gave me the key to his apartment. But I'm totally gonna ask when I see him." He seems to be excited about the prospect of teasing Ellis.

Gabe's thoughts get stuck on the part about Jordan having a key to Ellis' apartment. Okay, so he's obviously staying with Ellis for the two days. And they're obviously close if Ellis gave him a key. And Jordan is obviously queer and lights up when talking about Ellis. And—

Gabe stops right there. He's not going down that road. Just because Ellis has a friend who's interested in men doesn't mean he's interested in Ellis. And considering that Ellis freaked out when Gabe asked him out on a date, it's safe to assume they're simply good friends. And even if they were something else, it doesn't matter. Gabe might be a little heartbroken about the whole 'crushing on a straight customer' thing, but in reality he just wants Ellis to be happy. Jordan clearly adores him, and Gabe could never be upset about that.

He's looking for something to say when Zeke pops up next to him. "There you go," he says to Jordan. "A medium flat white, exactly one and a half pumps of hazelnut."

"Thank you." Jordan spares him a glance as he takes his coffee before looking back at Gabe. He raises the cup in cheers. "It was nice meeting you, Gabe. Have a good one."

Gabe smiles. "You too." Part of him is sad to see Jordan go because he'd love nothing more than to interrogate him on the topic of Ellis. Not that he would. He has no intention to make his silly infatuation glaringly obvious. It's bad enough that Ash and Zeke know.

"Wow. Small world," Zeke comments, looking after Jordan's disappearing form.

"Eavesdropping again?" Gabe asks, unimpressed but unsurprised. "And not really. He did say he found this place because he saw the coffee cups at Ellis' place."

"Which is weird and kinda gross."

Gabe shoots him a glare. "It's not and it's not." Even though he was just thinking the same.

"Aww, look at you, jumping to your man's defense." He winds an arm around Gabe's shoulders.

Gabe shrugs him off. "Not my man." It's unfair how much he likes the sound of that. Fuck, *if only.* He'd be so good to Ellis. So, so good. He'd be the *best.*

know. Whenever I step in there, I feel a little more like...myself. Like I can breathe. Like the world is not crashing down around me."

It sounds like bullshit even to his ears, but Jordan doesn't laugh. His gaze is soft and, if it's possible, a little melancholic.

"What's his name?"

Fighting and failing to suppress a smile, Ellis breathes out, "Gabriel."

Jordan's lips twitch. Ellis fails to see what's so funny. "You wanna ask him out?"

Guilt slams into him with a force that makes him gasp for a breath. "*He* asked *me* out. Wrote his number on the takeaway box last time I was there with a note '*Have dinner with me*'."

Jordan whistles. Ellis doesn't like how excited he looks. "Ballsy. Me likey. When was this?"

Ellis averts his eyes. "Saturday."

He can feel Jordan's burning stare on the side of his face.

"Please tell me you've been back since." The tone of his voice suggests he already knows the answer.

Ellis swallows. "I was going to go. But then Dawson called that Cal's at the hospital and...everything just snowballed from then on."

"Snowballed, my ass," Jordan says indignantly. "You bailed, Ellis, admit it."

"I didn't... I was going to say yes when I went there on Monday. I was." He looks at Jordan to prove he's telling the truth. "But...a part of me was..."

Jordan's stern face softens with understanding. "Relieved that you had an out?"

Shame burning under his skin, Ellis nods. "I don't want to give him false hope. I'm not even sure I'm attracted to him. He's a really nice person and I like talking to him, but that could be all there is to it."

What if he just feels a little attached because Gabriel treats him so kindly? What if he's just confusing attraction with something way more platonic? He'd never forgive himself if he started something with Gabriel, only to turn around days, weeks later and tell him he got it wrong, he actually doesn't like him *that* way.

"I suppose he's...cute. In a goofy way. The stuff that comes out of his mouth is honestly off the charts ridiculous, and then he gets all flustered and flushed when he realizes what he said. He makes the best coffee and sometimes writes little messages on the cups. And he always looks so damn earnest when he's listening to me prattle on about something and—What?"

Looking at Jordan, he finds himself on the receiving end of a very flat look. "Yeah, you're not attracted to him at all."

Ellis scowls, his cheeks burning. "Very helpful."

"How would you like me to help? Do you want me to kiss you again to see if it does anything for you?"

Ellis scrunches his nose instinctively. "Not really."

"Rude." Jordan pouts, then laughs, "I'm kidding."

Ellis rolls his eyes. "I don't want to hurt him, Jordan."

"Good. You can start by cutting the bullshit."

Ellis frowns. "What bullshit?"

"About not being sure if you're attracted to him and that being the reason why you're hiding instead of talking to him like a fucking adult."

"I...I'm not—"

"Yeah, you are," Jordan stands his ground, his eyes hard and intense. "If you were *that* unsure how you feel about him, you wouldn't have planned on going back and taking him up on the offer. You sure as hell wouldn't look like a love-sick puppy when you talk about him."

"I'm not a love-sick puppy!"

"Please. You all but waxed poetic about him just a minute ago."

"I did not—"

"Ellis." Jordan fixes him with a hard look that gradually turns into something more tender. "Stop it. Out of everyone, I'm the last person you need to pretend with."

Ellis exhales shakily, blinking back the sudden burning in his eyes. He feels Jordan shift and press closer to him until he can wrap an arm around his back.

"I know your dad fucked you up pretty good. I know you think you don't deserve good things, and you think you're not good enough. But you do, and you are. And even if you can't believe it just yet, you can still take a leap of faith. Everything will fall into place, eventually."

Ellis lets out a shuddering breath. "How can I take a leap when I don't know what's out there?"

Jordan hums, squeezing him a little tighter. "Sometimes you just have to risk the fall."

He can imagine few things scarier than that. "What if I crash and burn?"

Jordan takes a while to reply, and when he does, he sounds a little far away. "What if you don't? What if you find everything you've been looking for?"

Odds have never been in Ellis' favor. It's hard to believe they could be now, especially with all the things that could go wrong.

He carefully extracts himself from Jordan's embrace, feeling too raw, too split open.

"Okay. Your turn now." Hopefully, talking about Jordan will make him stop feeling like his whole being is an open wound.

"What do you mean?"

"You said I've been acting weird. Well, so have you. And—" he says before Jordan can open his big mouth and blurt out a lie. "If I can't bullshit you, the same goes for you."

After a long moment where Ellis almost thinks he won't get an answer, Jordan speaks. "Believe it or not, I'm kind of in the same boat. Just the opposite."

"I don't follow."

"I met someone," Jordan starts, a self-deprecating chuckle escaping him. "I was sure he was into me. Or at least queer. All touchy feely and shit. But I miscalculated. He's straight and has a girlfriend. *Had* a girlfriend."

"You hit on him?"

Jordan makes a face. "He was really chill about it, thank god. But we met again and...*he* pretty much came on to *me*."

"Really? And that's...not good?" It's clearly not, if Jordan's sour expression is anything to go by.

"I'm not interested in being someone's experiment."

Ellis laughs, confused. "You said, I quote, that I *'wouldn't be the first straight boy you led astray'* and now you're being all grouchy because a supposedly straight guy decided he wants to fuck you?" The humor is short-lived, Jordan's mood darkening and his jaw clenching. Wait a second. Did he say he's in the same boat as Ellis? That would mean... "You have feelings for him."

A muscle in Jordan's cheek jumps. He shrugs, the action stiff and somewhat angry. "I'm not...indifferent."

Ellis tries not to laugh, even though he's dying to tease him. "Have you seen him since he came on to you?"

Jordan seems to have found something very interesting on the ceiling because his eyes are glued to it. "I...might've hired him."

"What?"

Jordan squirms. "He's my PA."

"What?"

"I know, I know," he says despairingly. "But he needed a job, and I'm a weak, weak man."

Ellis closes his eyes, opening them slowly. "Tell me you're not fucking your assistant." Among all the shitstorm, Ellis can't afford to have someone from his team be sued for sexual harassment if things go south.

"I'm not fucking my assistant," Jordan says, very tersely. "Not for lack of trying on *his* part."

A light-bulb goes off in Ellis' brain. "I'll go out on a limb and say that you came all the way here in a spur of the moment because you are running away, aren't you?"

Jordan has the audacity to look insulted. "What? Of course not! I missed you and I knew you were going through a hard time."

Ellis just stares at him.

"Okay, fine!" Jordan throws his hands up. "I needed some distance.

I can't think for shit when he's around."

How relatable. "I'm sorry, Jay. Are you positive it's just the sex he wants?" He didn't think he'd see the day when Jordan would be the pining one.

Jordan huffs. "He claims it wouldn't be just the sex, but I'm not stupid. He's curious and he knows I'm into him and thinks I'm gonna cave."

Ellis bristles a little. "You hypocrite. You tell me to take a fucking leap even if there's a huge fucking chance I might end up hurting both Gabriel and myself, but you won't take a chance on the guy you want and who wants you back?"

"He doesn't *want* me. He's just saying it to get his way."

Ellis studies his profile since Jordan still won't look at him. "And you know that for sure?"

Jordan swallows, his voice raspy. "Yup."

"Liar." He instantly feels bad when he sees Jordan wince. Seems that the tough guy is not as tough when it comes to his heart instead of his dick. "Hey."

Jordan reluctantly looks at him.

Ellis smiles. "What's your guy's name?"

Jordan's eyes slide shut, the name rolling off his tongue like a melody. "Charlie."

"Tell me about him."

Chapter 13

GABE IS SURPRISED TO see Jordan again Saturday morning. He can't decide if he's relieved or disappointed that Ellis hasn't come with him. He'd love to see him, of course, but he can just imagine the awkward silence that would follow.

"Good morning," Jordan says cheerfully, though he looks like he'd love nothing more than to fall into bed and sleep until the cows come home. He's also lost the formal clothes and looks like a completely new person in his shorts and a white tee.

"Morning. Rough night?" Gabe asks teasingly.

"You know how to flatter a guy." Jordan pretends to pout. It looks ridiculous on him. "To answer your question: fun night."

Gabe's not sure about that. There's a sense of contentment coming from Jordan, probably due to having spent time with his friend, but there's something else too. Something sad and a little wistful. Gabe doesn't call him out on it, it's hardly his place. Instead, he focuses on brightening his energy, hoping some of it will transfer to Jordan.

"I see. Need a pick-me-up?"

Jordan lets out a dramatic groan. "Yes, please. Save me."

Gabe laughs. "You got it. Flat white, is it?"

"A large one this time." His eyes sparkle mischievously, watching Gabe's face with intense focus. "And I need a coffee for my friend too. He's a lightweight."

Gabe bites his lip to stop himself from blurting out Ellis' order.

"What kind of coffee?"

Jordan looks at him like he can see right through the bullshit. Could it be that he *knows* and is just taunting Gabe? But...that would mean Ellis has talked about him. Somehow, Gabe has a hard time believing that. Then again, if Ellis was drunk and Jordan managed to get him to talk...

"You probably know better than me since he's your regular. I mentioned him yesterday. Name's Ellis?"

Yup. There it is. Jordan totally knows.

"Right." Gabe sighs, giving up all pretense. "I don't think he's a regular anymore." He expects some pitying looks, or half-baked words of comfort, but Jordan surprises him again.

"Oh, he is. Believe me." His expression turns a little more serious. "He's been a little busy this week. Family stuff."

Is that supposed to be an explanation as to why Ellis hasn't shown up the whole week? And does that mean there's something new going on with Cal? Now that he thinks about it, Gabe hasn't seen him or Dawson in a few days. That's unusual.

Whatever it is, it's not his place to pry.

"So, one dirty chai on oat?"

Jordan's brows rise slowly. "I thought he gets this disgustingly strong black coffee."

Gabe shrugs. "He's been trying new things."

"Yes, I've heard," Jordan replies, his tone heavy with implication. "Shocking. Doesn't sound like him at all."

"It doesn't?" Gabe can't help but ask. It only confirms his previous assumption that Ellis has never dated a man.

"Nope. I've known him for seven years and he's, like, the most predictable person ever."

Gabe douses the spark of hope before it starts a fire. He needs to be logical about this. "He's had to make a lot of changes lately. I suppose changing his coffee order isn't such a big deal in the grand scheme."

"Probably not," Jordan says amicably. "Not like dating someone new. Especially if that someone is not his usual type."

Oh-kay. So Ellis told him *everything*.

"What's his usual type?" Gabe asks, trying not to sound too eager. He can guess the answer anyway.

Once again, he stands corrected.

"Leeches. Narcissists. You know; the works." He sounds bitter and angry about it, which makes Gabe like him a little more. "I can see how the idea of dating someone kind and genuine could throw him for a loop." He gives Gabe a meaningful look.

Gabe's breath catches, his heart hammering against his ribs. Fuck, he's hopeless. "Anything else?"

Jordan hums thoughtfully. "Ellis has a soft spot for blondes." He smirks, likely at Gabe's dumbstruck look. "You know what? I'm gonna take a couple of croissants too. Hangover food."

Taking a second to adjust to the sudden change of topic, Gabe blurts out, "Cinnamon rolls. Ellis likes cinnamon rolls."

Jordan's smile overtakes his whole face. "Make it one croissant and one cinnamon roll."

"On it."

Making the drink and packing everything up give Gabe a bit of a reprieve, but not much. He's glad Zeke is in the kitchen and can't witness the disaster that Gabe is. His hands shake with excitement and anxiety as he steams the milk, nearly burning it, and he struggles looking at Jordan as Jordan collects his order.

"Thanks, Gabe," he says softly, probably sensing how much of a mess Gabe is. He hesitates before leaning in, speaking softly despite no one else being around. "Hey. I'm not saying you should wait forever. But...be patient with him, okay? He's one of the best people I know. Scratch that. He *is* the best."

"I know," Gabe says, a little choked up. "Thank you, Jordan."

Jordan nods, then gives a wry smile that has an amused edge to it. "At least now that I know why you shot me down my ego isn't so bruised."

"Used to people falling at your feet, are you?" Gabe retorts, fighting a smile of his own. After the heart-to-heart they just had, he feels a deep sense of kinship towards Jordan.

Jordan shrugs, lips twitching. "Usually kneeling before me, but yeah."

"I have an old knee injury. We wouldn't work out anyway."

Jordan barks out a laugh, then makes Gabe blush by saying, "I can see why he likes you. Be good to him, okay?"

"I will." If he sees Ellis again at all.

"Later." Jordan winks, sauntering away.

"Bye."

Well, that's a thing that happened. Could this week get any weirder?

A note for Gabe: do not challenge the cosmos.

Not a half an hour after Jordan's left, Gabe gets a text from Dawson asking if he's seen Cal. Jordan's comment about Ellis' family drama pops into his mind and his stomach clenches with a foreboding feeling. He resists the temptation to fish for details and just texts him back that no, he hasn't seen Cal in days.

He gets a distraction from his worrying when Ash pops in shortly after, looking awfully satisfied for someone who looks like he woke up five minutes ago. Right. Last night was Friday night. That can only mean one thing.

"That smirk of yours makes me really uncomfortable," Gabe grumbles as Ash approaches him, giving Zeke a hello. "Had a good night?"

"Oh, yeah." Ash whistles. "You have no idea."

Gross. "I have some and I don't want any more."

Ash smirks. "Had a good morning? You seem...better."

Does he? He feels scattered and uprooted, but Jordan's visit did pull him out of his misery. Speaking of...

"You'll never guess who came in this morning."

"It can't be Ellis, because I would totally guess that."

"His friend who's visiting from Sydney."

"Well, shit." Ash laughs. "You can't make that up."

Gabe refrains from explaining how Jordan ended up in this café, figuring it's not important. "That's not all. He knew about me and my stupid crush."

"Hmm. So your boy talks about you. Good."

Gabe ignores the 'his boy' comment. "He basically asked me to be patient with Ellis. And to treat him right."

Ash hums what sounds like approval. "I like the implications of that."

"Me too," Gabe says with a laugh. "I'm just a little nervous to..."

"Rekindle the hope? Yeah, I get that."

"Jordan—Ellis' friend—mentioned Ellis has been busy with family stuff. You hear anything from Dawson?"

Ash gives him a chastising look that falls flat since it's accompanied by a smirk. "Patient confidentiality, Gabe. I do stick to the rules on occasion."

"What use are you to me then?" Gabe grumbles, even though he understands. But Ash would tell him if something serious happened, right? Or at least, he'd hint.

As if summoned, Dawson walks through the door just then, Donut following dutifully next to him. No sign of Cal, though.

"Dawson, hey! We were just talking about you."

Slowly, Ash turns around, leaning back with his elbows on the counter. "Hi. Fancy seeing you in the wild." His gaze dips lower. "This must be the famous Donut. Hello, there."

At the sound of his name, Donut's tail begins to wag, and he pulls on the leash. Dawson goes with him, so Ash can get some obligatory pets and scratches in. It's a cute scene, but Gabe is more focused on the dark cloud hanging over Dawson's head.

He rounds the counter, giving Donut a quick scratch before

turning his attention to Dawson.

"What's wrong?"

Instead of words, a wrecked sob escapes Dawson's lips.

Gabe's eyes widen, and he gets slammed with a wave of grief so strong it makes him waver. He does the only thing he knows to do, drawing Dawson into a hug. "Oh, Dawson."

Dawson clings to him, muffling his sobs in Gabe's shoulder. Gabe rubs his back, pulling away an inch. "Here, sit down." He leads Dawson to a free table, away from the rest of the customers. Not that there are many, thankfully.

"I'm sorry," Dawson says when they sit down and hides his blotchy face in his hands. "God, this is embarrassing. I didn't mean to come here and lose my shit."

"It's not embarrassing," Gabe says. "And you're welcome to lose your shit. We got you."

"Is this about Cal?" Ash asks, direct as ever.

Dawson ducks his head, his laugh full of self-deprecation. "Am I that obvious?"

"No," Ash says, regarding him with sympathy. "I just have a hunch for these things."

Dawson huffs, his mood lighting up a shade. It's clear Ash's presence makes him comfortable, and in any other situation it would be amusing. Ash usually has the opposite effect on people, but he and Dawson must have grown close during his therapy sessions.

"What happened?" Gabe asks. "Why were you asking if Cal's here?"

"Because I didn't want to bump into him. He...he had a heart attack. Spent two days in the hospital."

"Shit," Gabe and Ash say in unison. Gabe follows it with, "Is he okay?" Is this what Jordan meant when he said Ellis was busy with family stuff? Fucking hell. All this time Gabe has been mopey as fuck while Ellis was worrying about his brother.

"Yeah. He went home three days ago."

"Okay..." That doesn't really explain why Dawson is avoiding him.

"His memories came back."

Gabe gapes at him, sure he must've misheard. "How's that possible? It's been like...two months, no?"

"I don't know. But he remembers now."

"What else? There's something else."

Gabe doesn't know all that much about Dawson's past—about the person Cal was before his accident. But from the little Dawson has told him, Cal wasn't a good person. Not a good person at all. And yet, he can't shake the feeling there's something that's bothering Dawson even more.

"He said...stuff. Nonsense stuff." Dawson's emotions flare up with anger. "Made up this story that he's not the real Cal, that he's..." He gives an incredulous laugh. "A reaper, or something, and that he took over Cal's body when he was in the hospital after his accident. And some other stuff. I packed a bag, took Donut, and got out of there. No reason to stay and let him manipulate the fuck out of me because he can't handle the truth." He looks at Ash. "You were right. People don't change."

It takes Gabe a second—or ten—to process, but the puzzle pieces slowly slot together. "Oh. Oh!" He taps the table erratically. "So *that's* what that was."

"What was what?" asks Ash.

Gabe almost tells him, then remembers Dawson is there too. He holds up a finger and gives him a pinched smile. "Can you give us a sec?" Without waiting for a response, he slaps Ash's arm, silently mouthing, "Follow me."

Confused but definitely curious, Ash trails behind him. They hurry off behind the counter, far enough that Dawson can't hear. Then Gabe rounds on him, his hands flying through the air as he tries to summarize his huge epiphany.

"Okay, so this is crazy, but hey, what's new, right?"

Ash blinks at him. "Right..."

"Okay. So, you know that Cal used to be an asshole before, right? I mean, you definitely know more than me. Dawson always kind of hinted and I put two and two together, but he actually talks to you about this. Anyway, when he and Cal came here after the accident, I tried to get a read on him. Amnesia and all that. Pretty fascinating, right? It was the first time we ever met, and it was super weird. Like, I could tell he's a good person. Or not a *bad* person. Couldn't feel anything malicious from him. But there was this...shadow surrounding him. When I felt his emotions, it was like feeling them through a...veil. A barrier." He snaps his fingers. "Like an emotional condom!"

"Emotional condom."

"Right! And, like, it wasn't bad, but it put me on edge because I'd never felt anything like it before. I thought maybe he was confused because of the amnesia and stuff, but now it makes perfect sense!"

"It does?"

"Duh! Cal's not human!"

Ash's jaw drops a little, a stunned expression on his face. He looks over at Dawson, who's watching them anxiously, and says, "Holy shit."

"Right?!"

Ash swallows, looking uncharacteristically out of his depth. "Do we tell him?"

"Of course we tell him!"

"He won't believe it."

"We'll make him believe. Jesus, Ash, we can't let him leave here thinking the guy who loves him to hell and back—literally!—is a psycho who's trying to gaslight him."

Ash sighs. "Yeah, you're right. It would destroy him."

"I know." A lump forms in Gabe's throat, Dawson's emotions so raw and intense that they make him a little sick.

And then another realization slams into him.

Ellis.

Ellis doesn't know his brother is not his brother at all.

Fuck.

Sometimes Gabe really, really hates knowing things.

Maybe he'll never come back anyway and you won't have to worry about that.

He quickly banishes the thought. This is so not the time to pine and mope.

With Ash by his side, he heads towards Dawson, trying to summon a reassuring smile. This is good news, after all.

They both take a seat, Dawson's panicked eyes jumping between the two of them.

Gabe interlaces his fingers, his cheeks puffing out before he expels a sharp breath. "Dawson, this will sound crazy, but hear me out, yeah?"

Dawson scoffs. "Crazier than a reaper taking over a dead guy's body?"

Exchanging a look with Ash, Gabe jumps straight in. "Have you considered the possibility that Cal was telling the truth?"

"Um, no?" Dawson says in that way that indicates he totally thinks Gabe's pulling his leg.

"I think you should."

Dawson laughs, of course he does. The laugh dies, and he stills when he notices their solemn expressions. "Are you being serious?"

"Hear him out," Ash says gently.

"There are things you can't explain with logic," Gabe starts. "With science, sometimes, but not always. That doesn't mean they're not real."

"Like your superpowers?" Dawson quips.

Gabe smiles. "Like that, yeah."

"You can read people, Gabe. So can any good psychologist." Dawson nods towards Ash. "And you know how to make them feel better because you're a kind, empathetic person. It's amazing, but it's not magic."

Gabe doesn't take offense, though he is a little tired of all the skepticism. He's had this argument before. A hundred times.

A little demonstration should do it.

Slowly raising his hand to give him a chance to move back, he places it over Dawson's, deliberately sending a trickle of positive energy through the connection.

He knows when it reaches Dawson because his eyelids flutter, a peaceful expression replacing the anguished one. He aims his gaze down, eyes trailing over the floor as if he's expecting to find himself levitating. Gabe has had some people describe the feeling as floating above the ground before.

Dawson takes a gasping breath when Gabe withdraws his energy, breaking the connection.

"Could a regular empathetic person do that?" Gabe asks, not trying to sound smug or anything.

Dawson does a double take when his eyes land on Gabe's. He must be seeing the golden hue that always appears in his eyes when he uses his powers like that.

"What was that?" Dawson demands, not sounding particularly freaked out. Then again, it's probably not the weirdest thing that's happened to him lately.

"Magic," Gabe says with a small grin. He feels his eyelids begin to droop, a wave of exhaustion falling over him. Damn, he's going to feel dizzy for a good while, but it needed to be done. "I'm sorry. I try not to do this without consent, but you were being stubborn." Thankfully, he can't feel any irritation coming from Dawson. "I have…empathic abilities. There's more to it. Remember the first time you brought Cal here? After he was released from the hospital?" Dawson nods. "I talked to him. There was something about him I couldn't put my finger on. And for a moment there, we touched, and I…I didn't understand what I felt. I'd never felt anything like it. But whatever it was, it wasn't bad, it wasn't malicious." He holds Dawson's gaze. "But it wasn't human either."

Panic floods Dawson's gaze. "I—I don't…"

"I felt how much he cares for you," Gabe prowls on. "You're on his mind constantly, Dawson. Whoever this man is, he's not the person you knew. He's worlds better, and he loves you so much that I can feel it in my bones when you two are around."

"He's telling the truth," Ash takes over. "I've never met Cal, but I know Gabe. He's the real deal."

"How do you know?"

"I'm not the only one with superpowers," Gabe says, leaving it there.

"Another time," Ash says when Dawson looks at him for explanation. "I think you should talk to Cal."

"*Now* you're advocating for him?" Dawson bristles.

Ash shakes his head. "Do you remember the second time you came to see me?"

"Which part?"

"You said you were so happy you couldn't bring yourself to care about what anyone else thought. You said that when you are with Cal, you can be yourself. You said he makes you feel safe. Is it really so unbelievable that he might not be the man you thought he was?"

Dawson's face, and his energy, go through a complicated myriad of emotions, finally settling on something resembling an epiphany. "Can people hear you when they're comatose?" he asks Ash.

"What?"

"Cal said something about the hospital. About me and Kieran...going into his room. Could he have been aware of what was going on around him even when he was sedated?"

"Possibly," Ash says, very reluctantly. "Just because the conscious part of your brain is on vacation doesn't mean the whole thing shuts off. Kind of like when you're sleeping."

"I have to go." Dawson pushes his chair back, giving Donut's leash a gentle tug as he hurries outside.

Gabe looks at Ash, and they both shrug. They've done everything they could. Whatever Dawson does next is—

Gabe's vision blacks out, an urgent, high-pitched sound piercing through his ears. In the darkness, a golden line twists and curls in various shapes. *Words,* Gabe realizes as the first one appears.

"Gabe?" comes Ash's worried voice.

"Pen. Need a pen and paper.

A chair scrapes across the floor, and then two items are placed in his hands. "Here."

Gabe hurriedly scribbles the message down, his vision finally clearing once every word is on the paper. Hope fills his chest as he reads them.

If it isn't happy, it's not the end.

"Is that for Dawson?" Ash asks.

Fuck. Dawson.

Folding the paper in half, Gabe hurries after him, shouting his name.

Dawson stops, although reluctantly, and frowns when Gabe hands him the paper. "What is it?"

"I don't know," Gabe says. "I'm just a messenger."

With that, he walks back to the café, his mind whirring.

What a fucking day.

Chapter 14

ELLIS WAKES UP TO the sound of a door slamming shut. Groaning, he crawls out of bed, waiting for his double-vision to adjust before he attempts to walk. Keeping it on down-low and drinking lots of water yesterday has saved him a pounding headache, thank god, but he would kill for a cup of coffee regardless. A particular type of coffee.

He must be really desperate because he swears he can smell the spices and the dark scent of roasted coffee beans as he drags his ass into the living room. Great. Now he has hallucinations.

"Good morning, sleeping beauty!" Jordan yells, making Ellis jump and clutch a hand to his chest. He looks very pleased with that reaction, and Ellis glares at him.

"You've already been out?" How long had he slept?

"And I come bearing gifts."

His vision sharpening, Ellis takes note of the carrier tray with two cups of what's hopefully coffee in Jordan's hand, and a paper box in the other.

"Thank fuck." Good to know he wasn't hallucinating.

Except his brain must not be fully online yet, because it takes him an embarrassingly long time to realize that he *is* actually smelling the spices from the drink Gabriel always makes him. He's never mentioned that little detail to Jordan. At least he's pretty sure he hasn't.

And then it gets worse.

"Something wrong?" Jordan asks, expression deceptively innocent.

"Where did you get this?" Ellis demands, pointing a shaky finger at the coffee cups bearing a very familiar, very specific stamp.

Jordan's mask cracks, a knowing smirk taking its place. "Where do you think?"

"Jordan...what did you do?" A sense of doom settles in Ellis' stomach, making him feel nauseated.

Jordan must notice his growing panic because he shuts the lid on the teasing, sighing tiredly. "Calm down, will you? I didn't do anything. I was just curious what your sexuality crisis was all about."

"I don't have—" Something else hits Ellis. "How did you know where to go?"

Jordan's chest puffs out, and he looks very proud of himself as he starts talking. "Fun fact: I went to *Lost and Ground* yesterday while you were at work because I saw your little cup collection. And I talked to a very nice fellow named Gabe. I didn't think much of it until you started blabbering about being attracted to a certain barista and finally dropped his name."

"You just go around asking people's names?" Ellis grits out, focusing on evening out his breathing so as not to have a meltdown. Of course he totally forgot about the cups sitting in the kitchen.

"Just the hot ones," Jordan replies.

Ellis sucks in a sharp breath, his eyes narrowing.

Jordan, the dick, just laughs. "Tone it down before you turn green."

"Fuck you."

"Nice bloke, that Gabe," Jordan carries on as if he didn't hear him. "And well...hot. Shot me down, though. I wonder why."

He knows Jordan is just ragging him on, but that doesn't stop the rush of warmth in his chest at the implication that Gabriel isn't interested in anyone but Ellis. Especially since—he can finally admit it now—Jordan is ridiculously attractive. And not as fucked up in the head as Ellis.

"Aren't you in love with your PA?" he reminds him.

"Not in love," Jordan mutters, very unconvincingly.

"Uh-huh."

"And my dick still works."

"Quit it," Ellis says grimly, not wanting to imagine Jordan's dick anywhere near Gabriel.

"You need to start to get comfortable talking about dicks if you wanna date a person who has one."

Ellis almost tells him that's not what he meant when something else dawns on him. "You didn't tell him we know each other, did you?"

Jordan purses his lips. "Define 'tell him'."

"Jordan!"

"I didn't say it outright, but he got the message."

"Jordan!"

"You should go back soon. He was clearly bummed about you being MIA."

An insult dies on Ellis' tongue. "Was he mad?"

"Not mad. Just sad." Jordan's face is sympathetic as he adds, "He seems like a really good person."

Ellis swallows, a feeling of loss expanding through his chest. "He is."

"You're a really good person too. And he thinks the same." Jordan hands him the box. "I hear you like cinnamon rolls."

Ellis stares at it, at the smiley face Gabriel drew on the lid, and something snaps inside him. "I need to go."

"Nuh-uh." Jordan blocks the way with his body since his hands are full. "Coffee and sugar first." Cutting Ellis' protest short, he says, "You don't wanna be a dick when you talk to him, do you?"

Ellis deflates. Jordan's right. He's not thinking clearly and he's being hasty because he just had an epiphany. Besides, Gabriel is working now and he won't have time to listen to Ellis unravel his soul or whatever. He needs to think it through, wait until he can think straight. Or not so straight.

"Thank you. For coming all the way here. For keeping my ass in line." Sometimes he forgets how lucky he is to have a friend like Jordan. Other times, he curses his very existence.

"Oh, believe me. It's my pleasure."

"Does that mean it's my turn to meddle in your love life and give sound advice?" Ellis asks, rather daunted at the thought.

Jordan pretends to think it over. "Nah, you're good."

"Thank god."

I'm such a creep, Ellis thinks as he stands in front of *Lost and Ground,* watching Gabriel mop the floor. Mop the floor and use the handle as a mic while singing along with the song blasting from the speaker. Ellis can't hear all the lyrics, but the volume is high enough that he thinks he recognizes the song. *Is that Frozen?*

Gabriel throws his head back and lets out a very passionate and enthusiastic *Let it go.*

Ellis hadn't planned on being a creep, simply meaning to come here after the café has closed. He was hoping Gabriel would have the closing shift, but hadn't considered the door would be locked. Instead of trying to get his attention, Ellis carries on watching him. A curious, tingly feeling travels through his limbs as he does. He resists the compulsion to squash it down, ignore it until it goes away. He needs to do the exact opposite if he wants a shot at this...*thing* with Gabriel. Whatever it is.

Suddenly, Gabriel twirls around, twice, and ends up facing the front of the shop. It doesn't seem he's seen Ellis, continuing 'mopping' and swinging his hips to the beat.

Ellis knows the exact moment Gabriel notices him, because he goes from energetic and unhinged to stock-still. His eyes are wide as they stare at Ellis, and it takes him several seconds to move again.

He props the mop against a table and pulls his phone out, the music dying at once. He looks like a skittish animal as he slowly walks to the door, and damn if Ellis can't relate. It makes him feel a little better that he's not the only one out of his element.

The apron Gabriel's wearing today says *Better latte than never*, and Ellis almost laughs at the synchronicity. He truly hopes it's not too latte.

Holding Ellis' gaze, Gabriel flicks the lock open. There's a faint blush on his cheeks, making him look so much younger.

Ellis' heart leaps into his throat when the door is suddenly not in the way. It occurs to him this is the first time they've stood so close without anything between them, and is surprised at how much of a difference it makes. Right now, they're not a customer and an employee. A CEO and a barista. They're just...them.

"Is there any chance you didn't see that?" Gabriel says in lieu of a greeting, face scrunched up and so red it looks sunburned. It's unfairly endearing.

"See what?" Ellis says seriously.

Gabriel laughs, the sound sending a shockwave through Ellis' body. "Thanks. Um..." He looks over his shoulder. "We just closed, but I can make you—"

"No, that's... I know," Ellis hurries to say. "I was hoping to catch you before you left."

"Oh." Gabriel licks his lips. "Because..."

"I didn't want to talk with other people around. And with a counter between us."

Gabriel presses his lips together as if he's fighting back a big smile. It doesn't work. The skin around his eyes crinkles and two dimples appear in his cheeks, the sight knocking the breath out of Ellis.

"I'd like that." He steps aside to let Ellis in.

Ellis gets a whiff of cookie dough as he brushes past him, wondering if Gabriel is baking something. As he steps further into the café, smelling only cleaning chemicals and coffee, it occurs to him the scent must be coming from Gabriel. He wonders if he would taste cookie dough if Ellis leaned in and kissed him. The thought doesn't exactly shock him. It's not the first time he thought about kissing Gabriel, but it's the first time he actually thinks like he might.

One step at a time.

"So...you an Elsa fan?"

Gabriel groans and shoots him a betrayed look. "You couldn't keep up the pretense so I could save face, could you?"

"Sorry. If it makes you feel better, I rather enjoyed the show," Ellis says, attempting to keep a straight face and failing.

Gabriel huffs. "Well, it's not like this would be the first time I made a fool of myself."

Any humor that Ellis felt disappears. "I'm sorry for pulling that disappearing act."

Gabriel, always too nice for his own good, takes pity on him. "It's okay. I know. Dawson was here today. I heard about Cal. Are you okay?"

Ellis blinks, confused. This isn't what he had in mind, and it still takes him a minute to remember that Cal and Dawson are regulars at the café and that they talk to Gabriel about personal stuff. Clearly even more than they talk to Ellis.

It's been three days since Cal was discharged, and Ellis has checked on him a few times, only getting some short, ambiguous response that didn't lessen his worries in the slightest. And this morning he texted Dawson as well, but didn't get a reply until hours later. Something's been going on that he doesn't know about, but something is always going on. That's not an excuse for avoiding Gabriel after he opened himself up to Ellis.

"I'm okay. It was a bit of a health scare, but Cal's fine. I already gave him a speech." That earns him a small smile. "I wish I could blame everything on him but...I don't want to lie to you."

"You never have to lie to me," Gabriel says, his hands twitching at his sides as though he wants to reach out for Ellis. And fuck if Ellis doesn't want that too.

"Yeah. I'm starting to get that." He laughs nervously. "I'm sorry about Jordan. He has a big mouth and tends to meddle in other people's business."

Gabriel grins. "We have something in common, then."

"Oh no, not at all," Ellis disagrees. "You're a completely different breed."

Gabriel laughs. "Okay. But really, don't apologize for him. He actually put a stop to my pity party."

"Pity party?" Gabriel shrugs, and Ellis remembers Jordan saying how bummed and sad he looked when he thought Ellis wasn't coming back. "I'm sorry."

Gabriel shakes his head. "It's okay, Ellis. I get it. I do."

Why does he have to be so understanding all the fucking time? Why can't he just yell at Ellis and tell him to shove his excuses where the sun doesn't shine? It would be so much easier.

"Is the offer still on the table? Because I'd like to take you out for dinner," he says quicky before he can lose his nerve.

Doubt and panic creep in when Gabriel is quiet for a few very long seconds, staring at Ellis as if he spoke a different language.

"No can do," he says, and Ellis' heart plummets. "If anyone is taking anyone to dinner, it's me. I believe I asked first."

Ellis lets out a relieved breath. He'd call Gabriel out on scaring him like that, but he kinda deserved it, so...

"You did ask first," he admits, chuckling. "Well, then...I'd like to have dinner with you. Or lunch. Breakfast. I don't care."

"I don't care either."

"Cool."

"Cool."

They laugh, neither of them giving any indication of going anywhere.

"Do you wanna go now?" Ellis asks, feeling a little lost. Now that the hard part is over, he's not sure what to actually do.

Gabriel brightens at the idea, then pauses. "What about Jordan?"

"What about him?"

"I thought he's visiting this weekend."

"Oh. Yeah. He manages the Sydney office for me now. He's flying back tomorrow."

Gabriel gives a decisive nod. "You should spend time with your friend while you can."

"It's fine. Jordan doesn't mind." In fact, he was the one to push Ellis to do this.

"Maybe not. But you should still be with your friend."

"Really, it's not—"

"Ellis," Gabriel says, managing to sound both incredibly patient and mildly exasperated. "I'm not going anywhere. There's no expiration date on how I feel about you." He speaks slowly, as if to make sure the words are making it through Ellis' thick skull. "Go be with your friend. I think you both need it."

Ellis opens his mouth, but nothing comes out. He *does* want to spend time with Jordan, as aggravating as he can be. Having him back in his life has lifted a certain weight off Ellis' shoulders. Moving to the GC, despite having family here, has made him feel more isolated than ever. It's been so easy to forget that there is, in fact, a person out there who cares about him and misses him.

"Plus," Gabriel goes on, "I don't have a change of clothes. I'm all sweaty and probably smell gross."

"You smell nice," comes out of Ellis' mouth without going through his brain filter first. Good god, Gabriel must be rubbing off on him.

You'd like that, wouldn't you?

Shocked at his own thoughts, he scrambles for something to say. "Tomorrow, then? Dinner?"

Looking a little stunned, probably by Ellis' comment, Gabriel gives a firm nod. "Tomorrow it is. Unless you'll be socially tired?"

"Normally, I would be, but you kind of have the opposite effect on me," Ellis admits sheepishly, wondering when he'll stop saying such sappy shit. He's starting to worry that with Gabriel around, his self-control is destined to be pretty much non-existent.

Gabriel drops his gaze briefly, then lifts it back up. "Cool."

"Cool."

God, they're ridiculous. And so not cool.

"I'll see you tomorrow, then," Gabriel says.

"See you tomorrow," Ellis echoes, but doesn't move to leave. A part of him is afraid that once he steps outside, everything he's feeling right now will disappear. He's noticed that Gabriel's presence makes it easier to ground himself in his emotions, which otherwise just wreak major havoc.

"Ellis?"

"Yeah?"

"Can you give me your number?"

Pulling out his phone, Ellis negotiates whether to send a wave or a smiley face. He ends up typing out a simple *Hi* and hitting *send*.

"Just texted you."

Gabriel's phone pings with a notification, and he stares at it, then at Ellis. "You saved my number?"

Hearing the disbelief in Gabriel's voice makes the guilt come back with vigor. "I meant to text you. Take you up on the offer. But then Dawson called, and my head was a mess, and—"

"Ellis. It's okay," Gabriel puts an end to his babbling. He takes a couple steps forward, making Ellis' breath hitch. "Thank you for coming here today. I missed seeing you in the mornings."

"Same. The coffee in my office building sucks ass."

That gets a laugh out of Gabriel. It seems like he's about to say something, only he clamps his mouth shut and looks away, face turning red.

"What?"

"Nothing," Gabriel says quickly. Too quickly.

Ellis replays what he said. It must be something he—

And then it clicks. "You wanted to make another ass comment, didn't you?"

Gabriel's guilty expression is all the confirmation he needs.

"I'm sorry! It's like a reflex, I swear." He hides his face in his palms.

Ellis laughs so loud he surprises himself, his heart swelling with emotion. "You don't have to censor yourself for my sake."

Gabriel peeks at him through the web of his fingers. "But the shit I say makes you uncomfortable."

Ellis shrugs. "A little. But I told you before; I don't feel like it's a bad thing."

Slowly, as if weighing how sincere Ellis is being, Gabriel removes his hands, his trademark grin firmly in place. "Okay. In that case, ass comments are back on the menu."

"Excellent," Ellis says, wondering what he just got himself into. "So...tomorrow?"

Gabriel smiles. "Tomorrow."

Ellis nods, turning around and heading for the door before he does something reckless. Outside, he allows himself one last look back and nearly chokes on a laugh.

Gabriel is doing some ridiculous shimmy dance—without the mop, this time—and stumbles back when his gaze lands on Ellis, who's trying very hard to keep a serious expression.

Instead, Ellis waves at him, making him hide his face in his hands again, and starts walking to his car. He smiles like a lunatic as he gets into the driver's seat, and it only grows when his phone vibrates, revealing a message from Gabriel.

Gabriel: Kill me now, please.

Ellis laughs, hard enough that his shoulders shake. Is it always going to be like this with Gabriel? Is he always going to make Ellis feel everything a hundred times more intensely? The prospect is terrifying.

It's kind of wonderful too.

Ellis: No can do. I was promised dinner.

Gabriel: Ugh.

Grinning like a maniac, Ellis pockets the phone before his fingers grow a life of their own and type out something he'll regret.

He sits in the car for a while, just to digest everything that happened. And it's a *lot*.

He did it. He actually did it. He took a leap.

And now he's falling.

Chapter 15

HALF AN HOUR LATER, Ellis is no longer so sure about having Jordan as a friend and is seriously considering express-shipping him back to Sydney.

"No."

"Elliiis," Jordan whines. "You *have to*. I can teach you the basics—"

"Please do not teach me anything."

"—but you need to do some serious research. You can't just whip it out and expect it to go smoothly."

"I'm not whipping anything out."

Giving no indication he heard him, Jordan jovially carries on. "And I know I've only met Gabe twice, but I'll bet my left nut he's a firecracker in bed. You better brace yourself."

"Jordan, if you don't shut the fuck up, I'll help you," Ellis growls. He's starting to suspect that the burning sensation in his chest has less to do with acid reflux and more with jealousy. Not that he has any right to feel jealous. He and Gabriel aren't anything.

Yet.

Jordan has somehow managed to manifest a box of condoms out of thin air. "I know you've had a bit of a dry spell. These are extra lubed." He pitches the box to Ellis, who catches it on reflex.

"I'm not sleeping with him on the first date!" He yeets the box back at Jordan.

"You never know what'll happen."

"I know *this* will not happen." Not that his mind hasn't wandered...there. Not too far but to some...stuff.

He's wondered what Gabriel looks like under the funny aprons and baggy t-shirts. If the cookie dough scent still clings to him after a shower. If kissing him would taste just as sweet. If they were to lose their clothes, would he be as patient with Ellis as he's been so far? Would he get annoyed and frustrated if Ellis dragged his feet? He can't reconcile that reaction with Gabriel's lovely personality, but everyone has a breaking point. Gabriel won't wait for him forever.

Maybe Ellis made a mistake. Maybe he shouldn't have given Gabriel hope if he's not sure he can follow through. What if he's wasting Gabriel's time?

Jordan snaps his fingers in front of Ellis' face, frowning. "You got stuck in your own head again, didn't you?" He sighs. "Fuck, I'm sorry. I just got a bit too excited."

Ellis grimaces, the thoughts of his inadequacy promptly replaced by distaste.

"Not like that," Jordan says with a laugh. "Well, maybe a little. But I mean it, Ellis—this is fucking wonderful. And I'm so proud of you. I think Gabe could be really good for you."

Yeah, Ellis thinks so too. He just doubts he'd be good for Gabriel. "You're biased. Of course you'd get excited about me dating a man."

Jordan opens his mouth to protest but changes his mind. "Well, let's face it—your taste in women sucks. So far, your taste in men is loads better."

"Yeah, not sure about that. I kissed *you* after all."

Jordan gasps, propping his hands on his hips. "Do you know how many guys would kill to get a piece of *this*?"

"I hear that organ trafficking is a lucrative business."

"Ha ha." Jordan crosses his arms. "By the way, when did you last get tested?"

"Must have been a none-of-your-business weeks ago."

"Ellis..."

"I'm not an idiot. You think I didn't get tested after I caught my girlfriend blowing another guy?"

Jordan purses his lips. "Okay, fair point." He's about to say something else when his phone dings with a text. He pulls it out, a muscle in his jaw jumping. He looks like he's about to ignore whatever it is, but ends up unlocking the screen and reading the rest. His chest expands with a sharp breath and his ears turn red. It's a stark contrast to his pale complexion, and it takes Ellis aback. In all the time they've known each other, he's never seen Jordan blush, not even when he's drunk.

"What is it?"

Jordan's gaze lifts to him slowly, a little dazed. "Huh? Oh, nothing." He clears his throat, his eyes finding the text again.

Taking advantage of his distracted state, Ellis makes a grab for the phone, but Jordan pulls it out of his reach.

"Hey!"

"It's Charlie, isn't it?"

Jordan sputters. "No!"

"Uh-huh. Show me, then."

"Why?"

"Why not?"

"Because it's private."

Ellis lunges forward, his fingers missing the phone by an inch. Jordan screams and attempts to stuff the phone down the front of his jeans. Ellis catches his wrist, throwing his whole body against Jordan's, and they end up toppling over in a flurry of limbs.

Ellis lands on top and stabs a finger between Jordan's ribs, pulling a high-pitched squeak out of him. He rises up, pinning Jordan down with his weight, and tickles his sides. Jordan drops the phone as he laughs involuntarily, and Ellis snatches it, holding it out of reach when Jordan attempts to retrieve it.

His eyes skim the thread of messages—from Charlie, as he suspected—starting off tame and innocent and progressively turning explicit. The last one makes him gape. He reads it out loud.

"'I dreamed about our kiss again. I woke up so fucking hard. I came twice thinking of your—' Jordan!" Ellis shrieks. "You said you're not fucking him!"

Figuring struggle is futile, Jordan flops onto the floor, letting out a groan. "I'm not. It was just a kiss."

"Why would you kiss him in the first place? I thought you're trying to establish boundaries."

"Because he begged me for it, okay?! How was I supposed to say no? Plus, the kiss happened before I hired him. I didn't think we'd see each other again."

Ellis sighs, giving Jordan the phone back. "This is ridiculous. Are you seriously only gonna fuck guys who mean nothing to you instead of being with the one you want?"

Jordan looks away. "You don't get it."

"I get that you're a coward. You push me to put my heart on the line, but you won't do the same. What did you expect when you hired him, anyway?"

"I told you; he needed a job. And I have morals. I wouldn't fuck someone I work with. Thought it would help strengthen my resolve." He chuckles wryly. "Blew up in my face, didn't it?"

"Is sexting supposed to help with your resolve?"

"I'm not texting back anymore," Jordan defends. Now that he mentions it, Ellis remembers seeing mostly Charlie's texts.

"But you don't want him to stop," Ellis observes.

Jordan shrugs. "He'll get it out of his system eventually and lose interest."

Ellis can tell he doesn't really believe that. He pats Jordan's cheek. "You're an idiot. But I guess that's why we're friends."

Jordan huffs, chuckling. Slowly, he drags his gaze up and down Ellis' form, and his lips twists in a sly grin. "For a straight boy, you sure look good up there. Maybe you won't have to do as much research as I thought."

Ellis blushes fiercely as he takes stock of the position he ended up in, sitting astride Jordan's stomach. "Shut up." He goes to get up when his ass brushes against something hard. Closing his eyes, he takes a slow, deliberate breath. "Please tell me you have a gun in your pocket."

"You all but mounted me after I got a filthy text from the guy I'm crazy about. What did you expect?"

Ellis ungracefully stumbles to his feet, looking anywhere but Jordan's crotch. "Let's not talk about this, ever."

Looking way too pleased about Ellis' discomfort, Jordan stands up. "Look at it this way. You already got practice. If you ever straddle Gabe like that—"

"Not. Talking. About it."

"Spoilsport. Anyway, you know where you're taking him?"

"Uh, no. He insisted he take *me* out for dinner." Now that he said it out loud, he realizes how strange the prospect makes him feel.

Jordan's brows shoot up and he whistles. "Oh, I like him. I like him a lot, Ellis."

"Jordan..." Ellis growls a warning, making the dickhead laugh.

"I meant, I like him for you," Jordan placates. "Come on. Are you telling me it doesn't feel good to let someone else take care of shit for once?"

"I don't know. It just feels weird, waiting for him to let me know what we're doing. Like I should do something." He won't deny it feels nice to leave everything in Gabriel's hands, but it also makes him feel useless.

"Well, you can always express your gratitude by sucking his—"

"Jordan!"

"Oh god, you're so highly strung. It's hilarious."

"Glad I can provide a source of entertainment for you."

Ellis ignores the stirring in his groin as the image of himself on his knees in front of Gabriel involuntarily flashes in his mind. Ugh, fucking Jordan, giving him ideas.

Jordan pulls him into a one-armed hug. "You know I love you. Come on, let's watch some *GG*, that ought to help you relax."

Ellis sighs and lets himself be led to the sofa.

If he survives the date, it will be a miracle.

Gabriel texts him the next morning while Jordan is packing his suitcase, his flight 3 hours away.

"Is that your boy?" Jordan asks with a knowing smirk.

Ellis shoots him a look. "He's asking if there's anywhere I don't want to go. And if I have allergies."

"Aww, so considerate. Well, you have that dairy thing..."

"He already knows."

"Of course he does." Jordan scoffs. "Is there anywhere you don't wanna go?"

Wherever it's people-y, but he can't tell Gabriel that. Going out for dinner implies there will be people around. He'd hate to give Gabriel the impression that he's ashamed of being seen with another man. It's just that he's always hated the possibility of other people listening in on what he and his date are talking about. And Erika and his girlfriend before that both had a thing where they hated if Ellis tried to take their hand in public, let alone do anything else. He's not a huge fan of PDA, but even for him that was a bit extreme. Not that he's planning any PDA with Gabriel. It's the first date.

He could let me hold his hand, though.

Now he's blushing at the idea of holding hands. Fantastic.

He starts typing out a reply.

Ellis: Maybe nothing too fancy? Anything else is fine with me.

Ellis: No other allergies but I hate sea monsters.

The response is instantaneous.

Gabriel: LOL do I strike you as a fancy person? Were you expecting a Michelin star restaurant?

Gabriel: Did you mean sea creatures?

Ellis: No. I meant sea MONSTERS. That's what they are.

Gabriel: You're adorable. Got it. No sea monsters. <3

Biting his lip to hide a stupid grin, Ellis lifts his gaze from the phone. Jordan is spread out on the sofa, his arms folded behind his head and expression salacious.

"What?" Ellis demands irritably.

"You're blushing. Did Gabby say something that made you flustered?"

Ellis is really starting to hate all nicknames coming from Jordan. "No."

Jordan makes a *tsk* sound. "Is it my turn to fight you for your phone?"

Ellis sighs in resignation. "He called me adorable."

"Aww."

"Shut up."

"I definitely agree with him."

Before Ellis can commit a murder, another text comes through.

Gabriel: Okay. I have an idea you might like. Can you meet me at six at the café?

Ellis: Sure. What should I wear?

Gabriel: Something comfy that you don't mind getting messy.

Ellis must stare at the text for quite a while, because another one comes through.

Gabriel: That sounded a lot better in my head. Please ignore.

A sudden laugh bursts out of Ellis. Jordan gives him a questioning look.

Ellis: Something comfy. Got it.

Gabriel: <3

His stomach flutters at the heart emoji, making him feel like a teenager. Except he was never this smitten with anyone as a teen.

"What's the verdict?" Jordan asks.

"Not sure where he's taking me, but he said to wear something comfy."

Jordan's face lights up. That's not good. "Oh, you have to wear gray joggers."

Ellis frowns. "That's oddly specific. Why?"

Jordan looks like he's not sure if Ellis is joking or not. "My god, how are you this sheltered? Nevermind. Gray joggers. Now."

"I don't own gray joggers." He pauses. "I have dark blue ones."

Jordan dramatically flops back onto the sofa. "This is gonna be harder than I thought."

Ellis parks the car in his usual spot near the café, taking a few minutes to fortify himself before he goes to pick Gabriel up. Today has been *a lot.*

As sad as he was when he was dropping Jordan off at the airport, knowing it'd be a while before they'll get to see each other in person again, he was also undeniably relieved. He was *this* close to strangling his best friend and leaving him to the sharks, especially after he googled what the whole thing about gray joggers was about. Then Jordan insisted on a white t-shirt, which Ellis had planned on wearing, but decided against out of pure spite.

Despite Gabriel's insistence on something comfy, he still feels strange wearing jeans and a simple black t-shirt to a date. Then again, he's never been on a date that didn't include some fancy establishment.

At five to six, he finally gets his ass out of the car and heads to the café.

Gabriel isn't waiting outside, but the lights are on in the kitchen. The sign says *closed*, but when Ellis tries the door, it opens. Stepping inside, he's instantly hit with the familiar scent of sugar and spices.

"Gabriel?"

He hears a crash, and then Gabriel's head appears behind the pass. He's smiling wide.

"Hey! I'm sorry, I'm running late. Almost done here!"

"No, you're fine." There's some more crashing, a muttered curse. "You need help?"

"I'm good!" Gabriel yells, sounding anything but. "Just take a seat and look pretty. I'll be right there."

Not sure how to feel about being referred to as pretty, Ellis dutifully takes the chair closest to him, drumming his fingers on his thigh as he waits for Gabriel to finish whatever he's doing.

Gabriel emerges shortly, flushed and a little frantic but beaming. "Hey, you." He removes his apron, which says *Kiss the baker,* and throws it over the back of a chair.

Now that he got a proper look at Gabriel, seeing him in khaki shorts and a plain white t-shirt, Ellis doesn't feel underdressed anymore.

Running a hand through his hair, Gabriel gives Ellis a smile so wide it nearly blinds him. "Glad you could make it. When I woke up this morning, I wasn't sure I didn't dream the whole thing up. Had to check my texts to reassure myself."

"You're making it sound like I'm some sort of celebrity. I'm just a guy." Not even a remarkable one, unless being a dick counts. What Gabriel sees in him is beyond Ellis.

Gabriel's smile dims a little, but his eyes are soft and kind. They always are. "Well, you happen to be a guy I like, so there's that."

Ellis coughs awkwardly. Gabriel sure has a talent for flipping Ellis' world with a few words. "Yeah, okay. Fair enough."

Gabriel laughs. "You know, if you need me to tell you how much I like you in regular intervals, I can definitely do that."

Feeling the skin on the back of his neck burn, Ellis mumbles, "No, that's okay. I'd like to preserve some dignity."

Gabriel laughs again, and Ellis notices there's a smudge of something, maybe flour, on his cheek.

"You have a..." He gestures at his own cheek, curling his finger into his palms when he's hit with a sudden urge to reach out and wipe it away for Gabriel. He's seen way too many movies where this happens. Someone has a smudge or something on their face, and the other person helps them get it off, and then they gaze into each other's eyes, and before long they're kissing.

That's lame. And Ellis is not lame. Nope.

Gabriel swipes at his cheek, getting the smudge on the first try. He chuckles. "Icing sugar. Figures."

"You were baking?"

"Yeah, so..." His smile is nervous this time. "I cooked for us. I hope that's okay. I promise I'm not trying to skimp on you. I was trying to decide where to take you, but nothing felt quite right. Then I thought I could cook and invite you to my place, but didn't want to make you uncomfortable. Plus, my place is pretty small and my oven broke the other day. And then I thought, hey, maybe we could eat here, but that felt weird too."

Gabriel is out of breath by the time he finishes talking, and Ellis has to bite back a smile. "So we're doing..." He leaves off there.

"Oh! Yeah, so, I cooked, duh. And we're kinda having a picnic? On the beach. Is that okay?"

"It's perfect," Ellis says quickly when it looks like Gabriel is going to talk himself into a mini meltdown.

"Oh, thank god." Gabriel's shoulders sag with relief. Ellis chuckles, kind of pleased to learn he's not the only highly strung person on this date. "Okay, I just need to pack up everything quickly, and then we're out of here."

Ellis waits for him to finish up, not wanting to meddle and get in the way. When Gabriel emerges again, he's holding an esky in one hand, and what looks like a cake box in the other.

The whole scene is so laid back and unromantic that some of the tension Ellis hadn't realized has built up instantly dissipates. He's been totally overthinking the whole date thing.

"Could you take this? It's cinnamon rolls."

Ellis takes the box from him, saliva pooling in his mouth. "You made cinnamon rolls?"

"Mini ones. Fresh from the oven. I needed dessert that wouldn't melt."

"Brilliant." He's fucking missed the cinnamon rolls and practically inhaled the one Jordan brought him yesterday. "Do we need blankets or anything?" He doesn't know much about picnics, but he knows that.

Gabriel puffs up. "Done. Everything is set. Cutlery, plates. I negotiated candles and stuff, but thought it might be a bit overkill."

"They'd probably get blown out anyway."

"Probably. Unfortunately, I am a hopeless romantic that has no problem defying the force of nature."

Ellis snorts. "I figured."

After Gabriel has switched off the lights and locked up, they head to the beach around the corner. There are a few people walking or jogging along the shore, but Gabriel has strategically placed the picnic near the bushes. For privacy, would be Ellis' guess. The blanket is big enough that they could each sit in one corner and stretch out their legs, but they end up sitting almost next to each other.

"What would you like to drink? The choices are pretty narrow, but I have iced tea, Solo, or soda water."

"Iced tea is good." Carbonated drinks make him burp, but Gabriel doesn't need to know that.

"Gotcha." Gabriel hands him a can of iced tea and nods towards the horizon. "Pretty cool, isn't it?"

The sun has started setting, painting the sky in shades of orange and purple. Ellis isn't one for sunsets—or sunrises for that matter—but for some reason the sight gets to him this time.

"It is."

And okay, as Gabriel starts unpacking the food he's made—which, by the way, smells divine—Ellis has to admit there's something magical about the whole set-up. He gets why people do this.

"I apologize in advance." Gabriel holds out a container to Ellis. "There's no meat in this. I'm vegetarian and handling, you know, animal corpses is something I really can't do. It's fine when I'm eating out with someone who orders meat. I just can't touch it. Or smell it."

Did Gabriel seriously apologize for something like that after cooking all this for them? "No, that's fine. I actually don't eat much meat myself. When I do, I stick to chicken and fish. Have to keep an eye on my arteries."

Gabriel visibly relaxes. "I thought you don't eat sea monsters," he points out with a smile.

"Fish are not monsters," Ellis says with an eyeroll. "Well, some of them, maybe."

"Right, right. So, your arteries, huh?"

"Gift from my dad. Heart diseases run in the family. High cholesterol, blood pressure through the roof, and all that."

Gabriel's forehead furrows with concern. "That certainly explains why Cal had a heart attack before forty," he adds absentmindedly, then gives Ellis a startled look. "Wait, you're prone to heart conditions and you used to drink a five-shot long black for how long?"

"Since I was sixteen?" Ellis admits, smiling crookedly. "But it used to be only three shots. I just developed a tolerance."

"Ellis!" Gabriel yelps, scandalized.

Ellis laughs, warmed by the concern. With anyone else, he'd be annoyed that they were trying to lecture him. But if there's one thing he's learned about Gabriel, it's how much he cares even when he shouldn't. "I'm fine. Coffee is necessary for survival. And, as you know, I'm now very partial to a certain less lethal drink."

Gabriel huffs unhappily. "That's something, at least. But I'm starting to regret baking all these." He makes a show of taking away the box of cinnamon rolls.

Ellis snatches the box before it's out of his reach. "No no no, these are safe. Totally safe."

Gabriel laughs heartily, letting him have his way. "Whatever you say."

"I'll work it off."

"I'd like to be there to see that," Gabriel says, seemingly without thinking. His face twists in a grimace. "Sorry. Filter malfunction."

"I don't mind," Ellis says honestly, biting his lip so as not to laugh. Gabriel's mind is a chaotic, curious place, and Ellis maybe-not-so-secretly loves it, even if a part of him sometimes gets uncomfortable. The idea of Gabriel watching him as he works out is not...unpleasant. It sure would motivate him to give his best performance.

Feeling his skin warming up, Ellis shovels a forkful of food into his mouth. An unrestrained moan rumbles from his chest. "This is amazing."

"Yeah?" Gabriel asks, a little wide-eyed.

"Uh-huh." Ellis devours half of the container in under a minute, not even caring he probably looks like a pig. "I never realized how different a home-cooked meal could taste." Dawson cooked for him when he came over for dinner, but that was still when things were pretty crazy, and Ellis was stressed out of his mind. He couldn't even appreciate it properly.

"You parents didn't cook?"

Ellis almost laughs. "I'm not sure my dad ever even boiled water for tea."

"And your mum?"

Feeling his throat closing up, Ellis swallows with difficulty. "Never really knew her. She left when we were kids, though Cal remembers her better. Well, used to remember her. Not now, obviously. Our nannies would cook for us." He forces a smile. "But it was never this good."

Judging by Gabriel's intense gaze, he can see right through Ellis' attempt to downplay it. Thankfully, he doesn't call him out. "I'm happy to cook for you whenever you want."

"Be careful, or I might take you up on the offer," Ellis jokes. Gabriel is probably throwing it out there to make him feel better.

"Don't threaten me with a good time," Gabriel says, and they both laugh.

"Thank you. For all of this," Ellis says when they've been quiet for too long. "I've never been on a picnic before."

"Really?" Gabriel asks with disbelief. His expression changes into something smug. "Does that mean I'm your first?"

Ellis huffs, ignoring the squirming sensation in his gut. "Sure."

"Well, I'm glad you like it. I love picnics. Couldn't count how many I've had."

The squirming sensation turns into something sharp and bitter. Does that mean Gabriel does this for all his dates? Cooks for them, takes them to the beach to have dinner and watch the sunset?

Did you think you were special?

"Hey, you okay?" Gabriel asks, two lines of worry between his brows as he scans Ellis' face.

Ellis forces a smile. "Yeah, just thinking." He shivers when Gabriel's fingers graze his arm, sending a jolt of electricity through his body. Inadvertently, he leans into the touch.

"Hey." Gabriel gently prompts him to look at him, his gaze kind and honest. "There's no one else I'd rather be here with. I want you to know that."

Ellis releases a shuddery breath, mourning the loss of contact when Gabriel stops touching him. "How are you doing this?"

"Doing what?"

"How do you always know what to say? Are you a mind reader, or

and fed up he was with everything. How every little thing threatened to snap the last thread on his patience. How he *did* snap and rained all his shit on Gabriel. And how instead of fighting back, Gabriel just...took it. He stood there and looked at Ellis like he was seeing something no one else could, and instead of trying to get rid of Ellis as fast as possible, he was...kind. Understanding when any other person would've—should've—told him to go to hell.

He remembers leaving the café confused as fuck, practically shaking with it. He remembers taking the first sip of the coffee Gabriel had made and almost crying with the relief that had overtaken his whole body. He remembers being unable to explain away what had happened.

And it didn't stop there.

"Have you ever done it to me?"

Gabriel winces. "Somewhat? When you first came to the café—"

"I was a dick."

"You were angry and irritated," Gabriel corrects, his voice brooking no argument. "One didn't need to be an empath to see that. But that was only superficial. Underneath it all, you were tired and lonely. Felt like you're carrying the weight of the world on your shoulders." His thumb strokes the back of Ellis' hand. "I wanted to make it better."

"You did," Ellis croaks out. He wouldn't know where to start if he wanted to name all the ways Gabriel has made him feel better. With a raspy chuckle, he adds, "The coffee was really good."

"I may have added something special to it," Gabriel admits quietly. "You know how I said I can influence people's emotions by focusing hard enough? I can do that to inanimate objects too."

"You spiked my coffee?"

"Don't call it that!" Gabriel squawks. "God, you sound like Zeke. I did not spike it. I magically enhanced it."

"Magically enhanced it."

"You're taking this really well," Gabriel points out, eyeing him curiously.

Is he? What Gabriel is talking about does sound a lot like magic.

A superpower even. Ellis has never been much of a believer when it comes to the supernatural, but he never outright rejected it either. As a kid, he was afraid of ghosts—Cal used to tell him someone died in their house and their ghost haunted the place—and while he might not be afraid of the dark anymore, he still avoids horror movies to this day.

Compared to ghosts, what Gabriel is talking about doesn't sound too far-fetched.

"Ever since I stepped into the café, I've felt things I can't find a rational explanation for. So, this would explain a lot. It's good to know I'm not completely crazy."

"I promise you, I've never done anything to influence how you feel about me," Gabriel says, sounding frantic.

"That never crossed my mind," Ellis tells him. "I know why I feel the way I feel about you."

He instantly flushes. It's true, though. His feelings for Gabriel aren't some big mystery, not now that Ellis isn't in denial anymore. Gabriel is...Gabriel, and it's impossible not to like him. He was there to listen when Ellis had a lot on his mind, gave him a place to come back to when everything felt too heavy. Most importantly, he's made Ellis feel seen.

"So, you being attracted to men, that's not news to you?" Gabriel inquires. It's the first time either of them has brought up the topic of Ellis' sexuality, despite him practically ghosting Gabriel after being asked out. Gabriel really is letting him off very easily.

"It's not. Though, if you'd asked me a couple months ago, I'd have denied it." He probably has Jordan to thank for figuring shit out so quickly. "I don't... Look, my brother is gay, and so is my best friend. I never thought less of them for that. It's just..."

"It's different when it's you. When it's personal," Gabriel finishes for him. Of course he does. Ellis doesn't even need to say anything, and Gabriel just *knows*. It's crazy.

It's awesome.

"Yeah. My dad, he...he always doted on Cal. Looking back on it,

I feel sorry for him. Having someone constantly step on your heels, watch your every move—it sucks. But that's not how I thought of it when I was younger. I was so fucking jealous of him. Cal was the golden child and I was the black sheep. Never good enough. Never as good as my older brother. But when Cal came out..." He hesitates before continuing. Gabriel is understanding, but what he's about to say is so fucked up. "This will sound horrible, and I'm sorry for that. When Cal came out, that was the only time in my life that I was better than him. The first time he was a disappointment, and I was not."

Once again, he was worried about nothing because Gabriel simply nods, barely blinking at the shameful confession.

"Did your dad flip out?"

Ellis laughs without humor. "My dad never flipped out. He just looked at you like you were the worst thing to ever happen to him." He had been on the receiving end way too many times to not remember how exactly it felt. "They didn't even fight. Cal was as stubborn and spiteful as they come, and I think dad knew there was nothing he could do about it without making it worse. Like, if he tried to forbid Cal from seeing men, Cal would go out of his way to do the exact opposite. Dad only said one thing. He said: "At least I still have one son I don't have to be ashamed of."

Gabriel's face contorts in a grimace. "That's so fucked up."

Ellis swallows, gripping Gabriel's hand like a lifeline. "What's even more fucked up is how happy I was when he said it. I thought: finally, there's something I'm better at than Cal. As if you can be better at your sexuality." He shakes his head, wondering what on earth had been going on in his brain at the time. "I was only twelve back then, and rather anti-social, I wasn't really thinking of dating. But as I got older and started noticing things..."

"You pushed it down."

"And I kept at it even after Dad passed." But not anymore. He's *done*.

"Shit like that tends to stick with you. Like bubble gum," Gabriel says, making him laugh. He always makes Ellis laugh. "But despite everything, you're here now. With me."

"I am," Ellis chokes out. "Thank you."

"For what?"

"Seeing me." *And not hating what you see.* Feeling a little too exposed, Ellis switches topics. "Why did your eyes glow when we kissed? Were you using your, you know, powers?"

Gabriel blushes. "You know how I said I can control it to an extent?" Ellis nods. "Extent being the operative word here. My emotions can be...overwhelming to other people. I need to keep a cap on them." Gabriel clears his throat. "Kissing you kind of unraveled all my defenses."

Ellis has to press his lips together to not smile like a goof. "Is it weird that I find that flattering?"

Gabriel rolls his eyes good-naturedly. "No. You can feel flattered all you want. It's true. I know I've been a disaster since we met, so you'd be surprised to find I'm generally more composed than that. Even my filter works better with other people."

Ellis raises a skeptical eyebrow. "I sincerely doubt that."

"Hey!" Gabriel shoves him, and Ellis catches his wrist, placing Gabriel's hand on his chest.

"It's okay. I like it. A lot," he promises. "I never have to guess with you. You just put all your cards on the table. You're like no one I've ever met."

Gabriel huffs a laugh. "I can believe that." His fingers stroke Ellis' chest through his shirt, making it really difficult to keep his breathing even. Yet, he can't bring himself to tell Gabriel to stop.

"What about the messages on the cups? They felt personal."

"They were," Gabriel confirms. "They are. Sometimes I have a... I'm not sure I'd call it a vision. A compulsion, maybe. If there's something a person needs to hear, I feel compelled to tell them. I don't know where the messages come from. I don't really care. I know they help, and that's good enough for me."

You deserve good things.

Ellis still isn't sure it's true. He's done too many shitty things in his life to deserve anything good. But he desperately wants Gabriel, and Gabriel is so, so good. Ellis will do anything to deserve him.

"Jordan said you kept the cups with the messages I wrote you."

Correction: Gabriel is very, very bad. And his glee is positively evil.

Ellis takes a slow, deliberate breath that does absolutely nothing to calm him down. "I'm going to kill him. Slowly."

Gabriel lets him stew for a bit, taking apparent pleasure in Ellis' discomfort. But then his hand is climbing from Ellis' chest to his face, brushing his hair back. It feels so good Ellis has to try really hard to not make a sound.

"You do deserve good things, Ellis. It's okay if you don't believe it. I'll just have to keep proving it to you."

With his heart in his throat, Ellis manages to press out, "That could take a long time."

"I'm more than okay with that," Gabriel says, not deterred in the slightest. A cold gust of wind washes over them, and Gabriel shivers. "The wind's picking up. Do you want to head back?"

No. He doesn't want this to end just yet. "Okay."

"Or..." Gabriel trails off, regarding Ellis thoughtfully. "We could go to my place? No funny business, promise," he adds in a rush. "We'll just talk or watch a movie. I don't want to end the date yet. And we still haven't touched the cinnamon rolls."

Thank god.

"Sounds good." Hopefully he doesn't sound too eager. But if he does, it's okay. This is Gabriel after all. "Your place."

Chapter 16

"HERE WE ARE!" TWISTING the key, Gabe opens the door to his apartment. "It's small, but it's mine."

Inside, he slips out of his thongs and props his scooter against the wall. He chuckles. Ellis' reaction when Gabe told him he doesn't drive but rides a scooter to work was priceless. It got even better when he suggested Ellis take a ride with him. The look of horror on his face was something he'd love to have a picture of.

Holding the bags with the picnic leftovers, Ellis sweeps his gaze around the apartment. He actually looks intrigued, and not like he's only putting on a show. "I like it. It's cozy."

"It is, isn't it?" Gabe takes the bags from him and carries them to the kitchen. "What?" Ellis seems to be looking for something.

"Nothing. I just assumed you'd have a roommate."

Probably a nice way of saying: how do you afford this? Rentals on the Gold Coast are no joke. "This place would've been way more expensive, but the landlord has a soft spot for me."

Ellis snorts. "Of course they do. But I meant, I'd expect you to have a roommate because you seem so..."

"Social?"

"Yeah."

Ah yes. The common misconception.

Ellis' eyes brighten when Gabe unpacks the cinnamon rolls and gestures to the sofa. They take a seat close to each other, and Ellis wastes no time digging into the box.

"Well, this whole empath business has one big downside; I need to recharge. Like, a lot. I love people, but my god, they can be draining."

Pausing midchew with his cheeks bulging, Ellis' face twists with worry. Swallowing, he asks, "Do I drain you?"

"No. Not in the *least*." It's one of the reasons why Gabe likes being around him so much. Ellis might be a bit of a grump, but there is nothing draining or abrasive about him. Except for that stubble. That looks like it would cause a delicious burn on Gabe's—

Control yourself, for fuck's sake.

"Your energy is very caring. Soothing."

Ellis scoffs. "Yeah, right."

"Nuh-uh." Gabe waggles his finger in disapproval. "You don't get to argue with an empath."

"Whatever you say."

"I might need to move eventually," Gabe returns to the original topic. In fact, this is something that's been on his mind lately. "Even if the landlord doesn't increase the rent—which she should because this really is a steal—the rent we pay on the café has almost doubled since we first opened. And we're nearing the end of the lease agreement again, so that will suck."

"I thought the café's doing well."

"Most of the time it is. We took a hit during the pandemic, as most small businesses did, but it's gotten better. Our regulars were very supportive and loyal. But Zeke and I are both reluctant to increase our prices to match the current market. So we usually don't."

He can practically feel Ellis' internal cringe. For him as a businessman, the notion must be completely insane. To his credit, he doesn't lecture Gabe.

"I take it business management isn't in your blood?"

"Ugh, I hate it. I wish I could just give out free coffee and pastries." Leaning back and resting an arm on the back of the sofa, he angles his body so he's mostly facing Ellis. "You have any advice for me, Mr. Big CEO?"

"Nothing really helpful. Sometimes you just have to do things you'd rather avoid," he says, his voice somewhat hollow.

"You don't like your job, do you?" Gabe blurts out. He knew Ellis isn't crazy about his job, but until now he hadn't realized how unhappy he is.

"It's alright, I guess." When Gabe gives him a rather unimpressed look, he sighs. "It sucks."

"What would you rather do?"

"Honestly? I'd just like some fucking sleep." Ellis laughs, but it quickly dies down. "I'm joking. Things will calm down, eventually. It's been crazy because of the relocation and Cal and...yeah."

"You sneakily avoided the question," Gabe points out gently. "That's okay. You don't have to tell me."

"I don't know what I'd want to do. There's not much I'm good at."

"Is that you talking, or your dad?" Gabe challenges, hoping he's not overstepping. Ellis doesn't seem to have an answer to that. "And it's not about talent or anything. My question was what you would *like* to do."

Ellis contemplates it for a moment. "I have a bachelor's degree in Architectural Design. I took it as a prerequisite to my master's in Building Management. It was... I enjoyed it. Creating something brand new and unique, it was...satisfying."

It must have been more than satisfying, if the way Ellis' energy just lit up is any indication.

"Yeah, I bet. Architects are cool. It's like combining art and science."

Ellis scoffs. "I'm not an artist, nor a scientist. I'm just someone who bosses other people around."

"Would you rather someone boss *you* around? Because I volunteer."

Ellis' gaze snaps up to him, his eyes widening comically. He sputters through some unintelligible words, his face changing color.

"I'm joking," Gabe says unconvincingly. He *was* joking, but upon witnessing Ellis' reaction, the image has planted itself in his brain.

choice. It's not that I hated it, I actually found it very interesting and stimulating. But halfway through the course I realized I could never do it as a job. As a psychologist, you are a guide when people feel lost. You show them doors they never knew were there. You nudge them this way and that, but that's it. That's not me. I can't just sit and hope people will find their way. I'm more of a grab-them-by-the-collar-and-drag-them-in-the-right-direction-kicking-and-screaming kind of person." He bats his eyelashes. "I have a tendency to meddle."

"You? Meddle? No way."

Gabe pushes his shoulder. "Sod off."

"I think you made the right choice," Ellis says. "You're such a chatterbox. You'd end up getting your license revoked."

"You're not wrong, but I don't appreciate your tone." He tries to sound offended, but Ellis' smile tells him he failed. "Well, that's the story. I know it's ironic, but I found I have more of an impact on people's lives from where I am now."

"I can attest to that. We haven't known each other that long, but you've already changed my life."

Gabe can only stare at him. How did they go from teasing each other to Ellis dropping a bomb like that? A bomb that unleashed a swarm of butterflies in Gabe's stomach.

He'll blame his next words on the butterflies. "And it's only the first date. Imagine how I could change it on the second. Or third."

And now Ellis looks like a deer in the headlights. Great job, Gabe. So much for 'no funny business'. He wishes he could take the words back and shove them down his throat, then sew his mouth shut. Since he can't do that, he patiently waits for Ellis' reaction. Except his reaction is nothing like Gabe had expected.

"Do I need to wait until then?" Ellis' eyes widen, as if he can't believe what he just said.

Gabe can hardly believe it either. This is the man who freaked out when Gabe asked him out to dinner, the man who has never been with a guy, who is so scared of opening himself up that he rarely says what he wants.

Until now.

Or maybe not. Maybe it just came out. Maybe Ellis didn't mean it.

Gabe doesn't say anything, giving him time to take it back, to change his mind.

Only Ellis doesn't do either. He looks at Gabe, determination setting in his stormy-blue eyes.

Dear god.

"I'm ready to change your life whenever you want," Gabe says, not even recognizing his voice with how deep it is. It's both a way out for Ellis, and a promise. Because whatever Ellis tells him he wants, Gabe is *so* going to grant him his wish.

"Now would work," Ellis croaks out after what feels like a small eternity.

"Yeah?" It's a redundant question. He can feel the desire and anticipation rolling off Ellis, but it feels important to let him voice what he wants.

Ellis licks his lips. "Yeah."

Instead of throwing himself at him like a harlot, Gabe slowly inches closer, placing a hand on his knee. He needs to take this slow. Like, a-line-at-the-post-office slow. Ellis is overwhelmed as is, Gabe can feel that much. But he can also feel his nervous excitement.

He does his best to rein his energy in, not wanting to overwhelm him further. He probably doesn't do a good job, because the moment he touches him, a shudder wracks Ellis' body, his eyelids fluttering.

Crap. Too much.

He goes to move away, but doesn't get far. Ellis' mouth lands on his, firm and demanding, his fingers sliding into Gabe's hair and *pulling*.

An unrestrained moan is torn out of Gabe's throat, way too loud in the otherwise quiet room.

Ellis pulls back, looking disoriented and surprised. "You like that?"

"You found my weakness."

"Oh." Ellis' hands twitch where they are still entwined in Gabe's hair. He gives it a small, experimental tug, pulling another wrecked sound out of him. "I didn't even mean to do it. I just needed something to hold on to."

"Well, you can hold on to me like that any time. Except maybe not in public. I need to preserve some dignity."

"What dignity?"

Gabe gapes at him. "So this is how it's gonna be? *Fine.*" Throwing caution to the wind—and relying on his mojo to gauge how far he can go—Gabe pushes until Ellis lands flat on his back, a squeal of surprise escaping him.

Grinning devilishly, Gabe swings his leg over Ellis' thighs, straddling him. "Hi."

Ellis' throat bobs, the action really erotic for some reason. "Hey." He doesn't seem to know where to look first, his eyes jumping all over Gabe, his pupils dilated. Then his gaze drops to Gabe's shorts, tented at the front, and his lips part on a shocked inhale.

A quick glance downward tells Gabe he's not the only one with a situation. The realization brings an unexpected relief. Until now, he couldn't be sure how Ellis would react to the idea of being with a man.

As enticing as it is, Gabe doesn't let his gaze linger. Instead, he drags it up Ellis' stomach and chest until it lands on his flushed face.

"How's the view?" he asks cheekily.

Ellis gives a laugh that sounds like it's punched out of him. "I could stay here all day."

"Yeah? Even if the sofa barely fits half of you?" Ellis' legs are practically hanging off the arm rest.

"Even then." His hands settle on Gabe's hips, light and cautious. "Can I..."

"Whatever you want."

Ellis huffs. "I don't know what I want."

"Would you like to find out?"

A nod, shy and almost imperceptible, but it's more than enough. Gabe covers Ellis' hands with his, and slowly drags them both up until they slip under his shirt.

"Take off my shirt." He doesn't phrase it as a question, having noticed that Ellis responds better to direct 'orders'. It makes sense, given how often he's forced, and expected, to make all the decisions.

It works. There's barely any hesitation before Gabe is raising his arms and Ellis is tugging the shirt over his head, holding it like he doesn't know what to do with it.

Chuckling, Gabe takes it and dumps it on the floor without care. And then he waits, letting Ellis look his fill.

Gabe's never been body-shy—something he's really grateful for right now, because Ellis studies him like one would a work of art. It's an insane ego-boost, and Gabe's dick must agree, growing impossibly harder under the attention. An untapped voyeurism kink, maybe?

His abdominal muscles contract when Ellis touches them, the contact unexpected and a little cold against his skin.

"Sorry," Ellis mumbles, about to retract his hand.

Gabe catches it, holding it in place. "No. Touch me."

"Where?"

"Anywhere. Everywhere."

Ellis guffaws. "Thank god you're not demanding." And then he's touching Gabe.

Everywhere.

He drags his palms up and down Gabe's sides, making him giggle. Amused by the reaction, he moves them higher and inwards, his touch featherlight as it skims over Gabe's chest, grazing his nipples. Gabe's not very sensitive there, but that doesn't mean Ellis' touch isn't pleasant. A shudder goes through him when Ellis traces his collar-bones, so close to his neck where he *is* sensitive. Ellis doesn't continue that road, though, instead stroking Gabe's shoulders and sliding down his arms.

"Do you exercise? You look like you exercise." His fingertips skim over the swell of Gabe's biceps.

"Thanks," Gabe says with a chuckle. "My arms are ripped from all the pastry making. I used to go to the gym, but it became too expensive. Now I just stick to some bodyweight training. There's a yoga class every Sunday at the beach too. I go when I manage to get myself out of bed early." An image of Ellis in a downward dog pose jumps into his mind. *Oh yes, please.* "You should come with me sometime."

"Yeah, not sure about that. I don't really fancy being ass up in front of a bunch of strangers," Ellis says, like he just had the same thought.

More images. So many images. Ah, hell.

"Hmm. What about if it was just the two of us? A private yoga session."

Ellis' hands still on Gabe's thighs. His lips part, a look of contemplation on his face.

Jesus. Gabe was pretty much just teasing, especially since it's impossible to have missed the insinuation. But Ellis is actually *considering* it.

"I suppose...I could be amenable to that." Before Gabe can put together a coherent response, Ellis' hands slide to his knees. He blinks. "You're hairy."

It's such a blunt statement that a laugh bursts out of Gabe. "Yeah. An ape descendant and all that." Ellis seems rather fascinated with the discovery, rubbing circles into Gabe's knees as if gauging the sensation. "What do you think?"

"It's...different."

"Good different, or bad?"

"Good." Ellis doesn't even pause to think about it. "Definitely good." His gaze flicks upwards. "Your chest is smooth."

"Always has been," he says, just in case Ellis is wondering if he waxes. He tugs on the hem of Ellis' shirt. "What about yours?"

"Uh, a little hairy. Not much."

Gabe pushes the shirt up, revealing a sliver of skin and a happy trail disappearing into Ellis' pants. Mouth suddenly dry, he swallows. "Can I see?"

"Y-yeah."

They end up nearly chest to chest when Ellis sits up, eyes locking with Gabe's for a moment.

"Let me." Gabe stops him when Ellis goes to remove his shirt. He doesn't just take it off—he glides his hands up Ellis' sides, rucking the shirt up in the process.

Ellis shudders, his breath hitching when Gabe lets his thumbs brush dangerously close to his nipples. Bingo.

Filing the information away, Gabe finally wrestles the shirt off, struck momentarily speechless when all that exposed skin comes into view. Because Ellis is beautiful on the regular, but without clothes, he's breathtaking; all smooth, sun-kissed skin and sculpted muscles. There's a cute smattering of hair—way darker than Gabe's—around his pecs, growing thicker towards the center and running down all the way to his stomach.

"Take a picture, it will last longer," Ellis says with a nervous laugh, his ears turning pink. God, he's absolutely stunning when he's nervous, which makes it really hard to feel sorry for him.

Swallowing quickly before he starts drooling, Gabe makes a show of reaching into his pocket. "Can I? Thanks!"

Ellis' hand shoots out to grip his wrist. "What are you doing?"

"Taking a picture," Gabe says innocently.

Ellis sputters indignantly. "It's a saying! I was kidding!"

Trying not to laugh, Gabe summons a disappointed expression. Ellis sees right through him, a scowl replacing his panic.

"You dick. You're just messing with me."

"Me?" Gabe gives him his best doe-eyed look. "I would never."

Rolling his eyes dramatically, Ellis makes an attempt to dislodge Gabe and move away. "You know what? I'm going home."

Using his body weight, Gabe pins him down, keeping him in place with a hand to his chest. "You're not going anywhere. Not until I'm done with you," he growls.

A wave of heat slams into him, so sudden and intense it can't possibly be from him. His lungs convulse, a moan threatening to force itself out of his throat.

He looks at Ellis in shock. When he made the joke about bossing Ellis around, it wasn't completely unfounded. He's had a feeling Ellis might appreciate following orders instead of giving them for a while. He still hadn't expected such a visceral reaction.

"What—what are you going to do to me?"

Gabe allows his lips to stretch into a slow, feral grin. "Nothing you don't want." He braces himself on each side of Ellis' head, bracketing him in, their faces so close they share the same breath. He lets their fronts fit together, biting his lip when he feels Ellis' erection against his own. "And everything you do."

Ellis' shuddering breath caresses Gabe's lips. He can practically taste the kiss waiting for them.

"I—I don't even know what that is."

Dear god, this man is precious. Gabe wants to keep him.

"Good." Shifting his weight to one hand, Gabe's fingers sink into Ellis' hair, the action earning him a small whimper. "It means I get to discover it with you. You just have to let me in."

And it means I'll be the first person to watch you come undone, the possessive part of him adds greedily. He's starting to realize Ellis has held himself back his whole life, in all ways. Fuck, Gabe can't wait to be the one to show him everything. To see him open up to life and go for what he wants.

"Gabriel?"

"Yeah?"

"Kiss me."

It's the easiest thing ever to obey, his mouth descending on Ellis' and taking it in a searing kiss. There's no exploration, no tentativeness like before. Ellis opens up to him like they've done this a million times over, deepening the kiss when Gabe takes too long to do so.

Gabe half-laughs, half-groans, letting his teeth sink into Ellis' bottom lip. Not much, just a playful nip that has Ellis gasping, wrapping his arms around Gabe and squeezing. Their chests press together, two erratic heartbeats beating out of sync, though it's impossible to tell which one belongs to whom. Ellis' blunt fingernails scrape across Gabe's back, hips thrusting up like he can't help it. The rough, sinful drag of Ellis' cock against his sends a bolt of lightning through Gabe's veins.

He can feel himself unraveling. The binds preventing his energy from unleashing are barely holding together. He forces himself to slow down, to withdraw himself from the intensity of the moment. His muscles grow tenser, his breathing deeper as the kiss loses heat and his body finally starts listening again.

Ellis makes an unhappy sound, something between a growl and a huff. He tries to deepen the kiss again, urging Gabe to follow suit as he licks into his mouth. This time when his hips undulate, it's decidedly intentional. His desire pours into Gabe, warm and languid and too delicious to resist.

"Gabriel."

There's something unfairly sexy about that voice as it says Gabe's name.

"Hmm?" He doesn't trust himself to speak, afraid that if he gets even a little sidetracked, it's all over.

"You don't—you don't have to control yourself." There's something desperate in Ellis' voice. "Just let go."

"I can't," Gabe says regretfully. "It could be...it *would* be a lot. If I let go."

"I can handle it. I want to feel what you feel."

Fucking hell, this man will be the death of him. He'll ruin him, Gabe just knows it.

"You sure?"

Ellis' energy speaks volumes, needy and fervent as it reaches out to Gabe, wrapping around him like silk. But he needs to hear it, needs to make sure Ellis knows what he's asking.

"I'm sure," Ellis says, unwavering. He cradles Gabe's face between his palms, thumbs stroking over his cheekbones. "Let go."

It seems today will be a first for Gabe too. Never in his life has he thought he'd find someone like Ellis. Someone he could tell his secrets to without judgment, ridicule, or fear. Someone who wouldn't ask him to make himself smaller, who wouldn't want to tame him. Someone who'd want to see, and feel, all of him.

Any plan to do this slowly, to gradually untie the binds, goes to hell when their mouths find each other again. Ellis' energy wraps around him, burrows itself under Gabe's skin, and everything snaps.

Ellis makes a sound like it's been ripped out of him and tears his mouth away. His body convulses as if zapped with electricity, gripping Gabe's arms in a bruising hold. His eyes, wide with disbelief and something else, bore into Gabe's.

"Too much?" Gabe asks, already working on drawing everything back in, but it's harder than usual, Ellis' own energy preventing him from shutting himself down.

"No. I mean, yes." A trembling exhale leaves him, but otherwise he seems okay, despite having been hit with a freight train worth of suppressed emotions. "Do you really feel all that?"

"For you?" He smiles softly. "Yeah." If Ellis thought that Gabe's stupid smiles, malfunctioning filter, and off-handed ass comments were the extent of his feelings for him, this must be a hell of a shock.

"Show me."

"What?"

"Show me."

Show him what? He's already opened himself up to his limit. Now Ellis feels what Gabe feels and there's nothing—

Oh.

And just like that, Gabe remembers they were in the middle of something. More accurately, his dick reminds him by trying to tear a hole in his shorts. His mind swarms with ideas, with every possible way he could show Ellis how much he wants him, body and soul. He wants to erase the memory of every person who has ever made Ellis feel inadequate, not good enough. Of every person who's taken something from him and never given anything in return.

Ellis might not know what he wants, but he's trusting Gabe to find out, to take care of him.

Gabe will take such good care of him.

The next kiss has none of the urgency, but all of the heat, setting his insides on fire. He lets it consume him, lets himself get swept in it, in Ellis.

Ellis clings to him like he's lost in the ocean and Gabe is a buoy, the only thing that can save him, like he would drown if he let go. It occurs to Gabe that might be what Ellis thinks he needs—for someone to save him.

Gabe doesn't think that's true. Ellis doesn't need to be saved because he's done that himself a long time ago. He had no choice.

He doesn't need a savior. He just needs someone to see him. To love him.

I volunteer as tribute.

Ellis throws his head back, breaking the kiss when Gabe rolls his hips, slow and sinuous, letting him feel it. He kisses the corner of Ellis' mouth, his stubbly chin. "Good?"

"Mhmfm."

Smiling, Gabe continues to pepper kisses over his jaw, pressing one to the spot below his ear and making him shiver. Then he licks the spot, tasting salt and Ellis, just to see what happens.

He isn't disappointed.

Ellis' hands fly to his hips, holding him in place as he thrusts up, again and again, groaning with each drag of his cock against Gabe's.

Moving his mouth lower, Gabe kisses and licks over his throat, mindful not to leave any marks. Not yet, anyway. Ellis' stubble burns his lips in the best way, making them oversensitive and puffy. Out of curiosity, he carefully scrapes his teeth over Ellis' Adam's apple.

Ellis arches off the sofa, mumbling, "Gabe."

Gabe grins like a maniac, proud he's reduced Ellis to a state where he's not even able to say Gabe's full name.

His grin disappears, morphing into a drawn-out moan when Ellis sinks one hand into his hair and pulls. Probably a payback, not that Gabe's complaining.

Ellis continues delivering short, gentle tugs as Gabe works his way lower, trying to get his mouth on every inch of exposed skin. The tug is far from gentle when he licks and nips on Ellis' nipple, confirming his theory that Ellis is planning to match the torture with his own. Ironically, it seems like a win-win.

By the time Gabe has reached Ellis' tummy, they're both a mess,

Ellis' breathing shallow and ragged, and Gabe's scalp sensitive and tingling in the best way. Every time he does something Ellis loves, he's hit with a blast of desire and pleasure, which makes him feel *more* desire and pleasure, which makes his emotions amplify, which gets Ellis all riled up, which makes Gabe's emotions more intense. They get stuck in this emotional loop that just gets more and more intense.

It's fucking awesome.

Gabe presses a wet kiss below Ellis' bellybutton and props his chin there as he seeks out Ellis' gaze. Fingers hooking into the waistband of Ellis' pants, he raises an eyebrow. "Yes?"

The word is barely out when Ellis breathes out a shaky but decisive "Yes."

Lips curling into a grin, Gabe starts to tug the pants and underwear over Ellis' hips. He feels like a kid on a Christmas morning about to unwrap his most anticipated present; torn between wanting to tear into it at once, or take his time and really savor it.

He sucks a bruise into Ellis' hipbone when it's revealed, figuring no one will be looking there. It pulls a hiss out of Ellis, probably more from surprise than genuine pain. When Gabe looks at him, he finds him already looking back, eyes dark and glazed over, lips redder than Gabe has left them.

Another tug, and Ellis' cock springs free, so hard it slaps against his belly with an obscene sound. Groaning, Gabe works Ellis' clothes down to mid-thigh, unabashedly staring as Ellis' cock twitches, pre-come pooling on his stomach. He's uncut, a discovery that comes as a surprise but a welcomed one because Gabe has always had a bit of kink for that.

A choked off laugh comes from Ellis. "You're staring like you don't have one yourself." He's nervous, Gabe can feel it, the connection between them buzzing with it.

Curling a finger, he grazes the knuckle over Ellis' length. The touch is featherlight, but Ellis reacts as if he's seconds away from coming. It makes Gabe's already filthy mind whirr with possibilities. If Ellis is so responsive to a simple touch...

"The difference is, I've never wanted to choke on my cock."

Ellis' eyes fly wide open, some unintelligible sounds falling from his mouth.

Taking pity on him—or not, depends how you look at it—Gabe leans down and runs his tongue over the tip, Ellis' taste taking over his senses. Sharp pleasure pierces through his gut, and he knows it's coming from Ellis.

"Gab—Gabriel..."

Fuck yes. They've barely done anything, and Ellis already sounds utterly wrecked. Gabe wants him more wrecked, completely and utterly shattered so he can put him back together.

"I want to suck you off," he says, hardly recognizing his voice, rough and deep, as if he's already been throat-fucked instead of just planning on it. "Can I?"

This time, the yes takes a while to arrive, but Gabe can feel it filling the air around them and waits for Ellis to give it a voice.

"Yes."

Now that he's been granted permission, Gabe wastes no time reducing Ellis to a babbling, desperate mess. His fingers curl around the base of Ellis' cock, squeezing just this side of tight, before his lips wrap around the head, giving it a powerful suck. The muscles in Ellis' thighs contract and quiver as Gabe's mouth descends lower, taking him in fully until he can feel him bump the back of his throat. It's been a while since Gabe's done this, but it's like riding a bike. His throat relaxes easily, taking Ellis further and drawing an inhuman noise out of him.

"F-fuck." Ellis grips the edge of the sofa with one hand. Gabe reaches for it, thumb brushing over Ellis' knuckles until his fingers uncurl so he can lace them with his own. Sappy? Maybe. He just loves holding Ellis' hand. He then takes the other one and guides it to the back of his neck, giving him a meaningful look. He could use words, but that would require him to pull off Ellis' cock, and he's not willing to do that.

Ellis gets the memo, eyes wide and breath hitching. He hesitates for a long moment before his hold tightens and his hips rise a fraction, thrusting into Gabe's mouth.

A shameless moan vibrates from Gabe's throat. Ellis groans, starting to pump his hips and press down on Gabe's head. He's being gentle, considerate, and while Gabe would love to watch him lose control, he loves this too. It's so *Ellis*, always thinking of other people.

Gabe lets his eyes slide shut in bliss, focusing on the feeling of Ellis' cock moving inside his mouth, silky and hot, and so good he might come just from sucking him off.

Reaching down with his free hand, Gabe pries his shorts open, his eyes rolling into his head as he finally gets a hand on his own cock, squeezing hard at the base so he doesn't blow in two seconds flat.

"Fuck, are you—" Ellis' expression is full of disbelief, his gaze fixed on the hand working Gabe's dick. His cock swells and twitches in Gabe's mouth. "Stop."

Regretfully, Gabe pulls off, Ellis' cock popping out of his mouth with a lewd, slick sound. "What's wrong?" Is he so far gone he didn't notice something was going on?

Ellis strokes behind Gabe's ear. "Can we...together?"

Oooh. Fuck, yes.

With a feral grin, he pushes up onto his knees and stretches out over Ellis, their groins lining up.

Gabe stares at Ellis' mouth hungrily. "Do you object to being kissed after a blowjob?"

Ellis' cheeks flush a pretty pink color. He licks his lips. "Not even a little." He meets Gabe halfway, surging up and claiming his lips in a bruising kiss and licking into his mouth as if he wants to get a taste of himself. The groan that follows is unhinged, and when he pulls Gabe down by the hips so they can grind together, sparks go off behind Gabe's eyelids.

Gabe has a moment of regret that he hasn't taken Ellis' pants off completely. He'd give anything to have Ellis' legs wrapped around his waist, gripping him tight as he thrusts and thrusts, bringing them closer to the edge. He's too far gone to stop now.

The kiss becomes uncoordinated and sloppy as they rub against each other, hips thrusting and sweat breaking out on their bodies. Gabe shoves a hand between them, circling both their lengths and stroking.

Ellis' mouth breaks away, his expression starstruck. His gaze travels lower to watch what Gabe is doing, and his face sets with determination. Seconds later, his hand is joining Gabe's, trying to mimic his movements. It's reluctant and clumsy at first, but Gabe removes his hand and puts it around Ellis', guiding him.

"A little tighter. Don't overthink it. Just do what feels good."

Ellis huffs impatiently. "It all feels good."

Gabe tries not to look too proud of himself. "Good. Let yourself feel it."

And Ellis does. Gabe can feel his elation, nerves, and fascination. Ellis' head fell back for a minute, but now he's back to staring at where they're pressed together, the tendons in his neck straining with effort. His face and chest are flushed, his breath coming out in short, erratic puffs.

He makes a choked sound, his cock swelling against Gabe's, hips thrusting out of rhythm.

"Gabe—"

"Me too. Let go."

Ellis whimpers, his grip tightening further as his cock erupts, splashing come over his hand and belly. Some of it lands on Gabe's cock, and he moans, replacing Ellis' hand with his own when his rhythm falters.

It only takes a few more strokes before he's coming, adding to the mess on Ellis' belly. Ellis watches with avid fascination, wincing a little when Gabe continues to stroke them.

Gabe lets go, trying to catch his breath. He leans down to press a kiss to Ellis' sweaty forehead. "Was that okay?"

There's a moment of utter silence, and then Ellis laughs, hard enough that his shoulders shake with it. High on pleasure and oxytocin, his energy pulses, rubbing against Gabe's. Gabe soaks it up, enjoying its warmth and affection.

"I'll take that as a yes," he says, chuckling.

Ellis' eyes are bright and sparkling when he looks at him. His hands frame Gabe's face, drawing him in. Soft, wet lips land on his, the kiss sweet and unhurried, bordering on innocent. He presses their foreheads together when they pull apart.

"Where have you been?"

There's something rueful and almost sad in his voice. It wraps around Gabe's throat, choking him, making tears spring to his eyes.

"Looking for you," Gabe whispers, smiling as he looks into Ellis' eyes. "But you found me first."

"Yeah," Ellis says, voice thick with emotion. "I did."

"Now you're stuck with me."

Ellis laughs. "I can live with that."

Gabe grins and kisses him.

Chapter 17

ELLIS WOULD LIKE TO say he feels no different when he wakes up on Monday morning than he did yesterday before he'd gone home with Gabriel. That the best date ever and his first time doing anything sexual with a man haven't changed him on a visceral level. That stripping himself bare, literally and figuratively, in front of Gabriel and touching each other wasn't as groundbreaking as he'd expected.

He'd be the biggest liar in the world.

There's been a shift inside him, as if he were made up of puzzle-pieces and they'd all just slotted together. For the first time in...ever, he no longer feels like he's been dropped in the middle of a raging ocean with waves coming at him from all sides, trying to take him down. He's still in the ocean, but it's calm and not so deep, and he might even see the shore.

Even the black hole in his chest seems smaller now. It's been shrinking since Gabriel had come into his life and something else has started growing in its place. Something he's never felt before.

What's surprising is how none of these changes feel like they are in any way related to Gabriel being a man. As if his gender was just an afterthought now that Ellis has come to accept that part of himself. Yes, touching Gabriel's flat chest and hairy legs (he finds that really cute for some reason) was new, as was the feeling of another man's come painting his skin. It was new, and fascinating, and amazing, but not life-altering.

No, the life-altering part was Gabriel holding him like Ellis was made of glass and kissing him as if his own survival depended on it. Them holding hands as Gabriel went down on him was, in a strangely disturbing way, the sweetest thing Ellis has ever done. Would Gabriel hold his hand when their positions were reversed? The idea makes his cock twitch.

Standing naked in front of the built-in wardrobe mirror, he barely recognizes himself as he stares at his reflection. He's a mess, all wild hair and a baffled expression. There are small, bright-red bruises Gabriel has marked his hips and thighs with before he—

At the memory of Gabriel between his legs, taking him all the way into his mouth like he was starving for it, Ellis' cock is now fully hard.

He sighs, foreseeing a shower wank in his near future.

There are only two people in the line before Ellis when he gets to the café. Even though Gabriel is already serving the first, his eyes latch onto Ellis the moment he crosses the threshold, as if he can sense him there. As always, he smiles, wide and radiant, and waves excitedly.

Ellis waves back, the action tamer than Gabriel's, but he's pretty sure he's grinning like an idiot.

"Hi, stranger. Long time no see," Gabriel greets him once the lady before Ellis has moved over to the pick-up station.

"Yeah, it's been a while," Ellis says, chuckling. He doesn't miss how Gabriel not-so-subtly checks him out, his pupils dilating a little even though he's seen pretty much everything there is to see.

Ellis' skin suddenly feels very hot.

"No cinnamon roll today, I presume?" Gabriel says, all blasé and shit, the little menace.

"Yeah, no. I had, like, five for breakfast." Which is probably why he's been buzzing since then. Sugar rush. But what did Gabriel expect when he sent him off with the rest of the cinnamon rolls and whatever was left of their dinner (which will be Ellis' lunch today)?

Gabriel smiles, pleased, then heaves a sigh. "You know that if you end up at the hospital with a cardiac arrest, I'll feel guilty as hell, right?"

"I always thought it would be stress that killed me. But cinnamon rolls? I'll take it."

Gabriel winces. "Okay, my bad. No jokes about you dying, please." His hand hovers over the stacks of cups. "Size?"

"Above average," Ellis says, smirking. The bad pun was worth Gabriel's stunned reaction.

As he's scrambling for a response, Zeke calls out, "I bet."

Ellis blushes. He didn't mean to speak so loud.

Gabriel's head snaps to him. "Hands off. I called dibs."

Ellis gives him a raised eyebrow, his heart pounding with the unexpected display of possessiveness. "Called dibs, huh? Thanks for asking my opinion."

Gabriel fixes him with a haughty look. "Your opinion was loud and clear last night."

God, Gabriel is killing him today. Well, every day, but especially today. It seems that getting access to Ellis' dick has broken what little control he had over his brain-to-mouth filter. And he doesn't even look sorry for what comes out of said, and admittedly kissable, mouth.

Ellis clears his throat. "I'll have a large." As he longingly peruses the pastry display, he remembers something Gabriel told him yesterday. "And two dozen donuts."

Gabriel goes silent, then chuckles. "You going to see Cal, or what?"

"No. Just figured I could make Monday a bit more digestible for people at work." Which is a nice bonus, if not the main reason. Now that he knows the financial situation of the café, he wants to support it as much as he can.

Thankfully, Gabriel doesn't look suspicious. If anything, his eyes soften, as they often do when he's looking at Ellis. "Always thinking of other people, aren't you?" Before Ellis can formulate a response that doesn't involve stuttering and babbling, Gabriel has grabbed a large paper box and a pair of tongs. "Flavor?"

"Surprise me."

Gabriel likes that answer, his face lighting up. He's quick but mindful as he fills the box to the brim, then hands it to Ellis.

"Zeke!" he calls out even though Zeke is just a few steps away.

"Yeah, yeah," Zeke grumbles, swapping places with him. "Hey, hot stuff," he greets, lips pulling into a sly smirk. It looks very wrong.

"Uh, hi..." Ellis presses out. "I'll just...yeah." He scurries towards Gabriel to wait for his drink.

"Ignore him," Gabriel says, giving Zeke a side-eye. "He's trying to get a rise out of me."

"I can see he's succeeding," Ellis notes with amusement. "Does he know?"

Gabriel's expression morphs into one of guilt. "It was kind of written all over my face this morning. Probably still is."

"Yeah, I feel like everyone at work will know too. Amanda will know for sure," he realizes with mild horror. "That's my PA," he explains when Gabriel looks at him askance.

"Does that bother you?"

Ellis hates that Gabriel even has to ask—not that he can blame him. Ellis hasn't exactly given the impression of being 'out and proud'.

"Nosy people? Yeah. Them finding out? No." He just doesn't like mixing work with his personal life. It's bad enough he's friends with Jordan, but the guy practically bullied Ellis into befriending him.

Gabriel looks at him as if Ellis handed him a puppy, all starry-eyed and soft-looking. He leans over the counter, gesturing for Ellis to do the same.

Then he half-whispers, half-growls, "I really wanna kiss you right now."

Instantly, Ellis' gaze drops to his lips. "Would the management be okay with that?"

The lips in question curl at the corners. "Oh, they'd be game. Believe me."

"Okay."

Gabriel grabs him by the tie and pulls him into a hungry kiss. Ellis makes a muffled sound of surprise, having expected a simple, PDA-acceptable peck. Gabriel clearly had a different idea because once Ellis' lips part on a gasp, his tongue pushes in, relentless and demanding.

Ellis has to brace himself against the counter as he opens up, swallowing a moan as he tastes something sweet with an aftertaste he's come to associate with Gabriel.

"Get a room!" someone barks, a note of amusement in their voice.

They pull apart, and Ellis gives the intruder a side-eye. There's something familiar about the man, but he can't place him.

"Friend of yours?" he asks, since the man seems to be amused by their antics.

"Not anymore," Gabriel grumbles, getting a laugh out of Ellis.

The man approaches them, stopping in his tracks as he stares at Ellis.

"Hey. I know you," he says, managing to sound accusatory.

Now that he got a proper look at him, the memories come back to Ellis. "Right. You're Dawson's friend. Kevin, is it?" They've only met once, briefly, at the hospital when Cal was first brought in and Ellis had flown up from Sydney.

"Kieran!" not-Kevin corrects snappily. "And you're Dickhead's brother."

Okay. So Kieran apparently has feelings about Cal.

"Wait." Kieran's frown deepens. "Why were you kissing Gabe?" Now, that was definitely accusatory.

Gabriel sticks his tongue out. "Because I'm irresistible."

Kieran doesn't look happy, though Ellis fails to see how the situation concerns him. Maybe he's Gabriel's ex? The thought is very unsettling.

"Are you two a thing? Seriously?" Kieran points at Ellis. "Him?"

"Hey, cut it out," Gabriel bites out, all playfulness gone. He looks pissed, and it's so unusual and unexpected that Ellis finds it a teeny tiny bit hot. "What's your problem?"

A tall man with strawberry blond hair speaks from behind Kieran. "He needs a good whooping, would be my guess." Ellis watches as Kieran's eyes widen like he recognizes the voice, and he whirls around. "A bit of a drama queen, aren't you?"

"You," Kieran growls.

"Miss me?" The man's lips curl in a dangerous grin. Something about it reminds Ellis of Gabriel.

"Fuck you," Kieran spits out, seething. "What are you doing here? Are you *stalking* me?"

The man huffs. "Nothing that interesting. Just popping by to say hi to my favorite cousin." He nods towards Gabriel who manages an awkward wave. "Looking a little worn out. Rough night?"

Kieran's teeth flash, reminding Ellis of a rabid dog. "Fuck. You."

The man's smile only gets wider. "Keep saying that and you might get your wish."

Fingers digging into his palms, Kieran turns to Gabriel. "Is my drink done yet?"

"Oh!" Gabriel jumps, hastily looking for the docket. "Just a sec." What feels like five seconds later, he's putting the finished drink on the counter. "Here it is."

Kieran stalks forward and grabs the cup hard enough that some of the liquid splashes out of the sipper. "Your family sucks."

Gabriel gives a strained laugh. "You're not wrong."

Kieran strides away angrily, then nearly yeets his drink at the man when he calls, "See you around, Kieran."

Likely figuring the drink is too expensive to waste, he instead delivers a very passionate 'Fuck you' and all but runs away.

Ellis and Gabriel share a look when the coast is clear. "Ash?" Ellis guesses. Gabriel has only mentioned one cousin.

At the sound of his name, Ash's attention turns to him. "I see you've talked about me." He walks forward, all leisurely like he hasn't a care in the world, and holds his hand out. "You must be Ellis."

Oh. Gabriel has talked about him too?

"Yes." He takes Ash's hand. "It's nice to meet you." Mostly true. He's not sure how he feels about Ash's intense scrutiny.

"It really is," Ash drawls, his grip tightening a notch. Ellis has a strange sensation of being dissected.

"Ash!" Gabriel barks. "Cut it out."

Ellis frowns, not sure what Gabriel is referring to. Ash isn't really doing anything apart from making Ellis vaguely uncomfortable.

Ash, however, holds his hands up, his face the picture of innocence. His grin is shark-like when he speaks to Ellis. "I've heard *a lot* about you."

If Gabriel's flushed cheeks are anything to go by, Ellis can easily guess what that conversation entailed.

Getting the impression that Ash loves to make people uncomfortable, Ellis wills his expression to remain impassive. He smiles a little.

"Only the worst, I hope."

Ash lets out a hearty laugh, then looks at Gabriel. "I like him."

"Don't."

Ellis covers his smile by taking a sip of his drink. Something about seeing Gabriel all grumpy and irritated makes him want to laugh.

"Wow." Zeke pops up next to Gabriel. "What did you do to Kieran? I haven't seen anything that entertaining in a while."

"Nothing," Ash says in a way that makes it obvious it was something. "He's so highly strung, I don't even have to try to get him riled up."

"And why do you want to get him riled up?"

Ash just grins, and asks, "When was the last time you saw something entertaining?"

Zeke purses his lips and taps his chin. "Probably when Gabby lost control of his mouth and told the loverboy over here he'd like to eat his ass."

With a sharp inhale, the coffee shoots down the wrong pipe and Ellis chokes, coughing up a storm. Through the burning in his nose and the pain of his lungs being torn apart, he hears Gabriel sputtering.

"I didn't—that's not—" He turns pleading eyes to Ellis before fixing them on Zeke with a look of utter loathing. The effect is diminished by the bright-red color of his face. "I hate you."

Zeke doesn't seem to be taking it personally.

Ash, on the other hand, looks like all he needs is a bowl of popcorn and a comfortable chair.

"Um. Excuse me?" comes a meek voice. They all turn towards it, finding a young man standing awkwardly in front of the till. The look on his face suggests he overheard the whole thing. "Could I get a coffee, please?"

"Oh my god," Gabriel cries, folding his arms on the countertop and hiding his face in them. "Kill me now. Make it quick."

Zeke laughs, pats him on the back and leaves to serve the customer.

Now that he's recovered from the violent coughing fit, Ellis' mind races. He scours his brain, but while Gabriel seems fond of making ass jokes, he never actually insinuated...well, *that.* Zeke was just taking the piss and enjoying making Gabriel lose his composure.

Except...Gabriel's reaction wasn't an outright denial.

Maybe Ellis is just dumb and oblivious and completely missed the mark? Because if he did and Gabriel has actually been hinting at...um...doing that to him...

He fidgets, his skin hot and tight under his suit. He pulls at his tie, loosening the knot as unbidden images flood his mind. The idea feels weird and...just weird. He's not a prude, not really, but he probably leans towards the more vanilla side of things. He's not sure why Gabriel would want to do *that.* What would he get out of having Ellis naked and spread out on the bed, lying on his stomach as Gabriel gently pulls his cheeks apart and leans in to lick—

Ellis snaps back to reality, stunned by his own raging imagination. He takes a quick drink of his coffee to moisturize his Sahara-dry throat and adjusts his stance to cover up the growing erection in his pants. When he chances a look at Gabriel, he finds him watching Ellis with a surprised expression. Shit. Just how strongly was he projecting his emotions? Did he...did Gabriel feel that?

Feeling exposed and embarrassed, Ellis turns his attention to Ash.

Not a good idea. Ash is looking at him like he can read his mind, and given that he's Gabriel's cousin, it's not unlikely. Fuck. Could this be any more mortifying?

"So...Kieran is clearly fond of you," Ellis points out, hoping to steer the conversation elsewhere.

"Don't worry. He'll come around," Ash says, smiling salaciously.

Something hits Ellis then. "Wait. That was you flirting?" he asks with disbelief.

"That was Ash being a self-absorbed ass and trying to get into a straight guy's pants," Gabriel says, his tone all judgment and disapproval.

Ash snorts. "Nothing straight going on in there."

"Don't you think *I* would know?"

Ash slowly arches one brow. "Don't you think *I* would know better than you?"

Gabriel's eyes narrow, but he doesn't contradict him again.

"Are you talking about your mojo?" Ellis asks, curious. When he gets a perplexed look in response, it occurs to him he might've overstepped. Apologetic, he turns to Gabriel. "Was I not supposed to tell? I'm sorry."

"He knows?" Ash asks. He doesn't sound upset. Instead, he grins again, folding his arms and resting his hip against the counter. "Well, would you look at that. Am I hearing wedding bells?"

"Ash..." Gabriel growls in warning.

"Got it, got it," Ash placates, not without an eyeroll. "I'll get my usual and be out of your hair lickety-split."

Ellis has never seen Gabriel make a drink so fast.

"Now leave."

Unbothered, Ash takes his drink and salutes Ellis with it. "Pleasure to have made your acquaintance. Hopefully we'll be seeing more of each other from now on."

Managing a subdued 'See you', Ellis watches him go, still reeling from the whole interaction.

"So..." He turns to Gabriel. "That's Ash."

Gabriel makes a noise of despair. "I'm so, so sorry. You shouldn't have to deal with this."

"No, that's...that's fine. He seems like a funny guy." Even if the fun is on account of everyone else.

"Oh god, no." Gabriel shakes his head resolutely. "*No.*"

Laughing softly, Ellis takes Gabriel's hand. "Hey. I'm just glad I got to meet someone from your life. You know everybody from mine."

A reluctant smile appears on Gabriel's lips which is quickly replaced with annoyance. "I'd be happy to swap."

Ellis laughs, finding Gabriel's antics amusing. As much as he bitches about his cousin and Zeke, it's obvious how much he loves them.

"I have to go," he says regretfully after a glance at his watch. "See you tomorrow?"

"Yeah." Gabriel leans over the counter for a kiss. "Don't work too hard."

Ellis kisses him again, just because he can. "I'll do my best."

"You got laid."

Ellis almost trips over his own feet, precariously balancing the box of donuts. "What?"

Amanda studies his face. "You look different. Your skin is all glowy and shit."

"I have a new moisturizer." He shoves the box at her with a little more force than required. "Take these to the guys, will you?"

She flips the lid open. "You bought us donuts?" Her eyes narrow. "Moisturizer, my ass."

Ellis glares at her. "Do you have anything work-related to discuss with me?"

She reaches into the box and shoves a chocolate donut into her mouth, her eyes on Ellis.

Taking that as a no, he goes to his office. Maybe he should start looking for a new, less perceptive PA. Or at least someone who understands boundaries.

His phone vibrates with a text. He groans as he reads it.

Dawson: Ellis! You and Gabe?! What? When? HOW?!?!

For fuck's sake. Damn Kieran.
Ellis ignores the text, but more keep coming.

Dawson: Don't ignore me! I need answers!

Dawson: Elliiiiis

Cal: Can you please answer Dawson's texts? He's been randomly screaming for ten minutes.

Cal: Is it true about you and Gabe? I like Gabe. He's nice.

Cal: Does that mean we're on the same team now?

Ellis runs a hand over his face, letting out a groan as another text comes through. He relaxes when he sees it's from Gabriel.

Gabriel: Has your phone been blowing up too? xD

Ellis: Yup.

Gabriel: I'm gonna kill Kieran.

Ellis: Nah. Just send Ash his way.

"Well, you are."

"Okay."

"You're blushing."

"That's sunburn."

"It rained all day yesterday."

"The sun is really fierce in Queensland."

"As I said—" Gabriel leans in. "Adorable."

He doesn't resist when Gabriel walks him backwards and pushes him up against the glass door. In the back of his mind, he's aware anyone could walk by, or god forbid, try to walk in, but he can't summon the willpower to care. Not when Gabriel makes this growling, whimpering noise whenever Ellis nips at his lower lip, or when he pins Ellis in place using his own body. It still feels so wild to be with someone who matches his strength, who can give as much as he gets.

Ellis chases after him when Gabriel pulls away, letting out a long-suffering groan.

"I need to pull myself together before someone comes in," Gabriel says ruefully.

"Yeah. Probably a good idea."

And Ellis needs to do the same before showing up at work. If he hurries, he'll get there before Amanda and won't have to explain why he looks like he's had marathon sex.

Gabriel quickly checks with him before starting on his usual order. When he puts everything in front of Ellis, there's also a rectangular plastic container filled with something orange.

"It's lentil curry," Gabriel explains, unprompted. "Dairy-free."

"You cooked me lunch?" He was already baffled when Gabriel cooked for their first date, but going out of his way to make Ellis lunch?

"I always cook too much, then end up eating the same thing for three days. You liked my cooking, so..." He shrugs.

"I did. I do," Ellis presses out. He feels a little choked up, and not sure what the appropriate reaction would be. "Thank you," he says at last.

Gabriel gives him a sunny smile. Why does doing things for Ellis always make him look so damn happy? It doesn't make sense.

It's not until Ellis is back in his car that he sees the message Gabriel has left him on the coffee cup.

You're adorable xoxo

He shakes his head when he catches sight of himself in the rearview mirror, smiling like an idiot. He'd better wipe that look off his face before heading to work. He has no idea how he would explain that to Amanda.

The following morning, Ellis sleeps through his alarm once again. In retrospect, it probably wasn't the wisest to spend the better part of the night texting back and forth with Gabriel. This was followed by trying to get Jordan off his case when he called Ellis in the middle of the night to ask for 'spicy details' from his date. Which Ellis did not provide, much to Jordan's chagrin.

While he's not quite late for work, he won't be able to make it to *Lost and Ground*, not when he knows how easy it is to lose track of time when talking to Gabriel. Grumbling under his breath, he shoots Gabriel a text, apologizing for having to skip today. He doesn't get a reply, but figures the café is just busy at this time.

Out of desperation, he orders a coffee from the little café at the office to tide him over, except he manages to mess up the order. He really needs to remember what the drink Gabriel makes him is called. After explaining, very badly, to the barista what the drink tastes like—and getting an unimpressed look in return—he's served something that tastes like stale gingerbread cookie soaked in dishwater. Being in public is the only reason he doesn't spit it out on the floor, though he dumps the whole thing in the nearest bin. Not a great start to the day.

An hour before his lunch break, Amanda strolls into his office, unprompted as per usual, holding a plastic container and a large paper cup.

"You didn't tell me you're waiting for a delivery. A tad early, isn't it?"

Ellis frowns. "Delivery?"

"Mhmhm." She walks over and puts the items on his overflowing desk. "Some cutie popped by and dropped these off."

Cutie? That's when Ellis notices the *Lost and Ground* stamp on the cup. Wait, Gabriel is here? And he's come all the way to drop off Ellis' coffee and what seems to be yet another home-cooked meal?

Ellis stands so fast the chair rolls back and crashes into the window. "Is he still here? Why didn't you let him in?" He marches to the hallway, but doesn't see Gabriel. Dammit. Has he left? And how did he know where to go?

"Are we sending delivery guys straight to your office now?" Amanda retorts, voice amused.

"He's not a delivery guy. He's—" He draws a blank. Labels always annoyed him, but he could really use one right now. Isn't it too early to discuss where this is going, though?

Amanda watches him expectantly, her expression pinched as if she's trying not to smile. What has she to smile about?

"He's..." Fuck it. He can discuss it with Gabriel later. "My boyfriend." Okay. Wow. Why is *that* making him all weird and squirmy on the inside?

Amanda makes a thoughtful sound, pulling him out of his reverie. Something is off, Ellis realizes.

"You're not surprised?"

She sighs, throwing a blond lock over her shoulder. "We women can sense these things. Also..." She takes the cup, holding it out in front of Ellis so he can read the message scribbled below the lid.

Miss you. Hope you like Italian xx

She thrusts the cup at him, so he's forced to take it—and stare at it with his mouth hanging open.

"Well done. He's a cutie pie," she says approvingly. Way too approvingly.

"Amanda."

"Still clinging to that moisturizer excuse?"

"*Amanda*," he says firmly, only managing to make her laugh.

"Going, I'm going. Enjoy your lunch." She winks and strolls out, hips swinging and high heels clicking.

Boundaries. Ellis needs to establish some asap.

The scent of coffee and spices tickling his nose, he takes a long, blissful sip from the cup, letting out a little moan as it fills his mouth. Fuck, he needed this. Shame that Gabriel didn't stay so he could see him, but he was probably in a rush to get back. Hopefully Zeke isn't going to give him much crap for leaving in the middle of his shift.

Ellis: Did you ride all the way here from the café?

He starts to worry when it's been twenty minutes without a reply. How long does it take to get to the café on a scooter? Those things can go insanely fast, which isn't exactly reassuring. As far as Ellis is concerned, those death traps are no better than motorbikes, maybe worse since you can use them on the sidewalk. He knows that Gabriel's been using his since moving to the Gold Coast, but experience isn't everything. Something might've happened. Maybe he was rushing to get back and a car came out of—

The relief as his phone pings with a text is so intense it almost makes him nauseous.

Gabriel: The scooter is faster than a car :D

Ellis groans. Not. Reassuring. At all.

He refrains from giving Gabriel a lecture, not wanting to sound like a concerned parent.

Ellis: How did you know where to go?

Gabriel: I asked Cal. He was very helpful.

The fact that Gabriel knew Cal and Dawson before he knew Ellis still feels a little weird. Good on one hand—Ellis won't have to make introductions—but weird on the other.

Ellis: Thank you. You shouldn't have bothered, but thank you.

Gabriel: Nonsense. I couldn't possibly leave you uncaffeinated. It's in your employees' best interest.

Gabriel: And you can't live on takeout. I mean, you can. But I won't let you.

Dammit, Ellis is too old to get butterflies in his stomach. He's probably just hungry.

Ellis: My employees are very grateful.

Ellis: You should have told Amanda to let you in.

Gabriel: I figured you had a meeting or something. Didn't wanna intrude.

Ellis puts the phone down for a second in case he types something like *I always want to see you.* He's been too sappy lately, he needs to slow down. One sappy confession every other day should suffice.
When he's confident his fingers won't betray him, he picks up the phone again.

Ellis: Are you free tonight? We could go to the movies. Or something.

He can't remember the last time he's been to a movie, but that's what people do on a date, right?

Gabriel: I'm down! But only if you're not too tired after work.

Ellis: You can give me a magical boost.

Gabriel: Oh, I can do more than that ;) ;)

The butterflies move lower, wreaking utter havoc and making his pants uncomfortably tight.

Gabriel: You still there? Are we on?

Checking the time between the texts, it looks like Ellis zoned out for a good three minutes. He takes a deep breath, willing the butterflies to calm the fuck down.

Ellis: We're on.

Gabriel: xx

Aaand they're back. So is mild performance anxiety, because for all intents and purposes Ellis is still pretty much a virgin when it comes to gay sex. He kind of regrets not taking Jordan up on his offer to 'teach him stuff'. How desperate is he?

Obviously, Sunday night was amazing. As was Monday and Tuesday night when Ellis lay in bed, a hand on his cock and Gabriel in his thoughts as he stroked himself to the memory of Gabriel's mouth, and the weight of his body on top of him as he pressed Ellis into the sofa. What pushed him over the edge each time was the phantom feeling of Gabriel's come splashing across his skin, his cock pulsing in Ellis' hand.

Great. Now he's hard again.

Shooting his dick a betrayed look—even though technically it's Gabriel's fault—he tries to focus on the document glaring at him judgingly from the file in front of him. He lasts all of ten minutes before his thoughts wander again, the anxiety tickling the back of his mind.

They're just going to the movies, that doesn't mean anything is going to happen.

But if it does...

He heaves a sigh, slumping in his chair. Well, one thing is certain—he's not going to call Jordan to ask for pointers. He does have some dignity, after all. Which only leaves one option.

Making sure the sound is off on his phone, he pulls up a porn site. It's been so long since he's visited one that he's surprised when it loads, looking very different from what he remembers. Another thing that's different is that he has to look for videos in the gay section, momentarily worried there won't be much to work with. Maybe he should look for a solely gay site?

Turns out he needn't have worried. There's *plenty* to work with. And when he says plenty... God, he's always found the dick size of the male actors ridiculous in straight porn (and that's saying something, considering he's not exactly lacking in that department), but this is a whole new level.

There's...there's no way those *things* can fit in...other things. Thank god he's already gotten a look (and touch) at Gabriel's dick, which is perfectly proportionate to his tall and lean body. Impressive, but not scary. Well, yet. It will probably be a little scary if it goes anywhere near Ellis'...um...things. Not that Gabriel gave an indication (apart from the comment about making Ellis sore) that he's expecting anything, but Ellis is...well, curious. More than anything, he wants to give as good as he's got. He wants to make Gabriel feel as good—or better—as he's made Ellis.

He types *blowjob* into the search engine before he can chicken out. Instantly, he's assaulted with thumbnail after thumbnail of men choking on monster dicks. Yeah, that's a nope.

Eventually, he ventures into the amateur section. While the quality isn't as good, it's closer to what he's been looking for—like normal-sized dicks, for one. After a minute of scrolling, he bites the bullet and clicks on the video titled *Blowing bf in the shower*. He never understood the appeal of shower sex, and his knees ache just thinking about kneeling on the tiles, but both the resolution and the angle look good, which is what he needs if he actually wants to learn something.

Checking once again that the sound is off and shooting a nervous glance at the door, he presses *play*.

One thing he notices right away is how there's no cringy prelude to sex, no eyeroll-inducing premise that's supposed to tell a story. Just two guys who got horny and decided to record themselves, either for money or kicks or both. It's refreshingly different.

There's not much build-up, but it's not rushed either. A redhead in his early to mid-twenties is kneeling in front of another guy, his boyfriend presumably, whose face can't be seen because he's holding the camera, aiming it at the redhead. And at his own cock, which the redhead is slowly stroking to hardness, smirking and mouthing something Ellis can't make out.

The redhead licks his lips and leans forward to suck the cockhead into his mouth. His eyes flutter shut, then reopen, dark and glazed over as he stares right into the camera, then slowly slides down until the whole thing is in his mouth. His body jerks a little, probably from a triggered gag reflex, but he doesn't pull back to gasp for air. Instead, he relaxes, retreats a little so he can wrap a hand around the base, and starts to slide his mouth up and down.

When the other man's hand clasps the back of his neck, the redhead comes to a stop, but doesn't pull off. He just opens up wider, looking beyond the camera, and lets his boyfriend fuck his mouth with short, rapid thrusts. Tears gather in the corners of his eyes, but he looks completely relaxed, the green of his irises barely visible.

There's no sound, but just by looking at his blissed out expression, Ellis can practically hear his moans and the obscene, slurping sounds.

It's oddly fascinating to see him enjoy himself despite being the one giving the blowjob instead of receiving it. Ellis can't remember ever seeing any of his girlfriends get off on sucking his cock so much. It's the main reason why he's never felt very comfortable letting them do it to him, a part of his brain convinced they were just pushing themselves.

Interestingly enough, he felt no such concern when Gabriel studied his cock like it was a work of art, then gave him a heated look that could melt Antarctica and all but asked for permission to suck him off. With permission granted, he proceeded to give Ellis the most enthusiastic blowjob of his life.

Yeah, Gabriel definitely wasn't pushing himself, that's for sure.

Would Ellis like being on the giving end? For someone who'd never genuinely considered putting his mouth on another guy's dick a month ago, he sure has thought about it a lot in the past few days. He has a feeling he'll be thinking about it even more in the foreseeable future.

The faceless man's thrusts become erratic and he suddenly pulls out of the redhead's mouth, jerking his own cock until rope after rope of jizz cover the redhead's face, some of it landing in his waiting mouth.

Ellis' stomach swoops, his cock jerking in his pants. For a fraction of a second he sees himself in the redhead's place, all puffy lips and flushed cheeks as Gabriel tells him to be good and open up, then proceeds to come all over his face and on his tongue.

The intercom buzzes, scaring the living shit out of Ellis. His phone flies out of his hands, and he rams his knee into the desk, swallowing a curse.

"Your 11 o'clock is here," comes Amanda's voice, completely unaware she nearly sent another Reeves brother to the hospital.

Ellis presses the button with a trembling finger. "A-a minute."

He needs more than a minute, but at least his desk hides his hard-on. That will teach him not to watch porn at work. He even gave Cal shit for doing the same. So this is what karma feels like.

Chapter 19

ELLIS IS ALREADY WAITING outside the movie theater when Gabriel gets there, tires squealing as he comes to a quick stop in front of him after going 200 miles per hour. He swears he can smell burned rubber.

"Hey!" Gabriel gives him a toothy grin, taking off his helmet. "Where's your suit?"

"I made a stop at home." He didn't want to show up wearing the same clothes he'd stewed in the whole day. "Should you be riding so fast? It's getting dark."

"Don't worry, Mum. I was wearing a helmet."

"Doesn't mean you can't crash." And break something. Like his fucking spine.

Gabriel looks at him, mirth vanishing from his eyes and replaced by something softer. "You're too sweet." Cupping the back of Ellis' neck, he pulls him into a quick, chaste kiss. "If it bothers you so much, I promise I'll go slower from now on."

Ellis' shoulders relax. "Thank you."

He waits for Gabriel to secure his scooter and overhears him mumbling under his breath. He thinks he hears the word 'adorable'.

"What are we watching?" he asks as they step inside.

Gabriel scrolls on his phone. "Well, our options for this time were either *The Guardians of the Galaxy* or *The Nun*."

Ellis holds his breath. Fuck. He should've checked what's on. Or at least tell Gabriel he hates horror and gore when he was asked about his preferences.

"I went with *Guardians*," Gabriel finally says.

Thank fuck. "Sounds good to me."

"Yeah? You seen the first two?"

"The first one, I think. It's the one with the mentally unstable racoon, right? And a talking tree?"

Gabriel's lips twitch. "I'll count that as a no. We can change it to *The Nun* if you—"

"No! No, uh...this one is good."

Gabriel's brows are practically in his hairline, a hint of a smile tugging at the corner of his mouth. "Are you scared of horror movies?"

"No," Ellis says, probably too quickly to be believable. "I just find them lame. I mean, everyone is so dumb. Why would you go to a scary-looking house in the first place?"

Gabriel's lips purse, and it's obvious he's trying not to smile. Stepping towards Ellis, he runs a hand down his arm. "You know I'd protect you, right?"

Ellis gives him a flat look. "I'm not sure your mojo is suitable for banishing a demon."

"True," Gabriel concedes, his fingers tracing nonsensical patterns over Ellis' forearm. "Zeke, on the other hand, would be all over that."

"Would it work?"

"No. Everyone would die."

"Thought so."

Gabriel's hand finds Ellis', and their fingers intertwine. "So, *Guardians*?"

"Yes, please."

Gabriel smirks. "I actually went to see it before, but don't remember anything."

"How come?"

"I went with Ash and we bumped into Dawson and Kieran." He gives Ellis a pointed look. "Sat next to them too."

Ah. "Ash and Kieran?" That must have been even more interesting than the movie.

"Yup." Gabriel's expression is mildly grossed out. "Let's say I was distracted by Kieran's hostility and Ash's stupid dick." The expression is instantly replaced by one of regret. "That sounded a lot better in my head."

"Sure it did." God, he adores this man, even though he's a force of nature. Or maybe because of that.

Gabriel scowls. He looks like a grumpy kitten.

Ellis kisses him.

The movie is...fine. Truth be told, they could be watching *The Nun* and Ellis wouldn't notice. Because Gabriel has been driving him nuts, pun intended. His hand has been all over Ellis since they'd sat down, fingertips brushing featherlight over his forearm or drawing patterns into his palm. It's a testament to how depraved Ellis is that such an innocent action makes blood roar in his ears, his skin hot wherever Gabriel has touched.

All the stroking and caressing takes him back to when Gabriel was giving the same attention to a different part of his body. He's grateful for the dark, and his foresight to wear a pair of loose-fitting jeans.

Gabriel, on the other hand, seems engrossed in the movie, as if all the touching is something he does subconsciously, his other hand digging in a box of popcorn.

Ellis studies his profile, the way the light from the screen plays across his smooth skin. Something happens in the movie that makes his eyes crinkle and causes a dimple to appear in his cheek.

Ellis wants to kiss it.

As he contemplates actually doing it, Gabriel ceases the touching, slowly turning his neck to look at him. His eyes glow gold, lips curling into a smirk.

"You're making it very *hard* to concentrate, you know?" he whispers, loud enough to be heard over the speakers.

"I'm not doing anything," Ellis lies.

Amusement flashes in Gabriel's eyes. "My mojo disagrees."

Oh god. Can he feel the arousal thrumming under Ellis' skin? That's so humiliating.

"Maybe your mojo is malfunctioning. Like your filter." Deflection. That should work.

Not.

Gabriel's fingers wrap tight around his wrist. "That's what you think?"

"That's what I think."

Gabriel's teeth flash in a dangerous grin. He leans in until their faces are an inch apart. "So if I were to suggest we get out of here and go to my place where I would do some very indecent things to you, you'd say you'd rather stay and watch the movie?"

Ellis swallows, proud when the words come out steady. "It is a very good movie."

"Yeah? What is it about?"

"Aliens?"

Gabriel's lips press together. "Sure. Guess we'll stay, then." He molds back into his seat and slurps on his slushie.

Ellis stares. Is Gabriel really not going to do anything? He's not unaffected. Ellis can see it in his features, tense with anticipation and the way he's focusing intently on the movie. Does it mean they're playing chicken? Fine. Ellis can play.

He lasts 43 seconds.

"When you say indecent things..."

Gabriel doesn't even look away from the screen. "*Very* indecent things."

Ellis drums his fingers on his thigh. "I guess...we can watch the movie some other time."

Gabriel is out of his seat before Ellis has finished talking. "That's my man," he says, brushes pieces of popcorn from his clothes, and walks away.

Ellis tries to follow him calmly, not run.

It doesn't work.

Once the door to Gabriel's apartment closes behind them, Gabriel pounces like a wild cat, barely giving Ellis time to step out of his shoes. He shoves Ellis against the wall near the doorway, pulling a startled gasp out of him. Their mouths collide, Gabriel's tongue pushing between his lips. Tasting salt and sugar, Ellis moans, hooking his fingers into the waistband of Gabriel's pants and tugging him close. The hard ridge of Gabriel's cock presses against his, causing his thoughts to scatter until the only thing that remains is the sensation of Gabriel's body against his.

Gabriel rips his mouth away and growls, "Walk."

Blinking his eyes open, Ellis stares at him dazedly, unable to process the word. Gabriel huffs, stealing another kiss. Then Ellis is being walked—pushed—backwards, tripping twice because Gabriel won't stop kissing him.

He doesn't mind at all.

Once in the bedroom, Gabriel flicks on the lights, steps back to give Ellis a hungry once-over, and orders, "Naked. On the bed. Now." He gives no indication of doing the same, just stands there and looks at Ellis like he's a delicious meal.

Heart pounding, Ellis strips, equal parts nervous and excited under Gabriel's watchful eye. With a deep breath, he tugs his briefs down his legs and steps out of them, naked as per Gabriel's orders. He blushes when Gabriel's gaze lowers to his straining cock, and turns bright red when it twitches under the attention. Desire sweeps over him in pulsating waves, curling around him like a warm hug. It feels a little strange, like standing at the shore while water laps at your feet. It's not the first time he's felt something like this.

Is this...is he feeling what Gabriel is feeling?

"Ellis," Gabriel says, sounding impatient and out of breath. "Bed."

"Was something in the slushie or are you always this bossy?" Ellis asks, hoping the sass will cover up for the way his heart is hammering in his chest. He climbs onto the mattress, suddenly grateful for the support. His legs aren't jelly, but they feel unstable. Because a bossy, demanding Gabriel? That pushes buttons Ellis had no idea existed.

Slowly, Gabriel walks over, climbing on the bed on his hands and knees and caging Ellis in with his body. He hasn't lost a single piece of clothing, and the contrast does something to Ellis.

"Oh, you're about to find out very soon just how bossy I am." He leans down until his mouth hovers over Ellis'. The ring of gold around his irises hasn't disappeared since they left the theater. "And I have a feeling you're going to love it."

Heat flows to Ellis' face. "Tell your mojo to tone it down."

"Hard to do when you're projecting your emotions so strongly."

"Oh yeah? What am I projecting now?" He regrets the words right away, sure that Gabriel is going to enjoy the heck out of embarrassing him and making him squirm.

Turns out he's wrong. Gabriel doesn't tease him. What he does is much worse.

His mouth descends on Ellis in the tenderest of kisses, the gentleness sending a powerful quake through his body. "How badly you want to let go and have someone else take care of you for a change." Gabriel strokes his cheek with his knuckles, his eyes overflowing with a kaleidoscope of emotions. "I can do that. I'll take really good care of you, Ellis. Such good care."

Ellis grasps his hips, clinging to him so as to not completely shatter before they've even done anything. The reality dawns on him then, this startling realization that it's always going to be like this with Gabriel. He'll always be able to unravel Ellis with a few words or a single look. Hell, he could probably do it with less. Until now, it hadn't quite clicked how much power Gabriel holds over him. How little he'd need to completely destroy all of him.

It should send Ellis running for the hills.

Instead, he cradles Gabriel's lovely face between his palms and lets emotion bleed into his voice. "You've been doing that all along."

Gabriel's eyelids slide shut, the space between his brows furrowing as if he's in pain. But his energy slides against Ellis' like a soothing caress, diffusing into each other. Gabriel's energy is so pleasant and familiar that the whole process feels like one big, tight hug that promises to put all Ellis' broken pieces together one by one.

At once, the safe bubble cocooning them pulses with something urgent and raw, intense in a completely different way.

Gabriel's eyes spring open, the gleam in them unmistakable. Ellis has seen it before. He shudders as he remembers what will follow.

"I can do even better," Gabriel rasps out. He sucks at Ellis' lower lip and gives it a playful bite before pushing up to sit on his heels. "Turn onto your stomach."

The order does something to Ellis, whether it's the tone, the words, or the possibilities behind them. Blood turns into liquid fire in his veins, another fire burning low in his belly and causing his cock to throb and dribble. It's almost a relief when he rolls over, as if Gabriel not being able to see his face could hide his vulnerabilities. As if Gabriel can't feel every single thing.

Behind him, Gabriel utters a ragged "Fuck."

"What?" He casts a glance over his shoulder.

Gabriel's gaze is raking all over him, jumping back and forth like he can't decide where to look first. Reverently, he slides his palms up Ellis' toned calves. His legs aren't normally sensitive, but Gabriel's touch has positively turned them into an erogenous zone. Ellis shudders, the muscles of his legs flexing.

"You're fucking gorgeous. Ridiculously beautiful, really." Gabriel makes it sound like he's annoyed by the fact.

"I've put on weight since you started feeding me cinnamon rolls."

"Well, it's gone to all the right places." To make a point, he glides

In a stealthy attempt at extracting himself, he carefully peels Gabriel's arm off his chest and shuffles to the edge of the bed. And that's as far as he gets.

The human blanket wiggles, letting out an unfairly adorable yawn. A pair of pretty amber eyes flutter open, bleary and heavy-lidded.

"Hmm, good morning," Gabriel murmurs, wriggling closer and pulling Ellis exactly where he was before.

"Morning." Resigned to his fate, Ellis wraps an arm around him. "I should nickname you koala bear."

"I like that. Does that make you a eucalyptus tree? That would track. I kinda always want to climb you. "

Ellis gives a very undignified snort. "Sure. Just don't eat me."

"I already did." Gabriel's grin is wicked, just like him. He trails his finger over the raised edge of Ellis' cheek. "You blush so prettily."

Groaning, Ellis fits his palm over Gabriel's face. "Go away."

"Nooo. I want cuddles." He attaches himself to Ellis like a monkey, something hard and hot poking his hip.

Ellis swallows, his tongue gone dry. He's suddenly aware of his very naked state, and Gabriel's for that matter.

"Is that all you want?"

Gabriel blinks, as if he wasn't aware of his aroused state until Ellis pointed it out. He doesn't seem embarrassed in the least, and his smile is lopsided, a little sheepish. "I want a lot of things, but I'll take what I can get."

Here goes nothing. "How about my mouth?"

Empath or not, Gabriel didn't see that coming, not if his gaping-fish expression is anything to go by. "Where did that come from?"

Ellis shrugs. "I suppose overthinking and porn-watching do interesting things to the brain. And seeing you suck me off might have contributed a little."

"Porn-watching?"

"For research."

"Ah." Propping himself up, Gabriel looks at him, his free hand tracing patterns over Ellis' chest. It's very distracting. "What did you learn?"

"That I have a micro dick." That makes Gabriel laugh. "And that gay—or bi men clearly don't need to breathe."

Gabriel makes a thoughtful sound. "Maybe lay off the porn and just go with the flow."

"Is that innuendo?"

"I mean, if the shoe fits..."

Ellis catches his wrist, forcing their eyes to meet. "I'd like to try. I have a very vague idea what to do, but I want to make you feel good."

Gabriel's breath comes out shaky. "Technique or skill don't matter to me. I'll feel good if you feel good. I'll only enjoy it if you do."

It's obvious from the way he phrases it that he worries Ellis might be forcing himself. Fondness fills the space between his ribs. He leans forwards to kiss the worried expression off Gabriel's face.

"For an empath, you can be exceptionally dense sometimes."

"Excuse you," Gabriel complains, but his eyes are glued to Ellis' lips.

"Come on. Can't you feel it?"

Ellis is practically vibrating with it, this need mixed with curiosity and self-doubt that begs him to slide between Gabriel's legs and show him how good he can be if given the chance. He's always been a quick study, especially when properly motivated. Wanting to give back as much as he's received would do it, but the promise of seeing Gabriel come apart through his actions? Sign him the hell up.

"I can," Gabriel admits. "I just couldn't tell who it's coming from. I'm kind of nonstop horny for you, if you haven't noticed."

Ellis' shoulders begin to shake, a giddy feeling spreading through his limbs. Only Gabriel could say something like that and look so serious.

In a rare surge of confidence, he turns them until Gabriel is on his back with Ellis hovering over him. After a second of hesitation, Ellis lowers himself so he can roll their hips together, Gabriel's cock sliding against his and pulling simultaneous groans out of them.

Zeke has the gall to look confused. "Me? Nothing. Just chatting with your boo."

"Leave my *boo* alone."

Rolling his eyes, Zeke gets up and disappears somewhere in the kitchen under Gabriel's watchful gaze.

Ellis is still cringing at being referred to as boo when Gabriel nods at him. "Come on, I'll make your coffee."

Ellis follows him to the coffee machine, watching him work. It's oddly calming, especially since Gabriel makes everything look effortless.

"Was he bothering you? Do I need to kick his ass?" Gabriel asks seriously.

Ellis chuckles. "I'm tempted to say yes just to see you do that."

Gabriel sticks his tongue out, pouring hot milk over the mixture and putting a lid on it. "Here."

"Thank you." He leans in for a kiss. "See you tomorrow."

Gabriel kisses him again. "Can't wait."

Ellis: Did you know that Virgo and Aries aren't compatible?

Gabriel: I'm gonna kill Zeke.

Ellis: The match is less than 10%.

Gabriel: Stay away from the horoscope, Ellis.

Ellis: Do you think I'm uptight and pedantic?

Gabriel: OMG. If you read any more of that shit, so help me.

Ellis: ...You do have a temper.

Gabriel: Ellis!

Chapter 20

Gabriel: I have a situation.

Ellis stares at the text, a feeling of dread making his stomach drop. He just saw Gabriel a few hours ago when he was picking up his coffee. What could've possibly gone wrong since?

Nothing's gone wrong. You're just overreacting.

Surely, if it was something serious, Gabriel would've called instead of texting.

Unless he's being considerate, not wanting to interrupt you at work.

Stomach tied into knots, Ellis quickly texts back.

Ellis: Are you okay?

He's halfway out of his chair, ready to jump in the car and make his way to the café, but his phone buzzes again.

Gabriel: Can I call?

He doesn't bother texting this time. Instead, he hits the call button, relieved when Gabriel picks up before the first ring trails off.

"I'll take that as a yes," Gabriel says. Ellis can hear the smile in his voice and he sags back into the chair, letting out a huge breath of relief.

"Jesus, you scared the crap out of me."

"What? Why?"

"Your ominous texts!"

"Ominous?"

"Yes!"

"Uh-huh."

"It's not funny. I thought something had happened to you."

"If something had happened, I wouldn't be able to text, would I?"

"Totally irrelevant."

"Uh-huh." Now Gabriel is definitely laughing at him, and Ellis grunts a complaint. "I'd apologize, but I'm enjoying this mother-henning side of you. You're too cute for your own good."

At least they're on the phone and Gabriel can't see his face, red from embarrassment and indignation. "I'm not cute."

"I beg to differ," Gabriel hums. "But I do have a situation. I have to cancel our date."

Ellis' shoulders droop. As glad as he is the situation is nothing serious, he's been looking forward to spending the weekend together. As a surprise, he's booked a ferry to Stradbroke Island for Sunday. The whale season is coming to an end, but with a bit of luck they'd be able to spot some. And dolphins. Apparently, Gabriel is obsessed with those. The weather is supposed to be good too, mostly overcast but warm with no rain. It's fine, though. They can always reschedule.

"Oh," is all he says. He's tempted to ask for the reason, but doesn't want to pry in case it's something personal.

Luckily, Gabriel explains without prompting.

"I talked to my mum yesterday. We call every week, to catch up and stuff." A pause. "I might have mentioned you."

"Okay?"

Ellis' heart gives a little jump, both pleased and nervous. He understands why Gabriel might feel weird about admitting he talks to his mum about his new, um, boyfriend, since the relationship is so fresh. And he must've noticed that Ellis has a bit of commitment phobia. But being talked about to one's parents isn't that big of a deal.

It's not like his mum has met Ellis and—

"She wants to meet you."

Ellis chokes on air, wheezing as he struggles for a breath.

"Hello? Ellis?"

"I'm here," he coughs, gripping the edge of the desk for support. "I...uh...okay? Yeah, that's fine," he lies.

"Tomorrow."

"What?"

"She's flying down from Cairns."

"What?"

"I did try to stop her, but..." Gabriel huffs. "She's like me, times ten."

"God help us all."

"Rude. But accurate. Look, I get that it's crazy soon, so if you don't feel up for it I'll just distract her by taking her around the Coast. She's a huge fan of bodyboarding."

Despite his previous shock, Ellis smiles. He can almost see it—Gabriel's personality, amplified and wrapped in the body of a fifty-something-year-old woman as she rides the waves and screams excitedly. Ellis already likes her just for raising a man like Gabriel.

He shakes off a pang of yearning in his chest.

"No, don't do that. She's your mum." Knowing he'll probably regret it, he says, "It's fine. Yeah, it's soon, but...I'd be happy to meet her."

Gabriel is quiet for a moment. "Really?"

"Really. I told you, I want to get to know the people in your life."

Gabriel snorts. "You'll change your mind after tomorrow."

"Thanks for the vote of confidence," Ellis says drily. "Your dad's not coming?"

"Nah. We don't really keep in contact."

That gives Ellis a pause. Gabriel doesn't sound particularly upset about the fact, but it makes Ellis wonder why it's never been talked about before. The only thing he knows is that Gabriel's dad is an empath too.

"Ah, okay. When does she land?"

"Around noon, I think. She'll take an Uber to the café, and then we'll go from there. I'll finish early. Zeke will handle it by himself once the lunch rush is over."

Suddenly possessed by an altruistic spirit, Ellis says, "I can pick her up if you want."

Gabriel's voice is very soft. "That's sweet of you, but you don't have to. She's a Gen X, but she can operate a smartphone."

"I know," he says with a chuckle. "But there's no reason to when I can just drive down."

"Okay, but only if you're sure," Gabriel checks again. "Thank you. It means a lot."

"It's nothing."

"It's a lot," Gabriel insists, then laughs. "I kind of wish you'd said you didn't want to meet."

"Why?"

"Because I have a possessive streak a mile long when it comes to you and I'm not quite ready to share you yet."

Ellis opens his mouth, but no sound comes out. He thought he's gotten used to Gabriel blurting out random stuff that makes him momentarily speechless, but it's as if Gabriel's been upping his game, coming up with more and more brain cell-popping statements each time.

Ellis forces a laugh, grateful Gabriel can't see his face. "I'm sure your mum is a beautiful woman, but I can control myself."

"Funny," Gabriel deadpans. "It's just... Fuck, a part of me wishes I could lock you up and keep you to myself."

Ellis can feel more brain cells popping and dying. Except the ones that operate the function of his nether regions. Those seem to be on top of their game. "Um..."

Gabriel lets out a groan that sounds both frustrated and aroused. "God, you're adorable. I'd give anything to take you home right now and have my way with you. Ellis?"

"Shit." Ellis scrambles to fish his phone out from under the desk, didn't he? About himself?"

Ellis nods. "He did."

"And you haven't known each other long."

"A few weeks." Has it only been that short of a time? So much has changed, it's insane.

"But you believed him?"

"It's hard to be skeptical when you experience what he can do first hand."

Carrie makes a sound of approval, but a reproachful look overtakes her features. "He struggled a lot as a child. The sensitivity, the empathy... Poor boy was so confused. Didn't know what was happening to him. I didn't do a good job preparing him."

Ellis' heart aches. It hurts to imagine Gabriel as anything but happy and confident. "You knew from the start, then?"

Something about her changes, an air of melancholy wrapping around her. "He takes after his daddy, after all."

"But his dad couldn't help?"

"Hard to be of help when you walk out of your kid's life."

The information takes Ellis by surprise. Even more surprising is that Carrie doesn't sound resentful, or angry. Just...sad.

"You haven't talked about this, have you?" Carrie takes a guess, probably because Ellis has gone quiet.

"Gabriel said they don't talk."

"That's a very simple way to put it. What happened is—"

"Carrie?" he intervenes gently. "I think it's better if he tells me. On his own terms, when he's ready."

She stares at him, long enough that Ellis starts to worry he fucked up by cutting her off so harshly when she wanted to share something personal with him. But then she smiles, looking almost proud, and says, "Gabby sure knows how to pick them. Damn, if I was twenty years younger..."

"Oh my god, Carrie!" Ellis cries, getting whiplash from how fast this woman can switch gears.

"Gosh, you're cute."

Ellis shakes his head, refusing to believe this is his life now. "Your family is nuts."

She laughs, patting his thigh again. "Sorry, sweetie. You're so easy to tease. But don't worry, you're safe. I don't get the 'I'm-into-MILFs' vibe from you."

"Milfs?"

She looks at him, covering her mouth with her palm. "Oh dear."

It's so hard to keep up with new slang these days. Curious, Ellis types a quick text to Gabriel.

Ellis: What's a milf?

Gabriel: OMG. Get your ass over here right now!!!

Gabriel: You're not to be alone with my mum ever again!!!

He frowns. Is it something bad? He'll have to google it later.

Gabriel is standing in the middle of the café, arms crossed and tapping his foot like an angry parent. Carrie, bless her heart, doesn't take note of any of that and spreads her arms to envelope him in a bear hug.

"My boy!"

Gabriel's facade cracks a little. He covers it up by rolling his eyes and returning the hug like it's a huge imposition.

"What did we talk about, Mum?"

"Your hot boyfriend?"

"Mum!"

"You did not do him justice."

"When did you say you're flying back?"

"When did it become clear that you'd inherited it?"

"I was maybe a year and a half when my parents took me to the zoo. There was a kid that had fallen and hurt his knee. Started crying. And I started crying with him."

"It could've been a coincidence. People cry when they see other people cry."

"True. But their eyes usually don't start glowing."

"Oh." He forgot about that little detail.

"Long story short, Dad freaked the hell out. Spiraled into depression. He was convinced my life would be hell, like his was. Obviously, he was happy with Mum, but you can't expect someone to sort out your issues. Not that Mum didn't try. She's a nurse—fixing people is kind of her calling."

Ellis doesn't say that Gabriel managed to heal parts of him that had festered for decades. No, he can't fix Ellis, nothing probably can, but he's done more for him than he'll ever realize.

"So he left? Just like that?" A swell of rage rises inside Ellis. Maybe he's projecting his own shit, but the idea of Gabriel being abandoned by his dad as a defenseless child makes him see red and awakens his protective instincts.

"No. For months, he tried to make it work. When it became obvious he couldn't, he made sure we were taken care of. Left us enough money from his inheritance so we wouldn't struggle." Their gazes lock, and Ellis is stunned to find no trace of resentment in Gabriel's. "I know he didn't want to go, but he couldn't take care of me. He was convinced he'd ruin my life."

Ellis frowns. He doesn't really get how Gabriel can be so calm, so collected when talking about this. Sure, almost three decades have passed, but Ellis is proof that time does not heal everything.

"Mum never moved on," Gabriel carries on. "She still loves him, I can feel it. She even kept his name. Gave it to me too."

"Cleaver?"

Gabriel nods. "The family name." He chuckles. "When I was younger, I swore to change it once I turned 18."

"But you didn't."

"I've changed a lot over the years."

"So your mum says." It's still hard to picture Gabriel being any different. "Have they talked since?"

"No. Mum promised she wouldn't look for him, it would make everything harder. Dad never told anyone where he's going, not even his brother."

Sounds like a load of bullshit.

"So none of you know where he is?"

Gabriel bites his lip. "I do."

"You do? How?" Ellis demands, propping himself up on his elbow.

"I have my ways," Gabriel says vaguely. He laughs at Ellis' unimpressed expression. "Kieran."

"Dawson's friend?"

"I didn't want anyone close to me to know I was looking for him, so I couldn't ask Ash, nor Zeke. And I'm not very tech-savvy. My people-searching skills start and end with Facebook, which, shockingly, Dad doesn't have."

"Where did you find him?"

"Arrowtown."

"New Zealand?" Seems like Australia wasn't a big enough country to hide in.

"It's his home country."

Ellis blinks. "Wait a second, you're half-Kiwi?"

Gabriel pouts. "Don't discriminate."

"Oh no, this is a big deal. I'm not sure we can date anymore."

"Hilarious." Gabriel's features soften. "Arrowtown suits him. The place has, like, 3000 people. If I wasn't an idiot, I'd have been able to find him too. He owns a small business, makes furniture and stuff. He worked as a carpenter when he was still with Mum. It should've been obvious." Laughing, he says, "He even has a website. With his name and everything."

"Did you contact him?"

"Kinda."

"Kinda?"

Gabriel pulls on a loose thread on his shirt and mumbles, so low Ellis can barely make it out, "I kinda turned up on his doorstep."

"What?" Why is he surprised? Of course Gabriel would choose getting on a plane and flying over to some bumfuck town in New Zealand instead picking up the phone.

"I had something to say that I didn't want to do over the phone."

Okay. Fair enough. "What did you say?"

Gabriel's eyes become glassy. "That I forgive him."

"You forgive him," Ellis echoes, voice dripping with skepticism. He doesn't mean to be an asshole, he just doesn't understand how Gabriel could've found forgiveness without ever talking to his dad in the first place

To his relief, Gabriel doesn't look upset by Ellis' reaction.

"Contrary to the popular belief, I don't think forgiveness is for the person you're forgiving," he begins to explain. "It's for you. It's you, cutting yourself free from whatever's been keeping you stuck in the past. And you can't just decide to forgive. It needs to happen on its own, when you're ready."

"If it's for you, why did you feel like you needed to tell him?"

"From what Mum told me, I knew it broke his heart to leave. That he probably spent all these years drowning in self-hate and guilt. And I thought, if he's anything like me, hearing the words from me might finally give him peace."

"Did it?"

"I think so, yes," he says quietly. He strokes Ellis' fingers and forearm, as if he needs the contact to ground himself while getting swept up in the memories. "He was nice. Nothing like I imagined."

"Did you talk?"

"Not much. He did invite me in, though. Made tea." Ellis smiles, knowing Gabriel never drinks tea unless it's peppermint and he's sick. "He asked about me a little. I told him about the café and how I use my gift to help people. He seemed pretty relieved that I'm doing okay."

"That's good." Not that it means much. The guy still left his kid behind.

"I thought of leaving him my number if he ever wanted to get in touch."

"But you didn't," Ellis takes a guess.

"I didn't want to put that pressure on him. And frankly, I had no idea how to include him in my life if he was up to it anyway."

"Yeah, I get that." He studies Gabriel's face, getting a feeling there's more. "What is it?"

Gabriel squirms. "Since I visited him, I've been getting cards on my birthday."

"You think..."

"Yeah. They have a stamp from New Zealand, and the card never says anything other than *Happy Birthday*, handwritten. No signature either. And they always arrive at the café—which I told him about." He gives a watery laugh. "It's so stupid, but I always look forward to them."

Ellis wraps an arm around his waist, stroking his lower back. "It's not stupid."

Gabriel looks up at him, his gaze vulnerable. "It's not?"

"No." He kisses Gabriel's forehead. "It's not."

Gabriel makes a soft sound, like a whimper but not quite, and cranes his neck so he can catch Ellis' lips. The kiss is innocent, a plea for comfort, but there's a need behind it that makes Ellis' blood run hot, despite the topic of conversation being the furthest thing from arousing.

The kiss ends as quickly as it started, leaving him a little cold, but not for long. Gabriel snuggles into him, hiking his leg over Ellis' hip. Ellis holds him tight, continues caressing his back.

"Are you okay?" Gabriel doesn't feel upset, but there's something going on with him that makes Ellis a bit panicked.

"Yeah. Yeah, I'm good." It's a relief when Gabriel lifts his head, and his cheeks are dry. He's even smiling again. "It's just...you're the first person I've told about this. I didn't realize how good it would feel."

Ellis secretly preens. He's normally not the go-to person when someone needs comfort, or to get stuff off their chest. "I'm glad."

"Sometimes I still can't believe how much has changed."

"In what way?"

"For the longest time, I blamed him. My dad, I mean," he confesses like it's something shameful. "Blamed him for everything. For Mum never finding happiness with another person, for feeling so terribly alone most of my life. For not being there when I needed him, when my empathy felt like an unbearable burden, or when I was bullied for being too sensitive.

"And then one day I realized; this is how he felt too, probably still feels. Like the world is crashing down around you and you can't escape it. Like it will always be like this and you'll never find reprieve, because nobody will ever understand. At some point I realized; if I were in his shoes, I'd have done the same thing."

"I don't think you would," Ellis disagrees. He can't really imagine Gabriel like that.

"Not now," Gabriel concedes. "I'm a different person now. But I still don't want kids." He looks at Ellis, unsure and worried.

"You don't?" Gabriel always struck him as the type who'd want a whole litter. Hearing the opposite is, frankly, a huge relief.

Even though it feels too soon to have this conversation, Ellis is glad it's been brought up. His previous relationships, if they can even be called that, never felt serious enough to warrant a discussion about kids. But now, for the first time in his life, he sees a future with somebody.

"I love what I can do with this ability, but I never want anyone else to go through what I did." Gabriel sighs. "Not wanting kids is the reason my last girlfriend broke up with me."

Words of comfort on the tip of his tongue, Ellis stills. "Wait. Girlfriend?"

Gabriel gives him a curious look. "Yes?"

"Oh. I thought... I just kind of assumed you're gay."

Gabriel lets out a snort. "I can't believe it never came up. "

"I guess we were too busy talking about other things. Like my suppressed sexuality and your mojo."

"That would definitely explain it, yes," Gabriel agrees, eyes sparkling.

"I kinda like it. That we're both bi." It sounds stupid and makes no sense, but the thought that Gabriel could choose to be with a woman but ended up choosing Ellis makes him preen.

"Actually, I relate more to pansexuals."

Ellis blinks at him. "Uh...I'm sorry, I don't know that one." Idiot. He could at least make an effort to educate himself on the queer community since he belongs to it.

Gabriel strokes his arms, his smile infinitely patient. "That's okay. I'm happy to enlighten you." His lips purse contemplatively. "The easiest way to put it would be: when I'm attracted to someone, I'm attracted to them as a person. I don't really, well, *notice* what gender they are. Does that make sense?"

Instead of instantly agreeing, Ellis takes a few moments to really ponder the concept until something in his brain clicks. "Yeah, it does, actually." He licks his lips. "Well, I'm definitely bisexual."

Gabriel laughs. "Okay."

"Going back to the original topic—there are no kids in my future either. As you already know, I had my balls snipped a long time ago."

Gabriel visibly relaxes. "Can I ask why you did it?"

"Because I refused to take the risk of becoming a shitty parent like my dad." And he would be shitty. No need to transfer his mummy and daddy issues onto an innocent human being. He's relieved when Gabriel doesn't try to contradict him, probably understanding where Ellis is coming from. "Also, kids are annoying."

Gabriel laughs. "I like them. Just don't want to raise them."

"Does Ash want kids? I know you're not brothers, but you could be the favorite uncle who spoils his nephews and nieces rotten."

"God, I hope not," Gabriel breathes, his expression terrified. "Poor children." He heaves a sigh. "I'm probably not being fair to him. As much of a dick as he can be, I'll always be grateful to him.

"What did he do?"

"After finishing high school, I was lost. Had no idea what to do with myself, lived with my mum... You can imagine. Ash already lived here and I thought: maybe I can do what he did. Take off, start anew somewhere else. So I did. Moved in with him."

"I bet you loved that," Ellis says, not without sarcasm.

"Sure, if you like to listen to a different guy being fucked every other night." Gabriel's face twists with disgust. "As insufferable as he is, Ash pretty much saved my life. He's not like me, but he understands what it's like to be different. That was most important." He lets out a groan. "I hate to admit it, but he's a really good therapist."

"I'm glad you found some closure," Ellis tells him, still in awe of how strong and amazing of a person Gabriel is.

"Me too. But...I wish I could tell Mum. About Dad."

"Why don't you? Would she be mad that you looked him up?"

"It's complicated. Despite the promise, I think if she knew where he is, she'd want to see him."

"And you don't want that?"

"I'm...worried. For her, for him. When I went to see him, I didn't go with the intention of reviving the past, or making up for the lost time or whatever. But Mum would. She still loves him, Ellis." His eyes are pleading. "What would you do?"

"Nuh-uh. I'm the last person you should ask."

"That's not true," Gabriel disagrees. "We have a lot in common."

"I'm not like you," Ellis says, tasting bitterness in the words. "I'm not sure I'll ever find a way to forgive my mum for leaving. There's no closure for me."

"Your dad never talked about her? About what happened?"

"Not much. When he did, it was always in a way that made her look like the villain in the story. But seeing as my dad was a narcissist through and through, I soon learned I had to take everything he said with a grain of salt. A whole bag of salt, really."

"I'm sorry." Gabriel's hold on him tightens. He snuggles closer until their noses touch. "I wish there was something I could do. A way to give you peace."

God. Gabriel really has no idea. "You do. When I'm with you, it's the most peaceful I've ever felt." He takes Gabriel's hand, placing a kiss on his knuckles. "You're my solace."

It takes immense effort to defy his natural response to run and hide, to not look away when Gabriel's eyes bore into his, as if searching for the truth. He doesn't have to look deep; Ellis feels exposed on a visceral level, cracked open at the place he's spent all those years guarding, never letting anyone see.

Between one second and the next, Ellis finds himself on his back, blinking up at Gabriel's lovely face. He's looked at that face a million times, and each time he discovers something new, another thing to love. Like the tiny scar on his upper lip, which Ellis is definitely going to ask about later. For now, he just wants to kiss it.

He doesn't need to lift a finger. Gabriel's soft mouth descends on him, the kiss rougher and hungrier than Ellis would've done, but no less mind-blowing. A staggered moan reverberates between them when Gabriel's body covers his, his hard cock pressing against Ellis' stiffening one.

Gabriel peels his lips away to rasp out, "Ellis?"

"Yeah?"

A hand on his chest pushes him down when he tries to catch Gabriel's mouth again. He groans in frustration. What is Gabriel thinking, riling him up like that and then just—

"Will you fuck me?"

Ellis' brain short-circuits, losing its ability to form a semi-coherent thought. His visual imagination, on the other hand, lets loose. Unbidden images of Gabriel—of being inside him, connected on such a deep level—flood his mind. His body responds accordingly, making him feel feverish with how quickly it heats up, his mouth going dry when he tries to piece words together.

He goes to nod, when a very solid, alarming thought strikes him. "Your mum's next door."

Gabriel rolls his eyes. "Listen."

Not sure what he's supposed to be listening for, Ellis strains his ears. The muted sound of snoring reaches him.

"It's still weird."

"You don't seem to mind." Gabriel says smugly, rolling their hips together.

Ellis tries to glare at him, but his eyes roll back. "It's your fault," he grunts.

Gabriel's grin is proud. "I take full responsibility." Then the little shit does it again, bracing himself on Ellis' chest as he grinds against him.

"Shit," Ellis hisses, hands flying to Gabriel's hips to halt his movements.

It only makes Gabriel smile wider, eyes darkening with desire. "So? What do you say?"

This isn't fair. Gabriel knows full well Ellis is terrible at saying no to him—and that's on a good day. What is he supposed to do when Gabriel is pinning him down and looking at him like he wants to have him for dinner?

"You're very manipulative," Ellis says unhappily.

Gabriel bites his lip, as if that could somehow cover up the shit-eating grin trying to break free. "Is that a yes?"

Ellis scowls. "...Yes."

Then Gabriel is on him again, plundering his mouth. His body on top of Ellis is a comfortable weight, making him feel warm and safe and wanted. Not that feeling wanted is ever a problem with Gabriel. He always looks at Ellis like he's a present under the Christmas tree that he can't wait to unwrap.

Between needy kisses and wandering, impatient hands, the few clothes they're wearing disappear one by one, until it's just Gabriel's hot, sweat-slicked skin against his.

A large, warm hand wraps around Ellis' cock, giving it a firm stroke.

"I really want to feel your dick inside me."

"Jesus, Gabe," Ellis moans, thrusting into his hand.

Gabriel makes a pleased sound, starting to kiss Ellis' neck. "I like it when I get you to call me Gabe."

"I should call you menace," Ellis says, turning his head for more access, more kisses. He lets his eyes drift shut, just enjoying the sensation.

"Apt," Gabriel agrees. "Do you have lube and condoms?"

Ellis makes a vague gesture towards the nightstand.

"Sweet."

A gust of cold air washes over Ellis when Gabriel moves away to get the lube.

"Hmm, an unopened box. Did you want to be prepared?" Gabriel teases, examining the box of condoms Jordan has left behind.

"It's a long story."

Ellis found it when he came back from dropping Jordan off at the airport. His first instinct was to chuck it, but he couldn't bring himself to do it. He probably owes his friend a thanks.

There's the sound of a cap being flicked open, forcing Ellis to open his eyes.

The first thing he sees is Gabriel slicking his fingers, grinning seductively when he notices him looking. "Do you want to watch?"

Ellis can only nod. And when Gabriel reaches behind himself, rubbing the lube between his cheeks, it becomes a trial to even remember to breathe.

Then Gabriel does something that makes his body jolt, two vertical lines appearing between his brows. "Damn, it's really been a while," he says with a chuckle.

Instantly, alarm bells go off in Ellis' head. "Are you sure you want to do this? I'm not...you know..." He pointedly glances at his cock, standing tall and proud, inches away from Gabriel's.

Gabriel gives a hearty laugh. "I know, you're a big boy. Don't worry, I like the burn."

Christ on a cracker. "O-okay."

The moments that follow are one of the, well, *hardest* of Ellis' life. Because Gabriel is stunning when he's wearing a dirty apron and serving coffee. Breathtaking when he's seconds away from tipping over the edge, his face flushed and contorted in pleasure. But like this?

Pinning Ellis in place, hips rocking as he rides his fingers so he can get ready to take Ellis' cock, a look of complete bliss on his face as he gazes down at him...

He's a fucking vision. The stuff that dreams are made of.

Needing to touch, and needing to make sure it's real and not a hallucination, Ellis croaks out, "Can I—Can I try?"

A guttural groan rises from Gabriel's chest. "Fuck, yes." Withdrawing his fingers, he grabs the bottle of lube and squeezes a generous amount into Ellis' hand. He guides it between his cheeks, drawing a sharp breath from both of them. "Start with two," he instructs.

Swallowing hard, Ellis brings his trembling fingers to Gabriel's hole, just circling it at first. Gabriel's thighs clench, his cock twitching, pushing out a drop of precome.

"Jesus," Ellis chokes out, feeling a sudden need to taste it. He pulls his hand back, much to Gabriel's chagrin, and surges up to give him an apologetic kiss. Using it as a distraction, he smoothly flips them over so he can be on top.

Or attempts to.

"Fuck!" he gasps as a sharp pain pierces through his lower back.

Gabriel pushes up on his elbows, eyebrows pulled together. "What happened?"

"I think I threw out my back." This used to be his best move.

Gabriel's expression is stuck somewhere between sympathetic and entertained. "Yeah, sorry. I'm not exactly delicate."

"No shit." After a few controlled breaths, he tries to move, relieved to find his back is actually fine and he's just a big drama queen. "Okay. All good. Now, where were we?"

"You were about to finger me until I begged for your cock."

"Right. That." When did his voice get so squeaky? Jesus.

Enjoying Ellis' discomfort too much, Gabriel spreads his legs wide and lets his arms flop down by his head. His left eyebrow arches expectantly. "Well?"

"Impatient," Ellis chides, slotting himself into the inviting space

Gabriel has created for him.

"Nope. Horny."

"Yeah, yeah." Finding his fingers inconveniently dry, Ellis lubes them up again, waiting a few seconds to let it warm up.

"Elliiis," Gabriel whines, his bottom lip sticking out in a pout.

"Not impatient, huh?" He leans forward and takes Gabriel's cock into his mouth at the same time two of his fingers push inside.

"Shit!" Gabriel's back arches off the mattress, one of his hands shooting down and latching onto Ellis' bicep. "Fuck. Yeah, just like that."

Ellis barely registers the words, his ears filled with white noise. All of his senses are focused on the tight, soft heat enveloping his fingers and Gabriel's unique, sweet taste on his tongue. Whenever he withdraws his fingers, Gabriel's body tries to pull him back in, his blunt fingernails leaving half-moon shaped marks in his skin. Gabriel's head is thrown back, mouth slack and trying to form words Ellis can't hear, though he thinks he can read some of them. Words like *so good* and *more* and *please.*

It's an addictive feeling, being needed—wanted—so desperately.

There's a frantic tapping on his shoulder, trying to get his attention. Lightheaded and out of breath, he pulls off Gabriel's cock but doesn't remove his fingers. He doesn't even remember adding a third one.

"What?" God, he sounds like...well, like he was just wrecking his throat on a dick.

Gabriel, of course, notices, grinning like a Cheshire cat. "What? I need a break. You're way too good at that for a gay virgin."

Hello, praise kink. "Bisexual virgin. And I learn fast."

"Lucky me." He makes grabby hands. It's unfairly adorable. "Come here. I wanted to ride you, but I'm wiped. Sooo out of shape. You'll have to do the hard work."

"How optimistic to assume I'm in better shape after you've been feeding me all those cinnamon rolls."

Pulling his fingers out, he stretches himself over Gabriel, indulging in a slow make-out session. This is yet another first for him. He's had a lot of those lately, but not all of them have to do with being with a man. Having someone who understands him has nothing to do with Gabriel being a man. Being able to be completely himself around another person has nothing to do with Gabriel being a man. Having someone supporting him and listening to him has nothing to do with Gabriel being a man.

Pausing in the middle of sex just to kiss and touch each other, just to feel each other instead of barreling towards the finish line so it can finally be over has nothing to do with Gabriel being a man.

It has everything to do with Ellis finally realizing how he's wasted so many years spending his energy on people who didn't give two shits about him.

"Hey." Gabriel's palms frame his face, coaxing him to look up. "Where did you go?"

"Nowhere." He ducks his chin to brush their lips together. "I'm right where I want to be."

"Good." Gabriel smiles wide and catches his mouth in a short, deep kiss. "Now if you could get where *I* want you to be, that would be great."

Ellis laughs so hard his whole body shakes with it, not doing any favors to his erection that has started wilting while he was busy whining about the wasted years of his life. Thankfully, it only takes one filthy kiss from Gabriel, one look at his wantonly spread legs, and the problem is sorted.

Putting on a condom and slicking his cock with an over-generous amount of lube, Ellis lines up, his gaze locked with Gabriel's as he slowly pushes inside. It's not as slow as he'd like, because Gabriel keeps urging him on with hands on his buttocks, pulling him forward.

"Fuck," Ellis breathes when he's bottomed out. A bead of sweat slides down his temple, tickling a little. Gabriel feels... He doesn't have words for it. Only that he never wants this to end.

His heart plummets when he notices Gabriel's eyes are squeezed shut, his features filled with tension. "Are you—are you okay?" What makes it confusing is that he can't feel anything but warmth and happiness coming from Gabriel.

Finally, Gabriel's eyes open, swirling with gold that doesn't seem to fade. A small, beautiful smile blooms on his lips. "I'm perfect." He moves his hands to Ellis' back, pulling him down on top of him like he can't bear any distance between them. "You are perfect."

"Gabe," Ellis says shakily.

"Perfect," Gabriel insists. He repeats it as he kisses Ellis, as if trying to brand his lips with it. Then his lips move to form a new shape, new words. Ellis feels them in his soul before they're spoken, feels the air around them saturate with their power. "I love you."

Despite anticipating them, he's not ready when the words finally land, reshaping his whole reality. It shouldn't be a big deal. People say them all the time, not even meaning them.

He didn't realize it would feel like this when someone said them to him.

He reaches inside himself, searching for the words of reciprocation he knows are there, have been for a while now, just waiting to be released. Something doesn't let him, something rigid and cold, like a metal door, guarding the deepest parts of him.

His frustration must show on his face because Gabriel gives him an infinitely patient smile, then proceeds to hook his legs around Ellis' hips and chase his demons away with a kiss.

"Ellis?"

"Y-yeah?"

"You gonna give me an epic orgasm or what?"

Ellis stills, and then he laughs, because it's the only thing he can do. That, and give Gabriel what he wants. Hell, he'll give him anything he asks for.

"Yes, sir."

Gabriel sighs, like he's disappointed. "We've talked about this, Ellis. Do not poke my hibernating kinks unless you're ready to bear the consequences."

As far as threats go... "Another time, then."

"Another time," Gabriel agrees, wrapping his arms around Ellis and holding on tight.

For what could be minutes or hours, the world stops for Ellis, him and Gabriel the only two things in existence. He's not aware of anything but the way Gabriel clings to him, the way his hot breath caresses Ellis's skin as he pants into his neck, the wrecked sob-like moan he makes each time Ellis gets the angle just right.

It's all too soon when Gabriel starts chanting his name, his breath becoming labored and legs beginning to quake. Ellis is right there with him, because in this moment he can't even fathom his emotions being separate from Gabriel's, the two so closely intertwined it's impossible to tell them apart.

Needing to see Gabriel as they crash the wave together, Ellis seeks out his face, contorted in pleasure. His mouth is slack and red from their kisses, his eyes closed. They fly open when the tension snaps, glowing gold as his cock pulses and spills between them. His flabbergasted expression is the last thing Ellis sees before his orgasm slams into him, punching a cry out of him.

His arms give up, causing him to slump against Gabriel in a boneless heap.

"I'm sorry. Did I hurt you?"

Gabriel shakes his head, but is still wearing that dumbstruck expression.

"What's wrong?"

Gabriel's throat bobs. "Your eyes glowed gold."

"What?"

"Your eyes. When I looked at you just now, they were glowing."

Holy shit. "How's that possible?"

Gabriel chokes out a laugh. "Beats me. It's never happened before."

Well, that's helpful. "What about now?"

"They're blue again."

Ellis is oddly disappointed. "Oh."

"I think," Gabriel starts, caressing Ellis' sides. "I think the connection was just that strong. Our energies might've blended together."

"Oh." Seriously. Words. *Now.* "That's...pretty amazing. Right?"

"No. It's really fucking amazing," Gabriel corrects, grinning ear to ear.

Ellis grins back. "You're right."

"Shit. I can't feel my legs," Gabriel says, sounding happy about it.

"I can't feel my brain."

"Can you ever feel your brain?"

"I never thought about that."

They laugh, meeting each other halfway for a lazy, perfect kiss in a perfect moment.

The next moment is not perfect. The next moment is the stuff of nightmares coming to life.

"That was beautiful, boys," comes Carrie's voice from the other side of the wall.

For a long time, they just stare at each other, eyes like saucers and faces pale. Ellis can feel a laugh starting to vibrate in Gabriel's chest, his hands coming up to cover his mouth.

Ellis burrows his face in a pillow and screams.

Chapter 22

"ELLIS, COME ON. IT'S not a big deal," Gabe tells him for the gazillionth time. He's spent the better part of the morning convincing Ellis to leave the bedroom with no luck.

"I can never look your mother in the face ever again," Ellis whines, for the gazillionth time. The covers are pulled up to his chest, arms folded on his drawn up knees, hiding his flushed face.

If Gabe wasn't so annoyed, he'd find it adorable. Not annoyed at Ellis, but at his mum. Sure, he's not without guilt—it was his idea to have sex with his mother next door (who he assumed was fast asleep!), but there was no need for her to announce she was awake and had heard the whole thing. She totally did that on purpose!

Gabe will make her pay. After the best sex of his life with the man he's head over heels for, and being so attuned to each other that his energy sneaked over to mingle with Ellis', he wanted to bask in the afterglow and cuddle. Instead, he spent the night taming Ellis' anxiety and talking him out of moving to Siberia.

"Ellis, it's fiiine. She's caught me doing much worse." Well, she caught him jerking off, but it was just once (Gabe learned to lock the door after that), but Ellis doesn't need to know that.

"This is so embarrassing," Ellis mumbles into his arms, barely decipherable.

"Would it help if you imagined her naked?"

"Why on earth would I imagine your mother naked?!" Ellis shrieks.

"Well, that's what they tell you to do if you're nervous giving a presentation in front of a lot of people."

"I'm not giving a presentation!"

"The principle is the same."

"It's really not."

"Oh my god." He throws his hands up. "Just come out, will you? We'll miss the ferry." Maybe that wouldn't be such a bad thing. He's not sure how Ellis will handle spending the whole day with Mum.

Nope. They're going. Gabe wants to see dolphins and whales, and he won't let his twisted mother and secretly emotionally sensitive boyfriend ruin that.

Finally, fucking finally, Ellis drags himself out of bed, starting to put on his clothes. Gabe uses the time to text his mum.

Gabe: Not a word about you-know-what or you won't be invited to the wedding.

Mum: OMG THERE'S GONNA BE A WEDDING?!?!?!

Gabe: There could be, but you won't be there if you don't behave.

Mum: I'll behave, I promise!

Mum: What's the date?

Gabe pockets his phone, sighing. His life is hard.

True to her word, Mum keeps her big mouth shut, though Gabe can tell it's taking all her willpower. Whenever he feels her resolve cracking, he shoots her a warning glare. It works like a charm, exhausting as it is. Parents really do become children at some point in life.

When he's not keeping an eye on his unpredictable mother, he focuses on sending soothing energy in Ellis' direction. His boyfriend has been tense all the way to the island. It's not until they've disembarked and taken a short drive to Main Beach that he finally starts to relax.

Gabe hops out of the car, short of vibrating with excitement. "Is this where the dolphins are?"

Ellis seems amused by the enthusiasm. "We might spot some, but that's not why I took us here."

"Oh."

"Don't worry, we'll go see them before we have to head back. There's a better chance to spot them in the late afternoon, or at sunset. Whales too."

"Ah, okay! Good plan." Gabe looks at the vast expanse of the beach. "Are we going to swim?" The water is insanely blue, the kind that you see in Instagram pics after they've been put through a filter or photoshopped, and the waves are big enough to make him want to both jump in and steer clear.

"You can swim. Or..." Ellis opens the trunk and pulls out a pair of bodyboards.

Gabe's mum squeals when Ellis offers her one.

"Gabriel told me you like bodyboarding."

"I love it!" Squealing again, she grabs the board, hugging it to her chest like it's a cute animal. "Gosh, I haven't done this in a while. Cairns is shit when it comes to beaches."

"I know. Well, go crazy."

Mum takes it literally, running toward the waves without another word.

Gabe rolls his eyes, pretending his heart isn't melting like chocolate fondue. He already knew Ellis is thoughtful and caring, but this? Why does the man have to be so damn perfect? He's going to give Gabe a complex.

"I didn't know you owned bodyboards."

"I didn't. I picked them up yesterday, when you went to see Ash."

So. Damn. Perfect.

"Where's yours?" Gabe questions when Ellis hands him the other board.

"Yeah, no. I don't do that." He shakes his head resolutely.

"Have you tried it?"

"I've tried surfing."

Gabe laughs. "This is different. Better. More fun! You can just do whatever."

"I think I'll pass."

Gabe tries not to sulk. "What will you do?"

Ellis waves towards the beach. "Lie back and relax. Get a bit of color. Dip in if I get too hot."

"Hmm." Gabe lowers the board to the ground to free his hands and lock them behind Ellis' neck. "You might need to stay in the water forever, then."

It takes a minute for Ellis to get it, his cheeks turning pink. "You're impossible."

"Thank you."

Ellis huffs. "Don't you have waves to ride?"

Gabe presses himself closer to Ellis, letting their hips slot together. "I'd rather ride something else."

The pretty pink blush turns tomato red. Ellis scowls, pushing Gabe away. "Nope. Nuh-uh. Your horny ass already got us in trouble once. I'm scarred for life."

"I thought you liked my horny ass."

"Gabe!"

"Waves. Right. Going." He picks up the board and takes off, laughing at the image of Ellis glaring after him. Today's going to be fun!

Today *is* fun. Just not for Ellis.

After a lot of convincing, which turns to blackmailing when Ellis remains a stubborn mule, Gabe gets his way and watches Ellis ride his first wave, looking like he'd like to do literally anything else. He rides a second one, then a third. By the time he's on his tenth wave, he seems to be enjoying himself, even laughing when a particularly powerful wave makes him roll over and dive under.

Gabe secretly takes pictures and sends them to Dawson. What Ellis doesn't know can't hurt him, and can't make him mad at Gabe.

Ellis catches another wave, letting out a sudden cry of pain.

Gabe drops the phone, running towards him.

"Are you okay? What happened."

Ellis drags himself to the sand, standing up with a hiss. He cranes his neck to get a look at his left calf. "I think I got stung."

"Oh, shit." Gabe kneels to thoroughly inspect the sting. Relief floods him when he finds the affected area to be about half an inch in diameter. "Okay, it's not too bad. How much does it hurt?"

Ellis makes a face. "Just stings a little. It hurt like a bitch at first."

Gabe presses an apologetic kiss to Ellis' knee, earning a scandalized "Gabriel!"

He laughs. "Come on. The lifeguards will have something to soothe the sting."

"It's fine. I'll survive."

"The lifeguards, or I'll pee on it."

By now, Gabe is starting to worry Ellis' face is going to stay permanently red. Without a word, he heads to the lifeguards, Gabe following behind with a victorious grin.

When they come back to their towels, Ellis smelling faintly of vinegar, Gabe's mum is already waiting for them.

"Hey, where did you go off to?"

"Ellis got stung."

"Oh no." She jumps to her feet with more grace than a fifty-six-year-old woman should, wrapping Ellis in a hug. "Are you okay, sweetie?"

"I'm fine," Ellis says, clearly embarrassed. "They say there are mostly bluebottles here, so it's no big deal."

"That's good. Does it still hurt?"

"Not really. They put vinegar on it."

"Good, good. But you know, in case of an emergency, you can also pee on it."

Gabe cackles.

Ellis does not.

The rest of the day passes without Ellis dipping a single toe into the water.

Gabe doesn't blame him.

They have lunch at a cute local café serving out-of-this-world buddha bowls, though the coffee itself is subpar. Gabe starts to explain the importance of extraction times, freshness of the beans, and milk temperature. The amused smile Mum and Ellis share doesn't go unnoticed, but Gabe ignores them.

"It tastes good to me," Ellis says with a straight face, taking a sip of the underwhelming coffee.

Gabe doesn't talk to him for twenty minutes after that.

After visiting a couple of waterfalls and a few more beaches—Ellis has stubbornly stayed out of the water—they finally make their way to the highly anticipated dolphin sighting spot. Since it's the weekend,

Point Lookout is swarming with people, mainly families with kids. They still manage to spot a whole pod of dolphins close to the cliff.

"Oh my god! Looklooklook!" Gabe tugs on Ellis' arm, even though they're looking in the same direction.

Ellis chuckles, the sound warm and affectionate. "I can see them."

Gabe doesn't bother taking pictures, wanting to enjoy the moment and not miss anything. Plus, the dolphins are too far to take a proper picture.

They stay there for a while, making one last stop at Amity Point where Ellis thinks they might see some more. They arrive just in time to see two dolphins circling the pier. Gabe is a little disappointed they're not allowed to feed them, before remembering they didn't bring any food anyway.

The ferry takes them back to the mainland around eight, so by the time Ellis parks in his building, they're all bone tired and falling asleep on their feet. Especially Ellis, who looks like he's about to keel over. Poor guy is probably not used to this level of socializing and physical activity—not to mention the vicious bluebottle attack.

"I'm going to sleep like a baby," Gabe mumbles, burrowing himself under the covers.

Ellis answers with an agreeable 'Hmnpf' his eyes already shut.

Smiling, Gabe snuggles closer, pressing a kiss to Ellis' nose. It feels very warm. "Thank you for today. It was beyond amazing."

Ellis' eyelids slowly flutter open. "I'm glad."

"You had fun too, right?"

"I did," Ellis promises. "But I might need to recuperate for a few days. Or months."

Gabe stifles a laugh. "Well, you'll get some reprieve tomorrow. In less than fifteen hours, Mum will be on her sweet way home."

Ellis strokes his arm. "Are you going to miss her?"

"Nah."

"Gabriel."

"Okay, fine, maybe a tiny bit," he admits begrudgingly, earning a kiss to his forehead.

"Gabriel?"

"Yeah?"

"Am I sunburned? My face feels really tight."

Gabe flicks on the light, squinting before his vision adjusts. "Huh. You're a little flushed, but that should settle down by morning."

"You sure?"

"Oh yeah. It will be fine."

"I look like a lobster." Ellis stands in front of the mirror, studying his sore face. At least it doesn't look as bad as his shoulders, which seem to have literally taken the burn.

"It's not that bad," Gabe lies, torn between sympathy and wanting to laugh his ass off.

In the mirror, Ellis gives him a look that speaks volumes, causing him to burst out laughing.

"I'm sorry, I'm sorry." He steps behind Ellis to wrap his arms around him. "I know it must hurt. We'll grab you some aloe on our way from the airport."

Ellis lets out a dissatisfied grunt, but relaxes when Gabe gently rubs his favorite lotion with manuka honey into the burned skin.

They head for breakfast before driving Gabe's mum to the airport, arriving unnecessarily early because Ellis likes to have a head start 'just in case'.

"This was so lovely. Thank you, Ellis," Mum says, hugging him goodbye. Gabe notices him hiding a wince as Mum squeezes his sensitive shoulders a tad too hard.

"My pleasure," Ellis says, and Gabe can tell he's sincere. "Take care of yourself, Carrie."

"Same to you." She bear-hugs Gabe, kissing his cheeks despite his protests. "Okay, boys, I have to fly." She waves at them, heading for the security check. "See you in a few weeks."

They both pause mid-wave, blurting out a simultaneous "What?"

"It's almost Christmas! Don't tell me you forgot."

"No, I..." Gabe stutters. "I thought, since you came down now..."

"I've got plenty of annual leave hours left. Of course, I'll come see my boys for Christmas!"

"Right."

Oh god, Ellis is going to break up with him, isn't he? No way is he willing to host Gabe's mum twice in such a short period of time.

He chances a glance at Ellis, seeing the face of a man who's come to accept his fate.

"I'll have your room ready for you," Ellis promises.

"You're too sweet." She wipes away an imaginary tear. "I'm so happy to have such a wonderful son-in-law."

For the love of god. "Mum? Aren't you going to miss your flight?"

"Right, right. See you soon, boys. Love you."

"Bye, Mum." To Ellis, he says, "I'm so sorry. Please ignore everything she said."

Ellis laughs, but it's obvious the possible-matrimony comment threw him off. "It's fine. I mean, at least I have her approval as your boyfriend."

"That, you do. I think she likes you better than me."

"Only because I'm a new victim she can torment."

"You're not wrong."

"So...Christmas, huh?" A look of carefully contained horror passes over Ellis' face.

"We could get out of it. How difficult would it be to fabricate our deaths?" Gabe wonders.

"Not sure. But I'll look into it."

"That would be great."

Chapter 23

CAL AND DAWSON HAVE been insufferable ever since they'd found out about Gabe and Ellis, blowing up both their phones and demanding a double-date. Gabe would be happy to meet up, but he knows it might be a little too much for Ellis. After spending a weekend with Gabe's mum, he deserves a break. A long one.

But then Cal and Dawson begin to ambush Gabe at work and, well...Gabe can't keep hiding in the cold room forever. Double-date it is. At least he manages to talk them out of a romantic dinner, proposing a more harmless solution.

That was the thought behind it, anyway.

"I'm not sure about this," Ellis says, voice mildly terrified. He holds the leash in his hand like it's a time-bomb.

"What are you talking about? She loves you!" Dawson argues, gazing lovingly at the Pomeranian on the other end of the leash. It's true that she's taken a liking to Ellis, pawing at the door of her kennel when Ellis passed by. She even rolled onto her back, offering her tummy up for scratches when Dawson let her out.

Ellis' throat bobs. "She's scary."

As Gabe watches Lola rattle like a rabbit on speed, making noises not unlike a rusty car engine, he has to concede that Ellis does have a point.

"She is," Cal agrees, keeping a safe distance. The two must have a history. Gabe will ask about it later, when Ellis isn't listening.

"I think she's cute," Gabe chimes in, receiving a look of betrayal from Ellis.

"Do you want to swap?"

"Nope." Gabe is happy with his Jack Russel.

"Come on, Ellis. She's not that bad," Dawson tries to sway him.

"She really does like you. And she doesn't like anyone," Aubrey, who Gabe understands is some kind of supervisor at the shelter, confirms.

"She likes Dawson," Ellis insists.

"No, she *tolerates* me."

"Would you consider adopting?" Aubrey asks.

Ellis doesn't even get a syllable out before Dawson exclaims, "That's a great idea!"

"Hardly. I work long hours. She'd be lonely," Ellis bursts his bubble.

"I could walk her. We both could." Dawson nods towards Cal. "We have plenty of time on our hands."

Ellis is silent for a while. At first, Gabe assumes he's looking for a plausible excuse, but then something tickles his Spidey senses. It feels almost like regret.

"I don't know how to take care of a dog," Ellis says quietly.

"Didn't you say you had a Border Collie as a child?" Dawson asks.

"As a *child*. Our housekeeper took care of him most of the time." Another pulse of regret, stronger this time.

"It's not that hard," Dawson says.

"Why don't you take her?" Ellis retorts.

"Donut hates other dogs."

"Let us know if you change your mind," Aubrey says diplomatically, disappointment written in her face. "Lola's been with us for a long time. She'd love a real home."

Ellis' energy sours further, this time with guilt. "I'll keep that in mind."

Yeah, so dog-walking wasn't Gabe's greatest idea, as far as dates go. To be fair, he didn't foresee Ellis getting ambushed like that.

Gradually, Ellis' energy brightens once they start walking and chatting. He ends up at the front with Cal, while Gabe and Dawson stay behind.

"I still can't believe it," Dawson says, shaking his head incredulously. "You and Ellis. Ellis and you."

Gabe's aware he must be making some embarrassing, disgustingly smitten face, but who cares? "Pretty amazing, isn't it? Sometimes I can't believe he's actually mine." Just saying it out loud sounds fantastical. "What?" He feels Dawson's intense stare burning a hole into his face.

"Nothing. Just...it's so weird. I could never imagine Ellis in a relationship. He's so straightlaced and serious."

Gabe snorts. "Not so straight after all." That earns him a laugh. "And I'm pretty good at revealing his playful side."

"You're such a strange pair. It's awesome."

"It is."

"And he..." Dawson lowers his voice despite them being a good chunk of space behind. "He knows about you?"

"Yup."

"Wow." Dawson seems very astounded. "How did he take it?"

Gabe smiles at the memory of their first date. How scared he was to tell the truth, bracing himself for rejection that would sting more than being blown off because he's a man. But none of it ever happened because Ellis is, as it turns out, the most wonderful human being on the planet. And Gabe is so fucking lucky to call him *his*.

"I've never had anyone accept the truth about me so fast. Accept *me* so fast." His voice is thick with emotion, and he knows Dawson can hear it.

"He's a great guy."

"The best." Needing a distraction so he doesn't start happy-crying on a date, he asks, "How is it going with you two?"

"It's...good," Dawson gives a vague answer, but he's smiling. And even if he wasn't, Gabe can feel the warm, fluttery emotions coming from him. "We're taking it slow."

"Good idea."

Maybe Cal can sense they're talking about him because he looks back, his eyes instantly finding Dawson as if Gabe's not even there, and he smiles.

"He looks at you like you hung the moon," Gabe says, finding Dawson's shy smile endearing.

"Yeah?"

"You look at him like that too."

"Shut up."

Gabe laughs, but as he watches Cal and Ellis walk side by side, talking and laughing, his chest begins to feel constricted. He loves to see Ellis happy. Making him happy has been his number one priority ever since he got a feel of Ellis' energy. Of his heart. But keeping a secret from him makes everything feel tainted.

"Hey." He touches Dawson's elbow to get his attention. "There's something I wanted to bring up with you. I get you're still getting used to all this, but have you considered telling Ellis?"

Dawson blinks uncomprehendingly, and his features darken as the meaning finally sinks. "Why? What good would it do?"

"He thinks Cal is his brother."

"And they finally get along, unlike before."

Yeah, Gabe knows. That's why it would be so hard to tell him the truth. But it would be even harder to keep it from him forever. Gabe would always feel guilty, would always wonder if the good intentions justified the lie.

No, he doesn't want to live a life with Ellis where this ominous secret will forever hang over their heads like Damocles' Sword.

"He deserves to know, Dawson."

Dawson's eyes become stormy, taking Gabe by surprise. "You want to tell him his brother is dead? And in his place is a reaper? Really?"

Fuck. This really is a lose-lose scenario.

"I want him to know the truth," Gabe says, dejected. "I know it's not my place to tell him, so I'm asking you. I just... I love him, Dawson. And I can see myself..." *Growing old and wrinkly with him.* "Selfishly,

I don't want to spend my life knowing there's this huge thing I'm keeping from him."

He feels like a hypocrite. He's had no problem keeping a secret from his mum. Well, that's not true. It's not like it was an easy decision, but not seeing her every day definitely made it easier.

He's pleasantly surprised when Dawson actually considers it, going quiet for a long moment.

"And you think he'd believe us?"

Believing isn't the issue. It's what would come after. He has no idea how Ellis might react.

"He's more open-minded than you think."

Dawson gives a curt nod, not looking happy in the slightest. "I'll talk to Cal. See what he thinks."

Gabe releases a breath. "Thank you."

The rest of the walk passes in a quiet manner, at least for Gabe and Dawson. Tension stretches between them, but Gabe can't find it in himself to break it. He doesn't blame Dawson for being upset with him. This is hardly a topic you want to bring up on a date.

His heart skips a beat when it's Ellis who looks back this time, sending Gabe a look that makes a coil of warmth settle in his chest before it moves lower.

"You know," Dawson breaks the silence. "I might look at Cal like he hung the moon, but you're looking at Ellis like you're two seconds away from being arrested for public indecency."

Gabe doesn't bother denying it. "What can I say? I snatched the hotter brother."

Dawson snorts. "No, you didn't."

"Did too."

"You didn't—" Dawson hesitates, studying the two men in front of them. "I mean...it's pretty much a tie."

"Hey." Gabe slaps his shoulder. "No ogling."

Dawson raises an amused eyebrow. "I never took you for the possessive type."

"Me neither. I just have no self-control where Ellis is involved."

"Find it," Dawson says, unimpressed. "There are things I do not need to see."

"Prude."

Chapter 24

'If something is too good to be true, it probably is.'

Gabe doesn't know how many times he's heard that stupid saying, he just knows he hates it. If things seem *too* good, it doesn't mean something terrible's coming, that it's all just quiet before the storm. It doesn't mean the other shoe is waiting to drop. It simply means you finally have things you spent your whole life dreaming of. That's all.

So when December rolls around, marking the best time of his life, Gabe throws himself in head first. Because life is great. Ridiculously good, to be honest.

He and Ellis slip into a perfect little routine: Ellis stops at the café to pick up his coffee and lunch (yup, Gabe has officially turned into a good little wife, no regrets). Then they scandalize Zeke and the customers with some PDA before going about their respective days, always one emoji-filled text away.

Ellis has even reduced his working hours, much to his PA's chagrin, so he can meet Gabe for dinner most days without being in an insane rush. If they spend the night together, it's always at Ellis' place—because, let's face it, a latex mattress is what was missing from Gabe's life—and wake each other up with mutual handjobs.

Rinse, repeat, until the weekend comes, allowing for breaking up the routine and coming up with something more special.

Like last Sunday, when Gabe manipulated Ellis into coming to a beach yoga class with him. It was all orchestrated under the guise of *'increasing flexibility before arthritis sets in'*, but in reality Gabe just wanted to show his boyfriend off. Call him vain, but landing a gorgeous guy half of the Earth's population would lust after? Hell, yeah, he wants to show him off.

It worked a little too well.

Gabe underestimated how deep his possessive streak runs where Ellis is concerned. So, after enduring one full agonizing hour where he had to watch thirteen women (and one middle-aged man), including the instructor, drool and pant whenever Ellis took the pose of downward facing dog or warrior two, he was finally forced to admit he might have a bit of a problem. Just a tiny one.

Everything only got worse when the session had finished and the whole class flocked to Ellis like a shiver of sharks smelling blood. Ellis didn't make the situation any better when his polite persona took over, trying to indulge everyone in some small talk, totally unaware that one smile from him could cause a person to spontaneously orgasm.

His control run thin, Gabe all but dragged him away, ignoring the shocked expressions of the group and Ellis' confused one. Through gritted teeth, he ordered Ellis to get them home stat, curling his fingers into his palms so he wouldn't accidently start groping him while Ellis had to focus on driving.

Once the door shut behind them in Ellis' apartment, Gabe literally tore the clothes off him, pushed him onto the sofa—the bedroom was too fucking far—and swallowed his cock until he could feel it in his throat. Ellis was slick with sweat, his skin smelling and tasting of salt and musk, and Gabe went a little (more) feral because of it.

The first time he made Ellis come, it took less than two minutes. He never let him catch his breath before diving in for another round, in spite of Ellis' feeble protests. Whenever he pulled off, it was to suck and bite at Ellis' thighs and hips, the skin smooth and unmarked, but quickly turning various shades of red and purple.

Ellis was tugging Gabe's hair like it was a rope he was hanging onto, making it really hard to concentrate. But concentrate, Gabe did, sucking Ellis' cock like a hooker desperate for cash. In the heat of the moment, his fingers found their way between Ellis' cheeks. He felt Ellis tense for a second when he brushed his hole, but then he was opening his legs wider and angling his hips.

Eyes rolling into his head, Gabe circled one finger around Ellis' rim before pushing it in, shivering at the tightness that enveloped him.

And that was it. Ellis' body pulled taut like a bowstring stretched to its limit and filled Gabe's mouth for the second time, the force of his climax triggering Gabe's own.

When they both found their breath, Ellis asked, "What on earth was that?"

Gabe replied, "That was me, staking a claim on what's mine."

Ellis gave him *this* look and asked, "Why didn't you stake it before?"

Gabe decided that taking Ellis to his yoga classes could become a regular thing.

So, yeah. Life is good. Ridiculously good.

And then the other shoe drops.

On a Saturday morning, his legs still jelly from last night's sex and his side warm where Ellis is pressed up against it, Gabe wakes up to a text from Dawson. The foreboding feeling in his stomach is his first warning before he even reads it.

Dawson: I talked to Cal. He thinks you're right.

Dawson: I don't.

Dawson: He's ready when you are.

Gabe should be happy. This is what he wanted, for Ellis to know the truth. For himself to not have to keep secrets. And now, Cal finally agreed to spill the beans.

He *should* be happy. He should.

Gabe never thought that having someone's unconditional trust could hurt. But it does.

It hurts to know how much Ellis trusts him.

It hurts that he doesn't question it when Gabe tells him he needs Ellis to meet him at the café after it closes for the day. That he isn't at all suspicious when he comes in to find Dawson and Cal are there too.

And why should he be? He has no idea what life-altering truth he's about to learn, probably thinking this is a surprise double-date. And he doesn't even seem upset by not being given a heads-up.

No. He strolls into the café unwaveringly, sparing an easy 'Hey' to Cal and Dawson, before heading in Gabe's direction and kissing him like they've been apart for months, not eight hours.

The first time Gabe senses confusion in him is when he asks Ellis to take a seat with the rest of them. Still, Ellis does, not asking any questions.

It hurts in a way Gabe never expected.

It hurts even more when Cal starts talking.

The silence in the café is choking, actually physically choking. Gabe feels it like a vice around his throat, crushing his windpipe. He hasn't uttered a word since Cal started talking, none of them have. All of Gabe's focus has circled around Ellis, taking in every miniscule change in his energy. There hasn't been much change. Throughout Cal's delivery, Ellis' energy was one big flashing question mark.

"So, you're saying you're not actually Cal," Ellis finally speaks, his voice scarily flat. "That you are a...*reaper* and you took over his body, *Ghost Whisperer* style."

Cal looks at Dawson askance, receiving only a shrug in response. "I don't understand that reference. But yes. That's essentially it."

Ellis laughs, the sound bouncing off the walls in the empty café. When his gaze seeks out Gabe, waiting for confirmation that Cal is just messing around, it nearly kills Gabe to not be able to give it to him.

"It's true," he says, having to force the words out.

Ellis' expression blanches. "What?"

It takes everything not to reach for Ellis' hand. "They're telling the truth. I know because...because I felt it."

"You felt it."

"Cal. Who he truly is. I didn't put it together until recently, but it is the truth."

More silence, then Ellis laughs again. There's nothing amusing about it. It's the sound of confusion and denial, of being at a loss for how to react because the truth is simply not acceptable.

Whatever he sees in Gabe's face makes him stop, the first real trickle of fear and panic bleeding into his energy, tainting it.

"That's bullshit. That can't be—" He shakes his head. "It's not possible."

"You believed me when I told you about myself," Gabe reminds him.

Ellis frowns. "That's different. You... I felt it myself."

"You felt it with Cal too. How different he is." Gabe suggests gently, not wanting to upset him further, but needing for the truth to sink in.

He knows he's hit bullseye when the fear and panic grow stronger. He's not surprised that a part of Ellis always knew, deep down, that something about Cal wasn't right. But denial is a powerful tool.

"It's the amnesia," Ellis says. Everything about him screams desperation.

"Is it? All of it?"

Ellis is a rational man. He must've done his research when Cal woke up at the hospital with both his memory and personality wiped clean. He must've talked to doctors. He must've learned that in the history of amnesia, no one's ever got such a drastic personality transplant.

Ellis' features harden, his jaw locking. He looks angry, but Gabe can feel it's just a facade, can feel how scared he is.

Ellis turns to Cal, voice eerily calm. "If you're telling the truth, then where is my brother?"

Cal, to his credit, doesn't even flinch. "I harvested his soul. He's gone."

The next moment is the scariest of all. Ellis' walls rise sky-high, pushing Gabe out. Despite the turmoil of emotions he could feel coming from him just seconds ago, there is only a void and coldness.

"This is bullshit," Ellis hisses, the chair making a high-pitched noise as it's forcefully pushed back. He storms out of the café, Gabe ready to follow him, but it looks like Ellis just needs to get some air. He stays outside, pacing back and forth, hands pulling at his hair.

Gabe just wants to go over and hug him until the pain goes away.

"I told you he wouldn't believe it," Dawson says, dejected.

"He believes it," Gabe corrects him. "That's the problem."

All of a sudden, Ellis takes off. Gabe's on his feet in an instant, running after him. "Ellis? Ellis!" He catches up to him as Ellis is getting into his car. "Where are you going?"

"Home," Ellis snaps without looking at him.

"Do you want someone with you? Someone to talk to?"

"No."

Gabe's stomach rolls, threatening to empty its contents.

"Ellis, you're upset. You shouldn't drive."

"I'm fine." He slams the door shut.

Gabe presses his palms to the window before Ellis takes off. "Can you please text me when you get home?"

Forget about everything else. He just needs to know Ellis arrived home safe. He'd never survive it if he found out something happened to him because of Gabe.

Instead of brushing him off, like Gabe half-expects, Ellis gives a curt nod. It's not much, but Gabe will take it. As long as he knows Ellis is okay.

He's far from okay, and it's your fault.

He stands there helplessly as Ellis puts the car in motion and drives away.

Chapter 25

THE RINGING OF THE intercom jars Ellis out of the restless slumber he's drunk himself into. He peels his eyelids open, groaning at the sudden blast of light that hits them. He blindly searches for his phone to check the time, ignoring all the unread messages from Gabriel.

20:17

The intercom rings again.

What a fucking joke. Clearly, he can't even be granted enough time to grieve and process everything that's been dumped on him.

He takes a swig from the nearly half-empty bottle of whiskey and stomps over to the intercom.

"What?"

"Hi. It's me?" comes Cal's distorted voice. *No. Not Cal.*

"*Me* who? The reaper who killed my brother?" Ellis tries to sound angry, but the words come out slurred and pathetic, on the verge of a sob.

A stretch of silence follows. "Can I please come up?"

"Why?"

"Because you're my brother and I worry about you."

Closing his eyes in pain, Ellis rests his forehead against the wall. It's blissfully cold. "I'm not your brother."

"Yes, you are," Cal—*fuck, not Cal!*—says with the conviction of someone who's never been wrong in his life. "Can I come up?"

Fuck. If he doesn't talk to him now, he'll have the whole cavalry on his ass soon. Better to get it over with.

Ellis buzzes him in.

Soon, way too soon, there's a knock on the door. Ellis opens it.

"Make it quick." He turns around and wanders back to the sofa. He has no interest in being subjected to that deceptively crestfallen expression.

"You shouldn't be drinking," Cal—ugh, fuck it—says disapprovingly.

Ellis takes a long drink. "Why is that?"

"Nothing good ever comes of it."

That's not true. He gets to numb his stupid heart. That sounds pretty good to him.

"You don't want me sober right now."

Slowly, as if approaching a feral animal, Cal rounds the sofa, taking a spot on the far end. It leaves more than three feet of space between them, but it still makes Ellis feel cornered, makes him want to take off and just run until his lungs give up on him.

"He used to drink the same thing," Cal points out.

As if Ellis doesn't fucking know.

His eyes flit to the Paul John label. He never liked this stuff. He never liked whiskey. How pathetic is it that this swill is the first thing he thought of when he wanted to feel closer to his dead brother?

He slams the bottle on the coffee table, getting up on unsteady legs. "What do you want? If you're here to give me a lecture, you can fuck off."

Cal hangs his head, hands folded stiffly in his lap.

Ellis refuses to feel bad about it.

"Don't be mad at Gabe," Cal says. "All he wanted was for there to not be any secrets between you."

Ellis falters, short of falling on his face. He didn't even consider it might've been Gabriel who came up with the idea.

He probably felt bad about knowing something you didn't.

"Maybe there should be," he says bitterly. Sometimes, oblivion really is a blessing.

"You don't mean that."

"Don't fucking tell me how I feel."

Right now, he'd like nothing more than to turn back time and erase the conversation from his memory. Shame that amnesia isn't catching.

"Okay. I'm sorry." Cal's shoulders curl inwards. He bites his lip, his expression contemplative. "There's something I've been meaning to talk to you about."

"You gonna elaborate?" Ellis prompts impatiently when Cal just continues to sit there, making big eyes at him.

Cal nods, but even so it takes a good long moment before he does. "I haven't told Dawson this," he starts, wriggling his fingers. "I...don't know how to bring it up. But ever since the heart attack, something has changed. I started remembering."

"Yeah, you said that. Big scary reaper and all that." Ellis takes another swig from the bottle.

"I mean, I started remembering *everything*." When Ellis only stares at him uncomprehendingly, he explains, "I have Caledon's memories too."

"You what?"

Cal lets out a shuddering breath. "I remember his life. Bits and pieces. Something happens that triggers a memory, and then it's like being swept in a flood. I've started remembering more and more. The memories feel different from my own, they're shrouded in this—" He makes an all-encompassing gesture around his head. "Fog. It makes it easier to keep them separate from mine."

Great. Apparently, seeing someone else wear his brother's face wasn't blurring the lines enough. Now he also has his memories.

God, this is fucked up.

"Why are you telling me this?"

For the first time since he's stepped into the apartment, Cal smiles. "I remember you too."

There's an intense burning in Ellis' eyes. He turns his back to Cal, taking another much needed gulp from the bottle.

"Then you know that my brother and I never saw eye to eye."

"No, you didn't. But it's never that easy, is it?"

Ellis turns back with a confused frown.

Sighing, Cal stands up, taking a couple steps closer to him. "Back when I was..." His face contorts in a grimace. "Before Dawson," he settles on. "I'd spent a long time amongst humanity. Your kind is very confusing. A walking, talking contradiction. I've always found it fascinating, and very tragic, that you can hate somebody but love them at the same time." He cocks his head inquiringly, blue eyes boring into Ellis'. "Family is a complicated thing, isn't it?"

Ellis swallows heavily, once again presenting Cal with his back. The implication of Cal's words rings loud and deafening in his ears.

He's always wondered. Ever since they were kids, he's wondered if it was just him. If he was the only one who, despite their differences and all the bad blood, loved his brother more than anyone else in the world. Cal could hurt him, walk all over him, do his absolute worst, and Ellis would still come back running if his brother needed it. Ellis hated him for it, for reducing him to such a pathetic mess.

Unfortunately, he also loved him twice as much.

He thought that if he knew Cal felt the same way towards him, it would make things easier.

He was wrong.

"Why haven't you told Dawson yet?" he asks to turn attention to something else that isn't his trainwreck of a life. "Don't you think he'd like to know?"

A flash of fear passes over Cal's face. "I'm not sure. I think...finding out I have the memories of the person who made his life hell could make him feel unsafe around me. I can't go through that again."

Right. Because Cal—the real Cal—was, on top of his qualities, an abusive bastard who terrorized his husband for the better part of their marriage. And Ellis had no fucking idea.

"He fell in love with you even though he thought you're...him," he offers a half-baked consolation. He's not exactly in a supportive mood.

Cal offers him a grateful smile all the same. "That was when I didn't remember anything. After all, memories are what makes us.

Maybe knowing that I have Caledon's memories might make him afraid that—"

"You will start acting like him."

"I won't." Cal's eyes flash with determination. "As I said, the memories aren't as clear and sharp as mine. They're not as embedded. It's kind of like watching a movie, but more intense."

Ellis won't even try to imagine. "Some movie that must be."

A short laugh escapes Cal's lips. "Indeed." He shifts on his feet, casting the apartment a helpless glance before taking several steps towards Ellis. "I'll take my leave. I just wanted to tell you that losing Caledon doesn't mean you don't have a family. *We* are your family, if you'll have us. And I am your brother, if you'll have me." After some hesitation where his hands twitch indecisively at his sides, his arms come around Ellis in a loose hug.

Ellis accepts it passively, his body stiff as a board and the hand around the whiskey bottle squeezing so tight it's at risk of breaking.

It's a huge relief, accompanied by a strong sense of loss, when Cal finally leaves. The apartment falls into overwhelming silence, threatening to crush him.

Ellis locates his phone, sliding into the texts with Gabriel before he can chicken out.

The ignored texts force the tears he's been holding at bay to spill over.

Ellis: Home.

Gabriel: Thank you.

Gabriel: Whatever you do, please be safe.

Gabriel: I know you don't want to talk or see anybody (sorry for bombarding you with these, I'm just really worried) but if you need anything, I'm just a text/call away.

Gabriel: You're not alone, Ellis, no matter what it looks like.

You're not alone. You're not alone.

Ellis lets the words wrap around him like a safety blanket. Uses them to silence the voice in his head that's been trying to convince him of the opposite, the one that's been growing quieter since he'd met Gabriel, but which still sometimes takes over.

'*You're not alone.*'

'*We are your family, if you'll have us. And I am your brother, if you'll have me.*'

'*You're not alone.*'

He walks over to the sink and empties whatever is left of the whiskey down the drain before bringing his phone up again. Through shaking hands and blurry vision, he manages to type out three short words.

Ellis: I need you.

Seconds after he hits *send*, a reply comes through.

Gabriel: I'm on my way.

Chapter 26

THE TIME IT TAKES for the lift to reach Ellis' apartment seems to drag forever. Has it always been this slow? Or is Gabe just frantic? Considering he ran out of his apartment as though he had the hounds of hell on his ass after receiving the text from Ellis, chances are it's the latter. Even the Uber he took to get here seemed to go at sloth speed. Gabe regretted not taking the scooter, but he didn't trust himself not to end up in a ditch with how all over the place his mind is. But who could blame him? His phone had been glued to his hand since Ellis took off.

After a million years, the lift finally comes to a stop, dinging softly to announce its arrival. Gabe rushes to Ellis' door, hesitating for a second before delivering three, hopefully non-obnoxious knocks.

His heart breaks into a thousand pieces when Ellis opens the door.

"Hey," Gabe says shakily.

Even if he wasn't an empath, Ellis' face would say it all. He looks utterly shattered, his eyes glassy as if he's been drinking, and hair in disarray like he's been pulling on it.

Fuck. Gabe wants to hug him so bad. Hug him and hold him and shower him with kisses until the pain has no choice but to dissipate.

"Hey," Ellis says, voice rough. From drinking or crying, maybe both. He leaves the door wide open for Gabe before turning around. "Cal was here."

"He was? What did he say?"

Gabe's not sure how to feel about that. He didn't like the idea of Ellis being alone, but the man needs time to think, to process. Cal barging in on him only hours after the big revelation probably only pissed him off.

Ellis makes his way to the kitchen silently. He pulls a glass out of a cupboard and fills it under the tap.

Gabe lets out a breath of relief. While it's obvious Ellis has been drinking—the wavering gait and slightly slurred words are pretty telling—he must have decided it was enough. So maybe Cal coming by is a good thing after all?

Leaning back against the counter, Ellis downs half the glass in one go. "He wanted me to know he's still my brother, if I'll accept him."

Ellis' emotions are all over the place, Gabe has a hard time getting a read on them. The alcohol isn't helping either, creating a distortion.

"Will you?"

Ellis knocks back whatever is left in the glass, before slamming it on the counter. "How the fuck do I do that? He's..." His arm angrily shoots out. "He's supposed to be a freaking death-bringer."

"Maybe before. Now he's just...a man. A man who cares for you very much."

Ellis flinches, as if Gabe has slapped him. Despite the physical reaction, Gabe can feel his raw, vulnerable energy brighten with reluctant hope. Ellis might not be ready to accept this new Cal as his brother, but he's come to care for him since the accident. Of course he wants Cal to care for him too, reaper or not.

"How do you know?"

Gabe chuckles softly. "It's kind of my thing to know." Not to mention that if Cal didn't care, he wouldn't have come here to patch things up in the first place.

Ellis has no idea how much he's loved, by so many people.

"He said it was your idea to tell me."

It's Gabe's turn to flinch. "It was selfish. I adore you and I'd like to spend the rest of my life with you. And I couldn't imagine keeping a secret so big." He opens himself up to his limit, wanting to make sure that Ellis can feel the truth in the words. "I never want to have to lie to you."

Ellis groans, turning around to face the counter. "You won't even let me be mad at you, will you?" he grouses, like Gabe is being difficult.

The situation is not funny, but a smile fights its way to Gabe's lips. "Sorry?"

Ellis responds with an annoyed huff, his energy flaring up with the contradictory emotions of affection and irritation.

Is it wrong that Gabe finds that ridiculously adorable? Seizing the opportunity, he approaches Ellis and glues himself to his back, winding his arms around Ellis' waist.

Instead of tensing up as Gabe feared, Ellis' whole body relaxes, sinking back into Gabe like he's been waiting to be held. Gabe squeezes him tighter, burrowing his face in Ellis' nape, inhaling his familiar, comforting scent.

"What do I do, Gabriel?" Ellis asks quietly. If they weren't so close, Gabe probably wouldn't hear him.

Tentatively, he moves one hand from Ellis' waist and places it at the center of his chest. "You follow your heart."

The heart in question gives a powerful thump.

"My heart is a mess."

"Then it's a beautiful mess." Gabe kisses the side of his neck, reveling in the shiver that runs through Ellis' body. "I love the mess."

Ellis' shoulders droop. "Don't see what's to love."

"Don't do that," Gabe scolds, using a gentle but firm tone. He prompts Ellis to turn around, meeting resistance at first, but eventually Ellis lets him.

"Why me?" he asks, eyes downcast. "It could've been anyone else."

Gabe grits his teeth, fighting down an overwhelming surge of anger. If he had his way, he'd hunt down everyone who's even looked at Ellis the wrong way.

Fuck them. Fuck all of them. Everyone who's ever made Ellis feel like there's something wrong with him, like he doesn't deserve to be loved. Like he's anything less than absolutely perfect.

He takes Ellis' beautiful, sad face between his palms, coaxing him to look up.

"You're wrong," he tells him. "So very wrong. It couldn't have been anyone else. You were meant to find me. And I was meant to wait until you came along."

Despite his gift, and all the supernatural occurrences he's been a witness to, Gabe isn't a big believer in fate or destiny. He doesn't like the notion that a person is born into a life and has no control over what happens to them. What would be the point?

But if there's one thing that's become apparent ever since a beautiful, lonely stranger wandered into his café, it's that he and Ellis were meant to meet. They were always meant to find each other. He knew it the second Ellis stood in front of him, face filled with righteous anger and heart full of sadness. A part of his soul reached out, brushing against Gabe's as if saying: *Hey, it's you. I've been looking everywhere for you.*

Gabe senses the moment the tethers holding Ellis together start to crumble and he steps in before they completely break. He wraps his arms around him tight, saying nothing as Ellis shakes against him, his body jolting with suppressed sobs. He pays it no attention when his own eyes start to fill with tears, feeling Ellis' pain like his own. He invites the pain in, taking all of it willingly. He'll take anything if it means Ellis' heart will be a little lighter.

Gradually, the shaking subsides, Ellis' breath evening out. Even his energy, as raw as it still is, becomes more solid, like the broken pieces have finally started to come together.

"I'm sorry I took so long," he says, voice no longer slurred.

"I would've waited for as long as I had to," Gabe promises, kissing Ellis' temple. "But I admit, I'm glad you found me while I'm still in control of my bladder."

Ellis begins to shake again, for an entirely different reason. His booming, addictive laugh fills Gabe with bone-deep warmth. God, he loves making him laugh. He could live on that sound alone.

Loosening his hold, Ellis pulls back so he can look at Gabe. His cheeks are tear-streaked and blotchy, but there's a serenity in his gaze that wasn't there before.

"I..."

He doesn't get further than that. Gabe can tell he desperately wants to, his lips moving soundlessly and frustration filling his features when no words make it out.

After another failed attempt, Gabe covers Ellis' lips with his fingers and smiles.

"It's okay. I know."

Of course he knows. Ellis might struggle to say *I love you* with words, but he's said it in other ways, so many times. He's said it with his actions and his body. Each time was louder and clearer than if he shouted it into a megaphone.

Gabe doesn't need words. He just needs Ellis, exactly as he is.

Ellis releases a shaky breath, swaying forward until their foreheads touch. "Stay?"

Gabe kisses him. "Always."

Wild horses couldn't drag him away.

On Sunday morning, Gabe wakes first and just watches Ellis. His mouth is half-open, leaving a wet spot on the pillow, but his face is serene and worry free. Finally, after the night he had.

He'd managed to doze off for a bit before jolting awake and making a run—a stumble, really—for the bathroom. Gabe had knelt by his side and wiped sweat off his forehead and neck with a damp washcloth. He'd rubbed his back in soothing circles as Ellis' body purged the poisonous crap he'd ingested, promising everything would be okay. He'd helped Ellis brush his teeth, forced him to drink a glass of water, and half-carried him back to bed where he held him until he fell asleep.

Knowing Ellis will feel like a truck went over him when he wakes up, Gabe embarks on a search for a hangover breakfast. He's unimpressed, yet unsurprised, when he opens the fridge only to discover it completely deserted. Unless cans of gin and tonic and a bottle of sriracha sauce count.

Gabe closes the fridge with a huff. Shopping time it is.

Ellis stumbles into the kitchen, looking like death warmed over, just as Gabe's plating up scrambled eggs. He blinks at Gabe blearily, like he's never seen him in his life.

"Wow," Gabe says. "How are you still so cute when you look like crap?"

Ellis peels his eyes open. "A backhanded compliment like that... Did you wake up and choose violence?"

Gabe laughs. "Take a seat." He adds a slice of toast and some avocado to the plate, then carries it over to Ellis. "Do you feel like eating? I know they say something greasy like bacon or a burger is good for hangovers, but I don't think your arteries would be happy with that choice. Is this okay?"

"I..."

"What?" He starts to worry when Ellis only continues to stare at the plate.

"You made me breakfast."

"Obviously." He plates up for himself and takes a seat next to Ellis. "Hey, what's the big deal? I've made you lunch before."

"Yeah, I know. I just..." Ellis shakes his head, a small smile appearing on his lips. "Thank you." He kisses Gabe's cheek.

Gabe's smile is probably bigger than the situation calls for, but he doesn't give a damn. "How are you feeling? Still nauseous?"

Ellis puts on a thoughtful expression, chewing on a piece of egg. "Actually, no. My head feels like an over-inflated balloon, but it's not too bad." He pauses with the fork halfway to his mouth. "Did you do something?"

Gabe lets out a pleased sound. "I was hoping it would work. I haven't experimented much, so I didn't know if it would help at all."

"You used your mojo on me?"

"Yup."

"Huh. Wait." He fixes Gabe with a worried look. "Didn't it drain you?"

Gabe grins. "Yeah, but I slept it off."

Ellis doesn't look convinced. "You shouldn't have done that."

"It was a one-off. It's not like I'm planning to do it on the regular."

"You shouldn't have wasted your energy on me."

"Ellis," Gabe says, getting exasperated. "I'm ass over tits in love with you. Do you really think I won't do whatever it takes to make you feel better?"

Ellis gapes at him, cheeks flushed and his emotions all over the place, ranging from embarrassed to happy to panicked.

Gabe takes pity on him, changing the subject. "By the way, we really need to have a talk about your eating habits. The state of your fridge? A family of penguins could live there."

Ellis has the decency to look sheepish. "I usually eat out."

Gabe rolls his eyes.

"You went out to buy food? What time did you wake up?"

"Eight-ish, I think. I borrowed your keys. Hope it's okay."

"Of course," Ellis says quickly, getting Gabe's stomach all fluttery. "In fact..."

"Wha?" Gabe asks through a mouthful of toast.

Ellis bites back a smile. "Be right back." He disappears into his room, coming back with what looks and sounds like keys.

Gabe almost chokes on his food. Is Ellis seriously going to—

"I have a spare set," Ellis offers redundantly. He takes Gabe's free hand, lowering the keys into his open palm. "I want you to have it."

Gabe tries to stop his lower lip from wobbling. "Really? But...this is your safe place." He already knew Ellis trusts him, but this is his apartment. The one place he can be at peace when life gets too overwhelming. To give Gabe access like that...

"No." Ellis closes Gabe's fingers around the keys and kisses his knuckles. "*You* are my safe place."

Fuck. This is like a scene from a freaking rom-com. Thank god Gabe is already sitting, or he'd be swooning right now.

He surges forward, surprising Ellis with a greedy kiss. His grip tightens around the keys until they dig into his skin, the blast of pain grounding him, reminding him this is real.

Just yesterday, a part of him was sure it was over, that he'd lost everything and hurt the person he loves the most in the process.

Instead, he's got everything he never even dared to hope for. The other shoe has dropped, but they've come out even stronger on the other side.

If only he could make sure Ellis is never hurt again.

All things considered, today has been perfect. They've spent the day lazing around, eating pizza for lunch (and dinner), and binging half a season of *Gilmore Girls.*

Ellis is nice and relaxed, his head resting in Gabe's lap as Gabe plays with his hair, when his phone chimes.

Gabe can guess who the sender is by the way Ellis' whole body grows rigid.

"It's Cal," Ellis confirms without prompting.

"What's he saying?"

Ellis heaves himself into a seated position. "That he'll be there when—and if—I'm ready to talk."

"That's nice of him," Gabe says diplomatically.

"Yeah." Ellis gives a bitter laugh. "My brother was never nice."

Yeah, Gabe can imagine. "Do you miss him?"

Ellis laughs again. It's a broken sound, its sharp edges digging into Gabe's heart. "Pretty fucked up, isn't it?"

"No." He strokes Ellis' hair. "Not at all."

"I'm never going to get closure," Ellis says, leaning into the touch. "Not with my mum. Not with my dad. Not even Cal. I thought I did. After the car accident, we talked a lot. We...*connected*. I thought we got another shot at being a family. For real, this time."

"You still can be."

It's probably not the best idea to push the positive attitude. Ellis needs time to mourn, to be angry and sad, so he can move on. So it takes Gabe aback when Ellis seems to ponder the thought instead of outright refusing it.

"I think..."

"What?"

"I think I'd like to adopt Lola."

Oh-kay... That's not what Gabe expected. Where did that even come from? Nevermind.

"Really?"

Ellis shrugs, playing with a loose thread in his joggers. "It could be nice, giving a home to someone who doesn't have one. And I could use the company."

Gabe tries not to melt at the image of Ellis cuddling a fluffy dog like Lola. "I think it's a great idea! Dawson and I can take her out when you're at work! I mean..." He jingles the keys to the apartment. "I already have the keys."

Ellis chuckles, but his expression quickly turns serious. "Maybe you won't have to for long. I...I've been thinking of leaving the company."

Gabe's eyes nearly bulge out. "No shit?"

"No shit," Ellis says, laughing.

"Wait. You said leave, not sell."

"I thought of selling at first," Ellis explains. "But I'd still feel responsible for the employees. If I go through with it, I want to make sure they're in good hands."

Jesus, this man... Gabe's poor, overstimulated heart can't take it.

"So you'd still own it, but would have to find a new CEO?"

Ellis gives him a secretive smile. "Luckily, I know just the guy."

"Jordan?" Gabe takes a guess.

Ellis nods. "He stepped in when I needed someone to run the Sydney office for me. Given how much he loves to boss people around, I think he'll be happy to take over."

Oh god, let him take over. Ellis leaving the stupid job he hates would be the cherry on top of a spectacular cake.

"What would you do instead? Architecture?"

"Eventually. Maybe. I'd have to get a license and stuff, but..." He waves a hand dismissively. "That's a whole other thing. For now, I'd just like to...do nothing. Get a bit of a break." He smirks. "Go to the Maldives."

Gabe nods excitedly. "I like that plan."

"Yeah. Me too."

They end up making out for ages, with *GG* playing in the background, until Gabe starts yawning. Considering they've done absolutely nothing the whole day, he's remarkably tired.

"Shower?" Ellis suggests.

"Yes, please."

Turns out having Ellis' hands on him, caressing and stroking as he works lather into his skin, is a great way to wake Gabe up. All of him, it would seem. He looks down at his dick in betrayal while Ellis washes his back. *Down, little guy. No hanky panky when your man is having a crisis.* Surprisingly reasonable, his dick listens, wilting in disappointment.

Gabe's honorable intentions turn to dust when they slip under the covers. Instead of going to sleep cuddled up as he'd planned, Ellis' hands start to wander again. And then his lips. In no time at all, they're kissing again, Ellis using Gabe as his personal blanket. His energy is particularly needy today, scattered and erratic. Gabe can feel it reaching out to him, and he's more than happy to meet it halfway. He lets their energies blend together until it's almost impossible to tell them apart. He's hoping it would help Ellis settle, making him more grounded, but the opposite happens.

Ellis becomes more desperate, small, needy sounds escaping him between hungry kisses. He takes a tight hold of Gabe's neck, keeping him in place as he plunders his mouth, as though he's trying to pour himself inside him. As though connecting their energy isn't enough and he needs to connect their bodies too.

Despite his initial apprehension to start anything when Ellis is in such a vulnerable state, Gabe finds himself relenting. If what Ellis needs is a physical connection as well, that's fine by him. More than fine. Now that he's started to think about it, he wants to be as close to Ellis as possible.

"Yes? Would you like something?" Gabe asks, feigning nonchalance when the hard length of Ellis' cock slides against his own.

"Yeah. You."

Gabe grins. "Done." Pushing himself up, he slides open the bedside drawer to fetch lube and a condom. He flips the cap of the lube bottle open. "Do you want to watch?" He'd love to feel Ellis' fingers again, but having that dark, hungry gaze on him as he gets himself ready is just as good.

"I...um..."

And okay, a blushing Ellis is not an uncommon occurrence, but they've done this before. Why is he getting nervous now?

"Hey." Gabe brushes Ellis' hair off his forehead. He's starting to get worried, because Ellis won't look at him. "What's wrong? Do you not want to?" He was so sure this is what Ellis wanted.

His throat bobbing, Ellis shifts his gaze to meet Gabe's. "I want to feel you inside me."

This must be what a near-death experience feels like. Gabe's vision blurs, narrowing down to a thin tunnel, the rest of his senses checking out.

Ellis smirks, like he knows Gabe's brain just shut down for a moment. "Did I finally shut you up?"

The teasing successfully snaps him back. "Are you implying I never shut up?!"

Ellis laughs, no longer looking nervous, just hopeful. "Please?"

The gravity of the moment descends on Gabe like a heavy weight. "Are you sure? The timing is a bit..."

Seeking comfort in someone else's body is a normal response, but this is supposed to be Ellis' first time. Does Gabe really want to do it like that? What if Ellis regrets it later? Gabe couldn't live with himself.

A warm hand on his cheek snaps Gabe out of his whirring thoughts.

"I know," Ellis says, gratitude and adoration seeping out of him. "But I'm a right mess, and I want to be as close to you as possible. You're my solace, remember?"

Solace. Safe place.

Fuck. How is he supposed to say no to that?

You don't, genius. Shut up and make your man feel good.

"I remember." He nuzzles into Ellis' hand, pressing a kiss to his palm. "Turn over for me."

A shadow of disappointment falls over Ellis' face. "Can we do it face to face?"

"Oh, we absolutely will," Gabe promises, kissing him on the nose. "I just want to get you ready first. It will be more comfortable that way."

"Oh, okay." Ellis easily flips onto his stomach, stretching his body out like an overgrown, sexy cat. "You're the boss."

"Hmm, I like that."

One of these days, he's going to have a talk with Ellis about casually dropping statements like that. He obviously has no idea how twisted Gabe's mind can get.

That's for another time, though.

Gabe slides on a condom and reaches for the lube, pausing. Seeing Ellis like this, open and trusting, laying himself out in front of him like an offering, is a sight to behold. Gabe could see him like this a hundred times and it wouldn't get old.

Ellis turns his head to throw Gabe an impatient look. "What are you doing?"

"Appreciating the moment."

"Can you appreciate it more actively?"

Gabe shrugs. "Alright." He flops onto his belly between Ellis' parted thighs and grabs his firm cheeks, pulling them apart. Diving forward, he gives Ellis' hole an enthusiastic lick.

Ellis yelps, nearly jackknifing off the bed. "A little warning next time?" He glares at Gabe over his shoulder, but the effect is diminished by his flushed cheeks and hooded eyes.

"I'm being appreciative."

"You're being a menace."

"So you've said." He gently slaps Ellis' right cheek, drawing an appalled sound out of him. "Now, shush, and let me eat your gorgeous ass."

Ellis doesn't quite listen, still grumbling away, but Gabe pays him no mind. He licks and sucks at his hole until it's wet and pliant, relaxed enough that he can easily slide a finger inside. He goes slow, pausing as Ellis' heat envelopes him. Ellis has taken his finger before, but he's still mostly unused to it.

"Yes?" he asks to make sure.

In answer, Ellis further parts his legs and arches his back. *Sweet Jesus.*

Permission granted, Gabe takes his time opening Ellis up, sliding his finger in and out in a torturously slow pace. It doesn't matter he's tormenting himself too—he gets to see Ellis become unhinged, and there's nothing hotter than that.

"Fuck!" Fisting the sheets, Ellis keens when a second finger works itself inside his body, brushing right against his prostate. "Fuck. God."

Gabe tries to bite back a shit-eating grin, but the humor quickly leaves him. His breath catches when Ellis, who's apparently had it up to here with Gabe's leisurely pace, starts to move. He works his hips, pushing his ass back to get the fingers inside him deeper, then driving forward and thrusting his cock against the sheets.

Gabe watches the scene with poorly concealed wonder, not moving an inch and instead letting Ellis do the work. He only crooks his fingers when Ellis seems to get frustrated with looking for the right angle.

Gabe feels his fingers bump the bundle of nerves again, pulling a beautiful, porn-worthy wail out of Ellis.

"Yeah," he says raggedly, watching with fascination as his fingers repeatedly disappear into Ellis' hole. "Fuck yourself on my fingers. You're so fucking beautiful."

"Shut up," Ellis manages between breathy moans, shivering.

"Never."

Even as he's about to take another man's cock, it's the compliment that makes Ellis hide his face, his energy spiking with embarrassment.

It would be adorable if it wasn't so heart-wrenching.

Well then, Gabe will just have to get him used to it.

Challenge accepted.

He has just added a third finger, sucking in a breath at the insane tightness, when a pair of pleading blue eyes gaze back at him.

"G-Gabe..."

"Yeah. Come on."

Slowly withdrawing his fingers, he helps Ellis turn onto his back. He looks a wreck—a fucking beautiful wreck—all messy, sweat-soaked hair and bitten-red lips. The flush has spread from his face and neck to his chest, his whole body thrumming with anticipation.

How Gabe is going to survive this man welcoming him into his body, he has no clue.

"Gabriel."

"Yeah?"

"You're staring."

"You're beautiful."

Predictably, Ellis scowls, hands flying to his face. "Oh my god, stop it!"

"But it's true." He gently coaxes Ellis to reveal his face, dipping down to take his lips in a kiss. "Ready?"

Ellis nods mutely, eyes glazed over but fully present in the moment. His throat bobs, his breath suspending when Gabe's cock presses between his cheeks.

Gabe kisses him again, and again, and again, until he feels the tension gradually drain from him. "I'll never hurt you," he promises between kisses. With one hand braced next to Ellis' head, he hooks the other under Ellis' knee to open him up further. "Just breathe. Focus on me."

Their gazes lock, Ellis' full of so much trust and love it nearly chokes him.

"Always do."

Touching their foreheads together, Gabe pushes forward.

Chapter 26.5

IF ELLIS THOUGHT THAT being inside Gabriel was overwhelming, there isn't a suitable word to describe what he's feeling right now. Every spot where Gabriel is touching him feels on fire, but not the kind that burns; the kind that keeps you warm, safe, and protected. The kind you want to burrow under your skin and feel forever.

"E-Ellis? Are you okay?"

He understands why Gabriel is asking. Ellis' emotions are wreaking such havoc that not even an empath could make sense of them. The word *more* is echoing loudly in his mind, but he can't get his voice to work, can barely breathe. It's as though there's not enough room in his lungs for both air and Gabriel.

So instead, he wraps his arms around Gabriel's shoulders, raises his legs to lock them behind Gabriel's hips, and nods.

Gabriel releases a broken exhale, shifting his weight so he can draw his hips back, then forward. His cock slides deeper this time, hitting the same spot his fingers had before. Ellis throws his head back on a startled gasp, squeezing his eyes shut. Flecks and swirls of gold start to dance behind his eyelids, forming random shapes, then breaking apart again. Is this what Gabriel is seeing? Is this what he sees all the time?

Ellis would ask if he could speak, if he still had full control of himself, but it's hard to control anything right now. Gabriel seems to be everywhere at once, completely overtaking whatever is left of Ellis' senses. His sugary sweet scent is all around, filling Ellis' nose. His lips, swollen and wet, are raining kisses all over Ellis' face, whispering something Ellis is too far gone to understand.

Then Gabriel starts making these small, whimpering noises as he rocks into him, shallow and slow, arms shaking where he's holding himself up so as not to crush Ellis. His face is tucked into Ellis' neck, breath hot and damp where it hits his flushed skin on each exhale.

Ellis slides one hand from Gabriel's shoulders to grasp his thigh, pulling him forward, urging him on. Gabriel lets out a low whine, but he thrusts in deeper, hips stuttering as he tries to get used to the new pace. The way Gabriel fucks him is no longer careful and reverent, but powerful and wanting. The muscles of his back ripple where Ellis is clawing at it, his skin becoming slick with sweat. It's mad, and desperate, and something Ellis wants to feel over and over again.

An unfamiliar voice reaches his ears, and it takes him a while to realize it's his own, so breathy and raspy he doesn't even recognize it, mumbling a single word that sounds suspiciously like *please*. Gabriel catches his lips, coaxing his mouth open so he can taste the plea right from the source, giving Ellis everything he doesn't even know he's asking for.

There's not much Ellis can do besides hold on, and truth be told he doesn't want to. He wants this, exactly this, being surrounded by Gabriel in every way imaginable, letting him find pleasure in his body. There's no rush, no endgame to race toward, although they're both inevitably headed somewhere.

Ellis finds himself nearing the edge all too soon and he clings to Gabriel in a desperate attempt to slow the cresting wave inside him down. But then Gabriel starts to shake, making these broken, wounded sounds while whispering Ellis' name, and suddenly it no longer matters.

For all the intensity that's been building up, falling over the edge is almost indolent, like the sea washing against the shore. Warmth simmers in Ellis' belly, steady and unassuming, until it boils over, sending a rush of pulsing heat through him.

His cock spurts between them, rubbing against Gabriel's stomach.

Gabriel's cock swells and throbs inside him as he shivers, his hips driving forward hard and desperate. He stifles a whimper in Ellis' hair, his body giving a violent jolt before growing soft and pliant, pushing Ellis into the mattress.

Ellis lets out a happy sigh as Gabriel's weight settles on top of him, and he turns his head to press a kiss to Gabriel's overheated cheek.

With a mighty grunt, Gabriel pushes himself up so they can see each other's face. It's just in time that Ellis sees the last of the golden light simmering out from his eyes, and he wonders if his own eyes are glowing too. The answer is yes, if Gabriel's fascinated expression is anything to go by.

"Hi," Gabriel says, voice low and raspy, incongruous with his sunny, soft smile.

Ellis feels his lips stretch into a huge grin, nearly making his face hurt. "Hi."

They chuckle, and Gabriel dips down for a slow, unhurried kiss. He shifts on his hands and knees, starting to pull out.

"Wait." Ellis' legs squeeze tight around him, keeping him in place. "Not yet." His face is so hot it could cook eggs, but Gabriel doesn't laugh at him.

Instead, he lowers himself down on top of Ellis again, making a happy noise at the full body contact. "Okay. Anything you want."

Ellis wraps his arms around him, stroking his hair. God, he could stay like this forever, just soaking up Gabriel's warmth and inhaling his scent.

"Forever would be nice," he mumbles into Gabriel's neck. He's already said and done a lot of embarrassing and sappy things today, what's one more?

"That can be arranged," Gabriel promises, his energy pulsating with love and happiness.

Maybe being embarrassing and sappy isn't so bad after all.

Chapter 27

"I JUST WANT TO say how much I love that you're doing this," Dawson says. He sounds just as enthused as he did on the phone yesterday, when his ecstatic shriek almost pierced Ellis' eardrum.

After much agonizing and weighing the pros and cons, Ellis had finally made the decision to adopt Lola. To be frank, the cons list was much longer, but whenever he thought of discarding the idea, a cloud of longing fell over him. He couldn't stop thinking about Teddy, his childhood dog who had, for many years, been Ellis' only friend. Ellis was 19 when Teddy died, but he's never cried as much as he did that day. He never wanted to go through that again.

Yet, here he is.

"Good on you. You'll be walking her a lot," he tells Dawson.

That reminds him he needs to get another copy of his keys done. The idea of anyone other than Gabriel in his apartment doesn't thrill him, but he's brought this upon himself with this sudden need for company. Even if the company in question is a mentally unstable furry creature.

"You think I'll complain?" Dawson says with a snort. "Oh, by the way, we've brought a bunch of stuff to get you started." He gestures at his car, where Cal is silently hovering. "Some of Donut's toys that he never warmed up to, and a dog bed. And dry food he refuses to eat."

"Doesn't he need his bed?"

"He never sleeps in it. Likes to cuddle."

"Uh-huh. Thanks." That's not gonna happen with Ellis. No dog hair in his bed.

"Don't mention it." Dawson casts a nervous glance at Cal, then gives Ellis a tight-lipped smile. "I'll go get Aubrey. Get all the paperwork sorted."

Which means it will be just Ellis and Cal for a while. Yay.

"Okay. Thank you."

As expected, awkward, tense silence permeates the air. It makes Ellis roll his eyes—at himself, mainly. What is he, five? He sure acts like it, all sulky and broody. What is he even sulking about? Cal didn't even *do* anything other than try to maintain a connection with him.

And taking over your brother's body after reaping his soul.

Right. Almost forgot that little detail.

To be fair, Cal's given him plenty of space to sort out his thoughts. He's not even taking advantage of them being alone right now, leaving the ball in Ellis' court. It's not his fault Ellis is too emotionally constipated to work through his feelings.

With an irritated huff, Ellis walks over to Cal. "Hey," he says awkwardly.

Cal looks shocked to have been addressed, but his face lights right up. "Hi." A nervous smile curves his lips. "How are you?"

"Hanging in there," Ellis says truthfully. No reason to sugarcoat it.

Cal nods in understanding. "That's...good. Um..." He helplessly looks in the direction Dawson has disappeared in. "Dawson wanted to ask you, but was worried it would upset you..."

"What?"

"Would you and Gabe like to come over for Christmas? Or rather, Boxing Day? We're going to Dawson's sister's place for Christmas, but we could have a second Christmas together."

A second Christmas? Ellis doesn't even know if he can have one. He's both scared and excited to spend his first real Christmas with Gabriel and Carrie, not really knowing what to expect. How do normal people celebrate?

When he was growing up, Christmas was one big sham. Stiff, emotionless dinners and expensive, meaningless gifts. He hated the whole charade. And now he's supposed to play happy families again?

"Thanks for the invitation, but Gabriel's mum is coming to spend Christmas with us, and I have no idea how long she's planning to stay." He wouldn't be surprised if Carrie announced she's staying until the New Year.

Cal's hopeful expression shutters. "Oh. Well, she can come too. I'm sure Dawson would love it."

"Yeah, I...I don't know."

"Oh." Cal's shoulders sink. "That's alright. I understand it might be too much."

For fuck's sake. Cal's really killing that kicked puppy look. Now that Ellis thinks about it, it's a mystery he hadn't figured out on his own that his brother is long gone. Amnesia or not, his brother would've never pulled this off. He'd just rage and throw tantrums if he didn't get his way.

Cal was such a dick. So why does Ellis feel like crying whenever something reminds him he's never going to see him again? Sometimes the reality hits him so hard, he wishes he could have one last argument with Cal. How sad is that? He knows this isn't healthy. It's all kinds of fucked up, missing the person who made your life so damn difficult.

"You know what?" he says, resigned. "When I know what the plan is, I'll let you know if we can make it. That good with you?"

Cal perks up like it's the best news he's got all year. "Yes! That's perfect."

Ellis sighs. Now he has to buy more presents. Just great.

Once inside his apartment, Ellis sets down the bags filled with dog stuff and unclips Lola's leash. She takes off like a little orange bullet, instantly exploring everything.

"Just don't pee anywhere!" he calls after her.

Lola lifts her tiny, fluffy head from her important task of sniffing the sofa, a pair of big, black eyes fixating sharply on Ellis as if to convey: *Who the hell do you take me for? I'm a lady!* She then proceeds to jump on the sofa—an impressive move given her stature—and make herself comfortable on one of the pillows.

"Nuh-uh." Ellis wiggles his finger. "Furniture is off limits. Come on. Down, girl."

Lola, giving no inclination whatsoever to do so, shoots him a look that can only mean: *What are you going to do about it?*

Ellis answers by picking her up and putting her down. Throwing the dog bed in front of her, he says, "Here. That's yours."

Lola looks at the bed. Then at Ellis. She lets out a huff, her nose twitching.

"Go on," he prompts when she doesn't move.

Lola does go—on the sofa.

"Fuck's sake." Ellis picks her up again, placing her straight on the bed. "That's yours. This—" He points at the sofa. "Is for people."

Lola blinks at him, sitting on her haunches but not lying down.

Ellis sighs, turning around to unpack the toys and the food Dawson's given him. He's barely taken a step when there's movement behind him. He spins around to find Lola happily lounging on the sofa again.

He throws up his hands. "You know what? I don't have time for this. Have it your way."

What the heck did he get himself into?

He asks the same question when he's turning in for the night, the sound of claws on the hardwood floor coming closer and closer. He flips on the bedside lamp, unsurprised to see Lola hovering next to his bed. She lets out a high-pitched growl.

"No. Your bed is over there."

He put the bed outside his room and left the door open so she could see him. He's read somewhere that pets can get separation anxiety. That being said, Lola doesn't seem anxious. Just very dissatisfied with her living arrangements. She growls again, stomping her tiny feet.

"No," Ellis says firmly. Determined to ignore her, he switches the light off and attempts to go to sleep.

The growling continues for a while longer until it finally stops. Just when Ellis is about to celebrate victory, the mattress dips.

Ellis shoots up, flicking the light on again. "Are you kidding me?"

Lola innocently blinks at him from her spot at the foot of the bed.

"Okay, fine. But you're staying down there." He casts the room into darkness, too tired to argue with a four-legged bully.

He's already falling asleep when movement on the bed startles him. Something furry brushes his arm.

"Seriously?"

Lola answers with a whimper, her tiny tongue swiping across Ellis' hand.

He sighs, lifting the blanket. "Get in, you crazy bitch."

Lola doesn't waste time, crawling under the blanket and curling into a ball at Ellis' side, making a low noise of satisfaction.

Ellis stares at the darkened ceiling for the longest time, flooded with memories of his childhood. Of nights when he was home by himself, save for the housekeeper, his dad gone for business (or with a woman), and Cal sleeping over at a friend's place. Of staying up late, unable to sleep, and thinking of his mum. Of feeling so profoundly lonely he couldn't breathe, wishing there was somebody who'd love him, be with him. On those nights, he'd sneak Teddy into his room, finally falling asleep to the feeling of another heartbeat.

He curls his arm around Lola, stroking her soft fur. He's asleep within seconds.

Ellis wakes before his alarm, brought out of a surprisingly peaceful sleep by something trying to eat his face.

He scrunches his nose, opening his eyes to glare at Lola. "Thanks a lot."

Lola pants excitedly, a gust of her hot, stinky breath hitting Ellis straight in the face. "Fine. I'm up." *And in serious need of a shower.*

After the shower, he finds Lola sitting in front of the apartment door, waiting expectantly.

That's right. He now has a dog he has to walk. And pick up poo after. What was he thinking again?

"Okay, let me get dressed and we'll go."

Lola is, as one might've guessed, an energetic dog. Instead of walking *her*, Ellis ends up being dragged down the street and forced to a stop at every street lamp or trash bin. That itself isn't too bad.

The looks he gets from passers-by are.

It's not his fault a Pomeranian became attached to him! If he had his way, he'd get a Border Collie again, or a Labrador. Something a little more manly. As it is, the only thing missing is a blonde wig and he can star in a sequel of *Legally Blonde*.

A young woman jogging in the opposite direction stops in front of them, pulling out her earbuds. "Oh my god, she's so cute! It's a she, right?"

"Yeah," Ellis mumbles.

She crouches down to give Lola a pet, snatching her hand back when Lola snaps at her.

"Lo!" Ellis chastises. "Shit, I'm sorry. She doesn't do well with people." *Something we have in common.*

The woman seems unbothered. "Ah, no, my bad. I should've asked first. But she clearly loves you! How long have you had her, by the way?"

In a fit of internal panic, Ellis blurts out, probably a little too ardently, "She's not mine! I'm a... I'm dog-sitting for a friend."

The woman gives him a curious look but doesn't say anything.

"Don't look at me like that. I have an image to uphold," Ellis says after the woman has left, Lola giving him a look of utter betrayal. He only feels a little guilty.

Ellis senses something is wrong the moment he sets foot in the café, even though he can't tell what exactly. A feeling of anxiety and loss settles in his gut, which confuses him. This has always been a place that could alleviate his terrible mood just by him stepping in.

"Hey, there!" Gabriel greets him, all smiles as he puts a tray of freshly baked croissants on the counter. "How was the first night with your new baby?"

"Let's say I'm rethinking my choices," Ellis says jokingly, walking over to get his morning kiss. He's been looking forward to it the whole morning. As he gets closer, he becomes aware of Gabriel's puffy eyes and pink nose, and his heart sinks. "What's wrong?"

Gabriel's smile slips, his whole expression crumbling. "Dammit. I thought I'd pulled myself together." He angrily rubs at his eyes.

"Hey." For the first time, Ellis joins Gabriel behind the counter, pulling him into a hug. He wants to demand an explanation, but holds himself back, feeling like offering comfort is a priority now.

Gabriel clings to him, sniffling softly. "I'll ruin your suit."

"Fuck the suit." It pulls a watery laugh out of Gabriel. "What's going on?"

After a few hiccupping breaths, Gabriel says, "The café's closing down."

"What? Why?" Ellis' heart pounds. That can't be. This place is everything.

"You know how I mentioned our lease is coming to an end? Well, the owner decided to sell the place. He already has a buyer lined up and they want to open their own business."

Rage bubbles under Ellis' skin. He pushes it down so as not to upset Gabriel further. "I don't get it. Why didn't he offer to sell to you first?"

"He did. Sort of. He spoke to Zeke. Let him know there's a potential buyer, but that he wanted to give us a chance. But it's too much. The other guys offered a lot of money." Gabriel lets out a dejected sigh. "Zeke and I spent the whole night yesterday doing the math, but I'm still paying off my student loan, and he has a mortgage. They'd never lend us the money." He forces a smile. "Hey, it's okay. The business will keep running. Just not here."

While that's true, it doesn't sit right with Ellis. And not with Gabriel either, otherwise he wouldn't have reacted like this.

"But you love this place."

"Yeah," Gabriel says softly. "But sometimes you have to learn to let things go. Do me a favor and don't tell my mum when she comes over. She's a worry-wart. Kind of like you."

"Gabriel…" Ellis reaches for him, wanting to wipe the tears from his face and tell him it will be okay.

"Coffee!" Gabriel announces suddenly, moving out of Ellis' reach. "You need coffee. And a cinnamon roll. You look like Lola kept you up half the night." There it is again. That forced smile and cheerfulness.

It's so wrong it makes Ellis sick to his stomach.

He'll fix this. He'll fix it if it's the last thing he does.

Chapter 28

FOR HOW NERVOUS AND apprehensive Ellis has been about celebrating Christmas with Cal and Dawson, he feels remarkably...okay. Maybe celebrating with Gabriel and his mum had put him in a Christmassy mood? He hadn't known he even had that setting. Or maybe Gabriel secretly used his mojo on him again, boosting his mood or whatever. He doesn't care either way. He's just glad everything's not awkward and tense.

Dawson clearly went all out decorating the apartment, no doubt utilizing his artistic skills. Though it's obvious that Cal 'helped' decorate the Christmas tree, given how messy and disorganized some of the ornaments are. The tinsel, too, looks like it's been haphazardly thrown on. Kudos to Dawson for not pointing it out.

Ellis' own apartment doesn't look much different. He'd had no intention of getting a tree, let alone other rubbish, but Gabriel was so excited about the whole Christmas ritual that Ellis didn't have the heart to deny him. He stayed out of the decorating, though. It looked exhausting.

"This is amazing," Dawson says with the biggest smile on his face as they all sit down to eat. "You have no idea how happy it makes me that you're both here."

Donut, too, has joined them at the table, sitting on his haunches and waiting for something to accidentally fall on the floor (or straight into his mouth).

"Thank you for inviting us," Gabriel says. "How was your first Christmas?"

"Really nice!" Dawson gnaws at his bottom lip. "And a bit weird. My sister is still pretty distrustful of Cal, so..."

Gabriel snickers. "Judging by Cal's expression, 'pretty distrustful' is an understatement."

Cal indeed does look like he ate something very bitter. "I completely understand her reasoning." He says that, but his body language makes it obvious he's bummed about it.

Dawson places a comforting hand on Cal's shoulder. "She'll come around. You just have to give it time."

The way Cal looks at him can only be described as utterly smitten. "I'm not going anywhere."

Ellis looks away, feeling weird intruding on such an emotional moment.

"How about you?" Dawson asks, looking at Gabriel. "Your mum was here with you, right?"

"Yeah. Only stayed for two days, thank god."

Dawson laughs. "Too much?"

"I mean, *I* can handle her, but poor Ellis here was at his wit's end."

"I was not," Ellis protests. "It was fine. I'm getting used to her."

"I take it she's a handful, then?" Dawson asks.

"That, and she shamelessly flirts with Ellis," Gabriel says, managing to sound amused and annoyed at the same time.

Ellis' face grows hotter by at least ten degrees.

Dawson chokes on his mashed potatoes. "Seriously? I'm sorry, that's...kind of hilarious. Do you have the same taste in men?"

Gabriel huffs. "I think she just likes to stir shit up."

"Runs in the family?"

Gabriel throws a napkin at him.

The rest of dinner continues in the same spirit, with Gabriel and Dawson doing most of the talking, and generally keeping the atmosphere light and warm. It's...nice. Ellis can't tell if this is what celebrating as a family is supposed to feel like, but it's something he could easily get used to.

After dessert—which Gabriel has brought, and Dawson has begged the recipe for—they move to the living room to exchange presents. Ellis has never been good at picking gifts, and so was more than happy to leave the responsibility to Gabriel. He doesn't even know what Gabriel ended up buying.

Dawson opens his present first, eyes going wide and excited as he pages through what seems to be a very heavy cookbook. "This is amazing. I can't wait to try all of these! Thank you, thank you!"

Gabriel is next, unwrapping his present to reveal a pair of aprons with funny quotes and letting out an excited squeal.

Ellis smiles; he loves seeing Gabriel get excited over simple things.

He unwraps his present next, looking it over confusedly. "What's that?"

"It's a shakti mat," Dawson supplies unhelpfully. "It's supposed to relax you."

"It has spikes," Ellis comments with apprehension. "Isn't it painful?"

"When you're not used to it, but then it feels sooo good."

"Oh, I've tried that before!" Gabriel says. "Zeke has one of those. It's amazing."

"Right. Thank you." Ellis gives a polite smile, turning to Gabriel to whisper, "You can keep it."

Gabriel shoots him a disapproving look. "You're trying it. You're so tense all the time."

Ellis slowly drags his gaze from Gabriel's face down his chest and back up. "There are other ways to relax me."

Two spots of color appear high on Gabriel's cheeks. He licks his lips, his eyes narrowing. "Still trying it."

Ellis sighs. "Dammit." Worth a try.

Meanwhile, Cal has unwrapped his present. "Oh. What are these?" He studies the two books in his hands with great interest.

Ellis leans forward to get a better look, choking a little when he gets a glimpse of a half-naked man. Two half-naked men, actually! And this is supposed to be a present from him and Gabriel?!

"It's gay romance," Gabriel explains. "Paranormal gay romance."

Cal's expression brightens with intrigue. "Oh, amazing. Does it have vampires?"

"No vampires in these," Gabriel says with a chuckle. "But plenty of magic and spells. And book two has a morally ambiguous fae that is *sooo* hot."

"Gabriel picked the books, in case you were wondering," Ellis says, trying not to pout too much. He's *not* going to get jealous over a fictional character, goddammit.

"Thank you. I'm really looking forward to reading them." Cal pauses, studying the covers intently. "Did these men do something bad? Why are they tied up?"

"Both books have BDSM elements," Gabriel says breezily, while Ellis tries to blend into the sofa.

"Oh no," Dawson says. "Now he's gonna want to try it."

Cal looks between Gabriel and Dawson. "Why? What's BDSM?"

Dawson holds up a hand when Gabriel goes to explain. "I'll tell you later," he promises Cal.

Cal just shrugs, already flipping through the first book.

Ellis leans into Gabriel to whisper, "Porn. Really?"

"It's not porn. It's erotic gay romance!"

"Same difference."

"Don't be a prude. Don't you want to broaden Cal's horizons?"

Ellis shivers. "Meddling in my brother's sex life is the last thing I want to do."

Gabriel looks at him strangely, so Ellis replays his words back, going still.

He...he didn't mean it like that. Of course he knows Cal isn't really his brother. That doesn't change the fact he wears his face, which fucks with Ellis' head.

Before he can say anything, Dawson stands up. "Hey, guys, do you want to see my studio?"

Grateful for the distraction, Ellis nods.

"A few months ago. They never met, though."

That takes Ellis aback. "Because of the car accident?"

Cal shakes his head. "Because he didn't want to. He told her to never contact him again."

"What?"

Cal's brows pull together in a frown. "I think...he was too angry and hurt. He never forgave her for leaving."

Neither did Ellis. But if she ever reached out to him, if she wanted to meet him, wouldn't he jump on the opportunity to finally see her? Or would he run away?

You don't have to worry about that because she never wanted to see you anyway.

"She never contacted me."

Cal's expression is uncertain. "Maybe she thought you'd have the same reaction."

"And it was so hard to ask."

"Ellis—"

"Don't."

He doesn't want to hear it. Feeling a headache forming, he pinches the bridge of his nose.

Oblivious as ever, Cal pushes on. "Would you have wanted him to tell you?"

"Yes. No. I don't know." He doesn't know anything anymore. Whenever he thinks his life can't get more bizarre, he's proven wrong.

"I can show you the email," Cal offers. "I managed to log into some of Caledon's accounts when I started remembering things."

His heart pounding, Ellis takes a moment to consider it. Soon enough, he has his answer.

"Thanks, but...I don't think I'm ready for that."

Cal nods, like it makes perfect sense. Nothing makes any fucking sense anymore.

"You've been through a lot lately. You deserve a break."

"I really fucking do." Finally, something they can agree on. "Speaking of... I'm thinking of leaving the company."

Cal's brows shoot up. "Are you?"

"I'm still working on figuring everything out. But yeah, that's the plan."

"Good. That's good. I think it will be really good for you."

"Me too." He didn't really think Cal would have any objections, but it's a relief to have it confirmed. "And...thank you. For telling me."

"Of course."

"I'm sorry you have to live with Cal's memories."

Cal has probably been downplaying how confusing it is, especially given what happened with Dawson.

"It's...hard," Cal admits. "Not because they make me confused, but because I'm getting to know him. Who he was. But I don't want to know him. He'll always be the monster who hurt the man I love. I don't want to sympathize with him." He grimaces, his gaze full of apology. "I'm sorry. You shouldn't listen to this."

"No, I...I get it." It hurts, but he gets it. "I knew he wasn't a good person, but finding out what he did to Dawson... Turns out I didn't know him at all."

He'll always remember the sheer disbelief as Dawson confided in him. The moment of weakness when everything inside him screamed of denial and anger, when he wanted to accuse Dawson of lying. The gradually dawning horror as he watched Dawson fall apart in front of him. The numbness that spread through his body as he was forced to accept that his brother, the last family he had left, had caused someone so much pain. The emptiness the truth had left behind.

And yet...

"But you still miss him," Cal says. Not a question, a simple statement of fact. His voice is calm, without judgment or anger. "I have this memory..."

"What memory?" Ellis isn't sure he can handle any more revelations today, but he's intrigued by Cal's smile, small and reluctant, like he's about to share a secret.

"You're both very young. He's obviously older, stronger. You're at the beach, just the two of you because your dad had to work. He's trying to convince you to go surfing with him."

Not very specific. Their dad always 'had to work', so they wandered around. Cal was crazy about surfing and would pester him any chance he got. Called him a wuss when Ellis was too scared to try it, barely able to tread water in their private pool.

"You finally go with him," Cal continues. "He catches a wave, rides it all the way to the shore. You try to catch the next one, but it's too big and takes you down."

Oh.

Oh.

He remembers. Of course, he does. Why is Cal bringing it up now?

"He waits for you to come up, but when you do, another wave takes you under. The strap around your ankle is loose, and your board gets swept away. You get caught in a rip current, and it's taking you far from the shore."

"He saved me," Ellis whispers, not even trying to fight the incoming tears at this point. The memory wraps around him like the water that nearly killed him that day, lukewarm and inescapable. "He paddled all the way towards me, got me on his board, and swam us out of the current." A bitter laugh slips out of his lips. "I hated that he forced me into the water, but secretly he was my hero."

Unlike him, Cal knew the currents, but it was still dangerous to go so far. He was just a kid. But he didn't hesitate, didn't stop until Ellis clung to him, and he could get them back to safety.

"He was really scared he lost you. For a long time, he blamed himself for nearly getting you killed."

If Ellis closes his eyes, he can almost see it. Feel it. The two of them on the beach, out of breath and shaking. Cal's arms around him, squeezing tight as Ellis clings to him just as tightly, sobbing into his shoulder. The *I'm sorry, I'm so sorry,* chanted over and over in a soft, wrecked voice.

"Why are you telling me this?"

This time, he doesn't tense up when Cal steps into his space and pulls him into a hug. It's strange and unfamiliar, wrong in a way that's difficult to explain, but it's exactly what he needs. Even though he can't bring himself to reciprocate, he accepts it gratefully, allowing himself to revel in the comfort it brings.

After a long while, when Ellis has almost forgotten he's asked the question, Cal finally speaks.

"Because he'll always be a monster to me. He has to be. But he shouldn't be to you."

Ellis squeezes his eyes shut, drops his forehead to Cal's shoulder, and just *breathes.*

He doesn't know how long they stand there like that, but at some point, Dawson and Gabriel come back. To their credit, neither of them mentions what they walk in on, although Ellis gets a few strange glances before it's time to go home.

There's heaviness in his stomach when he waits with Gabriel for the lift to arrive. He can't shake the feeling there's something he should've said. When the compulsion becomes too strong, he turns to Gabriel. "Can you hold the lift?"

Gabriel gives him a surprised look. "Sure. Something wrong?"

"No, I just forgot something." He rushes back to the apartment, his hands shaking as he rings the bell.

Cal's the one to open the door. "Oh. Did you leave something here?" He steps aside to let him in, but Ellis stays outside.

"No. I just... I needed to say something."

Cal patiently waits for him to continue.

Ellis probably should've thought of what he wanted to say first.

"I've been thinking..."

"Yes?"

"There's no reason I can't have two brothers. For all I know, my dad has a bunch of illegitimate children anyway."

Cal stares at him for so long Ellis wonders if he actually spoke out loud. Finally, his throat bobs, a shaky smile appearing on his lips.

"I like that logic. I don't like being an only child."

Ellis laughs, a sense of peace finally settling over him.

Maybe everything will be okay after all.

"Are you going to get in touch with your mum?" Gabriel asks in the car on their way home.

Ellis spilled the beans about his mum once they were alone, feeling like he'd burst if he kept it bottled up. Telling Gabriel definitely lifted a lot of weight off his chest.

"One day, maybe. When I'm strong like you. But not right now."

Everything feels too fresh, too raw, too...just *too*. He's starting to understand why Cal didn't want to meet with her.

He feels Gabriel's energy brush against his own in a loving caress, all warmth and softness.

"You're the strongest person I know, Ellis. You and my mum."

He's not. He really isn't. He wishes he were more like Gabriel. More forgiving, more understanding, more empathetic. Unafraid to put his heart on the line, even if there's a big chance it's going to get crushed.

He's not brave at all, but he loves that Gabriel sees him that way. It makes him want to live up to the expectation.

"Seems that your mum and I have more in common than I thought."

Gabriel raises a curious eyebrow. "Oh, really? What else do you have in common?"

"We both like spicy food."

"Which *you* shouldn't eat, by the way," Gabriel reminds him. "What else?"

"We both hate horror movies."

"As does half the population. Next?"

"We both love you."

Ellis' heart pounds so hard it's in danger of bursting out of his chest. It doesn't help that instead of being his blabbering self, Gabriel is worryingly quiet.

Until he's not.

"Seriously?!" Gabriel yelps in indignation. "First time you tell me you love me and you have to bring my mum into it?"

"Sorry," Ellis mutters, trying not to laugh. "I'll try again later."

"Yeah, you better," Gabriel grunts, arms crossed sulkily. He's pretending to look out of the window, but Ellis can see his smile in the reflection.

After so much ado, saying the three words came naturally, like he's said them a million times before.

Shortly, they pull into the parking garage in Ellis' building.

"I have one more present for you at home," he tells Gabriel. He's almost more nervous about that than he was about the love-confession.

"Another one?"

"There's a limit?"

Gabriel actually ponders it. "Well, no, but...why now? Christmas was two days ago."

"It took a while to get sorted."

"Okay. But you're trying out your shakti mat first, before it miraculously disappears."

Dang. There goes Ellis' plan.

Ellis manages to delay the torture by insisting Lola needs to go for a walk first, taking deliberately longer. When they return, Gabriel has already spread the mat out on the floor.

"Do I have to?" Ellis asks miserably. The spikes are really scary.

"Yes! You'll love it, I promise."

Grumbling away, Ellis sheds his shirt and, so very gingerly, lies down on the mat.

"I can't do it," he announces after thirty seconds, the spikes digging into his back like a thousand tiny shark teeth. And people pay for this?

"Be patient!" Gabriel forces him back down when he attempts to sit up. "You need to stay like this for at least twenty minutes."

"It hurts!"

Gabriel smiles devilishly. "Stick with it and you'll get a reward."

Ellis stops struggling, eyeing Gabriel with suspicion. "You better be talking about sex."

Gabriel smirks. "Guess you'll have to wait and find out." He pats Ellis' tummy. "Twenty minutes."

"Fine."

Ellis is floating, his whole body buzzing and mind blissfully quiet. Something touches his face, Gabriel's voice bringing him to the present.

"It's been half an hour," he says, sounding smug. "You want to collect your reward now?"

Ellis doesn't bother opening his eyes. "I'm good." He's more than good. He could fall asleep like this.

"Excuse me?!"

"Just a few more minutes," Ellis mumbles. It's hard to even put a coherent sentence together, he's so relaxed.

"Unbelievable. I'll kill Cal and Dawson if this mat ruins our sex life."

"Hmm."

"Don't you have a present for me?"

Suddenly, Ellis is wide awake. "Oh. Right." He feels a little dizzy as he stumbles to his feet. "It's in the bedroom."

"That sounds promising," Gabriel drawls.

Ellis snorts. "Get your mind out of the gutter."

In the bedroom, he pulls a white envelope from the nightstand, taking a seat on the bed and signaling for Gabriel to do the same. "Try not to make a big deal out of it," he says as he hands Gabriel the envelope.

"In case no one's told you, that's a terrible way to prelude a situation," Gabriel teases, pulling out a folded sheet of paper.

Ellis holds his breath, watching Gabriel's face as he reads. His expressions range from confused, to disbelieving, to reluctantly hopeful.

When he's done, his doe-like eyes fix on Ellis. "What is this?"

The answer is obvious, but Ellis humors him anyway.

"It's an ownership transfer. For the café."

Gabriel's chin wobbles. "I don't understand."

Ellis brushes the back of his hand against Gabriel's cheek. "Yes, you do."

"What—How—" His eyes flit over the paper again, too fast to take any words in. "When did you do this?"

"Zeke gave me your landlord's number. We had a chat. I offered more money than the other guys." Ellis shrugs. "He was more than happy to accommodate me. Turns out he's getting a divorce and will be glad if he has any money left afterwards." He probably shouldn't be so happy about someone else's misfortune, but right now he doesn't give a crap.

Predictably, Gabriel freaks out. "Are you nuts?! Ellis, I know how much the original price was. And you offered more?!"

"Buying a café hardly made a dent in my savings."

"You just bought this apartment! It must've cost, like, a million!"

$1,230,000, but that's beside the point. "Yes, after selling my million-dollar apartment in Sydney."

"But—But—You can't—"

"I can. And I did."

"But—"

Rolling his eyes affectionately, Ellis takes Gabriel's face between his palms, putting a stop to his blabbering.

"Gabriel, I love the café. I love you." *So, so easy to say it now.* "The café is the reason we met. Do you really think I'd just stand by and let it get taken away?"

All the fight leaves Gabriel at once, his hands dropping to his lap. "Much better confession than the first one," he says, lips twitching. "But you put the contract in my name."

"Yeah. I didn't want you to worry that…if anything happened between us…that you'd lose the café."

"Ellis…"

"Not that anything will. But, you know. Shit happens. You never know, you might get fed up with me." It hurt to consider the possibility, but he had to be realistic. He would never want to put Gabriel in a position where he'd feel compelled to stay with Ellis for the sake of his livelihood.

Suddenly, Gabriel straddles his thighs, his fingers sinking into Ellis' hair and forcing him to look at him.

"Ellis."

"W-what?"

"You can be so dumb sometimes, you know that?"

"Um…"

"But…" He brushes his thumb over Ellis' parted lips. "You're the most loving, loyal, fucking amazing person I've ever met. I'll die before I let you go."

The fierceness of Gabriel's words renders him speechless. It takes all his effort to get out a simple "Okay."

"Okay," Gabriel repeats, seemingly satisfied with that answer. "By the way, I'm paying you back."

"What? No."

"Yes. Don't argue with me. Consider yourself our new landlord and we're paying you rent."

"I don't need the money."

"Tough because you're gonna get it. Ellis, it's a matter of dignity. Even if you convinced me to let it rest, you would have a hard time with Zeke. He won't accept charity."

"It's not—"

"I know. But you have to see our side too."

Ellis hesitates. Why is it such a big deal? He rarely spends money on the things he wants. He got an apartment because he needed it, just as he needed his car or his phone. For once, he invested money in something that truly matters to him, so why can't Gabriel just let it go?

Starting to accept defeat, Ellis relents. "Fine. But I won't let you pay whatever you've been paying until now." He remembers what Gabriel said about the rent starting to get too high. "I'll take 40%." That should be satisfactory, right?

Clearly not.

"That's ridiculous. We could easily afford to pay 80%."

"No."

"70?"

"No."

"Fine. 65%. That's my last word. And you're not allowed to pay for anything at the café ever again."

Judging by Gabriel's determined expression, there will be no swaying him.

Stubborn bastard, Ellis thinks fondly.

"Deal."

"Deal." Gabriel's smile is so big it almost doesn't fit his face. "Seal it with a kiss?"

Ellis laughs. He leans up, stopping abruptly. "I don't have to kiss Zeke too, do I?"

Gabriel's expression turns murderous. "Over my dead body. And his, if he tries to tell you otherwise."

Ellis laughs, shaking his head. As if he would let that happen.

"You're the only person I ever want to kiss. You're the only person I *want*."

"That's right. Now..." Gabriel pushes him flat on the bed. "I believe I promised you a reward."

Ellis grins, relaxing into the mattress and giving himself over to be ravished. "All yours."

Gabriel leans down, brushing their lips together. "All mine."

Epilogue

The headboard slams into the wall, the whole bed creaking ominously at the impact. At this rate, Ellis will have to start shopping for a new bedframe. He'll make sure to send Gabriel the bill.

Sinking his teeth into a pillow, he holds on for dear life as Gabriel fucks him into the mattress, their hips creating an obscene slapping sound each time Gabriel's cock drives into him. There's nothing else he can do in this position; his chest touching the sheets while his ass is in the air. Gabriel is keeping him in place with a tight grip that is just short of bruising, and his hands are tied to the headboard with his own tie.

Note to self: never ask Gabriel to help you dress.

Behind him, Gabriel lets out a grunt, coming to a brief stop. He adjusts his position, and the next thrust has Ellis crying out.

"Jackpot."

He can hear Gabriel's evil chuckle as he picks up the pace, hammering into Ellis' prostate on every thrust. Tears spring to his eyes at the combined sensations of pain and pleasure. He can feel the familiar tingle climbing up his spine, golden swirls beginning to dance behind his eyelids.

Gabriel lets out a guttural moan, probably from getting a taste of what Ellis is feeling.

Ellis wants him to have more than a taste, wants him to know exactly what he's making him feel. He opens himself up to his limit, giving Gabriel the full blast.

Gabriel's movements stutter, his grip on Ellis tightening. "I see what you did there," he says huskily, a note of amusement in his voice. His fingers sink into Ellis' hair, tugging gently, coaxing him to turn his head. "Look at me, sweetheart. Show me those eyes."

With a shaky breath, Ellis does as told, forcing his eyes to open. The angle is weird, and a bit uncomfortable, but he doesn't stop until their eyes meet.

Gabriel's are overflowing with gold, and Ellis knows his must be too. He can feel it, and he can see it in Gabriel's expression, all wonder and lust and love.

"There we go." Grinning proudly, Gabriel leans down to let their lips meet in an imperfect kiss. "I fucking love you."

Ellis shudders. "Ditto." He yelps when Gabriel's teeth sink into his shoulder. "I love you too."

"That's better," Gabriel says, kissing the sore spot. "Now, hold on tight."

The next few moments are a blur. Ellis isn't aware of much beyond the desperate sounds coming out of him and the scorching heat rapidly building in his belly. His whole body feels like a volcano about to erupt, and he screams when the tension finally snaps, painting everything around him in shades of gold.

His brain slowly coming back online, he struggles to breathe, only to find it's because he's being squashed into the mattress.

"Breathe. Need. Now," he gasps out, inhaling deeply when Gabriel finally pushes off him, his cock sliding out with a wet squelch that makes Ellis' ears burn.

"Oh, sorry. I think I blacked out a little," Gabriel mumbles, raining apologetic kisses over Ellis' shoulders. "Are you okay?" He starts untying Ellis' wrists, stroking the sore skin. "I didn't make it too tight, did I?"

That, he is worried about, but Ellis not being able to sit properly for a week is evidently no biggie.

"Ellis?"

"It's fine. Though some warning would have been nice."

He did not foresee Gabriel pouncing on him like a wild cat when Ellis stood in front of him in his slacks and an open shirt, asking which tie he should wear. He for sure did not foresee ending up tied to the bed with one of said ties, then railed into oblivion. At least Gabriel had half a mind to shut the door to get rid of Lola. Ellis doesn't care what anyone says—having sex in front of your pet is weird!

"Is that a complaint?"

"Consider it feedback."

"Uh-huh."

"And now I need to shower. *Again.*"

"Cry-baby." Gabriel gently smacks his asscheek. "Come on. I'll give you a hand."

"Not sure that's a good idea," Ellis grumbles, but takes Gabriel's hand and follows him to the bathroom. He bites his lip as a trickle of Gabriel's come slides down his thigh. His cock gives an interested twitch, so Ellis glares at it until it flops back down.

Despite being annoyed by having to take yet another shower, he has to admit it's nice having Gabriel's hands all over him, sudsing him up and massaging his tense muscles. That is, until one of those hands wanders between his cheeks under the pretense of cleaning him, but ultimately working two fingers inside him.

Ellis' arm shoots out for support as his body gives a surprised jolt. He looks back to give the bane of his existence a glare. "Are you kidding me?"

Gabriel innocently flutters his eyelashes. "What?"

"You know wha— Fuck!" He gasps when Gabriel presses on his prostate.

"Yes?"

How is Ellis supposed to talk when Gabriel keeps rubbing the same spot?

"Don't. We don't—ah, shit—we don't have time for this. We're probably already late."

"It's okay if we're a little late."

"No. We—ah, yeah, there—we can't be late. It's Dawson's f-first ever exhibition."

It's bad enough they had to leave early from Cal and Dawson's wedding (although it was advertised as *renewal of vows*), because *someone* came up with the brilliant idea of exchanging blowjobs in a public bathroom and ended up getting jizz on Ellis' pants.

Gabriel lets out a wistful sigh, withdrawing his fingers. "Guilt-tripping isn't fair game, you know?" He starts to wash the suds off.

"It's the only thing that works on you, you maniac."

"I'm only a maniac because you've been so busy lately."

"We live together. You see me every day."

"Doesn't matter. I still missed you."

Now who's guilt-tripping whom? Though Gabriel is right—Ellis *has* been busy. He hadn't realized how time-consuming it would be to prepare for the exams to become a licensed architect. It's a lot harder than he imagined.

"I missed you too," he admits quietly.

They switch positions, Ellis washing Gabriel this time. As he lets his hands roam over Gabriel's soft, wet skin, his mind starts to wander. Back to the wedding. To the thought that had crossed his mind back then and hasn't left him since.

"Hey, Gabriel."

"Yes, dear?"

Ellis huffs, pinching Gabriel's waist and getting his hand slapped.

"I've been thinking... I'd like to meet my mum."

Gabriel stills, turning around in Ellis' arms. "Really?"

"Yeah."

Gabriel tilts his head, probably trying to gauge Ellis' emotional state. "What brought this on?"

It's a fair question, considering Ellis hasn't mentioned her in a year and a half.

"I've been considering it since Cal and Dawson's wedding," he confesses. "It just kind of got to me, all of us being there. Even Dawson's sister and her family." Olivia has warmed up to Cal considerably over the years, but their relationship has never been the best. "It's nice when family gets together for something important."

"Something important?"

"Yeah. I mean..." He starts to lather up Gabriel's chest to have something to do. "I don't know what my mum is like. If she's even a good person." He holds Gabriel's gaze as he says the next part. "But if there's a possibility to mend the bridges, I'd like to have her at my wedding too."

Gabriel's brows furrow. "Your wedding? Who are you marrying?" He takes a step back. "Wait a minute. Is this a proposal?"

Ellis squirms. "No. It's foreshadowing."

Gabriel lets out a puff of air. "Well, thank god because as far as proposals go, this was abysmal. And I would hate for you to beat me to it."

"What?"

"What?"

"You said—"

"I'm just foreshadowing."

"Right."

They both stand very still, trying to keep impassive expressions.

"Do you think I should invite my dad to my hypothetical wedding?" Gabriel asks next.

"Would you like to have him at your hypothetical wedding?"

"I wouldn't hate it. But I'd have to tell mum first."

"Have you considered telling her?"

Gabriel sighs. "Every day."

Ellis closes the distance between them, tugging Gabriel under the spray to wash the soap off him. "Take your time. There's no rush."

"No? Because I was hoping to get married before 30."

"You're 31."

"You won't let me have any nice things, will you?" Gabriel

grumbles.

"That's not true. You can have anything you want."

"Guinea pigs?"

"No."

"Chinchillas?"

Ellis smiles. "No."

"Ugh. Guess I'll have to make do with you."

"Yeah, you have no choice."

Gabriel nods along. "A terrible imposition. Truly."

"I love you," Ellis says, his heart swelling to twice its size. "You're the best thing that's ever happened to me."

Gabriel stares at him. Then his gaze darkens, and he pushes Ellis up against the wall. "I changed my mind."

"What?"

Gabriel kisses him fiercely, his cock already hard and rubbing against Ellis'. "We can be late for the exhibition. I'll make it up to Dawson."

"Make it up how?" Ellis demands, hooking one leg over Gabriel's hip and wrapping a hand around both of them. He lets his head fall back, hissing as it hits cold hard tiles. The pain is quickly forgotten when Gabriel starts kissing his neck.

"He can be late to our wedding to get back at us," Gabriel suggests, voice trailing off into a moan.

"That sounds reasonable," Ellis concedes. He can't really argue when he has this beautiful man in his arms and his heart.

Yeah, they can be late.

Latte is better than never.

Author's note

THANK YOU SO MUCH for making it all the way here. I hope that Ellis and Gabe's story brought some light (and laughs) into your life.

In case you're wondering—yes, there will be bonus stories where Ellis meets his mom and Gabe his dad. It just didn't feel right to make it part of the main story.

I'm still planning on adding some bonus stories for Cal and Dawson as well. :)

If you've been wondering about the books Cal got as a Christmas present, those are real! You can check them out by searching for *Midnight Sun* and *First Snow* by Saga Nansen.

What's next

BOOK 3 – Ash and Kieran's story.

I don't have a title yet. I'll try to get the book out before the end of the year, but to be honest with you, Kieran isn't talking to me much. I think I pissed him off, eh.

You can already tell this will be (one-sided) enemies to lovers and possibly some D/s dynamic. I had no idea Ash was into that until I started writing Book 2 lol. Oh, and there will also be some time travel. To the future. *wink wink*

Book 4 – Zeke's story

That's it. I wasn't planning on it, but Zeke is a stubborn little bitch. Also refuses to tell me who his boo is, though I'm starting to get an inkling.

A "mafia" book

This story has been trying to get my attention ever since I finished Book 1, but I turned it away so I could focus and Ellis and Gabe. Since Kieran is being a little bitch, I might try writing this book at the same time as Book 3 in the series. We'll see which comes out first haha.

I'm using the term 'mafia' lightly, because while one of the MCs is a mafia boss, the story isn't dark or violent. I don't have a stomach for that. It's pretty much a story about a dangerous, formidable guy who falls for an innocent, vulnerable guy and becomes super protective of him. In short, it's trashy and swoony lol. I don't normally read mafia books, but I absolutely loved Just a bit Ruthless by Alessandra Hazard and Sainted by Jesse H Reign—so this book will have a similar vibe.

I'd like to say this is gonna be a standalone but...well, Should the Sky Fall was supposed to be a standalone too. Blew up in my face, didn't it?

A short story

I've been approached by an author who's putting together a group of authors who debuted in 2023. Each of us will write a brand new short story, and the whole collection will be available for free. The release date is sometime in July.

A soulmate story

It's not official yet, but in the second half of 2025, I might publish a story revolving around soulmates as a part of a multi-author series. When I know for sure it's going to happen, I'll let you know :)

Other works

WHO WE ARE
<u>Should the Sky Fall</u> (Book 1)
<u>Should Our Hearts Catch Fire</u> (Book 2)

NOVELLAS
<u>Unraveled</u>
(free if you sign up to the newsletter)
<u>Un/Tamed</u>

SHORT STORIES
<u>At Your Service</u> (free)

Stalk me

To stay updated about my upcoming releases, bonus scenes and freebies, visit my website **https://amithiaraine.com** and join my newsletter, or follow me on social media. I also have an author group on FB (Amithia Raine's Reality Escape) where I'm sharing snippets, pics and whatnot from what I'm working on.

I'm your regular anti-social weirdo who loves to escape reality by getting way too invested in the lives of fictional dudes, be it through reading or writing.

I was born and raised in the Czech Republic. In 2019, I ran away to Brisbane, Australia, where I made camp and have no plans on changing that. In real life, I'm a physiotherapist, and a coffee and sugar addict. In my other (way more interesting) life, I'm a sap who can't survive without two (or more) boys in love and a proper happily ever after.

I like my boys to be imperfect and a little broken. I like seeing them being put back together. I love slow burn, the kind of love that's flawed but pure and lasts forever. I like that inexplicable pull that transcends reason and time. I also may or may not have a weakness for 'trashy' romance, cliches, idiots in love and characters whose toxic inclinations would make a therapist run for the hills. Whatever my wandering soul craves in the moment.

Printed in Great Britain
by Amazon

AMITHIA RAINE

Should Our Hearts
CATCH FIRE

WHO WE ARE BOOK 2